THE COMF

Jeremy Sheldon was born in 1... where he still lives, working as a script-reader and a DJ. He studied at the University of East Anglia where he was awarded an MA in creative writing.

For more information, please try the following:

www.jezzaroona.com
www.escapecommittee.net

THE COMFORT ZONE

JEREMY SHELDON

Jonathan Cape
London

Published by Jonathan Cape 2002

2 4 6 8 10 9 7 5 3 1

First published in Great Britain in 2002 by
Jonathan Cape
Random House, 20 Vauxhall Bridge Road,
London SW1V 2SA

The Random House Group Limited Reg. No. 954009

Grateful acknowledgement is made to the following for permission
to reprint previously published material:

'Star Dust' Words by Mitchell Parish and Music by Hoagy Carmichael
© 1929, EMI Mills Music Inc, USA. Reproduced by permission of
Lawrence Wright Music Co Ltd, London WC2H 0QY.

The Long Goodbye by Raymond Chandler
(Penguin Books, 1959) © 1953 by Raymond
Chandler. Reproduced by permission of Penguin
Books Ltd.

While every effort has been made to obtain permission from owners
of copyright material reproduced herein, the publishers would like
to apologise for any omissions and will be pleased to incorporate
missing acknowledgements in any future editions.

A CIP catalogue record for this book
is available from the British Library

ISBN 0–224–06271–9

Papers used by Random House are natural,
recyclable products made from wood grown in sustainable forests;
the manufacturing processes conform to the environmental
regulations of the country of origin

Typeset by Palimpsest Book Production Limited,
Polmont, Stirlingshire
Printed and bound in Great Britain by
Mackays of Chatham PLC, Chatham, Kent

To Richard and Cissy Sheldon for their irreducible faith

Contents

LET'S GET OUTTA HERE

When I was a child, I spake as
a child, I understood as a child,
I thought as a child: but when I
became a man, I put away my
childish things.

Corinthians 13, xi

1

There are two types of people in this world. There are those who lay around on the floor as children and imagined what it would have been like if we all lived upside-down. And plainly there are those who didn't. Either you were the sort of person who imagined a scenario where everyone had huge lights coming out of the floor of their living-rooms – or you weren't. Take me, for example. As a child, I spent many an afternoon lying on the carpet in the paths of dusty sunbeams, imagining everyone having floor-level windows and staircase-shaped ceilings. But my wife, on the other hand (my *ex*-wife, actually) didn't. Never had. Never thought she might. End of story.

•

Not much else in life is like that. For instance: some people like football. They *love* it, are absolutely *crazy* for it. They go starry-eyed over memories of ruddy-faced men with perms and sideburns, can tell you the winners of the League Cup in 1962 and 1985 (Norwich City, both years) and drink their tea out of a 'lucky Bobby Moore mug' every Saturday morning during the season.

Then there are those who hate The Beautiful Game. They loathe it, won't let you talk about it at the dinner table and pretty soon you end up reading your weekly copy of *A Game of Two Halves* while you smoke 'your' fags in 'their' garden. My ex-wife was – and, to the best of my knowledge, still is – exactly that kind of person. To be fair, she grew up having a couple of fanatical Port Vale fans as parents (a vale of serious tears by anyone's standards) and it should have come as no surprise that she spent the next six years and three months doing anything she could to sabotage my viewing of *Match of the Day* and other sporting highlights. Tickets to abysmal plays, her mother, her birthday or an anniversary every so often. Candlelit dinners ('we always eat in front of the telly, I thought it would make a nice change . . .'), tropical underwear, cans of whipped cream and going into labour. These were all some of the diversionary tactics employed over that long and arduous campaign. She even tried going into labour a second time, one midweek evening a few years after her previous attempt, and I can still summon up the memory of the satisfied look that glittered in her eyes as she breathed deeply and told me that *it was time* through increasingly clenched teeth. Luckily the gods knew the truth on that occasion, saw what she was up to and rained off all the cup-ties that night. Furthermore, I'd learnt my lesson by then and had acquired a pocket-radio for hospital waiting-rooms, car journeys to dying aunts, school reunions (hers) and other eventualities. She hated it, of course, but that was fine by me. I just kept it out of harm's way in a box in the greenhouse and checked its batteries every Saturday afternoon between three and five o' clock.

Of course there are also all the other type of people as well: people who 'don't mind' football, people who 'catch the odd game after the news', who watch the Cup Final with their family each May the same way they sit down to the Queen's Speech every December. And there are people who simply couldn't care either way. The world is not, by any frantic tugging on the apron-strings of the imagination, simply divided into those who know where they were the night Gazza cried and those who cry when you try to put his framed picture up in the lounge. Football, unlike staring at the ceiling with a puzzled look on your face, is something that one can be neutral towards.

2

It was armed with these awarenesses and my pocket-radio (I'd 'won' it by saving the coupons from all the alfresco cigarettes I'd smoked during the first three years of my marriage) that I recently travelled to California to catch up with friends and relatives and to enjoy a little post-divorce R & R. Once there, I was to stay with my cousin Stephanie at her bungalow in Belmont a few miles south of San Francisco. According to my mother (who'd stayed there the previous summer), it sat high up on a hill amongst groves of eucalyptus trees. According to my mother, it was a paradise under unbroken skies. According to my mother, it was a sun-drenched utopia where crazy deer were known to crap into your swimming pool and jump out at your car at STOP signs.

And of course there was TV. Let me tell you now: *never* miss Tina Friggers' talkshow on KCUF, 10 a.m. Pacific time. I also recommend the luscious Maria (star of the eponymously titled *Maria!*) who lost me early on in each episode with her volcanic Spanish but quickly won my heart with her tartan trouser-suits and her passionate discussions on *Jovenes Alcoholicos* and *Allegados a los Famosos*.

You see, I spent my first mornings in California sitting by the pool, watching cable, trying out fruit-juice combinations and eating bags of *chips* until lunchtime before retreating inside to eat watermelon in front of MTV for the rest of the day. And by the Friday of the first week of my stay, things had escalated. I was up to six bags of chilli-flavoured Yam Slices with my talkshows and would spend the entire afternoon contemplating Life, the tailoring on Maria's white blouses and the possibilities of Stephanie's ceiling over several microbrews. Of course, if you haven't guessed already, this was one of my most recent reveries with regards the whole inverted-floor conundrum ... *except that something different happened this time!* There I was, lying on the polished floorboards, drunkenly spilling beer and cigarette ash all over my t-shirt and imagining how I would get socks out of an imaginary chest of drawers that I'd stuck into the corner of the ceiling, when I suddenly remembered another childhood musing that I'd never mentioned to anyone in my life.

Top Cat.

Do you remember? He lived in an alleyway on the wrong side of town, had a gang and a great signature tune, harassed a poor police officer named Dibble and generally lived it up. After a few verses of *Top Cat . . . ta tant ta ta ta . . . the most incredible leader of the pack*, I tried to remember the names of the rest of TC's gang other than Choo Choo, Brain and the regrettable Benny – couldn't – but ended up being reminded of another thing that used to puzzle me. You see, during the credits at the very end of every episode, TC used to hang up his snazzy purple waistcoat and hat, put on his polka-dot pyjamas, pop in his ear plugs, put up his television aerial for some light-night NFL action and climb wearily into his garbage-can/bed/office/studio-apartment, only to be helplessly whisked away by a dump-truck. Every episode this happened – and what had always worried me was how TC got back to the alleyway for the beginning of each subsequent episode. Did he jump out the back of the truck? And if so, did he drag his bin with him? Or did he ring Benny, Choo Choo, Brain (with his Droopy Dog eyes) and the others, and order them to come and get him?

Similarly, when Fred Flintstone got locked out of the house by his sabre-toothed pussycat at the end of every episode of

The Flintstones, did he resign himself to a night's sleep on the rock-hard doorstep? Wasn't there a back door he could resort to? Didn't Wilma get pissed off (or just *pissed*, as they say out there) at the regular-as-clockwork cries of 'WILMAAAAAA . . . !' every evening as she applied her curlers and prehistoric mudpack?

I was later to find out that, at least in this instance, popular consensus has Wilma open the door, while only one person believed that Fred started his next sunny day in Bedrock cruelly unshaven and bleary-eyed on the doorstep of the Flintstone household. But that afternoon I was alone with only my own questions for company. After a few hours of contemplation, I got up off the floor, fixed myself an iced tea and scanned the television pages for episodes of either cartoon, but found neither. If I'd wanted to, I could have watched four *Creature from the Black Lagoon* films all in a row, but I'd seen them the day before. So instead, I started preparing a salad and waited for Stephanie to get back from the city.

•

'Wilma let him in.'

'You reckon?'

'*Totally.*'

Steph took another spoonful of Fuzzy Munch, dipped her spoon into the tub of Furry Slop Pops and put it into her mouth, one hand under her chin to catch the drops. The air in her kitchen was warm and tangy.

'And that's your last answer?'

'Yup!' Little did I know that she would be the first of many people who believed as much.

'I think . . .' I started to reply, but then paused dramatically as I reached for the chopped-hazelnuts sprinkler. 'I think that if anything happened – and that's not to say that I'm convinced as to what *did* happen – then she left him on the doorstep. For the whole night. On purpose.'

'Oh come on, Jeremy!' A few beers never did any harm to Steph's sense of indignation.

'I mean it,' I said. 'Pass me the crushed-biscuit topping can you?'

She slid it across the table saloon-style, knowing that only my American relations are allowed to call me *Jeremy*, just as I never, ever, ever use the word *cookie*. 'Almost every show had Fred and Barney screwing things up. Betty and Wilma were always saving their asses . . .'

'Betty and Wilma fucked up too,' I replied. 'I can think of plenty of their scams that went wrong.'

Steph put down her ice-cream and handed me the phone.

'Call Jackie! See what *she* says!' she challenged.

As it turned out, Jackie (Steph's sister) was at an architects' dinner downtown, at a conference centre somewhere on Van Ness, and although the ringer on her cellphone had been switched to SOOTHE mode, it hadn't been turned off entirely and I might as well have gone right in there and played a drum solo.

'Waddya mean: "What happened to Fred at the end of *The Flintstones*?"' Jackie hissed down the line. 'Do you know what you've done? My phone just went off in the middle of Jay Szymanski's speech! In front of two hundred architects!'

I later discovered, after an intimate conversation with a beautiful designer called Alexis Vanek, that Jackie had dis-embowelled her handbag in her haste to find her bleeping phone and in the process managed to spill two bottles of wine over the curator of the Powers Institute and the visiting Chief of Police sitting on either side of her. And though Jay Szymanski, acclaimed designer of both Rosenfeld Memorial

Museums (Chicago and New York), might not have blinked an eyelid at the digitised *Fur Elise* that sounded out from amidst his seated audience, he hadn't been able to ignore the SWAT team of waiters that rushed to clear up the spreading mess and had needed to pause in the middle of the word *psychogeography* with an eyebrow impatiently raised.

I quickly summarised the terms of the dispute. There was a moment's silence at the other end of the line, if you didn't count the scurrying of waiters or the faltering voice echoing in the background.

'Wilma let him in. Of course she did. Now can I please hang up?'

I put the phone down. Steph was already stretched out on a sofa with a bottle of Chablis and looking at the ceiling.

'I told you so.'

Indeed she had.

'Steph? When you were a kid, did you ever stare up at the ceiling and . . .'

•

Over the weekend and the following week, I searched the TV listings for a glimpse of Fred or TC, something to jump-start my memory, but they didn't seem to be showing either cartoon in that part of the state. That left me with only raw human data, so I asked almost everyone I met what they thought, as long as it didn't seem obvious that the person in question would be offended. Steph, when I asked her, couldn't remember the end of *Top Cat* but claimed she did remember that at the end of every show she'd had to turn over as soon as possible to catch the end of *Wacky Races* because they'd clashed. Jackie wouldn't budge from her position, not even under duress, and I was still undecided. A few people couldn't remember seeing, or had never seen, both cartoons (which is to say that I asked my uncle and my grandmother next). But most had some recollection of one or the other and even a fair number of Jackie's architect friends offered me ideas on the subject and were no end of fun after I brought the whole thing up one evening, in a lobster restaurant on the top floor of the Embacadero Centre. I hadn't been sure how such a line of questioning would go down, but after a few rounds of tequila their answers had been prolific and many of them spent the rest of the evening trying to impersonate Fred and Barney or the giggling of Betty and Wilma, much to my and Jackie's surprise. Even the *maître d'* had a theory. Citing Fred's virility as his principal evidence and acknowledging with a shrug that it was Wilma's *duty* to let him in, he lingered by our table and solemnly expounded his belief that surely '*Monsieur Fleentston*' would have gone out for a big night of gambling and drinking with Barney and his other buddies from the quarry. 'A man az no uzzer course of action,' he added, with a brief smile for Ms Vanek who was sitting next to me (and whom he later escorted home), 'when a woman doz no return iz lov.'

In a way, it was good to know that there were other people like me out there, people troubled by the little things as well as the big. But what wasn't so great was that I was starting to get the same answers after a while. For every gem there were turkeys. For every 'Fred went on a bender' there were several people who gave Wilma the benefit of the doubt. Even my aunt, after presentations by both Steph and myself, concluded that Wilma was the key to the situation (all this said in a hushed tone you understand, with a sideways glance at my slumped uncle who was busy watching Jerry Rice receive his millionth pass for the 49ers that quarter). Did everyone think that Wilma let Fred back in? It seemed like it when I finally collated the results of my survey so that I could make some kind of sense of them.

They went something like this.

90.48% of the people questioned could remember seeing *The Flintstones*. 100% of these could remember the ending (I guess shouting 'WILMAAAAAA' at the top of your voice grabs attention) and of that figure a staggering 84.21% believed that Wilma let him in. Of this percentage, 71.88% were women. Incidentally, 0.026% of people who had seen *The Flintstones* confirmed the best of my suspicions and thought that it wasn't necessary 'to find closure for that particular narrative sequence as its meaning/outcome was formally, as well as arbitrarily, convened/deferred', that there was 'no necessary reason to make logical/chronological connections between the credits sequence and the main body of the narrative' and that the credits were 'a repeated syntagm anyway'. As it happened, 0.026% of people who had seen *The Flintstones* was a Doctor of Literature at Santa Cruz, an old college friend of Steph's that I met on my third weekend in America. And every time 0.026% got to a '/', she said the word 'stroke', which I thought was pretty sexy.

The other side of the coin was a much tidier affair. Of the people questioned, exactly one-third had seen *Top Cat* (23.81% had seen both) yet only 50% could remember the credits sequence. The overwhelming majority view – 90.86% to be exact – agreed that TC was cool. Very cool. Positively low temperature. After this, opinions varied with most – 57.14% – opting for the calling of the gang, although 0.00% of these couldn't remember any of their names other than Brain, Benny and Choo Choo. The Doctor of Literature, now 0.071% of all *Top Cat* viewers questioned, did her little bit as well and after dialling us a pizza from her bedside telephone, decided that TC was so cool that on reaching the depot, he simply had his trash can put on the next truck back to the alley ('he was under no pressure . . . he probably had a mini-bar in his trash can and kicked back with a highball') none the worse for the experience.

11

3

Start to finish, I was in San Francisco for six weeks. Enough time to learn to stop asking for 'twenty Marlboro' at the fag shop, to stop calling fags *fags*, to look in the right direction when crossing the road, to know that a *Café Borgia* was the brightest possible way to start the day. The best thing I'd seen, or nearly seen, had been a species of Amazonian fish in the aquarium at the California Academy of Sciences. It was so brazenly vile that it was prohibited from sharing a tank with any other creatures, and the little plastic sign above the tank (which had been empty for unspecified and wholly ominous reasons) informed that the fish had been known to attack straying cattle. Even schools of piranha were considered a soft target, and after looking around at the rest of the fish and a few belligerent octopi, I reckoned *that* fact alone made it the Leader of the Pack. The Big Chief. It was illegal just to own one in the State of California.

On my last day in America, I was still thinking about this absent fish and preparing to watch my last episode of *Maria!* – an episode about shark attack – when my mother called.

'Is Steph there?' she asked, after I'd enquired about the kids and reassured her that I'd visited my grandmother regularly.

'No. She's at work.' My mother would have known that Steph was at work, it being a Friday morning.

'That's a shame. And how are *you*? Have you packed?'

I paused, looking at my suitcases stacked by the front door. The last thing I wanted on my final morning in San Francisco was another 'I-never-liked-her-Are-you-feeling-better?' speech, however well intended.

'Mum?'

'Yeeess . . . ?' It is a peculiar trait of my mother's that she often sounds like Bela Lugosi's butler.

'Do you remember the end of *The Flintstones*, when Fred gets locked out?'

'Yes I do.'

This didn't surprise me. My mother is one of those people who, in spite of displaying many of the undesirable symptoms of prolonged parenthood, has a firm grasp of who Adam West and Burt Ward are and holds a healthy torch for the mercurial Jim Rockford.

'Well . . . what do you think happens? How does Fred get back inside the house? Or do you think that he sleeps the night on the doorstep?'

My mother didn't answer for a while and I guessed that she was thinking. But after a few minutes she still hadn't answered and I suggested that she thought that Wilma simply let Fred back in the house.

'Oh no!' she said in a tone of voice that I'd only heard her use once before. It was when I had accused her of preferring The Beatles over The Stones because she was soft. ('Oh no!' she had said, 'I just didn't like Mick Jagger's lips.')

'Oh no!' she said down the telephone. 'What I think happened was that while Fred was banging on the door, the director shouts, "Cut!" Fred then goes back to his trailer, gets into his normal clothes and drives home. Why do you ask?'

•

After I put the phone down, I pondered my mother's genius. Her answer took some beating. A moment of pure class. Even my Doctor of Literature friend couldn't have matched that. I thought about it again, thought of good ol' Fred marching back to his trailer, to his cellphone, his cigars, a cocaine habit, an LA Rams cheerleader or three and all the rest. 'Hey!' he would shout, 'this champagne ain't cold. Waddya all . . . *amateurs*?' before steaming off the lot in his red sports car.

Such a statement provoked questions beyond 'Would Fred's feet stick out the bottom of his Buick Wildcat?' Surely it raised all sorts of issues with regards TC and his stray gang of cool cats. What was the truth about Choo Choo's pink fur and cream polo-neck? Why were Brain's eyes so droopy (and why was he so aimless?) and how long would it be before Dibble cracked and confessed certain shocking truths about rehab, mere tabloid speculation up until then, to his Latin-American fans on *Maria!*?

I had little time to think about it that day. My plane was due to take off in a few hours and Maxine (Doctor Cigliuti to you) had been kind enough to offer to take me to the airport at around one o'clock. I'd be a liar if I said that things weren't a little awkward as we drove along the freeway to San Francisco International, and though we both cheered up after I'd given her a hug and said some nice things to her once we'd got out of the car, an uncomfortable silence returned while I was pulling my cases out of the trunk. I lit a cigarette to give my hands something to do and was looking up at the fading summer sky when she finally spoke up.

'Can I ask you something?'

'Sure. Anything you like.'

'I'm embarrassed.'

'Don't be.'

I turned to face her and saw hesitation in the pools of her eyes.

'It's just that I wanted to know if you were being serious.'

I took one of her hands in mine. I'm a shit when it comes to conversations like this. A real shit. Even my ex-wife will agree with me there.

14

'Are you referring to us sleeping together . . . ? I mean . . .
sort of . . . seeing . . .'

Her mouth spread wide in a smile.

'No, dumb-ass! I meant about *The Flintstones.*' She punched
me on the shoulder. 'And *Top Cat* too.'

I replied that I'd been serious.

'That's good. I'm glad. It's just that I never had a chance to
ask you if you get a show called *Magnum P.I.* in England.'

Magnum! I thought of Thomas, Rick, Higgins and the other
TC. In my mind I saw a titles sequence that included leopard-
print bikinis, magical Hawaiian sunsets, grass skirts and a big
red Ferrari.

'It's one of my favourite shows,' Maxine added and I looked
at my watch. There was still thirty minutes until check-in and
there was a Bagel Counter through the swing doors near to
where we were standing. I hurried her over and said it was my
turn to buy.

THE COMFORT ZONE

And this is where we wait
together, regardless of age,
our carts stocked with brightly
coloured goods.

Don DeLillo, *White Noise*

1

I often think back to a moment during the first round of THE GAME. Moll and I were standing by the delicatessen counter in the supermarket, staring at the tubs of shivering food on the other side of the glass.

'Look at the Calamata olives!' she said, pointing. 'They look like the gleaming husks of beetles!'

After three years together, I was used to Moll's prosodic reaction to many things, including bad computer games, the word *cunt* and egg mayonnaise. But she knows that I'm paralysed by insects more than anything else (along with injections, dentists and failure): *was she being deliberately mean?*

'Don't put me off . . . I'm concentrating!' I replied as I surreptitiously bit on another Chicken Penang Bite. 'I need to score at least another ten quid in the next few minutes if we're to stay in contention. I just saw Chip and Suki on their fifth packet of chocolate raisins over in aisle 26 – and Chip wasn't even looking green.'

'But they do! *Look!*' She pointed again. 'Imagine eating a quarter-pound of beetles, the crack of the shells as they split between your teeth, the writhing thoraxes . . .'

Suddenly it was me who was starting to turn green as Moll asked the girl behind the counter for a half-dozen scotch eggs.

'What do we actually want to pay for?' I asked.

'Some beers, some wine, some crisps – the others can pay me back when they come over tonight. But please don't get any cakes or biscuits. I've had enough of sleeping next to you after you've got so stoned that you pass out without brushing your teeth.'

'What do you mean by *that*?' I asked, and it was then that Moll snapped.

'We all fall asleep in our clothes once in a while but you seem to be turning it into a ritual. If you're not careful, you'll have to go to the dentist before the end of the summer, something which *you* despise and I despise hearing about.'

•

Once again, I'm left with the feeling that I'm learning too little too late. When had that sour note of frustration crept into her voice? Had it been there all summer? Or longer?

At the time, I put Moll's combative manner down to the content of her reading. The latest issue of *Sassy!* magazine had run a feature article entitled 'How To Argue!', the journalist citing 'Taking Turns', 'Calm Honest Responses' and 'Eye Contact' as the necessary components of any 'serious discussion', big ticks splashed on to the page next to photographs of a couple engaged in all three activities. Conversely, the journalist had also cast a damning verdict on such male tricks as the 'Looking-to-the-heavens-What-did-I-do?' response, the 'Hands-up-You-win' approach (typically employed within sixty seconds, with eyes widened) and the 'Glassy Stare'.

So there in the supermarket, I only imagined that Moll had simply been taking the opportunity to implement some new Agony-Aunt theory that she'd recently fixated on, as she often did and usually out of the blue. But now I realise that she was trying to tell me that she was ready to leave, that there wasn't anyone else (even if there seemed to be very soon afterwards) but that she'd had enough of *me*.

But if that's the case, then why did she stay around to play THE GAME?

•

Of course there are a multitude of theories discussed and dismissed by all of us involved with THE GAME, a 'shitload of reasons' (as The Doc might phrase it) as to why we had a competition to see who could steal and eat the most food from the supermarket. 'Swashbuckling in an age of microwave meals, CCTV and slow-motion replays,' Jefferson suggested when I raised the issue just the other day, perhaps seven months later when most of us were sitting in the pub watching Wimbledon knock Manchester United out of the FA Cup.

'I get bored shopping,' said Chip, 'always have done. When I eat meat what I really want to have done is looked the fucker in the eye and ripped out its throat with my own teeth.' Which separates him, I suppose, from those who simply said that they'd had nothing better to do.

'*We* did it because we knew that we were championship material from the start,' said The Gooners, who then started dancing around the TV room of the pub spilling their lager everywhere and singing their 'Oh-to . . . oh-to-be . . . oh-to-be-a . . . GOONA' victory song until a newsflash that Leeds were one-nil up at Highbury sent them humbly back to their seats.

'I also think we got carried away by the Euro '96 feelgood-factor,' said Jefferson.

'Bullshit. *You* got involved 'cos you're a thievin' scouser. It's in yer blood,' said The Doc.

•

As for me? Well, parts of me identified with most of those answers. But if anyone asked me why I played THE GAME, I would tell them it was because of Gazza and the inspiration of a simple trajectory one Saturday afternoon last June (remember the perfect turf and the Wembley weather, the ball looping up

21

through the air from his left foot to his right, Scots defenders on the floor or nowhere to be seen, the Dentist's Chair celebration, those Tears-in-Turin finally and thankfully a million years away from *that* Saturday afternoon at Wembley). I never felt like explaining it in any other terms.

'I think witnessing such moments of genius always stirs people up a bit,' I said to Calamity Claire, for example, during a retrospective moment by the jukebox. 'We all see it and want to get *out there* and achieve something.'

●

Of course Moll wasn't in the pub on the night Marcus Gayle's headed goal knocked United out of the FA Cup, or at least not in the same pub as us. And even though we talked about it a lot at the time, I still don't have her reasons.

2

It all happened during the summer of '96. Moll and I were living in the basement of my Aunt Jocasta's house in Chiswick and getting our rent paid by the Housing Benefit office because I was claiming the dole. Although a year had passed since we'd left university, I still wasn't working, was still unable to decide what-I-wanted-to-do-with-my-life: everything I could think of seemed not important enough to be a life's work, but too important to be merely a hobby.

It was a time spent in frantic apprehension of the dentist's chair (a real one), in fearful dread of the 'Butcher of Burlington Gardens' and his array of mouth-pumps, his arsenal of hypodermic weaponry, his oral torture-machines. It was the summer of the European Championships, a magical three weeks when everyone went football crazy. And it was a summer spent floating into the dole office with a portfolio of rejection letters painstakingly procured by a combination of careful targeting and contrived helplessness.

Did I have what it takes to be an On-Site Analyst for leading blue-chip manufacturers of FMCGs? Was I a team-playing, self-starting writer of 'Advertorials'?

I am aware of my lack of experience in the field of Industrial Liaison, I would write on bluntly worded application letters, *but believe that my interpersonal skills and an aptitude for quick learning will more than compensate.*

Out with the databased mailshot and in with the rejection letters. *You have not been successful with your application in this instance,* the companies would reply, leaving me with no other option than to surrender the evidence of my enterprise at the job centre once a fortnight and duly collect my winnings.

•

So there I was (and I wasn't the only one), spending the summer mixing records at parties and clubs for a little extra cash to supplement my giro and selling three-gram eighths of hash for the same reasons. Moll had recently started some part-time work-experience at a VT editing suite in Euston and the result was plenty of empty days for me to do whatever I wanted – which invariably meant watching the football whenever it was on, sunbathing in the park with my comics and smoking single-skin joints while I doodled down ideas (but not really) for the novel I was planning to write called *The Year I Stayed In.* Also, Chip from next door had pretty much taken to letting the part-timers run the off-licence which he managed ('you don't need to *sell* alcohol – *it sells itself,*' he would chortle) and the both of us would get high and meander along the High Road in the sunshine, stopping off at beer gardens and record shops as they passed us by, paying visits to the library with its cheap

video rental and to the supermarket with its bright colours and
its air-conditioning.

•

'Just because I'm a bit slack in a personal sense at the moment
doesn't mean that I have to stop caring about the planet,' I said,
handing the joint to Chip and taking a jam jar out of the white
plastic bag. 'And anyway: listen to this . . .'

We were standing by the recycling skips at the back of the
supermarket car-park. I pushed the jar through the little spyhole
and we heard the smash as it broke on the other side.

'Weird, isn't it?' I said.

'The sound reverberates inside the skip.'

'It's sort of violent . . .'

'. . . yet benevolent.'

'An action that's satisfyingly propitious . . .'

'. . . yet rewarding at a destructive level.'

'A morsel of cheap fulfilment . . .'

'. . . just when it was least looked for.'

'The crucial issue remains: do they plan it that way?'

'Of course they do.'

Chip took a large Ribena bottle out of the carrier bag. The
sound of the smash was even louder.

'It's good to help the environment.'

'Let's go. The Germany–Czech Republic game starts in an
hour and we've got shopping to do.'

The recycling skips were only the first round in the supermarket's continuity of cheap thrills. All I needed was four bottles of
Budweiser Budvar as an excuse to be in the building in the first
place (Grolsch if it was Holland playing, cans of Carlsberg Ice for
Denmark and so on) and if high-velocity skidding along the polished aisles on my own wire trolley wasn't sufficient entertainment then I could always examine everyone else's shopping.

•

There were plenty of other options if I needed them.

I could slip haemorrhoid cream through the bars of another customer's trolley or into their basket when they weren't looking and then watch them squirm when they arrived at the checkout. What were they going to do when they eventually noticed the offending tube (in their minds, it was the size of a courgette)?

Usually they either tried to hide it amongst the magazines by the till or else ran back to the Home Remedial shelves to replace it. Some tried to claim that they were the victim of a practical joke, resulting in much entertainment on the part of the cashier and other customers. And occasionally (and best of all) some just paid for it, trying to keep a straight face and not draw any attention to themselves. I even played the trick on my bank manager when I saw him buying groceries one lunchtime and watching *his* poker face cloud over as the cashier-girl passed the tube through the infra-red was a moment to *savour*.

•

If I wanted, I could search out Sonia, the prettiest girl out of all the supermarket staff, who usually worked at the cigarette counter. Talking to her was as easy as buying a scratchcard or a packet of Rizlas and she would occasionally ask me for a couple of eighths for her friends, which never hurt.

•

And sometimes there were free samples on offer at a makeshift counter in the supermarket entrance and I could nibble on a small cube of whatever cheese it was that was on trial, or perhaps sip on a thimble of some newly developed Chardonnay and see how many times I could get away with going back and asking for more.

•

But if all this got boring, or didn't suit the mood of the day, then I could simply stand there in the crowd that slowly divided itself over the tills and marvel at everybody: the pensioners with their frugal baskets of chocolate mints, ready-to-bake spotted dick and own-brand custard creams perched on top of four crates of cat food; the students with their cereals and tinned tomatoes, their economy pasta and special-offer wines; the Range-Rovered wives with two heaped trolleys and a clutch of food-and-wine magazines, credit cards poised and primed. The price of a four-pack bought me the right to check everyone out at the checkout, the parade of packets, tins, bags and boxes on the black rubber conveyor-belt telling its own story, divulging the details of other lives.

I would often find myself treading water in the sluggish queue at clocking-off time, amazed as people's shopping formed its own account of someone else's immediate future. *There they went*: one bake-in-the-tray Broccoli Mornay; one bag of apples; one tube of Rolos; one jumbo-size packet of crisps. I'd take a mental inventory of the shopping as it rolled down towards the chaos of plastic bags at the far end and I'd look up to see some gently perspiring first-jobber in a grey polyester suit (nineteen years old and now already half a decade younger than me) trying to pay and pack at the same time and evanescing bedsit vibes, an evening-in-front-of-the-TV and a late-pint-round-the-corner before the early night under the inevitably frayed duvet and another day's duty at the filing cabinet. *There they went*: the single rotund slab of Barbary Duck; the 365g jar of Gourmet à L'Orange Sauce; the black plastic tray of Sugar Snaps (already topped and tailed). I'd look up to see an opera-swilling, fringe-theatre-loving Chiswick dilettante waiting with open carrier bags, a copy of *Aria* poking out of an authentically scuffed leather satchel and a red spotted hankie spilling from his breast pocket.

Eventually I wondered if there was something intrusive about this point-of-sale voyeurism and I soon asked Chip if he analysed other people's shopping.

'Of course I do. It's a late-twentieth-century condition.'

Chip said it was called 'Social Profiling'.

'I do it all the time at the off-licence . . .'

'When you're there . . .'

'When I'm there.'

'Chip – you *work* there. You're the manager for fuck's sake! We're just customers here and we're still looking over our shoulders at everyone else's shopping.'

'They plan it that way. It may be a cheap thrill, but it's a thrill nonetheless.'

•

The problem with cheap thrills, of course, is that they can soon get expensive. The European Championships meant that there was an average of three hours of football programming each day to shop for and all of us were partial to the odd snack as we wheeled around amongst the tamarillos and galia melons. To start with we presented the empty wrappers, packets and Tetrapaks of the items that had fallen foul of our impatience to the disapproving eyes of the cashier-girls. After all, we weren't *criminals*. We were just bored. And *peckish*. But it didn't take long before the empty wrappers, packets and Tetrapaks stopped ending up on the conveyor-belt and started ending up in our pockets, in our record-bags, on the floor or stuffed under the mounds of glistening grapefruit.

'I could get used to this,' said Chip, as he deposited an empty Hot 'n' Spicy Pepparami wrapper behind the columns of toilet-paper in aisle 5.

'I think we already are,' I countered.

'Still this . . . this *grazing* lark,' he continued (Chip and I were pleased to have discovered the official terminology for our particular style of snacking), 'it's not *all* bad. I mean it takes *application* to know where to stash all this . . . *debris*.'

'It's a skill,' I suggested.

'You could almost turn the whole thing into a sport.'

Now *there* was an idea.

3

'Do you have any work to declare?'

'No.'

No way. Another fast-track-entry into the-world-of-media-sales had been denied me (O.T.E. rumoured to be *blah-blah-blah*) and my misspelt application to become a 'recriutment copyriter' for Paine, Toyle & Loss on Hammersmith Road had also met with rejection. I dutifully pushed my rejection letters across the desk down-at-the-dole-office, while a young black guy was going through a similar process at the adjacent signing-point.

'Have you worked at all this last fortnight?'

'No,' he replied, signing his name and smoothing out the creases of his hundred-pound Dolce & Gabbana jeans with the pale undersides of his fingers. I followed the line of his legs down to the floor where his feet lay cosseted in a sparkling pair of box-fresh Filas and he turned his head and winked.

A minute later, we were both pushing through the swing doors and stepping out into the street. As soon as we were out of sight, we shook hands.

'How's it going, Tevin?'

'Not bad, as it happens.'

'Where did you get your new trainers?'

'A mate's shop down in Tooting. He imports. I can sort you out if you want.'

'Not at the moment. I'm a bit skint. You got time for a drink?'

Tevin nodded and soon we were skinning up in a beer garden along the High Road and drinking Red Stripe from the bottle, talking about football and pot and records.

'Tevin – can I ask you a question?'

'Sure,' he said.

'How come you aren't like your brother or some of the other boys you roll around with?'

'What do you mean by that?' Tevin asked, flicking weed seeds off the table-top and on to the floor.

'Your brother and your other mates all dress *down* when it comes to signing on. They're probably in the multi-storey right now changing out of their Hilfiger and Ralph Lauren. But *you*? You go into the job centre with your big trainers, a new Armani jacket and all-the-rest and tell them blatantly that you haven't worked.'

•

Tevin, along with his brother, Reesey, and his cousins, used to serve-up in an area that spanned west from Shepherd's Bush Road as far as Hanwell, never straying further south than the river and never further north than the Hanger Lane Gyratory after a run-in with the Martin Family up in Wembley a couple of years back. Ounces, wraps of coke, pills, pagers, smart-cards for mobiles, SIMMs and SCSIs, satellite receivers – they were happy to deliver it all. And when it came to signing-on day, they'd leave their Golf GTis in a car-park nearby and change into six-year-old Air-Maxes and worn-out 501s before showing their faces. Sometimes they'd even take it in turns to sign on for each other. *We all look the same to them,* Tevin said on one occasion, *which is fine with us.*

•

'Yeah. I guess you're right.' Tevin cupped the joint and lit it. 'The thing is . . . I ain't really like Reesey or the others.'

'In what way?'

'Well . . . like I'm older than them, right?'

'Right.'

'An' they're all happy signing on and making the extra dollar selling. But *me*? I don't want to be signing on no more. I got my music and my screensavers and my HTML skills and all that. I don't want to still be serving up pills in a year's time. I will if I have to . . . *but that's different.*'

Tevin took another sip of his beer.

'So I guess I just front up to the system to remind me who I am, to remind me who I want to be . . . *and to give me a kick up the arse.*'

We drank up. Tevin wanted to show me the new hands-free kit he'd 'found' for his car. He also had a new Zoom Tube so we climbed in and went for a spin down the M4 as far as Heathrow before turning back, putting some old '92 Vibes 'n' Wishdokta on the tape-deck so that I could check out the bass.

'How's Chip?' Tevin asked as we sailed past Junction 2. 'Is he still running that off-licence or what? Every time I go in there looking for him, he ain't there.'

'He's not working much these days.'

'Enjoying the sunshine, is it?'

'Something like that. The both of us are trying to start something up at the moment.'

'What's that then?'

I told Tevin about our out-of-control snacking.

'So we thought we'd have a competition. We're sorting the

rules out at the moment and looking for possible competitors. You interested?'

'Reckon so.' Tevin laughed. 'It sounds . . . *interesting*.'

•

Supermarkets. Think about them one way and they're just shops, just *big* shops, just another fantastic convenience. Think about them another way and suddenly you're in the realm of Loyalty Cards and Reward Points, the land of absent clocks, artificial light and data-tracking.

'It's called a "Comfort Zone". They set their environmental controls at a steady 23°C during the summer,' announced Suki, Chip's girlfriend. Two days later, Moll, Chip, Suki and I were eating a meal that I'd made. Cooking for the four of us had become my duty on the days I cashed my giro.

'Because of the humidity problem that comes with air-conditioning,' she continued, 'they have to overcool the air and then re-heat it to the appropriate temperature.'

'That sounds good for the environment,' I said. 'And how the hell do you know that anyway?'

Suki shrugged.

'Part of me *loves* going to the supermarket. I feel so free,' said Moll. 'There's so much choice. I know that the reality is otherwise, of course, but never when I'm actually in a supermarket.'

'I was horrified when I noticed that they don't sell single-litre bottles of any of the major soft drinks any more,' said Suki. 'It's just an attempt to force us to increase our dosage.'

'The supermarket is like the Federation of Planets in *Star Trek*,' Chip chipped in. 'It doesn't matter who you are or what you look like – you can still be a member of the institution. All you've got to do is obey the rules, which is to say that you dutifully spend your money there . . .'

'Which is where *we* come in,' I interrupted.

Chip and I had both mentioned our preliminary ideas about THE GAME to Suki and Moll. And now we pushed our plates to one side and addressed the task of forming an official list of rules.

'Are we going to have teams?' asked Chip.

'We could have a mass free-for-all,' offered Suki, 'just get everyone we know to walk into the supermarket at the same time and start stealing.'

'What if someone gets caught?' asked Moll.

It took almost two hours of discussion before we came up with a set of ideas that looked even vaguely feasible. But eventually I had it all written down and made another pot of coffee before summarising everything back to the others.

First, we were going to put all of the teams into a hat and then make a draw which placed them in a knockout competition. Teams were to consist of two players – one doing the actual *eating* while the other acted as a look-out and general *aide-de-camp* – with *both* players permitted to conceal food packaging and price labels around their person. After all, we were going to score each game by totalling the cash-value of goods consumed and needed some easy way to keep a record.

The length of each leg of the competition had also been a difficult issue. An hour? Half an hour? Forty-five minutes? In the end I suggested twenty-two and a half minutes (half the length of half a football match) which seemed satisfactory, and it was agreed that both members of the team had to join the 'Five Items Only' queue before such time had elapsed.

'We'll get someone trustworthy to sit on the old people's benches behind the checkout line with a stopwatch,' I said, 'so that all you have to do is be seen to join the queue within the allotted time. That way, competitors can't be penalised for the sluggishness of other shoppers in the queue before them.'

'What?' objected Chip. 'We have to *buy* something as we go round so that we can get out at the end?'

'It seems inconsistent with the general premise, I know, but I can't see any other fair way of implementing closure on the GAME process.'

Suki suggested that if Chip was so worried about it, he could try buying some fruit. It was cheap, she told him, and might even be good for him.

•

And so it was that we had the basic format of THE GAME. Unsurprisingly, a lot of suggestions were discarded. The idea of a Vegetarian League was just one example. And though it seemed fair to allow contenders to take a tin-opener and items of cutlery in with them (the range of foodstuffs that it would have been possible to eat would have been too limited otherwise), a line had to be drawn at plates, bowls and similar receptacles, otherwise this would have made THE GAME 'ridiculous'.

4

Once the initial rules were decided, it was a matter of forming the teams. Tevin checked with Reesey and then logged in officially by mobile phone. Jan and Steve-from-up-the-road called in from up the road the following day. Chip and Suki already seemed to have devised a ten-aisle strategy.

A few days later I called The Doc and Calamity Claire. The Doc answered.

'A thievin' competition,' he concluded after I'd run through the details with him.

'It's not exactly *thieving*.'

'What is it then? How's it diff'rent?' The Doc sniffed

disdainfully. 'Just so's I know, y'know?' He'd been mixing records at Two Smoking Turntables until six that morning and I'd woken him which always made him a little bit haughty.

'It's different because we're not criminals,' I told him, 'we're not desperate. Nor are we trying to *gain* anything.'

'Y'what?'

'*Theft* means that the thief wants to *possess* or *consume* the thieved object for some reason generated by either the thieved object itself or by a value system to which the thieved object is linked. There's also the issue of the evasion of the economic system of sacrifice, of payment, of having the ready cash.'

'Yeah?'

'What we're engaging in is a totally different sort of exercise: a contest of mental agility and gastronomic fortitude; a head–to–head–single–leg–knockout–cup–competition requiring consumer knowledge and progressive moralities.'

The Doc blew his nose.

'Soun's like the diff'rence between thievin' and a thievin' *competition* to me. Not that I give a shit . . . I'm in.'

'Great. What about Claire?'

I heard him turn over and prod her. A muffled 'fuck off' came back in response before The Doc returned to the line.

'Make that both of us.'

So that was The Doc and Calamity Claire booked. I put the phone down, walked into the living-room and sat down next to Moll who was watching Turkey vs. Denmark.

'The Doc says that he and Claire will play,' I told her.

'I heard. Through the door.'

Moll looked tired. I thought that maybe the late nights she'd been working recently were getting to her so I tried to make her laugh.

'Did I tell you about the time Gazza told the President of

34

the Danish Football Association that he could speak Danish and then proceeded to do an imitation of the Swedish Chef from *The Muppet Show*?'

'Yes.'

'Smile if you like me . . .' I poked Moll in the ribs but she grimaced.

'Get off!'

'Who's winning?' I asked, starting to roll a joint, even though I knew that the game had only just kicked off, even though the score was displayed in the top left-hand corner of the screen along with the time.

'They've only just kicked off.'

We didn't say much for a while, just the odd comment on my part with regard to the Danish number two being 'surprisingly handy' and the observation that the Turkish centre-halves were sluggish in stepping-up-on-the-opposition-forwards. Moll was still being quiet and I wondered if she was having second thoughts about THE GAME.

'You want to play, don't you?' I asked.

'Want to play *what*?'

'THE GAME.'

'You sound like you're asking me to come outside and kick footballs at cars in the street after our homework's done.'

I looked across at her, trying to work out her mood, but her eyes just reflected back the twinkling lights of the television screen. I could just about make out the white dot of the ball pinging back and forth.

'It'll probably be just as much fun,' I ventured.

'I don't know if I really want to get involved.'

We both sat in silence again for a few moments, and then Moll turned to me and said that she'd play, that she'd be my partner for the whole competition.

'I just want to say, for the record, that I didn't like your definition of theft. Okay?'

•

(*How come?* I hadn't even been bullshitting! How else could one respond to that supernatural array of goods, mass-produced and beamed in from a multitude of different elsewheres, those vast corridors of food suddenly coming into being as I came in off the street, bored and stoned?)

•

'I just want to say, for the record, that I didn't like your definition of theft. Okay?'

I shuffled in my seat.

'*Okay.*'

'I thought it was limited and simplistic.'

'*Okay.* Jeez – I was just messing around.'

Okay. No problem. That was fine. Or was it?

Moll was subdued for the rest of the day and then left for another night shift over in Euston. Soon after, Jefferson arrived to drink a few bottles of Nastro Azzurro and to watch Italy vs. Germany. I thought about talking to him about Moll's increasingly erratic moods but remembered that he never had any good advice when it came to women and told him about THE GAME instead.

'I think I'll be good at this,' he said.

'What makes you say that?' I asked, but then had to wait until after we'd watched a replay of Zola scuffing a penalty before I got my answer.

'The *wanker* . . . he had the Germans at his mercy!' Jefferson shouted in disbelief before the conversation resumed. As it turned out, Jefferson had spent a couple of years at a boarding school up in Cheshire where he'd developed a flair for gluttony. 'They used to ration our tuck,' he said, 'with draconian precision. We were allowed, for example, *four* cans of Coke for each half of the term, *six* packets of crisps, two packets of Fruit Chews, two bars of chocolate and so on. Well, you can imagine what everybody did. The "four cans" rule meant that everybody brought back four 500ml supercans. The "six packet" rule for crisps meant that people arrived at the beginning of term with those huge multi-packs, or else six large cash-and-carry sacks – and I mean *sacks* – of Bar Snacks and Bombay Mix.

'It totally defeated the object of the rules. The school didn't want two hundred boys running about with unlimited sweets. And what did they get? Two hundred boys with a zero-level of patience devouring this unholy amount of *trash* in the first two hours of term, getting totally out of control on caffeine, tartrazine and e-numbers and then throwing up the first of their Christmas-sized bars of Dairy Milk just as they were climbing into bed.'

'So you're confident then?' I asked. 'Who's going to be your partner?'

'It'll have to be Jam . . . and *he* can do the eating come to think of it. I saw him eat twenty-two packets of Monster Munch . . .'

'What? At school?' I asked. Jam, along with guys like Dr Rob and Wavy Dave who now lived down Fulham Palace Road, were all childhood friends of Jefferson's from Liverpool.

'No. Last night, after we beat the Dutch. After we *thrashed* the Dutch. He says he was so stunned, and not just by the ten pints he'd drunk throughout the game, that he doesn't really know what came over him. Can't say I'm surprised. I mean, we beat them! Four-one! Their worst defeat in thirty-six years and *we* gave it to them. Didn't everyone go a little crazy last night?'

Thinking about how Moll had been acting, I wasn't sure. There were some things in life that I knew I could take for granted, some things that were as blatantly obvious as Danny Blind's foul on Paul Ince as he arrived in the penalty box at about twenty-two minutes past eight the night before. These included the fact that we had, indeed, *thrashed* the Dutch. We'd *tonked* them. We'd *battered* them. Choose your own combination of words out of *spanked, humiliated* and *humbled*. Over the ninety minutes, we'd delivered a football showcase that even started to absolve the pain of Turnip Taylor's final days and The Koeman Incident, with perhaps the third goal being the exhibition piece (Gazza taking the ball off Adams after a mistake by Ronald de Boer, exchanging the ball with *both* Anderton and McManaman before *strolling* into the box and slipping it to Sheringham who feints then passes to Shearer who gives it the-doomsday-treatment-off-the-bootlaces). That much was certain. *But what about Moll?*

After the game I'd travelled out to Vauxhall with my records. I'd been asked to mix a set at Bam Bam's, a small club near the station, by a friend-of-a-friend-of-a-friend for forty quid. Moll hadn't been sure if she was going to come because she thought that she might be called in to work at the last minute. But in the end she wasn't needed and tagged along with Suki.

•

Have I said how beautiful Moll was? Forget about turning-heads-in-the-pub or looking-good-on-your-arm or wolf-whistles-in-the-street – Moll was always too striking for any of this to be sufficient (however much she protests that her nose is too big or chest too flat). And it was that night, the night England put four past the Dutch in front of a packed Wembley, that I realised she was changing, that it was as if she was growing even more beautiful by the day.

I'm not talking about the-sunshine-bringing-out-the-best-in-people – what I saw was more than just a tan. Nor am I talking about a few beers and a night of historic football lending my contact lenses a rosy tint. Amidst the noise of the nightclub, the beat pounding four-to-the-floor and the-crowd-going-wild as I dropped another piano-break into the mix, my radar picked up on the way women narrowed their eyes at her before turning away to chat in groups at the bar. I registered, even across the distance of the dancefloor, the hormonal rustle filtering through the crowd of men that loitered near to her and Suki, and I asked myself if it had been always been that way.

I realised it hadn't. It was as if she'd started to effuse some sort of aura into the space around her, some sort of signal, some sort of sound (I faded a dub into the after-echoes of the piano-break). When had *that* started to happen? *And why hadn't I noticed?*

Later on, maybe as late as three or four in the morning, I was still pondering these same questions as the three of us slid back home in a mini-cab. And when Suki let herself in next door, leaving Moll and I fumbling for keys on our doorstep, I took my cue.

'You look beautiful,' I said, remembering what I'd seen from behind the turntables.

'Hurry up and let us in. It's got cold . . .'

'I mean it. You look beautiful.'

'Do I?'

'I think so.'

'But you're drunk.'

'So?'

'So . . . you're making me embarrassed.'

I looked for a glimmer of irony in her eyes but couldn't find it.

'What do you mean, *I make you embarrassed*?' I asked.

There was a pause. One of us managed to open the door and we went inside, both of us walking into the kitchen.

'I didn't mean anything by it,' Moll said, standing with her back to me as she poured herself a glass of water. 'I'm tired. Sorry. It came out wrong, that's all.'

'"Embarrassed" means *embarrassed* however tired you are, doesn't it?' The conversation wasn't going as I'd planned.

'I've apologised, haven't I?'

'Yes . . .' I let my voice trail off, trying to defuse the situation, and Moll said that she was going to get changed.

I sat down on a chair, not knowing what to think for a few minutes, and then walked along the short passage to our bedroom to find Moll already in bed, curled up in a ball and facing away from the door. I took my trainers off and curled up behind her.

'Are you asleep?'

'No.'

'Don't you think it's stupid when people say "Are you asleep?" and the other person says "No"?'

'Take your clothes off, brush your teeth and get into bed.'

'Are you okay?' I asked.

'Fine. I'm tired and I've probably got to work tomorrow.' A hand reached back and squeezed mine. 'Sleep well.'

●

I couldn't sleep for ages. And then, like I've said, the next day I called The Doc and Moll snapped at me afterwards leaving me even more perplexed. *What was the matter with her?* Over the next few days I cooked for her and did her laundry. I cleaned up and even sold some old records at the Music and Video Exchange on Goldhawk Road and spent the money on a new pair of trainers for her. It seemed to cheer her up a little bit but she still seemed to be avoiding me. Was it THE GAME that was making her anxious? I offered to cancel the whole project but she told me that she still wanted to take part.

And then one evening she came home from work and suggested that we go for a walk along the Thames. For a moment my heart yelped because I wondered if she had some bad news to tell me. But she seemed happier and talked about the commercial she'd been working on that day and even bought me dinner in one of the pubs on the towpath. There, we talked about things that had happened at university where we'd met and afterwards, as we walked back arm-in-arm through the leafy streets, she told me that we were celebrating.

'What?' I asked.

Moll told me she'd been offered a full-time editing job and I wrapped my arms around her and congratulated her.

'That's amazing.'

'I'm sorry I've been a bit *serious* recently,' she told me, 'I guess I've just been a bit tense because my work-experience was coming to an end and I wasn't sure what was going to happen.'

'That's alright. And there was me thinking that it was something else, THE GAME perhaps . . . or *me*.'

She squeezed my arm and kissed me.

5

A few days later, I awoke to find that Moll had already left for work. Having nothing else to do, I pulled on some clothes and wandered down the High Road with a joint.

It wasn't just the supermarket that set my pulse racing. The empty days often propelled me to the local Our Price where I'd loiter by the house CDs and leaf through the cases admiring the artwork, imagining what it would be like to be a world-class DJ and putting the shop-staff on edge because they all thought I was going to start shoplifting or removing the inlay booklets.

If I was feeling particularly brave, I'd take the bus up to the sports shops in Hammersmith or even into the West End and just gaze at the trainers. Up in the West End, they've got them all. All the sizes in all the colours: a trainer for every occasion. The latest Reebok Odyssey Hexes in white, black and Rio red for those days when you felt like you needed some 'front'. White Nike Tour Pluses in classic tennis-shoe design with the swoosh tastefully rendered in oxidised green for when you felt like you were 'on-top-of-things' ('postmodern Green Flash,' I suggested to my brother when I told him about them on the telephone: I told him that wearing uncomplicated trainers was the same as being secure in your own sexuality).

•

But once THE GAME got under way, the importance of these minor distractions dissipated. The draw, for instance, caused a stir of excitement as one would expect.

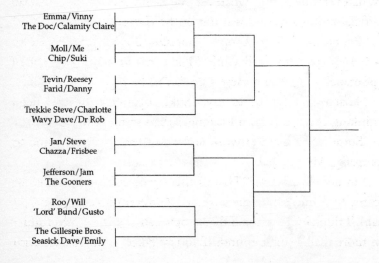

Competition hot-spots obviously included a first-round derby between the Chip–Suki team and Moll and me. Reesey and Tevin facing Farid and Danny had to be what football commentators liked to call 'the plum tie' and having the Jefferson–Jam team drawn against The Gooners was a satisfying nod to those Liverpool–Arsenal confrontations that have thrilled-audiences-down-through-the-ages.

●

'Friggin' scousers!' said The Hood, the designated 'eater' for The Gooners, when I rang him to let him know the results of the draw. 'They've got to be the favourites to win a stealing competition.'

'You Gooners, you're all the same.'

I told him he was just trying to start some of that good ol' siege-mentality that the Arsenal were so famous for. And when it came down to it, Jefferson and Jam *weren't* favourites. The unofficial book that Farid had started priced Chip and Suki as the most likely champions, with Reesey and Tevin as next strongest contenders.

●

Whatever the prices, whatever the odds, we decided that an official training-period was out of the question.

'People could just compile shopping-lists and then graze to a GAME-plan,' argued Chip. 'There has to be an element of spontaneity otherwise there's no fun to be had.'

'That's easy for us to say,' Suki suggested. 'We've been thinking about this for a lot longer than some of the others.'

'Some of us have to work and don't have as much time to prepare,' Moll added.

I mused for a while. 'There's also a problem with people just going back and eating the same old things round after round,' I said. 'I think the solution is that people can't eat the same product in more than a single round. If you've taken your chances with

Bali Satay Sticks in the first round, for instance, then you can't eat them in any of the subsequent rounds. That way, it doesn't matter if you've prepared for a lifetime, you'll still have to come up with other methods of scoring.'

'It'll be less boring,' Suki added and we all nodded.

Thus it was agreed that the first round would be played in two days' time, with each subsequent leg due to take place at three-day intervals so as to avoid unnecessary suspicion, and we duly called everyone to let them know.

6

'Have you got the stopwatch ready?'

'Yes. For the fourth time.' Moll brought it out from inside her t-shirt as proof.

It was the day of the first round. She'd decided to wear a light trench-coat as it could hold a large quantity of empty packaging without looking too out of place and she'd even stayed up a couple of hours the night before, stitching plastic carrier-bags into the linings of the pockets to prevent any staining. With a similar nod towards tactical thinking, I'd chosen to wear a pair of Adidas Scatbacks (in white, poppy and black with white traction pads and a three-stripe speed-lacing system) for extra-agility-in-the-field.

'Where's my penknife?' I panicked. I'd brought along a Swiss Army penknife with fork and spoon attachments that Aunt Jocasta had given me one Christmas, a present that I'd never thought I'd have any use for.

'It's in the back pocket of your jeans.' Moll put a hand on my shoulder. 'Look, don't start getting nervous or we'll never get anywhere.'

We were standing outside the main hall of the supermarket,

Me, Moll, Chip, Suki and Seb, who had been chosen to adjudicate the whole competition.

'Right people,' Seb said. 'I want to see fair play. Any questions? Yes? No?'

Moll, Chip, Suki and I all shook hands and wished each other luck.

'Right!' said Seb. 'Get set . . . *go*!'

Chip and Suki disappeared immediately.

'Where have *they* gone?' I asked.

'Never mind them,' Moll replied. 'We've got our own GAME-plan, haven't we?'

I nodded.

•

Which was really to run away from the truth of the matter. But Moll's small moment of reassurance seemed to do the trick. Later that afternoon, with the curtains drawn, Moll and I lay on our bed and reviewed our opening performance.

'I've never seen you quite so fired up, not even when you're mixing at the club,' Moll said as she stroked the swollen curve of my boiling stomach. 'The way you got started on those Belgian Chocolates . . . *brilliant*! We were already on a scoring ratio of £3.99 per 250g while Chip and Suki were messing about with chocolate raisins and Boasters.'

'In retrospect, I felt they lingered too long in the confectionery aisle,' I suggested. 'They got caught-in-possession . . .'

'You looked like Dan Akroyd in *Trading Places* when you stuffed all that Cooked Topside of Beef into your mouth.'

'Did I?'

The warm flush of success gradually crept through my veins as the gastric convulsions subsided little by little.

•

We'd won! We'd actually won!

•

'I thought it looked in the balance for a while,' I said to Moll. 'Chip can consume Lonza Stagionata like no other human being on the planet. How much do you reckon he ate?'

'I think he weighed in at about 400g. Suki admitted that he's been scaling down the amount he's been eating at home over the last few days.'

'On the sly?'

'On the sly.'

'That would explain his seven mandarin tartlets then . . .'

'*And* the six ready-to-eat chicken thighs oven-roasted with brown sugar . . .'

'– the four-pack of Yop Drinking Yoghurt . . .'

'– the whole pears canned in syrup.'

'He displayed nice technique on the tin-opener,' I concluded. As the victor, I had no problem with magnanimity. And there was no doubt about it: Chip and Suki had played to win right from the start. Chip had eaten big, looking for those big scores, those one-hundred-and-eighties, those royal-flushes, those golden-goals while we'd initially floundered.

'It just goes to show what you can do if you put your mind to it,' Moll suggested.

She was right (when *wasn't* she?). It had looked in-the-balance for a while. And with ten minutes left-on-the-clock, Chip and Suki had seemed ready to sprint-for-the-line while Moll and I argued by the delicatessen counter, acres-of-ground to catch up, a bag of Scotch Eggs and Vegetable Pakoras next on the menu and little else but straws-to-clutch-at once they'd been dealt with.

So how had we won?

•

I'd taken the healthy option. I'd gone for Lactobacillus casei

46

Shirota. On it's own, it only measured 2×10^{-3} millimetres long. Encountered in packs (packs of seven 65ml bottles of Yakult for £2.49 to be precise), it still didn't amount to much more than a mouthful.

I'd drunk nine packs – and washed them down with two jars of DeLuxe Goat's Cheese suspended in Grapeseed Oil (£3.49 per jar) for good measure. After that, there was no stopping me.

'The Yakult was a moment of inspiration.'

'Chip thought he'd already won . . .'

'He got complacent . . .'

'– his eyes-were-bigger-than-his-stomach . . .'

'– he thought victory was his . . .'

'– he saw tomorrow's headlines a-day-too-soon . . .'

7

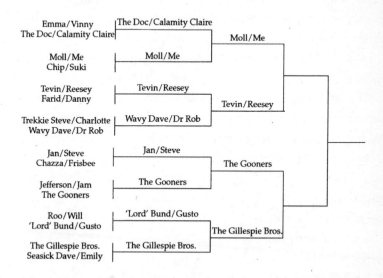

The first two rounds were completed without anyone getting arrested. Which is not to say that they passed without incident. Both teams of Scousers (Jefferson/Jam and the Wavy Dave/Dr Rob combo) were knocked out immediately, leading to much banter, while local boys, the Gillespie Brothers, represented West London with great style – or so *they'd* have it.

•

'DKNY innit?' Mark Gillespie said to me the day after the second round had been completed.

'What do you mean?'

'Me an' Sy go in there in our DKNY and our 'enri Lloyd and we're immediately intimidatin'. No member of starf's gonna challenge us when we're so well dressed.'

•

It was a similar line of thinking that had propelled Jan to wear his suit. But fashion choices hadn't constituted the only variety of attack-as-the-best-form-of-defence tactics he'd used. Jan had walked around the supermarket carrying a dictaphone and a clipboard, trying to behave in a manner that he described as 'conspicuously furtive'.

'I invaded their space with technology of my own. The authorities that run the supermarket, they're like an old prize-fighter gone soft, they're like America in Vietnam,' he'd confided. But then Jan was the sort of guy who claimed that NASA cleaned the space shuttles with Coca-Cola.

'Oh yeah?'

'Yeah. They're the fat cats that have got too used to being top dogs . . .'

I'd raised a hand to interrupt but Jan was on a roll.

'– controlling *their* environment with *their* surveillance systems,' he'd continued, '*their* bar-code readers, *their* weighing scales. Me? I walked into *their* yard with technology of my own . . .'

'With a dictaphone . . .'

'Yeah, a dictaphone. And *their* control system couldn't cope with it. I was a guerrilla-warrior marching into their HQ with a belt of hand-grenades taped to my body. I was a new type of Klingon Warbird de-cloaking off their starboard bow. I could have been *anyone* . . .'

'Are you sure?'

Jan took a breath.

'Well, the original idea was to look like some kind of store-detective or independent consultant taking notes on staff-performance levels and other business-operations criteria.'

'I see. *Conspicuously* furtive. And do you think it worked for you?'

'We wouldn't have made it to the second round otherwise. In the first round, I thought me and Steve-from-up-the-road were busted for sure. One of the shelf-stackers turned a corner and bumped into me just as I was trying to finish off a mouthful of Flavoured Surimi Shapes.'

'What happened?'

'I swallowed, cleared my throat and asked her where the Ferrero Rocher were, cool as a demi-cucumber. One look at my clipboard and she virtually went and bought them for me.'

•

All this talk of guerrilla warfare surprisingly bore some relation to reality. A day before the semi-finals, for example, Tevin and I were sitting in our usual beer garden and having a civilised drink in anticipation of the following day's clash, when he told me what had happened in his last tie.

'Y'know how you've got to be real careful, right, when you're eating the stuff and everything?' he said. 'Well, I was standing by the bubble-bath and some girl was chatting up Reesey over by the hairsprays when I see this guy in a beard staring at me.'

'Who was he?'

'I didn't know. So I started walking and got Reesey to take the girl's number and say that he'll call her later 'cause I think the guy's a store-detective or undercover police or something like that. But a few minutes later I bump into him again and this time I don't know what to think 'cause I catch *him* looking out for *me*. D'you know what I mean?'

I nodded. 'I think so.'

'And then we see him outside the store. *Outside the store*! I ask Reesey if he looks like five-oh and Reesey says that he has to be because of the shit haircut he's got and the shit clothes he's wearing and the both of us are getting ready to run for it when he comes right up to us and says: *Are you boys brothers?*'

'You're joking?'

'No joke!'

'So what happened?'

'He grabs me by my hand, tells me and Reesey that he's from Freedom Against Retail Tyranny, a coalition of "culture-terrorists", and that he's been in the supermarket spiking luxury ice-creams with laxative solution and a syringe. And then he asks what group *we're* from.'

'You what?'

'No joke! I almost pissed myself. He says that he's seen me and Reesey creeping around the supermarket and he wants to know what pressure-group we're working for.'

'What did you say?'

'I told him to watch out in case he did someone an injury . . . and Reesey sold him some skunk.'

•

In spite of these near-misses (and others), these false-alarms and cries-of-wolf, many things became clearer over the first two rounds of THE GAME, such as the need for certain tactical revisions. For instance, most teams in the second round opted to send the second member to get one of the numbered delicatessen tickets as soon as the clock started running while the designated 'eater' got busy with some solo scavenging around the yoghurts and desserts, or failing that, the pastry shelves.

Another general trend was to leave the consumption of liquid produce to the workings of biological necessity rather than to-go-out-and-try-and-win-THE-GAME by guzzling a couple of gallons of Ocean Spray Cranberry Juice. As 'Lord' Bund put it: 'After a dozen Kabanos, a brace of Mini Spring Rolls and a jar of Pitted Morello Cherries, you've *got* to drink a litre of Florida Breakfast Juice. It's not even a choice.'

Innovation also proved to be a valuable commodity. Teams that relied on easy manoeuvres like Parma Ham and Amaretto Truffles without recourse to adequate Plan Bs and Cs often found themselves getting in each other's way in a mutual race to snatch such items, or else stuck for good ideas when it came to the second round. Conversely, those teams that could execute that special move as and when THE GAME dictated usually found themselves with nothing but open road between them and the chequered flag.

And ultimately, as Moll and I found out, it all came down to each team's will-to-win. In our second round, we simply walked out into the supermarket and set about winning the tie, no-questions-asked, while The Doc and Calamity Claire allowed their minds to wander. While we were busy eating Gourmet Nut Selections and even managed to open and drain a bottle of Chateau Neuf du Pape while no one was looking, they ended up tasting all the cheeses on offer at the delicatessen counter and eventually couldn't be bothered to compete and paid for most of their shopping anyway.

8

And then the day of the semi-final arrived.

Moll and I got up late and drank tea in the kitchen while she munched on toast and flicked through a magazine. After that, we wandered out into the park across the road from the supermarket where we found Tevin and Reesey and Seb along with a few of the others who'd turned up to watch.

'Semi-final day,' concluded Tevin. 'We've got a crowd.'

'Shall we get going?' asked Seb.

The five of us left the others in a circle on the warm grass and trooped off towards the supermarket, Seb leading the way. In the entrance, he turned to face both teams.

'Right. You all know the rules.'

We nodded.

'See you in twenty-two and a half minutes then.'

He pulled his stopwatch out and held his thumb dramatically over the button.

'Get set . . .*Go!*'

Moll and I headed straight for the smoked salmon.

'An unoriginal manoeuvre, I know,' I told Moll, 'but we've been saving it. And as Bill Shankly said: "You've got to win THE GAME before you play THE GAME."'

'Stop talking and eat up.'

A supermarket manager strolled by as the blade of my penknife slipped along the greasy plastic but Moll got him to show her where the bin-liners were and I sauntered off in the other direction, rolling the slices into the smallest shapes possible before placing them in my mouth and swallowing, jamming them into mashed balls of pink flesh before gulping them down. A packet of Ocean Sticks followed, my hands squeezing the white slivers of reconstituted-non-specific-fish-product out of the polythene wrappers and straight down my throat. Moll returned with a delicatessen ticket.

'Should be about six minutes. We're fourth in the queue. Here . . . I got you a carton of Grape and Peach Juice.'

'Thanks.' I took it and put it inside my jacket. I'd rigged up a tube system that ran up from my inside pocket and down my left sleeve so that drinking a litre of fruit juice was only a matter a few simple scratches of the nose.

'We've made a good start, haven't we?' I asked Moll.

She agreed, but we then wasted the next six minutes entirely. I'd stripped a bunch of white seedless grapes into my outer pockets and was able to keep grabbing handfuls, but I was still only looking to notch up 99p for the whole lot.

'We need a big score soon. What are we going to go for?' I asked Moll.

'What about confectionery?'

We walked over to aisle 26 but two shelf-stackers were right in the middle of it, refilling the Pick 'n' Mix selection from huge cardboard boxes of sweets. At the other end of the aisle, we could see Reesey and Tevin standing there with matching expressions of disappointment.

'Let's hit the delicatessen counter,' Moll said decisively.

Our number came up just as we reached it.

'You order here while I raid the bakery,' I told Moll and tripped off and selected myself a Dairy Cream Fruit Choux Bun (a bit of a mouthful, I know, especially when you're chewing a mouthful of cream, glazed fruit and choux pastry and *especially* when you're doing this while your head's dipped into the cold blast of the freezer lockers so that it looks as if all you're doing is scrabbling for a Famous Fisherman's Pie). When I found Moll again, she'd filled a basket with a bottle of mouthwash along with the wrapped items from the delicatessen counter.

'For cover,' she explained, 'as well as for later. How do you feel?'

'Not too good – but I'll manage. What else have you got in there?'

Moll showed me and I gulped. A tub of Mushroom à la Greque, a tub of Isle of Skye Salmon Pâté and a thick wedge of Roquefort.

'Wasn't there anything else, anything less . . . *fragrant*?'

'For chrissakes, there isn't a lot left in the supermarket that's eligible. I did the best I could.'

The tub of Mushroom à la Greque slipped down easily enough and I told Moll it was a good choice. But then she unwrapped the other items and I had another moment of doubt.

'I can't do those,' I moaned, chorusing along with a sudden vicious gurgling that originated from somewhere within my stressed innards. 'I can't do them . . . I can't . . .'

'Why not? The cheese is £6.68 for a quarter. Another few mouthfuls and we've added 92p on to that . . .'

'I've eaten enough seafood to . . . to . . .'

'*Be a man!* You want to win, don't you?'

I stared at the food. What was it to be first? The pink translucent slush or the slab of soured cow's milk? More than ever before, I realised why people talked about being sick to the pit of their stomach.

'Quickly,' Moll urged. 'There's no one about.'

'But it's so big,' I complained.

'Of course it's big. That's why it's so expensive. That's why we'll win.'

A quarter of Roquefort cheese: eight (large) mouthfuls. I

took the first two relatively easily but the rest needed some courage.

'What if I throw up all over the floor?' I burped horribly, feeling a wedge of creamy cheese caked against the roof of my mouth. 'Does that disqualify us?'

'I don't know. I wouldn't have thought so. I think you said we have to be discovered playing THE GAME and vomiting wouldn't *necessarily* result in us being caught. Why? Are you about to?'

I gulped down some air. It tasted of bacon rinds and washing-powder.

'I don't think so.'

I didn't even bother to get out my spoon for the salmon pâté, instead dipping my hand into it and dredging out the pink paste with my fingers, wiping my hands on my t-shirt when I'd finished.

'You're swaying on your feet!' Moll pointed out.

'We still need a big score . . .'

'You've gone green again!'

'We still need a big score.' My mouth was on automatic for a few seconds, words just falling out of it. I took another sip of Grape and Peach Juice but it did little to help.

Then a quick look at the stopwatch told us we had about eight minutes left. Six pots of Flintstones Fromage Fraïs later and we still had four minutes to get to the checkouts. This gave us just enough time to deal with a jar of Fruttibosco Antipasto (£5.50), another hi-scoring product that we'd been saving for such a moment. The oil felt as if it was lining my throat, as if it was forming viscous reservoirs in the bottoms of my lungs, as if it was sealing up each and every blood-vessel.

'I don't feel very well. I don't think I can eat any more.'

Moll took hold of my elbow and guided me to the check-out. Reesey and Tevin were already there, Tevin looking equally troubled.

'I think he's payin' the price for the last two rounds,' Reesey said to Moll who agreed that THE GAME was a test of endurance as much as anything else.

'Are you alright?' I hissed at Tevin. I was virtually doubling up from stomach cramps.

'No.'

•

Seb met us on the other side of the tills and the five of us walked out of the supermarket, across the High Road and on to the grass where Jefferson, The Doc and the others were waiting.

'How did it go?' asked Chip.

'Anyone get caught?' asked Jam.

'You don't look very well,' Calamity Claire told me.

Tevin, Reesey, Moll and I emptied our pockets into two different piles and Seb made a list of what was in each before returning to the supermarket to verify the prices. In the meantime, the others milled around, everyone smoking joints except for Tevin and me who couldn't even manage a smile. I lay back and stretched myself out on the grass and closed my eyes, trying to focus on anything except the torture in my abdomen.

'You shouldn't lie down. It won't help your digestion.'

I opened my eyes. Moll was sitting next to me.

'I can't help it,' I said.

'Are you nervous?'

'I don't know. I don't know what I feel at the moment. Everything's numb.'

'Take deep breaths,' she said, stroking my hair.

And then Seb returned and sat down on another bench some distance away while he finished his lists, his notebook in one hand and a calculator in the other. All of us waited. After a few minutes he came over, a huge smile on his face.

•

56

'Who won? Who won?'

•

He put the two lists down on the ground and everyone huddled round. It took a few moments before I could get close enough to see them.

Moll/Me

Scottish Smoked Salmon	£9.95
White Seedless Grapes	£0.99
Mushroom à la Greque	£0.95
Roquefort Cheese	£6.68
Ocean Sticks	£1.05
Cape Grape & Peach Juice	£1.19
Fruttibosco Antipasto	£5.50
Flintstones Fromage Fraïs	£2.79
Isle of Skye Salmon Pâté	£0.92
Dairy Cream Fruit Choux Pastry	£0.69
Total	£30.71

Reesey/Tevin

Haribo Kola Bottles	£0.47
Dairy Cream Fruit Choux Pastry	£0.69
Kinder Surprise x 2	£0.84
Scottish Smoked Salmon x 2	£19.90
Bloom's Cooked Chicken Salami	£3.19
Frijj Drinking Yoghurt (Strawberry)	£0.75
Lemon Soufflé	£1.99
Lemon Sorbet	£1.39
Piel de Sapo Melon	£1.49
Total	£30.71

'I don't believe it!' said Suki.

'Double salmon! Nice tactics!' Jan congratulated Tevin and Reesey. Reesey explained that he'd watched Moll drag away the nearest manager and Tevin had stepped in and maximised his scoring potential.

'What do we do now?' Moll asked.

'A replay?' suggested Calamity Claire.

Seb reckoned that there had to be a period of extra-time and most agreed with him.

'Five more minutes and then we'll count up and see who's in front,' he said and Jefferson reckoned that we had to go back in there with all the empty packets and wrappers that we'd collected so far still in our pockets.

'It's an important fatigue on your competitive abilities,' he said and everyone else nodded.

•

Back we trooped, across the grass and back to the supermarket.

'I still can't believe this,' I said to Reesey. 'I feel *fucked*.'

'Are you ready?' Seb asked.

I looked across at Tevin and he smiled back weakly.

'Get set . . .*go*!'

This time Moll and I set off at a slower pace, going straight for the Special Selection shelves in aisle 1.

'I can't remember what we've already eaten from here.'

Moll *could*, however, and pulled me out a tray of Ackerman's Luxury Plain Chocolate Discs, some Rakusen's Chocolate Digestives from the Kosher shelves and I forced them down amongst a crowd of housewives milling around by the Fresh Meat and Gravy Powders. It took a while but Moll assured me it was worth it.

'Trust me,' she said, 'they're expensive.'

After that, we had seconds to get to the tills and I snatched a Single Mull of Kintrae portion from the Fancy Cheese Selection for good luck, while Moll grabbed a can of Coke so that we had something to pay for.

'Can you see Reesey and Tevin?' I asked and Moll shook her head but they soon came ambling up behind us, also with a solitary can of Coke.

'Are you lot having a picnic or something?' the cashier-girl asked.

'Something like that,' we all replied.

•

'I don't believe it!' Suki exclaimed yet again when we were back outside in the park five minutes later.

'Me neither. What is it with you lot? Are you all *gluttons* for punishment?' said The Doc before collapsing into a fit of laughter.

We were all standing around Seb's scrawling handwriting . . . *again*!

Moll/Me

Ackerman's Luxury Plain Chocolate Discs	£3.95
Rakusen's Chocolate Digestives	£0.90
Small Cheese Portion	£0.19
Total	£5.04

Reesey/Tevin

Cream Slices Double Pack	£1.09
Ackerman's Luxury Plain and Mint Chocolate Discs	£3.95
Total	£5.04

'You must have passed us as you came back from the bakery shelves,' Moll told Reesey.

Tevin and I were already staggering back across the grass towards the supermarket, the lowering sun streaking across our faces.

•

'I admit it,' exhaled Moll. 'I'm stuck. I can't think of anything else that you could eat.' We both stood motionless in the centre of the supermarket.

It had been decided that the 'penalty shoot-out' would take the form of a five-minute, one-product-only binge. Each team was to pick one product and eat as much of it as it could within the time allotted.

'I wish we'd left the Yakult until now. At the very least, it might make me feel better,' I said.

'I doubt it.'

Standing there, I could feel Moll sensing the-pressure-of-the-clock, but was helpless. I couldn't think of anything else either, not *then*, not as we stood in the central aisle surrounded by bustling shoppers. I looked about, my gaze taking in the shelf-stackers with their crates and sticker guns, the wheels of the trolleys, the signs that hung from the ceiling and labelled each aisle: Frozen Foods/Pastes & Spreads . . . Frozen Foods/Table Sauces . . . Canned Cat Food/Packet Cat Food . . . Canned Dog Food/Packet Dog Food . . . Tights & Socks/Home Remedials . . .

•

'Can you see anyone?'

'No not yet. What's holding you up?' Moll asked, watching my hands struggle with a family size jar of Vitamin C tablets.

'It's these childproof lids . . . I can't get them open quickly enough . . .'

'I'm not surprised . . .'

'Don't start . . .'

Moll put a hand on my shoulder. For a moment I thought she was comforting me. But then she spoke.

'Don't look up . . . but I can see one of the managers, standing at the end of the aisle by the tights and socks.'

Her voice was suddenly quiet, urgent.

'He's looking at us.'

'Are you sure?' I pretended to cough and upended another jar of tablets into my mouth. They were chalky and bitter but seemed good value at £5.50 for a few moments' nausea.

'Keep an eye on him,' I whispered, reaching for another bottle. 'These jars are worth a small mortgage. We're going to win, we're okay, we're going to win.'

'*There are two of them now.*'

'What are they doing?' (Another jar gone. I was sure that I had the white dust all over my face and looked like some out-of-control-gangster crazed on cocaine.)

'They're both looking at us and talking to each other . . . *wait* . . . Now one of them's speaking into a walkie-talkie.'

'Shit, shit, *shit*.' (And then another jar. Perhaps I was getting good at this . . .) I coughed. I was starting to gag but forced myself to keep on swallowing.

'What are they doing *now*?'

'There's still only two of them. They're just standing there. I think they've got us.'

'What about the other end of the aisle? Can we get out . . . ?'

'Yes . . . *no*! There's two of them there as well.'

I was starting to feel faint and the ground began to move in front of my eyes.

'I don't think I can manage another one,' I croaked weakly. 'I don't think I could manage *anything*.'

'It's too late. One of them's walking this way . . . the others are sealing off each end of the aisle.'

'That's it then . . .' I felt like I was about to suffocate in the air around me, in all 23°C of it.

'We're finished . . .' I said.

'Kiss me!'

'You what . . . ?'

'*Kiss me* . . . *NOW*! Maybe we'll embarrass them . . .'

'You reckon?'

'I don't know, do I?'

•

Like runaway lovers who've ducked into a side-alley during a chase sequence in an old romantic comedy, our arms slid around each other.

•

'I'm sorry about my breath,' I whispered, seconds before my lips met hers, 'I didn't manage to brush my teeth after I last ate.'

•

Moll's hands were at the back of my neck. I could see tears welling at the corners of her eyes as the space between us narrowed, then disappeared.

•

'That's okay,' she said. 'Lady had the same problem with Tramp, and that was on their first date,' she whispered between her immaculate teeth. 'Remember? In the alley behind the Italian restaurant?'

•

I wanted to laugh. I could see the two store managers approaching with a wary but determined gait and I wanted to laugh, but my lips were silenced by Moll's.

9

Unsurprisingly, there was the whole tap-on-the-shoulder routine to follow, a sordid débâcle in the manager's office and then in the interview room down at the local cop-shop after that.

No one at the supermarket bothered searching us until the

police came and when they did they were confused to say the least.

'Are you ill?' the constable asked me, sifting through the mound of litter on the table (it looked as if someone had taken a rubbish-bin from off the High Road and upended it on to the manager's desk).

'Actually, I feel a little bit better than I did a few minutes ago . . .'

'I don't mean *right now*,' he interrupted. 'I meant *in the head*.'

I shrugged my shoulders. The constable ran his eyes over the crumpled packets, the scooped-out pots, the empty wrapper for the Roquefort. He picked up the four empty jars of Health Care vitamin tablets and stared at them for a while.

'Are you a drug addict?' he tried.

'I don't think so.'

Moll fared similarly at the hands of a WPC before we were led outside and put in the back of the squad car. I wanted to make a joke about Mini Metros but didn't (Moll was unlikely to see-the-funny-side-of-it and I knew I'd just get in more trouble later) and in the distance I could see Reesey, Tevin and the others standing in the middle of the park as we were driven off down the High Road.

•

At the police station, we were officially charged, released on bail (Moll paid for both of us out of a savings account that I hadn't known about) and then sent out on to the streets with a clutch of Legal Aid forms, both of us due to appear at West London Magistrates' Court within a few months.

'I'll get us a taxi home,' I said when we were standing on Hammersmith Broadway

'Oh *will* you.'

I knew Moll was upset because she was chewing the butt of her cigarette and I tried to slide a conciliatory arm around her waist.

'Get your hands off me!'

I snapped my hand back.

Buses were streaming in and out of Hammersmith Station – 27s, 319s, 220s, 190s – but in the end KAB Cars saw us right and got us home for a fiver.

'I hate the way they do that,' I said, once we'd got home and let ourselves in.

'Do what?' Moll asked.

'I hate the way they drive you home at twenty-nine-point-nine miles per hour and then make attempts on the land-speed record once you've paid your money. It just doesn't seem fair. Anyway, where are the Rizlas? I'll roll a joint . . .'

Moll pulled the soggy mush of a Silk Cut out of her mouth.

'I'm going to go and pack my things.'

'What?'

'I'm going to go and pack my things. I've had enough. I'd appreciate you giving me an hour of space so I can sort it all out.'

•

Twenty-two minutes and thirty seconds later I went into the bedroom to try and talk to her. I'd smoked my joint but Moll hadn't come back into the kitchen. I had to talk to her, didn't I? Wasn't this all something that could be straightened out?

•

'Bored of being stoned already?' she asked when I knocked and opened the door. Black rubbish bags of clothes were lined up by the bed, a few crates already filled with books and videos. 'Anything I'm not sure is one hundred per cent mine I've put in the corner over there. You can have a look through it all and I'll take what you don't want when I come back to get the rest of my things.'

'Is this about drugs?' I asked her.

'Yes, that's right. I've turned into a moron moralist over the last two hours just because I've been arrested for shoplifting. *Is that how you think about me*?'

I sat down on the edge of the bed.

'Why are you going then? This *is* because of what happened this afternoon, isn't it?'

'No.'

'So you're coming back?'

'No.'

'So why are you going?' I asked after a deep breath, my head spinning.

'I don't need this . . .'

'We can talk about it later if you want. Just don't go now . . .'

'I don't mean that *I don't need this NOW.*' She paused. 'I mean that I don't need *this . . . any* of this . . . *all* of this . . .'

'You mean *me*.'

'Yes.' Moll lit another cigarette.

'But *you* said that you wanted to take part in THE GAME. It was *you* who wanted to play,' I said and quickly regretted it. It was the typical sort of mistake I make in arguments of this type.

'I think we're going backwards here . . .'

'Are we?'

'Look. Let's get one thing straight. *Yes*, I said that I'd take part in all of this. But I was doing it for you . . .'

'So this *is* about THE GAME.' I was starting to tremble with frustration.

65

'No. This is purely about *you*, about *you* and *me*, about *me* doing things for *you*.'

'Like what?' I asked.

'Like standing about and watching you mix records at night-clubs for hours on end . . .'

'So this is about DJing?'

'No. It's still about you.'

'What else . . . ?'

Moll sighed. 'You don't seem to be doing anything for yourself. So it's about you avoiding everything. I've been doing it too – until recently.'

Her anger suddenly seemed to drop. She came and sat next to me on the bed, though she made sure that we weren't touching each other. 'I'm to blame as well,' she said.

'For what?'

'*Can't you see?* We're both missing out at the moment, missing out on so much. I love the things you think. I love the things you talk about and the way you talk about them.'

'So what's the problem?'

'All of . . . *this*.' Moll gestured around the room. 'It can't go on. It just can't.'

'Like what?'

'Like you being on the dole. You put more effort into getting turned down for jobs than you do in looking for something that you *want* to do . . .'

'That's *my* choice isn't it?'

'Yes. It's *your* choice the same way it's *your* choice to let Housing Benefit pay the rent, the same way it's *your* choice to sell hash so that you can get stoned all day and afford new records and trainers. It's even *your* choice to spend all this time on a stupid competition that's ended up with us getting arrested.'

Moll lit another cigarette and I noticed that I wasn't the only one trembling. 'It's all so *comfortable* for you isn't it, not having to work, not having to do anything.'

I paused. 'It's been fun for you, hasn't it?'

'I don't know. I still want things to change even if it has. I still want a change . . . starting with us. *Fun* isn't so important any more to me, or at least not *your* kind of fun. I'm sorry if that's sounds hurtful but it's the truth. I've got a new job and it's something that I actually want to do. You've got to find the same.'

Sitting there on the bed, I wanted to say that I could change. I wanted to say that between the two of us we could make things different. But Moll was looking directly into my eyes and the words wouldn't come.

'You haven't noticed how you've stopped talking to me about what I'm interested in, or what I want to do unless it's the same as you,' she said. 'You're also scared of the future and now I'm convinced that it's you that's been holding yourself back rather than anything else. You'd rather just idle your time away and I've been suffering as a result. Just look at what happened today.'

•

'Convince yourself back the other way then?' I tried. Moll shook her head.

•

'Can't.'

•

Her voice was quiet, a whisper.

'I would say that there's a part of me that still loves you. But that's not the point. And it should be obvious anyway.'

67

10

We only spoke once on the telephone between the day she left and the day of our appearance in court. Legal Aid had suggested to me that incarceration was out of the question because it was my first offence but this only made me more worried.

'What if they've gone through their surveillance tapes and seen how much stuff we've stolen over the whole summer?' I asked Moll.

'They won't have. Don't be so paranoid.' There were voices and music in the background on her end of the line.

'How do you know? *And what if they have!* We won't be first-time offenders then, will we? We'll be more like *tenth*-time offenders. And it's not is if we can explain THE GAME to them.'

Moll told me that she was prepared to accept whatever happened. 'After all,' she concluded, 'it was *us* who committed the crime.'

I didn't have an answer to that and she said that she'd see me in court before hanging up.

•

Eventually our big day arrived. Moll turned up with private legal representation of her own (she'd borrowed the money from 'a non-mutual friend'; I wanted to accuse her of doing it just to hurt me) and we both apologised-to-society in front of anyone who'd listen. In return, we were sent away with £100 fines and criminal records. We'd also been made to pay the full cost of the produce we'd stolen

'We *must* have made a good team,' I said to Moll outside the doors to the building. She'd had her hair cut in a style I hadn't seen before and was wearing some new clothes including a new jacket that looked worryingly unisex. Some new boyfriend?

'I'm not coming back,' she said.

'I was talking about not getting seen on the security cameras at the supermarket. We must have been a good team otherwise they would have spotted us on tape and we wouldn't have got off so lightly.'

'I came here today prepared to take full responsibility for what I did.'

'Are you sure?'

'As much as I can be. I've still got some things round the flat, haven't I?'

'I've put them in boxes for you.'

'Thanks. I'll come round when you're out sometime next week. Leave a message on my answerphone to say when that'll be okay.'

'Okay.'

11

That was the last time I saw her. A few days later, I returned home to find her boxes gone and her key hanging on the hook magnetised to the door of the fridge.

And now, usually late at night, I often find myself thinking about the first time I saw her. It was in the checkout line at the supermarket in Fiveways, perhaps halfway through our first term up in Birmingham. I joined the queue behind her and started to unpack my basket before I noticed her. Then I looked up and saw her face, her green eyes scanning across a page of *Madame Bovary*. My heart palpitated. It flipped and flopped like a fish stranded on the wrong side of the waterline and gasping for oxygen. I looked away, but by then I knew that she'd noticed me noticing *her* and I stared down at her shopping sitting on the conveyor-belt in front of us, all the time hoping I wouldn't blush. Red onions, cos lettuce, a stick of celery, radishes, V8 juice, a gigantic pot of Marmite, clementines, a box of camomile tea, a granary loaf, a tub of natural yoghurt. A healthy selection, I thought to myself (healthier than mine). But amongst these were some anomalous choices: a jumbo bag of Monster Munch, the two packets of chocolate biscuits, Pom Bar Snack Teddies, fish fingers, a quarter-pound of peanut brittle.

Later I would learn how these items fitted into her life. The Snack Teddies were a habit that she'd picked up during a gap year spent living in France. The peanut brittle was something she only ever indulged in when she reached the halfway point in whatever novel she happened to be reading. She adored the strange, idiotic aliens on the TV advertisements hence the Monster Munch (pickled onion was her favourite flavour), and for a while there was nothing she liked to do more than stay up all night with me and watch parts of our combined video collection with a plate of fish fingers on her lap, the orange breadcrumbs smeared with thick-cut marmalade. We'd get stoned and watch my Cary Grant tapes (*Notorious*, *People Will Talk*, *Bringing Up Baby*, *North by Northwest*), or else watch her Russ Meyer collection – *Vixen*, *Supervixens*, *Beneath the Valley of the Ultravixens*, *The Lust Seekers*, *Beyond the Valley of the Dolls* ('Valley of the Molls,' she'd whisper into my ear).

•

As for THE GAME?

It turned out that Moll and I would have won our semi if we'd not been caught because Tevin had been forced to retire. His stomach had given up and he'd eventually been carried home by Reesey and The Doc. So Moll and I hadn't needed to eat a morsel: we'd have won the tie by default. To add insult to injury, The Gooners capitalised on the weak opposition to romp home to victory in the final three days later.

•

So that was it for Moll and I. Another semi-final lost on penalties, just like that other match, the semi-final between England and Germany that took place a few days later and placed England as tragic losers yet again.

•

But that's what happens, isn't it? Sometimes you win, and sometimes you're left with a bitter taste in your mouth. Does it help to cry over spilt milk?

HIGHER SOCIETY

What pleasure can it be for a
man of culture to see a
splendid beast impaled on a
huntsman's spear?

Marcus Tullius Cicero, *Ad Familiares VII*

1

First Saturday of the Christmas hols.

Usually I bound straight down the main stairs, not stopping for more than a second's glance at either the portrait of Granpa Charles in his regimental colours (painted just before he died at Passchendaele) or at Great-Granpa Nigel's hunting trophies. But tonight I stop and stare at the grim collection of stuffed heads mounted on the wall and I feel my skin prickle. *Is it because I turned sixteen a fortnight ago and I know what's coming?* I pause on the landing and look at them all closely for the first time in years. There are fifteen in total and though they're all different shapes, sizes and colours, some with straggly long hair and some with fearsome teeth, there's something uniform about all of them. Is it the expressions on the animals' faces, something about the muted colours of their preserved hides? Or is it because when I look at the collection closely, the animals don't seem to look so different, not once I've taken in the delicate tissue of their nostrils or their sad black eyes?

The sound of my mother interrupts my thoughts, her voice piercing through the thick oak door into the dust and silence of the hallway. She's in the kitchen, on the telephone, and I sit down on a step to listen when I hear her mention my name.

'Yes Timmy's back for the holidays. How's he getting on? Splendidly! Absolutely splendidly!'

Her voice drops a register for a couple of seconds, adopts the tone all mothers use when they're confiding in someone that they think they're going to get their way.

'They've all had to start choosing their universities and he's

75

having a few flutters about Oxford, says he wants to study . . .
now what did he call it . . . *Development*. What is it? God knows!
Something about Africa anyway and apparently one simply can't
do it at Oxford. Says he's going to have to apply to Southampton
or Reading or some other awful *town*. Can you imagine it? Me?
Dragging *my* mother to Southampton for his graduation?'

There's a pause while she laughs and I imagine her holding
the receiver in her right hand and making her palms-up 'I'm at
a loss (but not really)' gesture with her left.

'Well, Pru,' she continues, back at full volume, 'that's *exactly*
what I said. I said: "With an Eton and Oxford education, you'll
never look back in this world." Yes, it *was* brave of me . . . no,
they don't like being contradicted at that age . . . but I had to
say *something*! One simply can't lose sight of reality in life. "Go to
Oxford," I said to him, "and do something sensible like History
just like your father did. It's not as if it can do you any harm. If
you're still interested in Africa in a few years' time, then we'll
pay for you to go on safari in your gap year just like we did with
Simon and Rupert." *Simon and Rupert?* They're fine, absolutely
fine. Simon's doing very well . . . probably already spent his
entire Christmas bonus on Daisy! And Rupert will be back
from Bosnia on Christmas Eve. He's doing wonderfully . . .'

•

The eavesdropping continues throughout dinner. Mother, Father
and I perch at one end of the dining-table, a couple of candles
sending our restless shadows slithering all over the ceiling, and
I let my parents' voices wash over each ear for an hour.
They mostly chirp away about Simon and Rupert, both of
them concluding that Simon's firm will ride through the latest
'nervous time for the City' and that people in Bosnia 'don't
know how lucky they are to have people like Rupert keeping
their peace'. At the end of the meal, Father puts his knife and

fork together and leans back in his chair and I watch as he picks at a piece of meat between his teeth, preferring to dig it out with a fingernail than use a toothpick.

'The problem with your average Slav,' he says, 'is that he's as stubborn as a mule. Absolutely intractable. Rather play silly buggers just to make a point than find a solution. Always been the case, right through history.'

Mother agrees and then sighs. 'Yugoslavia was always such a beautiful place.'

They pause, having exhausted all the usual topics of conversation that they find it easy to agree upon (namely the successes of Simon and Rupert) and then turn their attention to me. Mother takes another sip of the heavy claret and asks me to explain 'Development', tells me that she 'really wants to get to the bottom of it'. Father duly answers her, lighting a cigar.

'Useless idealism,' he says, a cloud of smoke appearing in front of his face, 'nothing more than the intellectualisation of hand-outs.'

A predictable chain of events ensues. Before too long, the two of them have ticked off the Third World for being both 'irresponsible' and 'lazy' with regards debt repayment, asked what would have happened if '*we* hadn't bailed them out' and *tut-tutted* about 'the grunge contingent' who were 'always trying to change the world from the job centre'. Father laughs loudly at this as if he's never told this joke before, as if it isn't a predictable part of the same old hideous ritual that he forces everyone else to endure every time he has an audience. (For instance, I remember Simon bringing home a vegetarian literature student for Sunday lunch during *his* Oxford days. With much embarrassment, she'd had to decline not only the roast but also the vegetables because all of them had been doused in meat stock at some stage of their preparation and Father mercilessly took this as a cue to make her squirm throughout the meal as he tumbled through a routine of jokes about the 'grunge contingent', 'herbivorous job-dodgers' and 'giro revolutionaries'.)

'Another thing about these provincial universities,' he continues, 'is that they're a breeding ground for hunt saboteurs and the like.' He *hurrumphs*, taps his cigar over the ashtray. 'It's little wonder they don't offer Development at Oxford or Cambridge. I don't see Oxbridge graduates wasting their time with such nonsense. Too busy working all the hours God sends, too busy driving towards success, too busy making the economy function while these surly, unwashed longhairs waste away their time grazing on tax-payers' money and spoiling respectable people's legitimate sport.'

Mother nods her head in agreement. She says that she sees them at the supermarket at the weekends. 'I have to hold my nose when I'm behind one of them in the queue for the checkout,' she says and adds that it's the children she feels sorry for.

•

Of course, the conversation strays from hunting to shooting as it always does at this time of year, both of them telling me how much I must be looking forward to my 'big day'. Luckily I'm able to escape before they get too involved by offering to clear the plates and I leave the both of them in the dining room talking about 'that dreadful Keith Sliney', the man Father's invited to the Boxing Day shoot so that he can be persuaded to operate corporate events on the estate.

Later I'm upstairs in my bedroom listening to The Smiths and leaning out of the window to smoke a cigarette so that my room won't stink. *Could dinner have been worse?* Sometimes my parents hardly speak at all, instead taking turns to make short statements to each other across the dinner table, eyes not engaged with life in its present tense, both of them happy to let the other's grunts serve as agreement, as punctuation, as indication to speak, breathe or swallow.

What are their intimate conversations like? I wonder. *Do they have any?* It's hard to believe that they still try. It's also hard to remember a time when they used to talk to each other with any degree of tenderness, without being suspicious that my memory is loaded with childish idealism. What I *can* remember is Rupert's 'surprise' trip home from Sandhurst one weekend maybe six years ago. The two of us played a few frames of billiards in the library on the Sunday afternoon and then went for a walk down through the herb garden and out into the orchard. It was late September, fallen apples carpeting the orchard floor, sluggish wasps quivering amongst the craters burrowed out of their brown, pulpy flesh. Rupert looked terribly serious and I wondered what was the matter.

'Father's been seeing a woman,' he said once we'd made it as far as the first of the sheep fields, and then named her. She was a family friend and I remembered how a couple of years earlier I'd once overheard her whisper to another woman, during tea at the village cricket match, that she was 'the latest in a long line' to find out that my father 'had the biggest cock in Wiltshire'. At the edge of the orchard, sitting on the fence, I almost wanted to laugh at my earlier innocence and tried to look terribly serious too. *Is he . . . moving on?* I asked. Rupert shook his head. He seemed to tower above me, his hand ruffling my hair. 'There's nothing to worry about,' he said. 'Everything's going to be fine.' Mother and Father were staying together and all that the three of us had to do was to be good and to be brave.

2

The next morning I wake up just before eight and I'm sitting up in bed stretching when I hear Mother knock on the door.

'Don't be too long!' she calls out and tells me that Alan's already waiting for me.

'Won't be,' I reply, already pulling on some old cords and a jumper. Downstairs, Father's sitting at the table in the kitchen, newspaper in one static hand, triangle of toast in the other, the serrated edge of a half-moon bitten out of it, butter oozing around the teeth-marks. 'Don't be late for Alan,' he says, his eyes never leaving the newsprint, and I grab a piece of toast and a mug of coffee, swallowing them both down in a couple of mouthfuls before heading out of the back door.

Alan's waiting by the Land Rover, its engine already running. 'Morn', Master Timothy.'

'Morning, Alan.'

'How was your term? You working yourself hard?'

I say that I have been and he nods and then tells me to help him load the guns into the back.

'You forgotten all the things I taught you during the summer?'

'Of course not, Alan.'

'Good.'

We both climb into the front and drive off, trees and fields soon rattling past, the green curve of the horizon bouncing up and down on the other side of the mud-spattered windshield.

'This morning,' he continues, 'I'm going to take you up to Bleadon's.'

Bleadon's Copse: one of nine different drives on the estate

and the one reserved for the family's traditional Boxing Day Shoot. Father believes that this is one of the reasons he's going *to screw a fortune out of that bastard Sliney.* 'All these wide-boys, Yanks and Nips want to do,' he often says, 'is to pull on a Barbour and yomp around the countryside. All *we'll* do is cart them round from drive to drive, make them feel we're going to a whole lot of trouble, let them plug away at some cheap game and send them back to London with a brace and the bill.'

Alan is a little more economical in his reaction to Father's plans. 'Your father, Master Rupert and Master Simon,' he says to me, raising his voice so he can be heard above the sound of the engine, 'their first shoots were special occasions. Nothing makes me more proud than the sight of one of you youngsters joining the grown-ups. But after this year . . .' He breaks off and sighs.

'At least you'll get *your big day* before everything's changed. After this year, it'll all be different.'

•

I think back to the first Boxing Day after Rupert turned sixteen (he's ten years older than me so I must have been six) and I remember how I stood in my thick dressing gown by a window in the drawing-room and watched Alan drive Father and Rupert away in the first Land Rover, the rest of the cars falling into line behind them with the other guests on board.

'When can I go with Rupert?' I asked Mother who'd waved them all off from the doorstep before coming back inside, holding hands with Simon who followed behind her, the cheated adrenaline not quite faded from his face (he'd desperately wanted to join them).

'When you're old enough.'

She explained that since the end of the Civil War, every Lovington man has traditionally gone up to Bleadon's for his first shoot on the first Boxing Day after his sixteenth birthday.

'It's Simon's turn next,' she'd said. 'You'll have to wait a while for yours.'

With each passing year, the pattern of the day's events grew more and more familiar, the men arriving mid-morning and standing around on the gravel for a while before setting off, swigging sloe gin from silver hip flasks while they chatted, letting cigarette smoke and freezing breath mingle in the morning air. Rupert, sensible as ever, would always spend the time checking over the equipment, his eyes bright with excitement, while Father moved from friend to friend, always ready with a jovial slap on the back and a Christmas joke. It became routine to watch the convoy disappear up the drive, to spend the day reading in my bedroom as the faint echo of gunfire drifted as far as the house, to run small errands for Mother in the kitchen as she supervised the preparations for tea and for dinner. The men would return mid-afternoon, their boots caked with dirt and blood, Father sitting down in the rocking chair by the oven to pull off his Hunters and letting out a sigh as he lit his first cigar of the day, a wired tension in his eyes slowly subsiding, the corridors of the house full of the mouth-watering smell of the cooking meat, the sound of chattering voices and footsteps echoing through the corridors as guests returned upstairs to their bedrooms to bathe and change clothes. And a couple of years later, Simon duly joined them and it became just as habitual to listen to his and Rupert's bantering as to which of them had been the most successful as it was to open presents the day before.

•

And now? To be honest, now that it's bearing down on me, I don't want 'my big day'. It's all anyone seems to want to talk to me about (unless they want to lecture me about Oxford) and all I want to do is run away. Over the last few winters, I've been able to shut it out of my mind. But then one morning, halfway through the summer, Alan set up the targets as I always knew he would, and I reported to him each day afterwards, my heart throbbing with increasing fear.

I started with 'manners' (as Alan calls them), lessons on the correct way a 'sportsman' carries a gun, how he cleans it, how he stores it and so on. Then I started shooting with a four-ten, learning how to break the breech and load the cartridges and letting off rounds at targets stuck in the ground fifty yards away. Soon, after a fortnight, Alan graduated me on to a twenty bore. 'This is what you'll use when it comes to the real thing,' he said, letting me balance the weight of the gun between both hands. 'It's a bigger gun,' he'd said needlessly, 'not as big as your father's, but certainly enough for now.'

From the last two weeks of August up until the beginning of term, I practised almost every day with the twenty bore under Alan's scrutinising gaze, needing a recoil pad for the first few days until my body learnt to accept the pounding kick of the butt. By the time I went back to school to start my A levels, I had a dark bruise on my right shoulder. Other boys had similar bruises and would show them off to each other, brag about the size of gun they were going to use over the approaching Christmas hols, about how many they were 'going to bag' when it came to their first time. *Me?* I tried not to join in and would shrink away from any gathering of my contemporaries when they were talking enthusiastically about 'letting them have it with both barrels', hands miming the action of lifting the gun-muzzle and pulling through with the target while their fingers squeezed off imaginary rounds at the imaginary game their minds seemed intent on obliterating. By the end of term, a first shoot fast approaching for all of us who had just turned sixteen, the levels of anticipation amongst many of them had reached a wild intensity. *You have to drink the blood of your first kill* was one rumour that was produced by this gory whirlpool of conjectures. *You become a sex beast* was

83

another rumour touted by a boy in my Geography class. He was convinced that a successful day's shooting transformed you into an uncontrollable ravisher of women. 'My elder brother told me,' he claimed. 'He says the killing releases something inside of you,' though nothing I'd experienced at home seemed to verify this. Sure, there was a certain exhilaration that I could sense in the air when the men returned from Bleadon's, but that was all it was, surely?

Thus it wasn't hard for me to be scornful of such unruly fantasies. But as the term drew to a close, I realised that I was one of very few who were dreading the impending hols. To keep me from worrying about it, I tried burying myself in my schoolwork. I wrapped myself around the intricacies of my English Literature papers. '*Macbeth* is Shakespeare's most mature and profound vision of evil' was one essay topic I covered. 'Discuss how *Measure for Measure* investigates the tension between the Old Testament value of justice and the New Testament ideal of mercy' was another. I also threw myself at my piano lessons, practising for a couple of hours every day, but it didn't help. My fingers seemed to move automatically while my mind remained free to think about the dulled crack of the ammunition inside the muffled vacuum of the ear-protectors, about what kind of damage the spreading pellets could do to live flesh. And now I'm up on Bleadon's.

•

'That's where they'll come out,' Alan explains.

Up on Bleadon's, Alan and I take up a position eighty or so yards away from the edge of the trees, the ground dipping in between and giving me a clear shot across the whole width of the copse. 'There . . . there . . . and *there*,' he points with his finger and we set up targets on the same spots.

3

The days roll by, Christmas getting nearer and nearer.

If asked, most of the family prefer the summer when the sun seems to hang in the sky for ever, saturating everything with glowing colour from early morning until the doves return through the twilight to the dovecote just as dinner is served under the rhododendron tree. In contrast, I've always preferred the winter. The estate and the surrounding countryside seem particularly beautiful at this time of year and normally I spend much of my time outside. In the mornings, I can look out over the fields, crows wheeling through their twisted patterns in the crystalline air above sheets of groundfrost, my breath always carrying with it that brittle edge that lets me know I'm *alive*. Late in the afternoon, the world gets even colder, the sun lost behind clouds over Salisbury Plain, the white haze of the horizon awash with diffusions of pink and cold purple until suddenly there is no more light and everything is lost to the darkness.

This year I feel differently and as soon as I've finished practising with Alan, I spend most of my time inside listening to the radio, or else reading the books set for the following term's classes: *Journey's End*, *Far from the Madding Crowd* and a collection of Yeats' poetry. One evening, in the middle of the week before Christmas, I'm reading 'Leda and the Swan' when I hear the sound of engines coming down the upper drive. I look out of my window and see two blue lorries come to a standstill in front of the house, a logo emblazoned across their sides in white letters. *Cavanger & Sons of Warminster*. Father's game dealers. Tom Cavanger, the eldest of old Will Cavanger's three sons and current proprietor of the business, climbs out of the cab of the first lorry. There's the sound of the back door being unbolted before Father and Alan stride into sight.

'Mr Lovington. How are you, sir?'

'Very good. Now what have you got for us?' Father asks briskly.

'A hundred. Young and healthy.' His voice billows with deference. 'I know you often have a special day here at Everleigh Hall this time of year so I've got you the best, no sad flappers, just healthy young'uns with a lot of life in 'em.'

'Good!' Father replies. 'We don't want them to collapse the moment they're released.'

'We certainly don't,' Cavanger replies. From the treacle in his voice it's clear that Cavanger already knows about Keith Sliney and that he might be returning to Everleigh Hall more than his customary once a year if things go as Father's planned.

Alan gets into the cab of the first lorry and leads the other to the game-pens while Father takes Cavanger inside the house. They come back out ten minutes later, Cavanger repeating to Father that the animals he's brought are top grade, that all he has to do 'is ask' if we ever need anything *more reasonable* in the future and Father *hurrumphs* before he shakes his hand and walks back inside.

•

Over dinner, Father can't decide whether he's offended or delighted by Cavanger's over-familiarity. He calls him an 'obsequious little shit' several times and spits that he won't be propositioned on his own land – but also concludes that he's glad that Cavanger's 'on board'.

'We can get some real lame ducks for next to nothing,' he tells Mother. 'Take the margin up to something respectable.' Afterwards, Mother goes upstairs early and Father goes to his study to make some telephone calls while I pull on a coat and walk down to the game-pens.

Some families, like that of my friend James Biddestone who lives over in Tidcombe, are indiscriminate as to what they'll shoot. 'As long as it can move,' I've heard James' father declare and the game-pens on his land bear out this belief. They're simple breeze-block igloos, the concrete floors awash with rotten straw and congealing excrement. The animals they buy are little more than zombies. Many of them are malformed or have missing limbs or missing eyes, atrophied vocal cords (where do they come from?). Once delivered, they're kept manacled to the sides of the shelter on short chains that allow them to do nothing more strenuous than huddle together for warmth under the shredded rags that lie around amongst the toxic puddles. And when it comes to the morning of a shoot, the Biddestones' groundsmen hose them down before carting them up to the drive and then use the same hoses to scour down the pens later in the day. Father, on the other hand, claims to have the most humane facilities in the county: insulated sheds with gas-fired air heaters and concrete latrines at one end. The animals, allowed to roam freely around their spacious cages, even get mashed oats and milk twice a day and are let out into a stockade for an hour each morning and afternoon.

I open the door to the first pen.

There are maybe thirty of them inside. Many are sleeping, the sound of their ragged breathing joining with the faint background roar of the gas flues. In the orange glow of the heat lamps, a few skip and scrape across the floor, stopping every so often and looking about, bending to sniff the feeding troughs and each other. I walk inside, shut the door (I gag for a second at the smell. It may be 'clean' in here but it still stinks like a pig shed) and make my way down the central aisle between the two cages on either side. Some of them jerk their heads around at my intrusion, eyes holding me for a second. And then one of them, a female, comes closer and stoops towards me, her dark eyes looming close through the wire mesh. She has a blanket pulled around her shoulders that's scarcely large enough to cover the jutting spars of her ribcage and the pale curves of her small breasts, and when she bends her head to one side to look at me, she exposes the soft flesh of her neck.

'Hello,' I say in a soft voice, returning her stare. I realise that we're both probably the same age and we stay like that for a few moments, the two of us facing each other.

'Hello,' I say again, 'You're a beauty, aren't you.' I wonder if I can reach my hand through the wire and stroke her hair, her skin, but she looks me up and down one more time before scurrying back across to the far corner where I see two bodies churning amongst the straw. She crouches, sniffs the back of one of the writhing animals, grunts, runs her hand and then her tongue along its spine before sliding herself amongst the grappling pair.

•

The next morning Mother exclaims that she is horrified.

'Do you know what happened over in Fosbury last night?' she asks over breakfast.

She goes on to tell me that the Marshwoods woke up this morning to discover that their game-pens have been raided by saboteurs. Apparently fifty animals have been released and the authorities are still combing the countryside for some of them.

'Camilla's been crying her eyes out to me on the telephone already this morning. The police and Alasdair are agreed that it's likely to be an inside job as one of the groundsmen they took on at the beginning of the autumn can't be found. They're resigned to the fact that he must have been an infiltrator.' She sips her tea and straightens her cardigan. 'These ghastly *people*,' she sighs, as if they didn't deserve to be labelled as such. 'You give them a job. They accept your food, your money and they take lodgings from you. To make things worse, the bugger stole some of their possessions: silver, money . . .' She trails off, confident that her point has been made. 'Can you imagine if anything like this ever happened to us? I'd feel *violated*. When I heard, I thanked God that we have such trustworthy staff.'

I wrap up half of the croissant I'm eating in a napkin, stuff it into my pocket and tell Mother I'm going outside to look for Alan. Eventually I find him by the game-pens fixing reinforced padlocks to all the doors and gates.

'You heard?' he asks, nodding to me as I approach before focusing his attention back on his tools.

'Yes. Mother's just been telling me.'

'Well I've got to fix the pens up, make sure they're all secure. I want you to pace round the stockade and check the fence, make sure there aren't any gaps or weak points. If there are, remember where and tell me in a minute. We can go up to Bleadon's and practise after that.'

The steel-mesh fences, twelve foot high and topped with razor-wire, seem secure. The animals on the other side are out getting their morning exercise, eyelids twitching in the sunlight, and I see now that many of them are the same age as me or younger. As I pace my way round the stockade, my eyes search for the female that I was looking at last night and eventually I see her and walk around to where she is. A couple of feet away from the wire, she's amongst a whole trembling crowd of males and females and most of them draw back as I approach. But she stays where she is, her black eyes bright and curious, nostrils faintly rippling. *Does she recognise me?* I check that Alan's not watching and then break off a bit of croissant and poke it through the fence. She arches her head away from my outstretched fingers so I toss the piece through the fence on to the grass in front of her and for a moment it looks unbelievably stupid, a torn piece of patisserie lying there amongst the leaves and the grass. But then she crouches down (I notice the rangy muscles running up the insides of her thighs, the wild jute of her scrambled pubic hair), and sniffs at it before picking it up and putting it in her mouth. I wait to see if she swallows it or spits it out and feel relieved when she chews. *What are you thinking?* I wonder when our eyes meet again. Her lips part, her tongue trembles in her mouth, and she bleats out a soft warble. I step a little closer, only half aware that I'm pressing my face against the fence, and hold out another piece of pastry. This time she moves her face towards it. *Will she take it?* My skin anticipates the soft embrace of her lips and tongue closing around my fingers and I feel her warm breath on my fingertips as they approach the damp cavern of her mouth.

•

Mother drives me over to Ludgershall so that Dr Sputtinger can clean up the wound. After a few swabs with cotton wool and disinfectant, it looks no more serious than a couple of paper cuts. 'What happened?' Sputtinger asks, fixing a bandage around my hand. Mother answers.

'For some reason, he decided that one of my *pains-au-chocolat* would make a good breakfast for one of the animals. Unfortunately the young thing wanted his fingers too. I can't believe he's been so silly. Lucky he's got quick hands or who knows what might have happened!'

Sputtinger chuckles along with her, jokes that if I want a girlfriend then I should go to some parties and then gives me a jab 'just to be on the safe side'.

This isn't the end of my humiliation. Later in the day, Father returns from a shoot in Bishopstone and booms with laughter as Mother furnishes him with the details of my day. And a few days later, on Christmas Eve, Simon and Daisy arrive mid-morning in a new Coupé, brandishing smiles and bottles of Scotch, and Mother fills them in on the family news including an account of my 'escapade' while they place a pile of wrapped presents under the tree in the library. Then she goes through the whole story again when Rupert arrives in the evening.

'Looks like someone needs a girlfriend,' he jokes and Father asks what's wrong with the girls who work down at the pub. 'I hear they'll fuck anyone for Babycham,' he guffaws, too drunk to take any heed of Mother's hisses of feigned offence, and I cringe behind my consommé. Luckily I've drunk enough wine by the end of the meal so that I can go to bed early without need of an excuse. And upstairs, I lie on my bed, going through the motions of smoking a cigarette, the spinning of the room soon blending seamlessly with the onslaught of my dreams until I'm hideously lost as to what's true or false. At some point I'm on the front doorstep of the house with the whole family, Daisy included, polishing the guns and waiting for the Biddestones to arrive so that we can draw lots to see who gets to shoot each other first. At other times, it's *me* that's writhing around on the ground in the game-pen, *her* fingernails tearing strips out of my back, my windpipe choked by knotted clumps of her hair.

4

Christmas Day is either a tragedy or comedy depending on one's point of view. It starts with breakfast, all the main players assembling in the kitchen one by one. The rest of the family are hungover having stayed up drinking long after I went upstairs and are in the middle of a second round of Bloody Marys when the taxi arrives with Granpa Humphrey. Half an hour later Great-Aunt Gillian arrives with Great-Uncle Benjamin and we all make our way to St Francis's in the village, Simon pushing Humphrey's wheelchair and me pushing Benjamin's, the four of us falling some way behind Father and Rupert who talk about tomorrow the whole way down to the village, Mother, Daisy and Gillian walking maybe twenty yards in front of them.

Inside the church, we take our usual places near the front on the left side of the aisle, Father grandly shaking hands with the several offered in his direction. And as usual, Humphrey's emphysema makes him cough approximately once every ninety seconds, a succulently venomous gurgle that makes me want to pull out a handkerchief and wipe my hands. Reverend Peters deals with this repeated interruption with huge doses of pious understanding. 'This festival, inspired by a birth in the village of Bethlehem two thousand years ago, is a festival of life . . . of forgiving,' he intones halfway through his speech, pausing immaculately as Humphrey's lungs sound out another report and testing my resolve not to laugh. 'A festival of . . . understanding . . . and compassion.' This is by no means the entirety of the floorshow. Great-Uncle Benjamin is prone to bouts of nervous twitching that cause him to flinch every so often as if he'd been poked in the kidneys. This wouldn't be such a problem in isolation, but the spasm also comes with a sound effect like a compressed, high-pitched hiccup. *Only ten times louder.* By the time we're all kneeling to say the Lord's Prayer, Humphrey sounds like a twenty-gun salute while Benjamin froths about in his wheelchair doing his best imitation of a broken accordion being used as an occasional football.

After the service, Mother, Gillian, Daisy and Simon return to the house with Benjamin and Humphrey while Father and Rupert go to The Fallen Sparrow for a 'traditional pint' and insist that I come along. Many of the local men in the pub will be beating tomorrow and Father makes a big show of introducing me to them all and buying them a drink, playing his Lord-of-the-Manor role with consummate ease. A few of them track me with sideways glances, especially the teenagers loitering around the pool-table who've already left the local school and have started work on the farms or in the local factories. Their eyes seem to ask what makes me so different from them and when Father announces that it's time to go, I'm only too happy to leave and barely pause to mumble a polite goodbye.

•

By the end of lunch everyone's drunk again. Humphrey and Benjamin still persist in punctuating everything with some kind of visceral accompaniment (they add clipped belching and syrupy farts to their repertoire) and once we've all moved to the library to open presents, Gillian falls asleep in an armchair, the rumble of her sherry-soaked snores supplying a rolling timpani to this concert of emissions and squeaks.

We open presents for the next hour, those of us still awake either faking surprise at having been given a present we wanted (and knowing in advance that we were going to receive it), or else faking gratitude at having been given something we didn't want. I have to do the worst of both, Mother and Father having given me a brand-new shooting jacket, leather cartridge-bag and ear-protectors.

'All from Holland and Holland,' Father tells me, 'the *best*.' Humphrey takes a rest from his spluttering to tell me that 'they'll last a lifetime' and I almost find myself *hurrumphing*.

I spend the remainder of the day watching Mother and Father grow increasingly brusque with each other, watching Simon and Rupert play billiards with a bottle of scotch each, watching Daisy grow more and more uncomfortable as the Lovington clan descend into increasing disarray.

'I remember,' Benjamin bellows, burying his snout of a nose

93

into a cauldron of port, 'your – *heech* – Great-Uncle Giles' first shoot. Must have been – *heech* – back in 'thirteen. Absolute lion of a man, went on to be a fine racquets player too until they carted him – *heech* – off to Ypres. He bagged thirty-three that year, amazed everyone, never been bested. And then there was my Uncle Cranston. One of the rascals hid in a tree and jumped out at him – *heech* – and had his hands around Cranston's neck before any of us could do a damned thing about it. Had to finish him off with his hunting knife, right bloody mess everywhere. And did I tell I about – *heech* – you Great-Uncle Giles' first shoot . . . ?'

5

That night, I sleep for a few hours, my body creased up with nervousness, and I wake up at about five, my spine stiff, my stomach boiling away. When I get out of bed to be sick in the washbasin, I think to myself that it's going to be okay, that I've got the flu. But my head clears as I rinse my mouth out and I realise that there's nothing wrong with me and I lie down on my bed again and stare uselessly at the ceiling.

Half an hour later I get up again when I hear noises outside. I put on a dressing gown and tiptoe up to a bathroom on the floor above where there's a better view and I see that the sound is coming from the game-pens. The doors are open, the glow from the heaters effusing a milky orange nimbus out into the night. Through this walk the animals. It's too far to make out anything but the vaguest of shapes but even at this distance I can see their lean figures padding out into the stockade. The night air carries across the echoes of gamekeepers' shouts, the rattling of chains and barking dogs. The sound of engines heaving into activity coincides with the distant glare of headlamps suddenly piercing through the darkness and a wave of fear ripples through the crowd of shadows. Soon there's the metallic clanging of the lorries being shut up and locked, the shifting of gears as they pull away and up the track to Bleadon's.

•

Mother tries not to look too pleased with herself when I appear in the kitchen in my plus-fours and waistcoat.

'Oh Timmy darling! You look so grown up. I'm very, very proud,' she gushes and then busies herself pouring me a coffee and dishing out a plate of kedgeree that feels like sand and sawdust in my mouth. A few minutes later Father walks in and says that Keith Sliney has just called from his car to say that he's five minutes away and would I come out to meet him. I nod, pushing my knife and fork together, and follow him outside.

'Everything ready?' Father says as we both wait on the gravel.

'Yes.'

'Are you nervous?'

'No.'

'It doesn't matter if you are. I was. Rupert *wasn't*, of course, but Simon *was*, even if he'll never admit to it. You'll get over it once the action's started.'

Sliney's car glides down the drive and comes to a halt in front of us, a midnight-blue Porsche with tinted windows and cream upholstery.

'Gaudy little shit!' Father grunts and then suddenly puts on a relaxed smile as Sliney climbs out of his car.

'Mr Lovington. Nice to meet you finally.' He offers his hand and Father takes it, telling Sliney to call him 'Edward'.

'I've brought a friend,' Sliney says. 'I thought it'd be okay.'

'Absolutely,' Father replies, eyes sweeping over her fur coat and highlights. 'The more the merrier.' The blonde that gets out from the passenger seat introduces herself as Carol and Father says he's delighted to meet her before leading us inside. Over coffee in the kitchen, Father and Sliney talk about how long it takes to get to Everleigh from London and both of them agree it's an easy journey while Mother is left to gossip with Carol. 'What a nice place you have here,' Carol says to her and I notice Mother wince.

'Did you see *her*?' she asks minutes later, shutting the kitchen door behind her once they've been shown to their room. 'He could have let us know about her in advance. I mean, really . . . it's as if he's just picked her up in a nightclub, exchanged her heels for wellingtons and asked her to tag along. And *him*? He looked very mail-order.'

'He's a shit,' Father agrees. 'So what? We show him and his floozy a fantastic time until tomorrow morning when we get shot of them, a good job done.'

•

By ten o'clock, everyone's arrived. There are the regulars like Harry Aster, old 'Jock' McKinney and Andy Tretton who turn up every year. And there are the less frequent faces, men like Will Connell and Tom Shipton, old school friends of Father's whom he only sees once every few years. They all pat me on the back and shake my hand, many of them wishing me luck, others even going as far as saying, 'Well done!'

'You ready, Master Timothy?' Alan asks, coming up beside me and placing a heavy hand on my shoulder.

'Yes, Alan.'

'You're not going to forget everything now, are you?' he asks, the corners of his mouth breaking into a smile, and I say that I won't.

'Good lad. Well it's time.'

Father nods and everyone climbs into their allotted vehicle, Sliney coming in the first Land Rover with Father and me, Alan up front in the driver's seat. On the way up, Father makes conversation by telling Sliney about the tradition of the Boxing Day shoot 'here in Everleigh', pointing out other drives as we pass them.

Up on Bleadon's, I can't help but notice how quiet it is. The air is motionless. I'm given the fifth and central gun as a matter of course, while Sliney and my Father take the positions either side of me, the others then drawing pegs and taking up their positions to our left and right. Rupert comes up to me and wishes me luck and at some point I hear Alan remind me to enjoy myself.

'Don't get nervous and snatch at the shot,' he whispers soothingly and then retreats a few feet behind me.

The last thing I hear before I put on my ear-protectors over my cap is the sound of rattling cages and chains, of the dogs barking somewhere on the other side of the copse. Then everything's reduced to a muffled blur. Alan hands me my gun and as I slot the two cartridges into the breech with uncertain fingers, I can see out of the corner of my eye the other men watching me as they sit back on shooting-sticks, lifting hip flasks to their mouths one final time or else grinding cigarettes out in the mud with their boots.

Standing there, the gun heavy in my hand, I focus on the dense wall of trees eighty yards away, trying to shift my mind away from my heart that's beating a countdown, from the inside of my gloves where I can feel the sweat soaking into the lining. Down the shallow hill, Bleadon's is nothing more than a dark impenetrable mass in front of me. And then suddenly, amidst its rambling texture of greens and browns, I can make out the odd figure flitting from behind one tree-trunk to another. I gulp,

97

almost swallow my tongue, remember Alan telling me to *wait until they clear the edge of the copse*. My body stiffens as they get nearer, pale arms swinging wildly as they run through the trees towards us.

Then the first naked body appears. Then *another . . . and another . . .* bare feet flashing through the mist that's hugging the ground. My stomach flips. I feel the hairs rise on the back of my neck. As I flick the safety-catch, I almost look around at Alan but I know he'll just narrow his eyes and nod.

Now one of the animals runs towards me, clearly in range, and if I don't shoot then he'll soon be ridiculously close. I raise my gun and shut my eyes for a second, the first trigger giving way to the pressure of my finger with oiled exactness. When I open my eyes again, I see that the first round has missed completely and the animal, now only forty yards away, has broken sharply to my left. The barrels follow and the second trigger gives way as smoothly as the first. Another pounding kick of the butt. The figure, up until now more like a ghost, suddenly becomes substantial. It catches the load above the left buttock and topples sideways into the mud. To my right, I see Rupert raise his gun and let off both barrels with casual efficiency, his hands moving as easily as if they were lighting a cigarette, and behind him the muzzle flash and gunsmoke stretches out in a line.

Then I freeze completely. I can't do it. I can't go on and I cradle the gun uselessly against my chest. Father notices and I see him mutter something to himself before swinging his hulking twelve bore up into the air and firing another thunderous burst. This goes on for half an hour, wave after wave of animals released into the copse only to come out the other side to be slaughtered. On the ground in front me, the bodies stretch out towards the treeline, some lying still, others thrashing about, eyes white with pain, hands clutching at the gaping tears in their flesh. Then for a few seconds, the air becomes still again and I realise that everyone's stopped firing. From the other side of the copse, a red smoke flare soars up towards the turbulent clouds and I don't see who's the first to suddenly charge forward, but I think it's Harry Aster, snapping his breech shut and darting towards the trees. Father and Keith Sliney advance too, their eyes seething with frenzied determination, and I find myself straggling along behind them, all of us surging forward in a line over the falling ground, feet trampling over dead and wounded. Amidst the confusion, I can make out Rupert at the front of the crowd, understandably the quickest over the uneven ground, and I watch him kneel perhaps twenty yards from the trees and let off at least four rounds before the next nearest person draws up alongside of him. Soon the whole group has formed up in a tight wedge in front of me and I watch them loose off load after load as the animals stumble into range. I'm not sure how long this goes on for because my mind relays its images in time with the muted roar of the guns. But eventually the barrage stops and I see Father, Alan and Rupert enter into a short discussion before leading us into Bleadon's in a line. As we stalk through the copse, we find most of the animals quivering with fear. Some have climbed the branches, looking for some kind of escape route that doesn't exist. Others simply cower on the ground and the men take turns to fire from short range. Next to me, Simon paces forward, his face spattered with blood and when one of them springs out from behind a fallen tree-trunk, I see his eyes flash as his first round catches the animal squarely between the shoulders and catapults it into a ditch.

An hour later Father raises a hand and calls our advance to a halt. He consults Alan and then signals that it's time to head back towards the house.

It's over.

Soon the Land Rovers come into sight as we all trudge back out of Bleadon's and I take off my ear-protectors to find that the air is full of the dull groans of the animals that lie on the ground waiting for the last pulses of life to drain out of them, though these are soon drowned out by the chatter of the men as they gather in the centre of the clear ground.

'How many?' I hear Rupert ask Simon as I walk closer.

'Not sure. Fifteen? Sixteen?'

Harry Aster hands around cigarettes. 'Better than last year?' he asks the group, swigging from his hip flask and wiping his mouth on his sleeve before handing it to me. 'I saw you get *your* first one, Timmy. Congratulations, young man.'

I don't say anything but take a sip of sloe gin. Sliney, Father and Alan walk up and soon we're all assembled in a circle. Harry Aster repeats that he saw me get my first one.

'Yes,' Father replies, 'he did.'

Looking down, I suddenly realise that we're all standing by the corpse of the female that bit my finger, liquid weeping from her ruptured midriff, limbs splayed, one eyelid half-closed, the other wide open, blood seeping through the grooves of her white teeth. Her mouth is a clotted cylinder of chipped teeth and blood.

'Time for the *blooding*,' Father says.

'Blooding?' I ask, taking a step backwards but finding myself blocked by a stout wall of tweed.

'To celebrate you first kill, Master Timothy,' says Alan, almost grudgingly. 'It's traditional. A rite of passage.'

I look around the ring of faces and they stare back at me almost hungrily.

'Alan,' I hear my father say, 'I believe the honour falls to you.'

'Yes sir.' Alan strides into the centre of the circle. 'Master Timothy?'

I don't move but the wall of tweed and leather closes around me and I watch, horrified, as Alan crouches down beside the body of the female and saws at her wrist with a hunting knife until her right hand comes free. 'Here we are,' he murmurs as he walks towards me, raising the sopping hand and swiping it across my cheeks.

•

Alan drives us back. Rupert rides with me and Sliney and they talk about SA80s and the different types of ammunition used by the Army as we roll down the hill. Father, however, sits in the front and doesn't look at me once or say a word to me. Back at the house, Alan collects the guns for cleaning, his hands invisibly accepting tips from each guest, but when I hand him my gun, he thanks me but refuses my folded twenty-pound note.

'No need for a tip, Master Timothy.' He pauses and looks at the ground. 'Not on your first time.'

In the kitchen, Mother puts down her glass of wine and asks me if I've enjoyed myself. I reply that I was nervous, not sure whether I should tell her the truth, just as Father and Sliney walk through the kitchen door.

'Ever been on safari?' Father's saying to him. Sliney shakes his head. 'You should be our guest next summer,' Father says, slapping him on the back and offering him a drink. 'Nothing like chasing those jungle-bunnies across the plain from the back of a jeep, the hot wind in your face, the African sun beating down.'

I hover by the stove where I can smell a game pie cooking away in preparation for the hunt dinner later on. 'Did it go well?' Mother asks Father.

'It went fine,' he replies, looking at me but saying nothing more.

Mother tells Sliney that Carol went up to their room half an hour ago, that she is waiting for him, and Sliney says to Father that they can talk later and takes his drink upstairs with him. Father then announces to Mother that he's going upstairs too. He pauses after he says it, making eye-contact with Mother for a couple of seconds before turning and leaving the room. Then the door shuts and Mother sighs, a hand moving to her hair.

'You said you were nervous.'

I nod.

'You won't be,' she says, 'as you get older.'

She lingers for a moment longer and then tells me that she's going upstairs to talk to Father. And once she's left, I'm alone in the kitchen.

I sit down in the rocking chair by the stove to soak up the warmth, to let my breathing settle. I let my body slouch, let my head come to rest on the back of the chair and shut my eyes. It takes a little time to get the images out of my mind, the crippled slump of the bodies as they fell to the ground, the sight of the dogs scrabbling at the throats of the wounded. It seems to help when I imagine the rooms around me, familiar images of home, and I let my mind drift out beyond the kitchen to the four corners of the house. I can hear noises coming from the garages, the spluttering of the pipes in the basement, footsteps on the gravel somewhere outside. I let my mind wander out of the kitchen door and up the main stairs, past the portrait of Granpa Charles, past the bloodless stares of Great-Granpa Nigel's trophies hanging on the walls (the animals don't seem to look so different, not once I've taken in the delicate tissue of their nostrils or their sad black eyes), up to the bedrooms where I can hear the sound of adults talking, the opening and shutting of cupboards, the running of baths and showers. After a while I can pick out the fainter traces of background noise, light footfalls on carpet, the distant murmur of carols being sung on the World Service somewhere on the top floor, the metallic sound of bedsprings and luggage being unzipped, the shutting of doors and windows. These sounds are distant, like the whisper of rhythmic breathing, like the faint wind outside the window, almost as faint as the gentle creaking from down the corridor where fresh game has been hung in the pantry, toes dangling towards the ground and swaying inches from the sawdust.

INK

What's done cannot be undone.
To bed, to bed, to bed.

William Shakespeare, *Macbeth*

1

Jack awoke to the sound of the Westerkerk clocktower booming out over the rooftops of Amsterdam. Where was he? Whose house was he in? The bells that had shaken him out of his dreamless sleep, a dark and shapeless blackout from which he emerged thirsty and nauseous, fell silent and Jack started to remember the night before just as his hangover burst into horrifying life.

I'm in the shit, he thought to himself immediately as he twisted on to his back, his face peeling away from the pillow, a hand moving to his forehead: *I am definitely in the shit!* Now there were hazy recollections of his drunken arrival at Johanna's house the night before: the way the door had pitched and yawed in front of him as he stretched out a hand to ring the bell; the sound of Coco's anxious voice saying that she'd been worried to death and asking him where he'd been; the disarray of his gurgled answers. Her tone had hardened when she'd smelt the alcohol coming off his breath in thick waves and she'd shrieked later at the sight of his bandaged arm. By that time, Jack had been incapable of anything but sprawling across their bed and listening to her repeated insistence that she 'just didn't understand' while the ceiling spiralled dangerously above him.

Jack raised his throbbing limb and contemplated the dressing and the translucent quadrant of surgical tape. The material was blotted with small rosettes of blood that were fringed by yellow rings the colour of clouded urine. The flesh underneath ached and caused Jack to exhale, to remember both the whirring of the tattooist's needle and how *it* had looked when freshly completed, the black ink glistening amongst droplets of blood the colour of strawberry cordial.

He got out of bed and stumbled towards the adjacent bathroom where he drained off the ball of heat in his bladder and then deposited himself under the falling spray of the shower with his right arm extended into the dry air. When it came to brushing his teeth, he was obliged to swipe at his gums uselessly with the toothbrush in his left hand and afterwards he dried and dressed himself with the same awkwardness. After that there was nothing else he could do but go downstairs and face her.

Negotiating the steep ravine of the staircase, Jack shuffled into the kitchen and saw Coco crouched by the open dishwasher. She didn't look up and didn't say anything. So Jack didn't say anything. The Silent Treatment. All things considered, this was probably best. He opened the fridge door, pulled out a bottle of water and sat down at the small, round table where he watched Coco load dirty bowls and mugs in between the plastic spokes. Finally she spoke as she wiped the table in front of him.

'Does it hurt?'

'What?' Jack asked, half mesmerised by the ebb and flow of his hangover. The nausea now seemed tangible, *muscular*, organised in waves of contractions.

'Does it hurt – the tattoo?'

'A little bit.'

Coco's eyes stayed fixed on the surface of the table where her hand moved in circular motions.

'Does it need re-dressing?'

'The guy told me to leave it for two days. Where's Johanna?'

'She's gone out to have breakfast with some friends.'

Of course she had, thought Jack, how discreet. 'And Marie?' he asked.

'In her room getting ready. I thought we could go to the

Rijksmuseum this afternoon and then have lunch in Vondelpark. And then I want to take Marie shopping.'

'Sounds good,' Jack croaked as Coco lapsed back into silence and proceeded to make a small breakfast for him. Without another word, and with her back to him, she buttered toast at the counter and poured his tea before setting it down in front of him and going upstairs.

•

Half an hour later The Silent Treatment had been temporarily suspended in favour of The Talking Torture. Jack, Coco and Marie walked south along Prinsengracht, Jack and Coco always a yard apart and not holding hands, talking about anything except the night before or why Jack had been so late arriving at the house or what he'd been doing. At one point Coco pointed out a small chest of drawers outside an antique shop and asked Jack if he thought it would suit their bedroom back in London.

'That's what I love about Amsterdam,' she said. 'You walk down these canals and you can't tell if some of these houses are museums or galleries or shops or just *homes*.' Then she told Jack how her work had gone in Amsterdam the last few days and what she and Marie had done in the evenings, all the time not looking at him as she gave him the list of names, times and places.

'We got to Schipol an hour late and the train service to Centraal Station had been suspended . . . it was so muggy . . . Marie was ecstatic to see Johanna again . . . she took us to this amazing Indonesian restaurant called Temple Doeloe . . . Marie and I had rijstaffel . . . on Tuesday we met our opposite numbers at TRS . . . the night before last we went to the Muziektheatre . . . Marie and Johanna spent the afternoon at Anne Frank's House . . . Paul Scheider told me yesterday that he wants me to think about heading the new team.'

109

Jack listened, struggling to inject enthusiasm into his murmured replies. 'Mmmm,' he agreed. 'Really?' he sighed (inside he winced at another internal lurch, another visceral plea for help). It was hard to know what to say if they weren't going to talk about *it* – and it was hard to know where to look, especially with his eyeballs pulsating so ferociously. Jack definitely didn't want to look Coco in the eye and settled for focusing on Marie as she hopped and skipped a little way ahead of them, her pigtails flapping behind her. Occasionally Marie paused to take a photograph of a houseboat with her new camera or to turn around and wave at them. At least *she* was happy.

A few bridges further on and the three of them stopped at a canalside café for bagels and a drink. Marie sat twisted in her chair so she could reach over and stroke a cat that dozed on some nearby steps, singing the words of a nursery rhyme as she ran her fingers through its fur. And Coco was still talking and Jack was still hoping that the fresh air and the breakfast he'd eaten were going to make some kind of impact on the way he was feeling. *Wasn't that the point of forcing down the food and the liquid?* he asked himself. Wasn't that the reason for being outside and upright when he should have been in bed with a joint and the television turned down low: *that it was all meant to make him feel better?* Jack didn't feel better. He felt worse. For brief spells the vertigo would fade and his head seemed to shrink back to its normal size only for the pressure behind his eyes to return minutes later. His face itself felt numb and bloodless, the skin stretched into a grimace as if he were freefalling towards the ground, his heart not so much beating as *sobbing*, each breath a source of hope as his stomach clenched and crumpled. And Coco was still talking.

'Look at those houses . . . that's what I love about it here . . .

so open . . . the Dutch never bother about net curtains or any of that *English* crap . . .'

'Really?' Jack picked up his coffee cup but put it down again. His hands were trembling too much. He'd spill it all over himself.

'It's a pity . . . the rubbish in this city is enough of a problem as it is without there being a strike . . . hasn't been collected since Monday . . . piled up in the streets everywhere . . . there isn't even going to be any transport for the whole of *next* Monday . . . we'll have to get a taxi back to the airport . . .'

'Mmmmm,' Jack agreed, rubbing the bridge of his nose between his thumb and forefinger and wishing more than ever that he could be transported through time, either forward to the next day or back to the day before, it didn't matter, anything not to be sitting right *there* and right *then*. And Coco was still talking, and not talking about *it* but wondering whether they should see the East Wing of the Rijksmuseum first or a special exhibition of medieval carvings she'd read about in the *Financial Times*. 'I think it's already been shown in London so this might be our last . . . *will you look at that*!'

Jack wearily turned his head to see what Coco was pointing at. On the ground near the edge of the bank (and near another pile of rubbish sacks) lay a solitary leather boot, a small size that suggested it had belonged to a woman. In a way it looked no more extraordinary than the beer cans and junk-food cartons that lay around it, just another piece of flotsam left over from Amsterdam's Friday night.

'What kind of girl loses one shoe?' Jack heard Coco say, but didn't pay her much attention as his eyes desperately searched the cobbles for the boot's partner. 'Probably the sort of girl who wears shoes like that,' she said. 'Look! It's got little feathers *glued* to the sides at the heel. How *naff* . . .'

Jack couldn't see the other one anywhere, just the right half of the pair a few yards away from them. It stood the right way up, its buckle straps broken and hanging down loosely at its sides, the toe pointing out over the canal as if marking the spot where its wearer had taken a final step before flinging herself into the water. 'Losing both shoes you could put down to carelessness or drunkenness – but to lose one?' Jack heard Coco ask. 'It makes me think something more *disturbed* has happened . . . I mean, who loses one shoe? Who would want to take off *just one?*'

2

Coco had first mentioned the trip to Amsterdam back in March five months earlier. After another stagnant day at his word-processor, Jack had collected Marie from school as usual and walked her home through the drizzle across Brook Green. Back inside the warmth of the flat, he let her watch cartoons for an hour (and watched them with her) before she started her homework on the kitchen table and Jack started on a vegetable stew. Her class had been set the task of writing 'a story' describing their mothers.

'How do you spell *slissiter?*' Marie asked at one point, chewing her pencil.

'S-O-L-I-C-I-T-O-R,' Jack replied, coring the seeds out of a red pepper.

'And what about *cumpny?*'

'C-O-M-P-A-N-Y,' he replied, crushing garlic and rock salt into a paste with a flat butter knife. 'I thought you knew how to use a dictionary?'

'I do.' Silence. 'How do you spell *ryter?*'

'W–R–I–T–E–R.' Jack couldn't resist seeing what she'd written and wiped his hands on a cloth as he peered over her shoulder.

my Mummy is called Coco and is big with brown hair and brown eyes. my Mummy wears a soot and wears ear rings and is a soliciter. She works in the city. Sometimes she is very seriuss and very tired. Usually she is fun and tels jokes. She works for a company. my Mummy is french and english. Jack is english and he is a writer. Jack also does cleening and cooking.

'Well done,' Jack said, 'but you need to check your spelling.' He was writing out a list of corrections on a piece of scrap paper when Coco came through the door and looked to see what they were doing.

'A fat grouchy prostitute,' she whispered in his ear once she'd read Marie's piece. 'You told her what to write, didn't you!'

Marie made her amendments, gathered up her things and took them up to her bedroom while Coco poured a glass of wine from the open bottle in the fridge and sat down at the table. It was then that she told Jack about her trip to Amsterdam.

'The firm want me to go over for the third week of July and help wrap up the merger. Anyway, you know how I hate staying in hotels . . .'

Jack had nodded.

'So I rang Johanna to see if I could stay with her and she said that it was a great idea and also suggested I bring Marie with me for a holiday so that they can spend some time together. Do you think it's a good idea?'

•

Johanna was Maarten's mother and Maarten was Marie's father. Coco and Jack had 'done' the subject of Coco and Maarten the second night they'd slept together because they'd been 'doing' the whole subject of Coco and Marie at the time and you couldn't talk about one thing without talking about the other. Lying in her bed at her flat in Olympia, Coco told Jack how she'd met Maarten while they'd studied politics together at the Université de Lyon almost a decade before, both of them shunning other simultaneously casual relationships to move into a bedsit together on the north bank of the Saône, under the shadow of the grey cathedral. 'It was pretty grimy really,' Coco had admitted, 'just a mattress, a sink, a couple of gas rings and no heating in the winter. It sounds like a cliché, I know, but that's how it was!'

It *did* sound like a cliché, Jack thought as he listened, but it also sounded better than his three years in Nottingham spent trying not to get beaten up by the local metal fans (Nottingham still had them – *why?*) and only getting laid once every two and a quarter terms when everyone else seemed to be getting a couple of 'bunk-ups' a week. And Jack imagined how grimy it had been, whole weeks at a time spent in frowsy orgasmic bliss with nothing but more sex to keep the cold away, their room a caramel glow of candlelight bouncing off tumblers of wine and upturned copies of Spinoza (Maarten's) and Mill (hers). There would have been the beautiful spring mornings and the suffocating heat at siesta-time during the summer, the cloudy skies of tragic autumn afternoons, the leaves falling as the two of them walked through the dark streets back towards their bed.

'My parents came to Lyon to visit me but it was really to check out Maarten of course,' Coco had told him. 'They expected the worst so they saw the worst. One look at my mother's face told me she was praying that we'd split up. Which of course we did though perhaps not in the way she expected.'

Coco discovered that she was pregnant four months before her final exams and Maarten had disappeared from Lyon two months later.

'Just gone! I arrived back at the flat to find that all he'd left was a copy of *Ethics* with a note scrawled inside.'

'What did it say?' Jack had asked.

'I don't know. Once I saw his handwriting all over the inside cover I got so angry that I threw the book out the window. I went down half an hour later to look for it, after I'd stopped crying, but someone must have picked it up and walked off with it. It's funny to think that a complete stranger in Lyon has a copy of *Ethics* with Maarten's message to me written inside.'

Astonishingly, Coco passed all her papers first time and Marie was born four months later. At the same time, Coco's English mother separated from her Corsican father and moved back to England. Coco followed her, wanting to put Lyon in the past, and moved into the same house in Barnes and plans for postgraduate studies were dismissed in favour of re-training in the law which ultimately led to her job at Scheider & Rex.

'And now I'm here,' she'd said, wrapped in Jack's arms.

•

Jack's friends were impressed when he first introduced Coco to them at a pub the following Friday night.

'Not bad, Jack, not bad!' Al had said while Coco was at the bar buying drinks.

'Italian?' Chris had asked.

'She's really nice – not like the miserable poets you usually go out with,' Sophie had observed. 'She tells jokes and talks to us rather than sitting in the corner consumed by angst.'

'How old?' Geoff had asked.

'Thanks . . . err Corsican actually, or at least her father's Corsican and her mother's English . . . she's thirty.'

'*Thirty!*'

'Thirty.'

'She'll want a kid,' Chris tutted into his pint.

'I don't think women reach thirty and suddenly want children,' Jack replied. 'It's not like a deadline. And anyway, she's already got one. A seven-year-old girl called Marie.'

'Where's the father?'

'Somewhere in the Far East – Indonesia or some place like that. He flew the coop just before Marie was born and only shows up every couple of years.'

'And you've met her?'

'I've met her.'

'*Already?*'

'Why not?'

His friends hadn't had an answer and Jack was pleased that their surprise at the five-year age gap between him and Coco and at her having a seven-year-old child had been revealed as the hollow product of twentysomething foolishness. Maybe she *was* five years older than him. Maybe she was a solicitor and earned five times more than he did (at the time he'd been working part-time at Cinemaniacs Videos on the Uxbridge Road while he attempted to finish his first novel) – but weren't these material concerns meant to be irrelevant? When he moved into Coco's flat three months later, Jack fielded another round of enquiries as to the suitability of the relationship. Was he ready to settle down? Was he ready to play the role of a father?

'What can I tell you? I love her, and Marie. Isn't that all that counts?' He and Geoff and Al were in the pub a couple of nights before he was due to move out of his bedsit. 'And as for *settling down*, it wouldn't seem so strange to everyone else if it was *her* that was moving in with *me* or if it was me that had the better-paid job.'

●

'Do you think it's a good idea?' Coco had asked him. 'Marie and I would fly out on the Monday night and you could have the week here on your own, get some writing done and fly out on the Friday afternoon. You said you were going to finish around then so maybe this all works out for the best?'

Jack *had* said that his book would be finished by the end of July. That had been last August when he'd moved in and when he'd reached a halfway point in his novel. The problem was that he was still only halfway through. He was only *ever* halfway through and though there were occasional flashes of progress, Jack sometimes felt that he was doomed to never continue beyond the first hundred pages. He'd given up the drudgery of the video store to write at home in the day and look after the flat, to accompany Marie to and from school, to increase the stability of his life so that writing would become easier instead of harder. But by the time Coco and Marie were packing their cases for Amsterdam, Jack was still looking at the same passages that he'd been toiling over at Christmas, still sensing the same flaws, the same problems, and was too ashamed to admit to Coco that he was still stuck.

'Take care and see you on Friday,' she'd said to him, the taxi waiting in the road behind her to take her and Marie to the airport. 'Hope your work goes well. We'll call.'

The taxi had driven away down the road and Jack had gone back inside the flat and slumped down on the sofa where he spent the next few days scrupulously avoiding the word-processor, instead getting stoned (usually he was never allowed to smoke in the flat) and watching *Teletubbies* and cooking programmes, or else the black-and-whites they showed on Channel 4 during the day. Was Coco getting frustrated with him? Or was he projecting his own frustrations on to her? he would ask himself. Would she understand how or why he was finding it difficult to write? Or was that an impossibility given that he himself had few or no answers? Coco telephoned twice over the next few days, briefly letting Jack know that she and Marie were well, and Jack would lie to her, saying that he was making progress. And then Friday had arrived and seemingly before he knew it, Jack was rushing to the station to catch his train to Gatwick.

•

At Schipol Airport, Jack arrived to find the train service to Centraal Station suspended on account of engineering works being carried out on the line.

'You can take a bus to Zuid WTC and proceed by metro from there,' the ticket clerk told him from the other side of the glass.

Jack anticipated the journey taking an extra hour as it always did when this kind of thing happened and he only had a few hours to himself in Amsterdam before he was due at Johanna's house: his plans to spend the afternoon in a coffeeshop looked as if they were doomed and he'd probably not get another chance. But then the replacement bus service delivered him to the metro connection in no time at all and in the hot carriage, his travel-bag clamped between his legs, Jack pulled out a map and realised that he could recoup some of his preciously planned afternoon by getting out at an earlier station rather than going the whole way to the end of the line. At Nieuwmarkt, the escalator brought him up into the sunshine and into familiar territory. The coffeeshop he'd planned to go to, Basjoe, a small place run by three Surinamese brothers, was only five minutes away. Smiling, Jack crossed over the cobbled square, past a Chinese supermarket and benches where men slept in the baking heat, their breathing heavy from early-afternoon drinking, and walked down the side of the wide canal. He looked at his watch. It was a little after a quarter past two and he'd agreed to be at Johanna's on Prinsengracht at five. It would take twenty minutes to get across the city from

Basjoe so he had a whole two hours to idle away. He'd lost no time at all.

Basjoe seemed unchanged since he'd been there as a student a few years earlier: the same advertisement on the cigarette machine in the corner, the same newspaper racks mounted on the brown walls, the same indolent dub on the hi-fi system. From his table, Jack asked for a couple of grams of Silver Haze and a 7up and once he'd rolled a joint and lit it, he pulled out his copy of *The Long Goodbye* and began reading.

I drove back to Hollywood feeling like a short length of chewed string. It was too early to eat, and too hot. I turned on the fan in my office. It didn't make the air any cooler, just a little more lively. Outside on the boulevard the traffic bawled endlessly. Inside my head thoughts stuck together like flies on fly paper . . .

Damn right! sighed Jack putting the book down and taking another drag on the joint. It *was* hot and it was hard to read and not be distracted by the people outside walking past the window in front of him, the girls wheeling past on bicycles, their summer dresses flattened against their bodies (*cling! cling!* the small bells on the handlebars sounded), the taxis and cars slowing to make the turn right outside the door to the coffeeshop. Jack picked up the book and tried again.

I drove back to Hollywood feeling like a short length of . . . it was no good. There was too much noise inside as well, the sound of the bassline and the chattering voices. Four Americans sat at a table near the counter talking about which had been better, the Bubblegum at Grey Area or the Crystal at Abraxas. At another table sat a couple who weren't talking but staring down at their orange juices with ditched eyes, the boy every so often the victim of a bout of violent coughing. Two locals sat at the table nearest the door talking in Dutch and on a stool at the counter, a girl in a leather jacket and short black dress sat on her own, drumming her fingernails on the wood. Jack took another drag on his joint and turned back to his book.

I drove back to Hollywood feeling like a short length of chewed string. It was too early to eat, and too hot. I turned the . . . this time Jack closed the book before laying it back down on the table. He wasn't going to be able to read and decided to put the book back in his bag, determined to enjoy getting high while the world passed by outside. He looked down at his watch. Ten to three. When he looked up again he saw that the girl at the bar had moved to the table directly next to his and that she was staring at him.

'What's wrong?' she asked. Her voice was American.

'Pardon me?' Jack looked at her again to check that he didn't know her. He didn't.

'I asked, "What's wrong?"'

'What do you mean?' Jack replied.

'You're sat there looking at your watch and re-reading *The Long Goodbye* . . .'

'How do you know I'm re-reading it?' Jack interrupted.

'The cover's all beat up.'

'I could have bought it in a second-hand shop.'

'Yeah, you could have. You telling me you bought it second-hand?'

'No. I'm re-reading it. You're right,' Jack smiled.

The girl smiled back.

'So what's wrong?' she asked as she got up from her table and sat down at his. 'No one re-reads *The Long Goodbye* unless there's something going wrong in their life. Chandler's self-pitying enough at the best of times – *but in that one?* Sheesh! You got Terry Lennox: the human ghost, the lost soul who isn't lost, the murderer who isn't a murderer, the suicide who isn't even a suicide! And what does Marlowe do? Gets himself beaten up and thrown in jail for the guy . . . when he's not too busy lighting up cigarettes and pouring spare cups of coffee as a tribute to the guy's memory!'

'You think Marlowe's a . . .'

'A *chump?*' she interrupted. Jack passed her the joint. 'No, not really.' She took a drag and held it in for a few seconds. 'I guess I love *The Long Goodbye*,' she said, smoke signals appearing in front of her lips. 'I mean, *anyone* would fall for Terry Lennox.' She took another drag – more smoke signals. 'I would.'

Jack looked at her more closely. She looked as if she was in her early twenties, maybe a little younger. And if anyone looked like a human ghost, it was her. Her skin looked as if it had been violently and repeatedly scrubbed, bleached except where the skin mottled into dark rings around her eyes. The small black dress skimmed the tops of her thighs, revealing the spokes of her legs which crossed at the bony points of her knees before disappearing into cavernous motorcycle boots. On each boot, Jack noticed, were glued two small feathers that slanted backwards and upwards from each side of her heel.

'You seem to know a lot about Raymond Chandler. Do you study him?' he asked.

'I went out with a college lecturer for a while. Back when I lived in Los Angeles. So anyway, you haven't told me what's wrong yet.'

'Do I really look that miserable?'

'Maybe. The name's Wilma. Hi.' She extended a hand.

'Jack,' he said, shaking the hand and feeling the bones of her fingers.

'I'm sorry I kind of grabbed you, Jack,' she said stubbing out the joint in the ashtray and starting to roll another from a small ziploc she pulled out of a pocket. 'To tell you the truth, I'm a little bit tense.'

'Why's that?'

'I'm about to have a tattoo. At five o' clock. I just came in here to have a smoke and relax but I guess I'm too nervous. That's why I came over. You looked like you couldn't concentrate anyway.'

'I couldn't,' Jack said. 'I don't know why I even tried.'

'You want a drink?' Wilma asked. 'I need a beer.'

'Sure. A beer would be good.'

'I know a coffeeshop near the tattooist's where they serve alcohol. Why don't we smoke this on the way?' They were silent for a while as Jack watched her raise the cigarette paper to her mouth and run her tongue along its gummed edge. After that they walked out of Basjoe, turned right and walked along a short street to the Achterburgwal where they turned right again, lighting the joint as they walked past the Amsterdam Grand and a couple of coffeeshops with tables scattered out over the pavement. Still not talking, they took a left over another bridge, passing the joint between them. These streets were busier. Around them milled groups of men in football shirts with carrier bags stacked with cans of lager, kids with backpacks slung over their shoulders and dreadlocks tied back in bunches, black guys in dirty shellsuits standing in groups at the street corners whispering, 'Coke? Ecstasy? Coke? Ecstasy?' or else saying nothing at all but staring at everyone with wild eyes as they walked past. Then Jack followed Wilma deeper into the red-light district, past the sex shops and theatres advertising 'live shows'. From the steps, brutish men with shaved heads and expensive suits called out to the people passing by while prostitutes in Lycra bodystockings and high heels looked down on them all, impassive behind the glass doors of their cubicles. Occasionally Wilma acknowledged an acquaintance and returned a greeting with a turn of her head and a brisk 'Hiya!' or 'How ya doin'?' Then they turned left again and walked down a street lined with nothing else but cubicles and at the end they came out on to Warmoesstraat. 'In here,' said Wilma before ducking into a coffeeshop called Green Peace.

Inside the sound system was blaring out Pink Floyd's *Wish You Were Here*. Where else in the world do they still play Pink Floyd albums in bars? Jack laughed to himself as his ears hummed with the sound of ambient synthesizers. At the bar he ordered a couple of pints from a wrecked American who air-guitared with twitching hands while the glasses filled. When he was sitting back down with Wilma at a table by the huge window, she started talking again.

'You see over there?' She pointed through the glass at a shop-front across the street. 'That's where I'm having it done.'

Jack looked over at the huge posters in the windows with small images dotted over them like nursery wallpaper and the name of the place painted in large letters on to the glass: Victor's Body Shop.

'Is this your first tattoo?' Jack asked.

'No. My sixth.'

'Sixth?'

'Yeah. You'd have thought they'd get easier, that you wouldn't get so nervous. But you don't. Or at least I don't.' She sipped at her beer. 'Maybe it's because after your first time, you know how much pain to expect.'

'Where have you got them? If you don't mind me asking.' Jack looked across at her. He couldn't see any tattoos, just her piercings: the two rings through her left nostril, the stud in her tongue that flashed and bobbed as she spoke, the bar through her right eyebrow, the graveyard of crosses that hung from her earlobes. Who knew what lay underneath her jacket or her dress?

'I don't mind. I'll show them to you if you like.' Wilma bent down and slid her right ankle out of its boot. On the pale skin sat the black shape of a reptile, about four inches long. It looked as if it was climbing up her leg, its tail whiplashing behind it.

'A lizard?'

'A gecko,' Wilma replied. 'This was the first one I ever got done, in LA when I was sixteen. Thought it wouldn't hurt, but it hurt like *shit*. The vibrations from the needle sent shockwaves all the way up my shin-bone and into my kneecap . . . took an hour and a half. See the way the guy did the claws and everything?'

Now Wilma pulled off her leather jacket revealing the long spindles of her fleshless arms. On the outside of her left bicep was a figure of eight lying on its side. Infinity. 'I got this one done next. It hurt less because of where it is but took three hours. You see how thick it is and how neat the curves are?' The loops were as thick as one of Jack's fingers. Wilma twisted in her seat and bared the outside of her other bicep at him. Marked on to the skin was the cartoon face of Wilma Flintstone, her hair marked out in a spiral above the triangular face and the points of her eyes. 'You get the show in England?' she asked.

'All the time.'

'Got this one done at the same time and at the same place, on Haight in San Francisco. Turned out the guy was a cartoon freak and loved all those old Hanna-Barbera shows. He kept shouting 'Wilmaaaaa!' every so often to make me laugh. My mom named me after her.'

'How long did that one take?'

'Another hour and a half. This one hurt worse. It's all outline which means the needle cuts slightly deeper. *As for this baby . . .*'

She turned her back to him, gathered her hair into a bunch over her shoulder and told him to unzip her. As Jack's fingers took hold of the metal tag and started to move downwards, he thought of Coco in a business meeting with her colleagues. He imagined that they would be sitting around a table in a boardroom, everyone in suits and talking about . . .

'Not the whole way!' Wilma laughed, interrupting his thoughts. Jack pulled the zipper down perhaps six inches, perhaps a little more, and the black material parted to reveal the white surface of her skin. Christ! he thought. He'd almost lowered his mouth and kissed the back of her neck. A reflex, he told himself, it was just a reflex. You unzip a girl's dress and your instinct's going to start taking over.

'What do you think?' Wilma asked. Across her shoulder-blades there was a set of four concentric rings, two black and two white (the bleached pink of her skin), each band half an inch wide. In the middle was a black circle perhaps one and a half inches in diameter.

'Put your hand on it,' Wilma said. Jack put his hand on it and stretched his fingers apart. The whole design was as wide as the distance between the tip of his thumb and little finger. What was it? A target? A black hole? A dark sun? Or just a set of concentric rings around a black circle? Underneath, the skin felt cold.

'That must have been painful,' he said.

'Painful! I wish it'd been that simple.' She was still turned away from him and Jack let his eyes wander down from the top of her neck to where her spine jutted out like a knotted rope. Again there was the urge to bend down and place his lips against her skin and again he thought of Coco . . . and *Christ!* They were in a coffeeshop in full public view and he had to be at Johanna's house in an hour. It would take half an hour to walk across town which meant . . .

'I was in the chair for eight hours,' Wilma said, still leaning away from him, 'at a place called Barbarians in Greenwich Village. I almost blacked out from the pain about four times and had to stop after five hours.' She now sat up straight which Jack took as a cue to zip up her dress. 'Almost didn't go back to have it finished.' She swivelled on the seat and was facing him again. 'But I did.' She drained her beer. 'I couldn't lie on my back for a fortnight afterwards. I got one more around my belly-button, a snake eating its own tail. I got it done at Victor's but I guess I can't show you that one without stripping off.'

Now Jack and Wilma both started rolling joints. Wilma went up to the bar saying that she needed something stronger and asked the wrecked American for a bottle of vodka from out of the freezer which he gave her and which, Jack noticed, she didn't pay for.

'You ever want one?' she asked when she returned to their table.

'What?'

'A tattoo?'

'I did once, but I never dared to take it any further.'

'Why not?'

'A combination of things really. I'm shit scared about pain and I could never think about what I wanted. I mean, they last for *ever*. I know people have them lasered off and so on, but essentially they're permanent. I toyed with the idea of having a seahorse or something but I could never find an image that made it seem worth facing up to the pain.'

Listening to himself, Jack felt a little cowardly. He'd wanted a tattoo since he was sixteen but he'd been frightened. And here was this girl who'd spent *days* under the tattooist's needle. He almost expected Wilma to laugh at him, but instead she told him that he should take a look in the window across the road.

'If you want one then you should get one,' she said to him.

'Even if it's only small. It would only take half an hour.' She laughed and smoke spurted out her nostrils. 'Easier than a trip to the dentist.'

'I couldn't,' Jack replied, suddenly feeling like he could at least take a look through the window. He looked at his watch. It was a quarter past four. Why not go across the street with her and take a look? He wouldn't see anything he wanted and he had to be making his way over to Johanna's in fifteen minutes in any case. Why not go over and take a look and then say goodbye to Wilma and return to what suddenly felt like normal life?

'Why not?' Wilma asked.

'Why not *what*?' Jack asked, forgetting what she'd last said.

'Why couldn't you get a tattoo?'

'My girlfriend would freak.'

'That's not a reason.'

'Yes it is,' Jack replied, suddenly a little indignant. Wilma knew nothing about him and Coco. Yet it was the first time he'd mentioned Coco all afternoon.

'No it's not. You just said you wanted a tattoo since you were sixteen. How old are you now? Twenty-four? Twenty-five?'

Jack replied that he was twenty-five.

'So how long have you been thinking about this?' Wilma continued. 'Nine fucking years.' She refilled both their glasses, Jack suddenly realising that he'd emptied his. 'All I'm saying is that you should come across the street with me and see what it's all about. I bet you've never even taken a look at a tattooist's.'

This was true. He'd thought about getting a tattoo many times, but never been anywhere near a tattoo parlour.

'Okay,' he said. 'We'll finish these joints and these drinks and I'll come and take a look.' In his mind, Jack told himself that he'd walk across the street with her and politely inspect the place and by then it would be four-thirty and time to say goodbye and walk through the city to Johanna's house where he'd find Coco and Marie waiting for him.

Now they sat in silence, both of them smoking. Every so often Jack sneaked glances at her, the way her throat rippled as she swallowed more vodka, the way her dress gripped her pinched torso (*cling! cling!* trilled the bicycle bells in the street outside), the faint camber of her breasts lying above the tapered angles of her ribcage and waist. In five minutes they'd finished their drinks and smoked their joints down to the roach. Then Wilma shrugged on her leather jacket and picked up the bottle which was now only half full and slotted it into the inside pocket before they cut through the ambling bodies that swayed up and down Warmoesstraat and came to a standstill outside Victor's Body Shop.

'What are you going to have done this time?' Jack asked Wilma as they stood facing the glass looking at the sample designs on the other side. He realised that she hadn't told him.

'I got the image in my pocket. Here! Take a look.' From a breast pocket, Wilma pulled out a folded piece of paper. It was a photocopy from a textbook of some sort, two columns of text around a picture of an African carving.

'It's a juju doll,' Wilma said. 'Come on, I'll introduce you to Victor,' and without another word she pushed her way inside. Jack stood in the street for a second and looked at his watch. 4.29. He had a minute before he was due to set off, he thought as he followed her through the swing doors.

The inside of the parlour was spacious and brightly lit. Wilma and Jack leaned on the small counter and Wilma rang the bell. Out of a doorway appeared a tall blond man who recognised Wilma with a smile.

'Hi Wilma.'

'Hi there, Victor. How ya doin'?'

'Okay. Had a lot of tourists in today.'

'Meet my friend Jack. He's thinking about having his first.'

'Hiya,' Jack nodded and Victor nodded back.

Victor was as pale as Wilma, and almost as skinny. Long, gangling arms sprouted out of his faded Motorhead vest, his skin a swirling tangle of colours and shapes. Every inch of his arms was decorated with some kind of design: twisting curlicues in black, green and red whose overall pattern Jack couldn't determine; an eagle on his left forearm pictured in a steep dive, its talons outstretched; a series of five bands that ringed around his right bicep; an approximation of the internal bones mapped out across the backs of his fingers and hands. As he ran one of these through his hair, Jack could see that even the shaved mound of his armpit had been tattooed with a pop-art explosion, the word *BLAM!* skewing out its centre.

'Do you know what you want?' Victor asked. 'We've got plenty of examples that might help you decide on something if you haven't.'

'I'll take a look.'

Jack left Wilma and Victor talking and wandered over to the large black ring-binders that sat on the small shelf running around the perimeter of the room. Telling himself that he'd say goodbye to Wilma as soon as he had a chance, he opened one and leafed through its laminated pages. The sample designs were arranged thematically as far as he could tell: a selection of skulls stared back up at him and a variety of cowled Grim Reapers beckoned towards him with skeletal fingers; a series of moons and stars came next followed by a crowd of naked women with muscular breasts and hips, some of them leaning back over the bonnets of hotrods, others astride huge motorcycles. *Blowtorch*

Bitch . . . Bad Motherfucker . . . Born to Lose. There were pages of superheroes: Superman, Spiderman and the Silver Surfer as well as a whole page of Batman designs and Bat-signals. Another folder contained pages of miscellaneous symbols: the zig-zags of lightning bolts; the variegated stripes of a barcode, the fused apostrophes of *yin* and *yang*; the Star of David; the symbols for radiation and for pi; the black sphere of an eightball; an apple with a bite taken out of it; a spider's web; an *ohm*; Thor's Hammer; a marijuana leaf; a handprint and two footprints. At the back was a section containing the Celtic Runes and their translations and examples of Arabic and Indian script: *Peace . . . Strength . . . Inner Fire.* Chinese characters followed: *Dragon . . . Tiger . . . Warrior . . . Truth.*

'Anything grab you?' Wilma was now looking over his shoulder.

'Not really,' Jack replied. 'I guess I wouldn't choose anything I'd seen here because . . . .well, it wouldn't really seem individual.'

He looked down at Wilma's boots, the feathers slanting back from the anklebones, and then glanced at his watch again. It was ten minutes to five.

'No it wouldn't, but maybe something you've seen's inspired you?' he heard Wilma reply. If he left straight away he'd only be twenty minutes late. Coco could be running late too, what with her colleagues inviting her to join them for the inevitable round of drinks . . .

'Victor says his brother Frank is free for the rest of the afternoon. You could have a small one done at the same time as me. It's up to you.'

Jack looked at his watch again but realised this was avoiding the real issue. He suddenly knew as he looked down at Wilma's legs that he wasn't frightened of the pain. Christ! He'd have a small one, high up on his upper arm where it had to be least painful. *How would Coco react if he came home with a tattoo?* She'd be shocked at first, he admitted to himself, but she'd soon adjust, wouldn't she? It wasn't as if she was a prude and *everybody* had tattoos these days. You saw them *everywhere*. Even people at Scheider & Rex had them. At a summer party the year before, to which 'spouses' and 'partners' had been invited, hadn't a drunk secretary hiked up her skirt and showed the dolphin marked on the outside of her thigh to a whole group of onlookers? Jack turned so that he was facing Wilma. Behind her, Victor leafed through a magazine.

'You should wait if you can't think of anything,' Wilma told him.

•

Fifteen minutes later, after smoking another joint in the street outside and drinking more vodka, Jack and Wilma were being led through a short passageway to a back room that looked like a barber's shop. Four swivel-chairs stood opposite four mirrors and Jack sat in one while Wilma sat across the aisle in another.

'Where are you going to have yours?' he asked.

'At the base of my back and a little bit to the left. About two inches long. Just a sentimental thing, you know?'

Victor walked in from washing his hands and pulled up a low stool beside Wilma. 'Only a small one today, huh?'

'Only a small one . . . *here!*' Wilma pointed to the space above her left buttock. 'About two inches long,' she repeated. Victor placed his finger and thumb on the area she'd pointed to.

'This big?'

Wilma nodded.

'Okay. I'll do a sketch in biro and you can check it.' Victor set the photocopied image of the juju doll on the counter beside him while Wilma got up, spun her chair round and then sat back down on it with her legs spread either side of the metal spine and her chest against the backrest. With both hands, she reached back and flipped up her skirt so that the skin was exposed, but also the two curves of her buttocks, the black delta of her underwear puckering up where her skin met the surface of the chair. At that moment Victor's brother took the nearest stool next to Jack and held out his hand.

'Hi!'

Jack shook it, tearing his eyes away from Wilma.

'Victor says you've chosen something.'

'A winged boot on my right arm. Do you know what I mean?'

'Like Mercury in Roman mythology?'

Jack nodded and Frank started to make a small sketch.

'Barefoot, a sandal or a boot?' he asked without emphasis.

'A boot. Definitely a boot.'

'With feather details or without?' Frank's hand continued moving above the paper.

'*With* . . . if you can fit them in,' Jack replied. 'I only want it small, about an inch across.'

Frank nodded. 'I think we can have a little detail.' The pen in Frank's hand dipped and scurried across the paper a few more times and then he passed it to Jack.

'Like this?'

Jack looked at Frank's drawing and nodded. A simple leather boot with elements of shading, the texture of the feathers suggested more than realised. Frank then guided Jack's chair to a position in front of the cubicle mirror and Jack took a last look at Wilma and the pale slope of her lower back which Victor was swabbing with alcohol before turning to face his own reflection. He looked pale and drunk. The whites of his eyes were fractured with red lines, his black stubble darkening every second (he'd shaved meticulously that morning yet there it was, rising through his skin), his broad nose greasy under the lights, the hint of a second chin sagging below his jawline. Jack looked for signs of nervousness in his eyes but found that he was staring back at himself almost without expression. In the mirror he saw Frank pull his stool closer and ask him to take off his jacket.

'First I am going to do a rough sketch on your arm with a pen so you can check the size and the proportions,' Frank told him and Jack nodded again. He shifted his weight in the chair so that his back was upright and tried to relax as Frank took hold of his arm and started to work on the surface of the skin with the tip of a biro. Immediately Jack felt himself tensing. Christ! The guy was just drawing on him and already his insides were squirming. Jack wondered what the needle would feel like, alternating this with trying to put the anticipation of pain out of his mind. All the people he'd ever spoken to on the subject of getting a tattoo talked about how painful it had been. They were almost reverent when it came to the pain (Jack felt the pen dig and probe the flesh of his arm) and used the same tone of voice as people who talked proudly of surviving broken arms, troublesome wisdom teeth, lengthy root-canal treatment and extracted tonsils. Jack hadn't broken anything, still possessed both his tonsils intact and had never been in the dentist's chair for more than twenty minutes of polite preventative inspection, so he still had no idea what to expect. And even Wilma had admitted that the pain had at times threatened to be unbearable.

'Take a look.' Frank had withdrawn his hand to reveal the outline of the image in blue biro. 'Like that?'

'Like that.'

'What colour do you want?'

'Black.'

'Okay. I'll get myself ready and then we'll start.' Frank now swabbed down the small counter to his right with a disinfectant spray and then laid out a sheet of paper he tore from a roll and taped down its edges. On this he set out the needle and the ink and then pulled on surgical gloves. It was at this point that Jack felt his bowels freeze and his heartbeat jolt upwards into a higher gear. Suddenly he was scared, a feeling that intensified as he felt Frank swab away at his arm, and as Jack looked away, there was the sound of the needles, a flanging whirr . . . and then the first *sensation*, like burning, on the skin of his arm.

'I'm going to do the general outline first. Okay?'

'Okay.'

Jack gritted his teeth and tried to centre his thoughts on the sensation of his molars grinding together. Frank was now talking to him in an easy-going tone, asking him questions about London, whether various clubs he'd frequented still existed, whether Jack had been to certain bars that he used to go to. Apparently Frank had lived there for a year when he was twenty.

'What were you doing in London?' Jack asked, steeling himself against the pain. It felt as if someone was taking a cheese-grater to his arm and grinding it mercilessly up and down against his skin.

'Nothing really,' Frank replied, 'I played keyboards in a band. I worked in a bar for a while, only for a short time. I designed the artwork for a record that a friend of mine made and drew a comic strip for a rock fanzine. I was really into graffiti back then so that took up a lot of my time.'

Jack, who had been the reluctant holder of many low-paid jobs in a variety of low-paying industries, had once spent a summer vacation working for Septex Services, a private company to whom other institutions (most notably London Transport and British Telecom) handed out cleaning contracts. Expecting to be a 'litter picker', Jack had been detailed to the 'graffiti squad' and had spent the summer wrapped in a protective plastic suit spraying detergent at the scrawled surfaces of buses and tubes, of bus stops and tube stations, the arches of flyovers and bridges, the scratched and pitted surfaces of phone kiosks and letterboxes. The shift lasted six hours, Jack clamping on his facemask at midnight and not taking it off again for six hours as his team scoured away the paint and ink down at the depot, or else outside on the streets of the sleeping city, the scribbles and doodles slowly fading in the acid foam that originated in the tanks strapped to his back. Jack initially decided against sharing this with Frank. Maybe graffiti artists hated the cleaners the same way gangsters hated the police? But feeling the relentless searing pain in his arm, Jack needed something to talk about. The conversation was like a relay race, a baton being handed from sentence to sentence. If one of them didn't keep talking then the baton would drop and Jack wouldn't have anything to say or anything to listen to and he'd be back to clenching his teeth against the pain. So he told Frank about his job and it turned out that Frank had been in London the same summer that Jack had worked for Septex.

'That's amazing,' Jack remarked. 'I hope I didn't destroy something you'd done.'

'Wouldn't matter to me if you had,' Frank replied. 'Some guys, they feel good when they see one of theirs up on a wall day after day. Me? The moment of satisfaction comes the second it's finished, when you stand back and see it for the first time, when you can still smell the fumes coming off the wet paint. Of course, the moment is only a moment and then you're running away in case you were about to get caught. Most of them I never saw again after that.'

'It sounds a bit like tattoos.'

'Very similar,' Frank agreed. 'Once a customer's left here I often never see the design again. Just a quick moment before I dress the skin and that's it. They pay and go.'

Now Frank started talking about other things he'd done in London. As Jack listened (he was concentrating and felt the beads of sweat collecting on his forehead), he forced himself to look into Frank's eyes, at the marbling of blues and greys in the wide rings of his irises, the miniature brown hairs that sprouted out between his eyebrows, the creases at the side of his mouth, the translucent yellow of his teeth, the tiny white swelling of pus at the base of a follicle under his lower lip.

'I even wrote a novel,' Frank was telling him and Jack sighed internally because at least he could talk about this and not think about the sharp *twangs* in his upper arm.

'What kind? I mean, what was it about?' Jack heard his voice tremble now, and thought that he felt the needle dig a little deeper into his arm, the bite of the agony finding a new edge as the metal probed deeper into his flesh.

'A science-fiction novel. You like science fiction?'

'Y-yes,' replied Jack, thinking that he only liked science-fiction *films*, that he'd never read a science-fiction *novel*.

'It's about . . .'

Now Jack could hardly control his thoughts. He heard Frank's voice sure enough, telling him of how the novel dealt with three 'timelines' – one in the present day, one in the Pleistocene era a million and a half years ago, the third occurring a hundred and fifty years into the future – but through his mind paraded a stream of images: Coco when she had said goodbye to him a few days before; Marie when he had first been introduced to her; Wilma flipping up her dress to reveal her buttocks and thighs minutes earlier; his parents; an old girlfriend whom he'd taken to Amsterdam the second time he'd visited (they'd split up, arguing on their second night in the city). How many people did Frank see in pain? Jack wondered to himself. How many widened eyes and crimped mouths and strange conversations – how much seeping blood?

'I-I-I'm writing a book t-t-too,' Jack heard himself stammer. The fingernails of his left hand were biting into the sweaty surface of his palm.

'Oh yeah? What about?'

'It's a-about a writer who m-meets this woman one day a year . . .' Jack warbled. His eyes were now locked on to Frank's and not leaving them, not for a moment, 'e-e-every year for eight years.'

'Is he single or married?' Frank asked.

'Married.'

'Happily?'

'H-h-he thinks so,' replied Jack, thinking that it was amazing to look into another person's eyes for so long and with such *need*. When did he ever look into Coco's eyes with as much longing? 'But then one day he meets this woman, a teenage sweetheart of his who h-h-he hasn't s-seen for ages . . .'

When did he ever look into Coco's eyes with as much longing? As they talked (and Frank seemed perfectly at ease returning his gaze every few seconds as he looked up from the point of the needle) Jack watched Frank's eyelids blink, watched his eyeballs twitch in their sockets.

'And what happens?'

'W-well they meet in a bar . . . b-by accident,' Jack heard himself say. His right arm now felt dead, saturated with pain. He was on the verge of screaming out that he wanted Frank to stop and getting up out of the chair and running through the streets outside. '– a-and they start talking . . .'

'Does he feel guilty?'

'When?'

'When he starts talking to his teenage sweetheart?'

'Err . . .' Just when Jack thought that things couldn't get any worse, he again felt the needle drive deeper into his arm, the pitch of the electric buzzing again modulating for a second, as if it were coming up against a greater resistance. For a second, Jack's mind saw his arm disappearing in a gush of blood and gristle.

'I g–g–guess so . . . I mean, *y-yes!*'

'And do they sleep with each other?'

Jack was straining for words and at the same time fighting for breath, fighting back tears and fighting to stay in the chair. Now his mouth moved and he heard words that sounded as if he was speaking them.

'Well . . . it's a c-case of . . .'

Now Jack couldn't speak. He felt himself giving in to the agony, surrendering to it. And yet he still heard his voice though he hardly sensed his mouth moving or his mind processing any information other than the fact that Frank was looking straight at him and that the needle felt as if it was probing *even deeper* . . . that he felt his eyes widen at a sudden stabbing . . . that he saw Frank's eyes widen almost imperceptibly in silent recognition of what he was feeling . . .

'That's it. Take a look.'

'It's finished?' Jack was suddenly aware that the whirring of the needle had stopped.

'All done,' Frank replied, sitting back in his stool.

Jack looked down at his arm and saw the black ink glistening on his arm. It looked like black oil, the shaded boot like a slick sitting on the surface of the skin rather than indelibly inserted into the meat of his arm through thousands of perforations, the outline of the feathers and the wings almost *dripping* as if they'd been drawn on with a fountain pen. Jack felt a smile slide across his face, a shit-eating grin that corresponded with the rush that surged through him.

'You like it?'

'I love it.'

Frank dressed Jack's arm and gave him a leaflet with information on how to let the skin heal. Wilma was going to be another fifteen minutes so Jack rolled himself a small joint and smoked it out on the street, almost wallowing in the sensation of his pumping adrenaline. When he went back inside, Wilma was standing with Victor and Frank by the front desk.

'How much do I owe you?' asked Jack.

'A hundred and twenty guilders,' Frank replied. Jack paid the money and shook their hands.

Then he and Wilma walked out into Warmoesstraat, the sun starting to sink behind the buildings on either side of the street. Jack checked his watch. It was half-past six. He was late whatever way he looked at it and he was in *trouble* whatever way he looked at it. *Fuck it!* he thought as he felt Wilma slide an arm round his.

'I need a drink and a smoke and another drink,' he told her. 'Shall we go back to Green Peace?'

'Can we go somewhere quieter?'

Jack searched her question for further intimacy (her hand had squeezed his forearm) but her tone was blank, preoccupied.

'Follow me,' she said with more energy and Jack felt her weight guide him through the crowds, past the bars that poured music out into air, along narrow streets where the neon lights shimmered above doorways and the grim shapes of the waiting women. They turned a few corners and walked south down the Oudezijds Voorburgwal, past coffeeshops where drinkers crowded the pavements and the cycle paths and held up traffic. After a while they crossed Rokin and the Spui and reached a part of the city that was quieter, passing windows through which Jack saw families eating dinner, couples watching television, an old woman watering her plants. He wondered what Coco was doing and thought of how worried she must be, but also realised that thinking about her elicited no remorse, no desire to suddenly change direction and walk to wherever she was. After they'd walked a few more streets, Wilma and Jack stopped at a bar called Momentum where they drank Long Island Ice Teas in quick gulps, the filters crumpling in their fingers as they sucked the life out of their cigarettes. Then they moved on to The Zoo, a coffeeshop where Wilma again seemed to know the barman and again came away with a bottle of tequila without paying for it. Outside, they found a table overlooking the canal, sat down and passed the bottle between them. They'd hardly said a word to each other since leaving Victor's. Now Wilma spoke.

'How do you feel?'

'Amazing. I've never felt like I did when it was all over. A huge rush just crashing through me . . .' Jack stopped to sluice back more tequila. 'Better than coke, better than speed, better than anything. I felt *omnipotent*!'

'It's a real kick, isn't it,' Wilma agreed. She was sitting with her chair pulled up alongside his and Jack realised that he had his left arm across the back of her chair. 'How does *it* feel?' she asked.

'A little sore. You?'

'Sore. Gotta keep drinking,' she said as Jack pulled out his bag of Silver Haze and poured the rest of the contents into a rolling paper.

'I heard what you were saying to Frank. You never told me you were a writer?'

'You never asked. And anyway I'm still writing my first book so I don't know if I can call myself a writer quite yet.'

'I knew you were a writer. That's what I told myself when I saw you reading *The Long Goodbye*. You do anything else?'

'I used to but not any more. I live with my girlfriend and she more or less supports us.'

'What does she do?' Wilma asked.

'She's a corporate solicitor. I stay at home and write in the mornings. In the afternoons I clean the house, pick up her daughter Marie from school and do the laundry and the cooking and things like that.'

Wilma was silent. Jack was silent.

'Sounds like a good arrangement. Better than cleaning graffiti,' she said after a while. Jack didn't reply and instead lit the joint. He waited for Wilma to break the silence but she didn't say anything. He looked at his watch – it was now a quarter to nine.

'The thing is,' he started, handing her the joint, 'it doesn't feel like a good arrangement at the moment. I can't seem to write and I can't seem to explain to myself *why* – and I certainly can't explain it to her . . .'

'What's her name?'

'Coco. Really it's Chantal but everyone calls her Coco outside of work.'

'And does she put any pressure on you?'

'I used to think that she didn't. But these days . . . .'

'Jack. Can I ask you a question?'

'Sure.'

'How long have you been feeling like this?' Her voice was quiet and steady.

'About six months.'

'And have you spoken to her about it?'

'No. I guess I don't know what to say to her. I mean, what would I tell her? I keep thinking that at any moment my writing will come together and that I'll feel happier and get a clearer picture of how I feel about her.'

'You should talk to her.'

'And say *what*?' he asked. Wilma passed the joint back to Jack and he took in a deep lungful of smoke, the juices collecting on the surface of his tongue. 'Before I met her I lived in a bedsit and worked at shitty places doing shitty jobs and I never had enough energy to write. Or maybe I just couldn't write and living in a bedsit just made everything feel even worse, as if my whole life was moving towards a dead end. Now I live in a comfortable place where I don't have to share a bathroom with the mad postmen and winos who used to live in the same building as me. I don't have to worry about how I'm going to make the bills or the rent or whether my computer's about to get stolen. I'd feel pretty stupid telling her that I felt . . . *dissatisfied*.'

'That's a whole list of negatives and more about your living conditions than about her.'

They were silent again, smoking the joint until it was dead. Jack got up and went inside to buy a couple more grams and by the time he came out it was ten past nine.

'Okay,' he said, lifting their bottle to his lips, 'at ten o'clock I go and find her.'

'Where is she?'

'At Johanna's house. Johanna is Marie's grandmother. That's where I'm meant to be meeting Coco . . . where I *was* meant to be meeting Coco.'

'At what time?'

Now Jack laughed.

'At five.'

'Is she gonna be mad at you?' Wilma asked.

'She's going to be furious,' Jack replied. 'Too late now to do anything about it.' He started rolling another joint, hands moving instinctively. 'Let's drink. Christ! I haven't had a day like this for too long.'

'I got one more question.'

'What's that?'

'In your novel: does the guy sleep with his teenage sweet-heart, the woman he meets one day each year? You were about to tell Frank but you got interrupted.'

'He wants to when he first runs into her again — and at one point he thinks that he will. But they just have an amazing afternoon together, talking about their lives and explaining how they've changed since they were kids and what they want out of their futures.'

'And they decide to meet again, on that same day each year?'

'How did you know?'

'A lucky guess.'

'Well, you're right. They plan to meet for just one day the following year, and also the year after that, the central character never telling his wife about it — it's his secret.'

'What happens?' Wilma asked.

'Well, I've still got to write this bit, but one year she doesn't show up. The next year he goes back thinking that there's a small chance she'll be at their rendezvous. But again, she's not there. This time he tries to track her down, and when he finally manages to contact one of her parents, they tell him she died.'

•

A clock somewhere struck ten as Jack stood up and scrabbled through his pockets. The tequila was half empty, the second bag of Silver Haze empty save for a few green crumbs, and he swayed a little unsteadily on his feet as he searched for the piece of paper on which he had written Johanna's address.

'Where the fuck is it? If I've lost it I'm *really* in trouble.' It wasn't in any of his jacket pockets nor in his travel-bag. Eventually he found it folded up in a corner of his now empty wallet, where he'd put it before leaving the flat in Olympia so that he wouldn't lose it.

'Where the hell is this?' he said, squinting at his own handwriting. Wilma took the note from him.

'Hmmm . . . Prinsenstraat. It's about twenty minutes away. I'll take you there.'

Jack shouldered his bag and felt Wilma slide her arm round his. Again, he felt her weight guiding him through the streets and along the banks of the canals, the fluid reflections of the streetlights and the glow of the lit windows bobbing on the surface of the dark water. As they walked, they passed couples walking hand-in-hand and Jack imagined what it would be like to spend the night with Wilma, to walk with her through the streets cloaked in intimacy until they found themselves outside where she lived. They'd go upstairs and lie down on her bed and smoke a last joint and then roll towards each other's bodies. Later, they'd talk about *The Long Goodbye* and *The Big Sleep*, something he could never do with Coco.

'What about you?' Jack asked.

'What about me?'

'I don't know anything about you except that you had a tattoo done in LA, then one in San Francisco, another in New York and one in Amsterdam . . .'

144

'I had *two* done in San Francisco,' Wilma interrupted. 'And now I've had *two* done in Amsterdam. And you know that I went out with a college professor in LA who was obsessed with Raymond Chandler.'

'And I know *that*. What else?'

'What else?' She stopped for a second and Jack found that he was standing facing her, the tall houses looming up behind her.

'I guess it doesn't matter if I tell you,' she said, fumbling for a cigarette. As she lit it, Jack saw the flame trembling – maybe it was just the breeze? 'I have a habit of getting myself into bad relationships with bad guys. Like with the college professor in LA. He used to treat me like shit. You want to know more?' Jack nodded.

'The last few months I've been going with a guy in Amsterdam. Not a nice guy. Maybe you know the type? The sort that trades in drugs and prostitutes and likes to call them his "business interests". Well, I left him about a fortnight ago after he kicked me down the stairs one too many times and I asked an old boyfriend to lend me some money so I could get clear of him. Now I've spent the money so I've got to go back. At least for a while.'

Jack wanted to ask her why she didn't leave Amsterdam, fly back to America or somewhere else in the world, but he knew that she wouldn't have an answer. He even thought of looking in his wallet to see how much money he had to give her – but realised that of the three hundred guilders he'd arrived in Amsterdam with, he only had about fifteen left jangling around in his pocket.

'What's he going to do when you go back? Does he even want you back?'

'Oh he wants me back alright, if only for the sake of his

wounded ego. And he won't do anything to me, at least not physically, at least not straight away. Maybe this time I'll be able to work out a better plan.'

They walked on, arm-in-arm again, Jack again thinking about what it would be like to spend the night with her, to wake up with her and spend long leisurely mornings in Basjoe. No more having to hear about the latest developments at Scheider & Rex, no more school runs (though he would miss Marie terribly), no more ironing the 'family laundry' (what was he *doing* ironing the 'family laundry'?). By the time they reached the address on Prinsenstraat, it was half-past ten.

'This is it. You want that one there.' Wilma pointed at a house about twenty yards away. They turned towards each other and Jack looked at her face, the point of her nose, the crease where her lips met, the points where her eyelashes met her eyelids. The dark hairs (the same colour as her roots, Jack noticed) seemed stitched into the skin rather than growing out of it.

'Is she going to throw a fit?' Wilma asked.

Jack nodded. 'Probably.'

'Well I hope you come out the other side okay.'

'You too,' Jack replied.

'Me too.'

Jack kissed her on the cheek, feeling the dangling crosses of her earrings brush against his skin. 'Take care of yourself,' he said.

'Always do,' she replied. Already she was moving away from him and back towards the centre of the city. She rounded a corner, looking back at him for a second before she disappeared from view. And then Jack turned and started walking towards the house. All the lights seemed to be switched on and he felt his eyes twitch with every step. He took a deep breath a couple of feet from the door. Coco would be fine, he told himself. She'd be more relieved that he'd finally arrived rather than angry that he was so late. Jack took another deep breath and then reached towards the buzzer.

•

If Jack had spent the afternoon too drunk to realise that he was stoned and too stoned to realise that he was drunk, then he'd spent the last four hours too full of adrenaline and excitement to realise that he was both too drunk and too stoned. Now the adrenaline seemed to evaporate from his bloodstream, the ability to stand upright or focus his eyes or form words deserting him. He reached for the buzzer a second time. It kept moving but eventually his hand tracked it down and he leaned against it. Somewhere in his skull a buzzer sounded. Best to play it simple, he told himself, just apologise and try and be as charming as possible. It was only half-past ten so it wasn't like it was the middle of the night. The door was pulled open and Coco stood there, backlit by the lamps burning in the hallway.

'I'mshorryI'mlate.'

'Where have you been?'

'I . . .'

'Where have you been? Where have you been?' Coco's voice steadily rose in volume. Jack thought that she couldn't repeat herself again but he was wrong.

'Where have you been?'

'I . . . I . . .' Jack pushed past her into the hallway and put his bag down.

'Where have you been?' she asked again, now hissing quietly. 'I've been almost worried to death . . . Marie's been asking what the hell's going on . . . I would have called the police except that Johanna told me that they wouldn't do anything for a couple of days.'

'I'vebeenintown . . . aroundtown . . .'

'And you didn't think to call? We've been sitting here for over four hours wondering what's happened to you . . . I thought you'd been hit by a tram or something . . .' Coco's nose twitched. 'You've been drinking.'

'I . . . I . . .'

'You've been drinking. You're totally drunk.'

Now there was another presence in the hallway. A woman in her sixties appeared at a doorjamb, thin, petite, immaculately dressed. Johanna, thought Jack, remarking that she looked uncannily like Coco's mother. He held out his hand. 'Hi . . . pleeshedt'meetyou,' he heard himself say. The old woman paused before taking his hand with a tentative grasp and he noticed that she shared a look with Coco before disappearing back through the doorway.

'WhereshMarie . . . IwantoseeMarie . . . ishshestillawake?'

'She's asleep. Finally. Who have you been drinking with? On your own? You're totally drunk. How much have you had?'

'Whereshourbedroom . . . Ineedtoputmythingshaway . . .'

'*We* are going upstairs where you are going to tell me where you've been this afternoon. I think I deserve an explanation.'

Coco pushed past him and led the way up the steep flight of stairs. Jack followed, hands and feet working together as if he were climbing a rope ladder or a cliff-face. To make matters worse there was another flight of stairs to be negotiated after the first and another to crawl up after that. By the time he followed Coco into their bedroom Jack was gagging for breath, his t-shirt a wet rag.

'I'lljushthangupmyjacketandthenshayhellotoJohanna.'

Jack took his jacket off and threw it on the bed. The room seemed desperate to keel over on to one side so Jack let it, sprawling out on to the bed.

'What the hell are *these*?'

Her voice now seemed distant, metallic, impersonal, like a public-address system at an airport.

'I'llgetupinashecond . . .'

'Did you hear me? I asked what the hell are these doing on you jacket?' She was pulling at a long blonde hair that had meshed itself against the fabric.

'Idunno.'

'You don't . . .*you've hurt yourself!*'

'Wha?'

'You've hurt yourself?' Coco stared at the bandage on Jack's arm.

'Ishatattoo . . . itdushen'thurtshomushnow.'

'A tattoo, Jack! What the *fuck* have you done to yourself?'

Coco was finally silent for a moment and Jack closed his eyes. The ceiling was spinning and rolling and Jack felt himself gag. *I don't understand . . . I don't understand . . . I don't understand.* Jack slithered across the bed and reached for a metal wastepaper basket and felt the whiplash of his stomach muscles, acids on his tongue. There was a second and third set of convulsions rising through his neck before he could wipe his mouth on his sleeve and sigh, a cold sweat collecting around his neck, on his forehead, at the small of his back. At least now he could lie back and let it all go.

3

'What kind of girl loses one shoe?' Jack heard Coco say, but didn't pay her much attention as his eyes scanned the cobbles for the boot's partner. At the same time (and picturing the tattoo on his arm concealed by the stained dressing) he remembered the men standing outside the prostitutes' cubicles the afternoon before, men with faces like Rottweilers, with mouths like clenched fists and Wilma telling him how she'd been kicked down the stairs.

'Probably the sort of girl who wears shoes like that,' Coco said. 'Look! It's got little feathers *glued* to the sides. How *naff* . . .'

Suddenly Jack wanted to search the city for her, maybe ask the wrecked American at Green Peace where he might find her and check that she was okay, or else ask Victor or the guys at Basjoe. But he knew it was impossible. What could he say to Coco? How could he explain it? Jack looked at Marie stroking the cat and knew that he couldn't just get up and leave.

'Losing both shoes you could put down to carelessness or drunkenness – but to lose one? It makes me think something more *disturbed* has happened . . . I mean, who loses one shoe? Who would want to take off *just one*?'

In the deep-sea chamber of his suffering head Jack heard Coco's words echo and reverberate. Did she always talk this much? Now she was talking about how she'd lost her shoes at a law-school ball because she'd 'been so drunk'. *We were walking around Fulham Palace . . . me and this guy called Rollo Banbury.* She'd lost both shoes – but of course she'd never have lost *just one*. Coco carried on talking, going on and on and on. Did she ever stop? Would she ever stop? Something was growing inside Jack, an inner voice getting louder and louder. Why didn't she *ever* stop talking? Did he really want to know about Rollo Banbury and the law-school ball? And what kind of person used the word *naff* anyway? Soon this voice seemed to blank out everything else. Jack saw her mouth move but then glanced across the canal at the streets of Amsterdam and almost stood up from his chair, not hearing any voice other than his own telling him that if he didn't do something soon he'd explode.

OFF THE WRIST

The guilty catch themselves.

Anon

Adam realised that he was feeling a little drunk, and more than a little bewildered: how had they got on to the subject of sex?

He was sitting opposite Kate in the university bar. One moment they were talking about the seminar they'd just attended, the last class of the term on the German Democratic Republic; the next moment, Kate was comparing sex with music, chortling into her third pint of cider as she discussed genres, track listings and the 'difficult third album', taking the conceit to ridiculous extremes while Adam tried not to squirm too much in his seat. Initially, part of Adam had liked the fact that she was talking to him about sex as if he was one of the girls. But after a while, he wasn't so sure. The plus point was that while she was talking to him about sex, things seemed pretty sexy between them (and Adam did so desperately want to have sex with Kate). But every so often, this feeling would be sidelined in favour of another conclusion: what if she was talking to him like he was one of the girls because that was how she thought about him. Just one of the girls. The speccy dweeb who she sat next to in History. Adam could imagine her talking to her friends later on. *So, do you fancy him then?* they'd ask. *Him!* she'd scoff. *Of course I don't. I mean, he's a lovely guy and all that, of course he is, great for going for a pint with after class and for helping me when I haven't done the background reading or when I'm stuck on an essay. But I don't think of him like that, no way. I just don't. He's more like a friend, y'know, a mate, one of the . . .*

'Most guys wonder why they're just one-hit wonders,' Kate

sighed, slurring slightly as she rolled a cigarette. 'They should try making real music rather than three-minute pop songs.' She sounded throatily conspiratorial.

'So what's your favourite album then?' Adam asked, trying to sound salacious and innocent at the same time. Wasn't that how it was done, this flirting thing?

'I dunno, one of those prog-rock concept albums, you know, one of those records that goes on for hours and comes in four parts.' Kate broke down into laughter again before composing herself. 'No, seriously,' and now she looked Adam straight in the eyes, 'I reckon a girl wants variety. She doesn't just want one thing all the time. Sometimes she wants soul – deep, meditative and lingering; sometimes she wants rock – hard, uncompromising and unrelenting; on a Saturday night she might want something predatory, something hip-grinding and funky, something like *Saturday Night Fever*; but on a Sunday morning she'll want something totally different, something a little more blissed out, something like "Sunday Morning" by The Velvet Underground, d'you know it?'

Adam nodded his head, though her directness was definitely starting to make him feel uneasy, and in spite of the fact that he'd never heard any 'Velvet Underground'. He'd never listened to music whilst growing up, and still didn't really take much interest. When he was younger, he'd occasionally listened to whatever was on the radio, not because he liked it but simply because it was there, or else spent his time trying to avoid listening to the growling sounds his elder brother seemed addicted to locking himself away with, the curtains drawn, the patchouli joss-stick smoking away in the corner. His brother had been an obsessive goth ('*Goth*, Dad, not goth*ic*,' he'd whined incessantly throughout his adolescence), spending six years of his youth dressing in black clothes that had washed out to grey, not going outside and continually arguing with their mum as to whether she really did understand why he needed to crimp his hair before attending his grandmother's sixty-fifth birthday party.

Now his brother managed a call-centre up in Scotland and listened to whatever his wife listened to. And Adam had moved on to listening to whatever his flatmates listened to: house and garage – but also drum 'n' bass, hip hop and rap, R 'n' B. And there was always the radio.

'So anyway, are we going or what?' Kate asked briskly while she waved at someone she knew on the other side of the room.

'Where?'

'Out.'

'Oh right . . .' Adam hadn't been prepared for Kate to take the initiative.

'You were telling me before class that your flatmates knew some people who knew the guys who'd hired out the room above The Blushing Bride tomorrow night for a party. Shall we go?'

'Errr . . .'

Adam had been building up to asking Kate out in the classroom earlier on, while they'd been waiting for Professor Thornton to arrive, planning to casually insert his request into the conversation they were having about the last weekend of term. But he'd only got as far as mentioning the party, all the while preparing himself for the inevitable and imminent knockback, ('That's *sweet*,' she would tell him, 'but I've already got *plans* . . .') when 'Thumbscrews' Thornton had stumbled in, a fraying pile of belligerent tweed and corduroy, and the room had fallen into a fearful silence. Now, after class, Adam couldn't believe that he'd been spared the necessity of being persuasive.

'Errr . . . yeah . . . let's go,' he said. 'Yeah, let's. I mean . . . er . . . the party starts at ten so we could meet for dinner beforehand . . . if you like.' Adam felt as if dinner was something he should offer her.

'Well we could. But you know what I say . . .' Kate stopped to gulp at her pint. 'Eating is *cheating*. You get pissed more cheaply on an empty stomach,' she gulped again, 'and I'm skint right now. D'you know The Brazen Cow?'

Adam did. It was a tough-looking drinker out on the ring road, in reality called The Grazing Cow but renamed by the city's wittier students.

'They do pound–a–pint house lager there. We could get in early, get a few down us and then get to the party later on. If we're hungry we can stop by the chippy next to the cinema. See what happens, eh?'

Kate drained the rest of her pint and then shovelled her stuff from off the table and into her bag.

'So, shall I come round yours around seven?' she asked. 'You live on Stanley Street, don't you? That's nearer to the Cow than my place.'

'Yeah,' Adam nodded, 'it is. And seven would be good. Seven would be great. See you then.'

'What number?'

'Number forty-three.'

'Great, see you there, got to go, bye.'

Adam watched Kate walk off, her hips as they swung away from him, the back pockets of her jeans, the waistband of her pants visible above the faded blue denim, a strip of bare skin between this and her t-shirt. And Adam was still thinking about this strip of skin as he boarded the bus home twenty minutes later. He had kissed Janine, the last girl he'd been out with (they'd been out to the pub three times and got as far as stripping down to their underwear and fooling around on her mattress after the last of these excursions), on that exact spot, on the skin at the base of her spine, but he couldn't remember what it *felt* like. If Adam concentrated long enough on the memory of kissing Janine there, he was able to imagine kissing Kate there. But he still couldn't remember what it had *felt* like. Adam tried to remember what it had been like with Franny, the last girl he'd fooled around with before Janine, but that had been ages ago, a whole . . .

Adam's thoughts were interrupted by a guttural cough and he looked up to see a pensioner staring down at him. She was glaring. Glaring. For a second, Adam blushed, imagining that she was reading his mind, but then he realised that she merely wanted to sit down and was indignant that he hadn't yet given up his seat.

'Please,' he said, rising. He was getting off soon anyway.

•

The walk from the bus-stop took ten minutes and as Adam trudged through the dark streets, he observed the variety of Christmas decorations hanging in each lounge window that he passed, the gaudy tinsel and the neon Santas. When he arrived back home, Adam found that his flatmates were staying in for the evening. Elton was in the hallway as he came in through the front door, on the telephone to Samantha, his 'girl back home' in Peterborough.

'I know babes, I know,' he purred into the receiver, 'I find it hard too . . . no, I really do, but we've managed to be apart for ten weeks already and still stay together . . . yeah, I know the holiday's only a few weeks, but we'll have the whole summer to be with each other, won't we . . .'

Elton put his hand over the mouthpiece and winked at Adam.

159

'You alright, mate?'

'Yeah.'

'Yeah?'

'Yeah.'

'The others are in the lounge. I better get back to *this*.'

Elton rolled his eyes and then went back to murmuring at Samantha while Adam proceeded into the lounge to find Danny, Simon and Paulo on their hands and knees, the PlayStation flickering away in the corner.

'These friggin' carpets.' This from Danny as he rummaged through the plastic laundry basket that served as the lounge bin, somewhere to empty ashtrays and throw beer cans and pizza boxes. 'Small light-brown dots alternating with small dark-brown dots. How the fuck are we expected to find lost dope on this?'

'What about looking across the floor at ground level,' suggested Simon as he pressed the side of his head against the carpet and scanned the area in front of his face with a bicycle lamp. Paulo was picking up each cushion in turn and shaking it down as if it were a potentially armed suspect, at the same time asking Danny to visualise the last time he'd 'seen it' and suggesting that he 'retrace his steps'.

'If you tell me to retrace my steps one more fucking time, I'll . . .'

'You'll do what . . .'

'– I'll . . .'

'Found it!' Simon held the lost eighth aloft. 'It was down here, in this Chicken Basket box under the sofa. Someone get some beers from the fridge.'

Elton walked in at that point with an armful of cans so they all sat down.

'That Samantha on the phone?' Simon asked.

'Yeah.'

'She still giving you a hard time mate?'

'Yeah. A bit. But she still doesn't want to split up so I guess I'll get to shag her all Easter holidays.'

'Who're you seeing tomorrow night?'

'Some Scottish bird. Lucy.'

'Shit football team, the Scottish,' offered Simon, picking up his bong.

'But I've also got to have lunch with that Diana girl again, tomorrow in the afternoon. She'd better not want to come to the party as well.'

'*Oh . . . Diana*,' chorused Andy, Paulo and Danny as they always did when her name was mentioned, to a tune that Adam had been reliably informed was Ultravox's 'Vienna'.

'Where're you going for lunch?'

'Her place,' smirked Elton.

'She got any flatmates?'

'Nah.' Elton smirked again, folding his arms behind his head, 'She lives on her own. Got a classy one-bedroom flat above that posh delicatessen on Potter Street.'

'What about you, Adam?' asked Danny. 'You asked that Kate out yet, the one you've been ogling all term?'

'Errr . . .'

'You *did!*'

'Errr . . .'

'I don't believe it,' scoffed Paulo, 'and she's coming to the party with you tomorrow?'

Adam nodded, deciding not to confuse the matter by admitting that it had been the other way around, that *she'd* asked *him* out. 'She wants to go to The Grazing Cow first.'

'The Brazen Cow! She wants to get tanked up, mate. You're *in there . . .*'

'Adam, you've fucking pulled, mate . . .'

'You'll be Clearing the Pipes like the rest of us tomorrow night . . .'

'Well I don't know about that . . .'

•

Clearing the Pipes. Adam shifted in his seat, sipped at his can of beer, stared at his knees, laughed nervously. Clearing the Pipes was something the other four regularly indulged in before a night out at the Campus Disco or one of the city's various nightclubs. There was always the same sequence of events: they'd each loiter in their own rooms with music blaring and get ready, splashing themselves with aftershave and pulling on clean clothes and polished shoes before they assembled in the lounge to wait for their mini-cab, a final joint passing from one hair-gelled head to the next. And then the cab would honk its horn outside and they'd all stand up to leave. *Everyone clear?* one of them would ask. *Clear!* the others would reply in turn, like a disciplined squadron of paratroopers preparing to jump into enemy territory, which would mean that they'd all had a wank earlier on. Adam sometimes went out with them (he didn't really like nightclubs – he hated dancing and he could never hear what anyone was saying). But he'd never joined in when it came to Clearing the Pipes. In the beginning, they'd asked him why not.

'You should give it a go,' Elton once told him. 'What if you pull tonight? You'll have a full tank, you'll be jumpy, you could . . . *misfire*. Why not whack one off before you go out? If you pull, then you'll really be able to knock the back end out of her.'

'You only get one chance to make a first impression,' Danny had advised.

'You don't want word going round all the girls that you

162

can't *deliver*,' Paulo told him, 'or you'll never score in this city again.'

Adam had told them that it just wasn't 'his thing', which was vague enough to have the others shrugging their shoulders and muttering things like 'Whatever, mate' and 'Up to you'. It was easier than trying to explain what he really felt, that their preparatory masturbation seemed somehow . . . *dishonest?* And after a while, the guys seemed to forget about it anyway, not bothering to address their comments to him as they headed for the front door the same way they'd grown used to not offering him joints or cigarettes when a packet was passed round (Adam was the only one among them who didn't smoke).

•

The banter continued for a little while and then gradually dissipated, finding other targets and other subjects. And then it faded away altogether as they became increasingly drunk and stoned and fixated on their computer game.

Around midnight, Adam stood up and said that he was going to bed. He'd thought that he was tired enough to fall asleep straight away – but up in his room, he found himself lying there in his boxer shorts and t-shirt, staring at the ceiling and thinking about Kate. Danny had been right, Adam thought to himself, he *had* been ogling Kate each time. Right from the very first seminar, Adam had found his eyes continually flicking across the classroom and coming to rest on her. Did she sense him staring at her? he'd wondered each time, feeling guilty but also unable to stop himself. Kate dressed simply, jeans and woollen v-necked sweaters that seemed demure but also seemed to plunge towards the crease of her cleavage. There was that charcoal polo neck she often wore, made out of a fabric that moulded itself to her arms and breasts.

One time, Adam had peered over the rim of his copy of

163

Anatomy of a Dictatorship and secretly watched her yawn, right from the moment her eyelids had started to lower themselves languorously towards her cheeks and her lungs began to draw in air, through the moment she gathered her arms up behind her head (her breasts now seemed to be moving *towards* him at an incredible rate), to the moment her lips parted and the hem of her jumper lifted away from her belt buckle and revealed the soft skin of her belly.

Lying there in bed, thinking about the silver ring that pierced her navel, Adam felt the muscles between his legs bunch and flex, the tension gently rising in unison with the restlessness in his fingertips. Beneath the ring, the waistband of Kate's jeans pouted at him and he imagined unzipping her. Somewhere among the thoughts flying around his head, Adam heard the voices of the others downstairs. *What if you pull . . . you don't want word going around* . . . Adam thought of Kate lying back on his bed as he approached her (he wanted her to suffocate with pleasure; he wanted her to look at him *afterwards* with damp eyes, her breath redolent with satisfied desires), and found that he had a palm wrapped around the solid trunk of his erection. For a second, Adam considered ignoring it, considered rolling over, shutting his eyes and falling asleep, considered allowing the following day to come flying towards him with its fresh potential. But then his hand started moving, kneading and rolling the skin. She would be there in his bed, stretching back in her white underwear. During the moment itself (tomorrow night? *Tomorrow night!*), Kate would run her hands through his hair, trace out shapes over the back of his neck and ears. Adam would cup her breast, his body repeatedly dipping towards her, and Kate would moan, as if surprised at some new sensation, her arms clawing uselessly at the sheets, her heels grinding into his buttocks . . . Adam felt his body convulse and then freeze

164

for a single, breathless pulse. Seconds later, every cell of his body was sinking back into the mattress, his lungs quickening to compensate for that lost heartbeat of oxygen.

And then nothing. Adam was back in his bedroom staring at the shadows on the ceiling but also looking down on himself as he lay there in his bed, his cock damp in his hand and the duvet already sticking to his stomach.

•

Adam awoke the next morning before any of the others. Standing in the lounge amongst the ash and grease of the night before with a cup of coffee, he shuddered at the thought of Kate arriving at the house later and having to sit among all the mess. But as he sipped at his mug, Adam reasoned that it didn't matter. He and Kate could go to the pub straight away. And as the others had pointed out to him, and as he himself realised with decreasing scepticism (and more than a few tremors of confusion), he had indeed *pulled*. Adam tried to be logical. He had fancied Kate Williams for the whole term. And now she'd asked him out, to the Cow to get drunk, and then to a party. *See what happens, eh?* A logical analysis of the situation so far pointed to . . . Adam swallowed, and then drained his coffee before picking up his jacket and heading off to catch the bus.

The city centre was busy: raincoated women cloyed the damp aisles of the market with their trolleys and prams and bags of shopping; spruced couples, arms linked, drifted over the cobblestones on their way to buy appliances and new clothes; children ran from shop to shop spending their pocket-money on sweets and comics. After another coffee and a croissant in a bakery, Adam felt more resolute about the evening ahead of him, perhaps even started to look forward to it. At the local music store, he pulled a copy of *Saturday Night Fever* from the rack, John Travolta poised on the cover, The Bee Gees grinning above him (were they considered bad or good? Adam could never work out what other people thought) but he had needed to ask a shop assistant about The Velvet Underground.

'Excuse me,' he asked, 'have you got "Sunday Morning" by The Velvet Underground?'

The shop assistant grunted and Adam wondered if he knew that he was buying a CD he'd never heard and probably wouldn't like (or, more mysteriously, wouldn't *understand*) just because he might be sleeping with a girl in his class later on that day unless she had a sudden change of heart in which case he'd be stuck with it . . .

'"Sunday Morning" is a *track* on a Velvet Underground *album*,' the shop assistant sighed. 'Do you want it?'

'Errr . . . yes?'

'Follow me.'

The shop assistant led Adam across the shop without a word, automatically stopping by a rack and wearily pulling the CD out from amongst hundreds of others as if its location was hardwired into his brain.

'Ah, the one with the banana on the cover,' said Adam cheerily. For some reason, the image was familiar to him. The shop assistant grunted again and then led him all the way back to the counter.

'That'll be £9.99.'

Adam paid and left, a smile fixed to his face. Outside the shop, he was so pleased with himself that he couldn't help but take the CD out for another look.

There it was: 'Sunday Morning', track one.

Adam had lunch in Chicken Basket and then took the bus back home where he found Simon and Danny slouched in the living room in their dressing gowns, smoking a joint as they watched the French Open, transfixed at that moment by a slow-motion replay of Marie Pierce winning the last point.

'Would you take a look at that,' Simon was saying, 'would you take a look at *that!* Muscle tone, aggression . . . she's beautiful, a fucking goddess.' Danny, head and mouth bent down to a mound of Frosties, stared at the screen over the edge of his bowl. He wasn't really listening, but then Simon wasn't really talking to him anyway.

'You can forget about frigging Anna Kournikova . . . will you look at *that* . . . Kournikova's a fucking child compared to *that.*' Simon waved the burning point of the joint towards the screen. 'Look at that cross-court top-spin forehand . . . fucking perfect . . . at least Pierce can fucking play . . . breasts *and* talent . . . a gifted hitter of the ball, a fucking natural, each shot just coming off the wrist . . . alright Adam? You alright, mate?'

'Yeah.'

'Yeah?'

'Yeah.'

Adam stayed and watched for a while, and then sloped upstairs to his room. Sitting on the bed, he decided that he would tidy up. Adam tried to picture the way he would lead Kate in through the front door and up the stairs later on when they came back from the party, tried to picture what she would see when she first walked in. Adam wanted it to be perfect, and put on his new Velvet Underground CD while he paced around the room stuffing dirty clothes into cupboards, changing his bedclothes (Adam grimaced when he thought of the night before), organising his books into neater piles and opening the window. Soon he was finished, the room arranged so as to look unarranged, the carpet clear of the debris, the condoms he had dutifully bought months earlier lined up inside the top drawer of his bedside table. Adam had bought them from a machine in a pub toilet because he'd been unable to face the girls behind the counters in any of the local chemists. He had been sure that they would imagine him with an erection and shuddered at the thought. Now Adam imagined himself with an erection, but this time with Kate's fingers running up and down its length. Adam sat back down on his bed and pictured the two of them together and again heard the advice of the others from the night before. Should he try Clearing the Pipes this one time? What did he have to lose? Was it really so *dishonest?* Adam scratched at the skin behind his ear. He should try it, he told himself, surely it was harmless?

But then there was the question of how soon to try it before the date? Should he try before he and Kate left for the pub, or later? Adam realised that there wouldn't be time after they'd left the house. He couldn't imagine slipping away into the pub toilets later on and giving it a go while everyone else outside the cubicle was chatting and taking pills and smoking joints. No, he thought, he would definitely have to do it before leaving the house. The next question Adam asked himself was how long should he wait. Right until the last possible minute? Or should he get it over and done with? Looking down at his straining crotch, Adam paused for a second. *He could do it straight away*, he told himself, *at least then it would be done.* He looked at his watch. It was coming up to four o'clock. Was there any point in waiting? How much difference could a few hours make? Surprised at his own decisiveness, Adam cleared his mind and reached towards his flies only for Simon to burst into his room.

'Wha?'

'Only me – you alright, mate?'

168

'Yeah.' Adam hoped he wasn't blushing as he tried surreptitiously to twist his body away from Simon.

'I just wanted to ask if I could borrow a t-shirt. You got any clean ones?'

'Yeah – in that drawer over there.' Adam pointed and Simon took one out. 'This one okay?'

Adam nodded.

'Thanks, mate.'

Once Simon had shut the door behind him, Adam took in a deep breath. There was no way he could have a wank in his bedroom while the others were in the house. As Simon had just proved, someone could walk in at any minute. Adam thought about locking himself in the toilet and paced across the landing. Shutting himself inside and quickly lowering the seat, Adam was about to unroll some toilet paper when he gagged. Someone had stunk the place out! Adam tried to ignore the stench but the smell was even worse than in the public toilets in town (he would only dare enter *them* for an accelerated piss, and then only when he was desperate). Staring back at the poster of the tennis player scratching her bum Blu-tacked to the inside of the door above a picture of the England squad, Adam tried one more time to overcome the desire to flee, tried to cajole itself into an erection, to wheedle his cock into action, but it was no good. The air in there was swampy with warmth and odour, almost solid, almost *fibrous*, and Adam was forced to emerge and return to his bedroom.

Back on his bed, Adam suddenly felt lost and slumped back on his pillows wondering what to do. He lay there in silence for a while, a cold throb of panic insinuating itself into his breathing and across the back of his neck, and he caught himself imagining him and Kate in bed together again. But this time she wasn't moaning nor running her hands along his spine nor grinding her body against him as she surrendered to the freefall of pleasure. No, Adam was imagining Kate turning away from him as he shamefully pulled himself out of her, unable to stifle a quiet sigh of disappointment as she resigned herself to getting more sleep than she'd intended, her thought that it had hardly been worth putting the condom on in the first place almost audible in the darkness . . . Adam snapped himself upright. Sod it! he muttered, and trudged back across the landing towards the loo. It's just a smell, he told himself, it would all be over in moments and then he could get on with preparing for the evening ahead, start looking forward to it again, go out and have a good . . . Adam turned the handle to the door to find that it was locked.

'Who's that?' Paulo's voice.

'Sorry . . . er . . . it's Adam.'

'You alright, mate?'

'Yeah.'

'Look, mate, I think I might be a while. You desperate?' Adam heard the pages of a magazine being turned over, a turgid cough, a whiff of cigarette smoke.

'No, it's okay, don't worry about it,' he replied.

Once more back in his bedroom, and by now feeling the panic starting to take hold of him, by the roots of his hair, by the throat, Adam buried his face in his hands. It was going to be a disaster, he told himself, it was going to be a catastrophe unless he . . . Adam gritted his teeth and told himself in the most authoritative tones he possessed that there was nothing else he could do but get it over and done with right there and right then. No one was going to come in, he told himself. How long could it take anyway? What was the mathematical probability of being interrupted? The others seemed to manage it, no problem, so why shouldn't he? Adam's fingers closed around his zip and . . . .

'Oi, mate!' Elton burst into his room and Adam almost burst into tears. 'Oi, mate, you got any shower gel I can borrow?' Adam stammered. His mouth couldn't form words for a second, not that it seemed to matter to Elton. 'I'd get some myself but the corner shop's run out.' Elton paused to leer. 'I ended up shagging Diana all afternoon, mate. Better get cleaned up before I go out with Lucy, if you know what I mean.'

It took all of Adam's self-control not to simper when really he felt like curling into a ball and sobbing. 'It's over there,' he pointed to the shelf where he kept his toiletries, 'help yourself.'

'Cheers, mate. You've saved my life.'

Elton helped himself and Adam got up off the bed and slouched downstairs into the lounge. Simon and Danny were sitting on the sofa watching a *South Park* video, sniggering every so often and bending their heads for a series of hits from the bong.

'Alright, mate – what you been up to?' Danny asked.

'Nothing,' Adam replied, almost too quickly.

'Cool,' said Danny.

Adam sat down and stared at the screen, not really taking in the cartoon, instead looking at his watch repeatedly and wondering what he could do. It was well past five o'clock. Kate would be arriving in two hours, he told himself. Where could he go? Adam briefly considered a wider range of options, desperate plans that had previously seemed ridiculous. *The end of the garden behind the rotting structure their landlord laughably called a shed?* No good – it was raining, and he'd be spotted by the neighbours in any case. *The phone-box on the corner?* He'd get

171

himself arrested. *He could do it in the toilets in the betting shop across the street, or else he could hide under his bed or shut himself in his wardrobe or . . .* Adam told himself to stop being stupid. He would just have to wait until the toilet or the bathroom were free. Simple as that.

He sank back into the sofa and tried to relax. But it soon became impossible: neither room looked destined to be free ever again. Elton seemed to have *installed* himself in the bathroom, Adam was able to hear him humming as he splashed away under the shower on all three occasions that he went up to check. And Paulo remained locked in the toilet, still smoking cigarettes and still flipping through the pages of his magazine. Around six o'clock, Paulo suddenly appeared in the lounge. But before Adam could move, Danny was up out of his seat and walking out the door muttering that he 'had to take a crap'. Adam couldn't believe it. He almost felt like lashing out at something, at somebody (he even thought about trying to run up the stairs and beat Danny to it). But in the end he resigned himself to defeat. *This* was his destiny, he told himself, *this* was all he deserved: a night doomed with sexual failure.

•

Adam was still cursing himself a quarter of an hour later, and simultaneously half-believing that he was cursed, when the phone rang in the hall. Simon got up to answer it (it was his turn) and after a while came back into the lounge with the news.

'That was Jezza and Farid. They say there's been a big session going on at their house all afternoon. They've had some girls over from the art college and they want us to go round and help them out. I said we'd be over by half-past for a drink and that we can try and take them all out to the party later. Sound good?'

Suddenly the house was a flurry of activity, doors slamming, music being turned up, insults being hurled back and forth from bedroom to bedroom. Within ten minutes, Adam watched as all four of them assembled back in the lounge in fresh clothes, the air sharp with the scent of their aftershaves.

'We ready, boys?' Elton asked. He'd called Lucy and told her to meet him later at The Blushing Bride.

'Have a good one tonight, Adam. See you at the party later on, mate.'

'Yeah . . . and good luck,' offered Danny. 'Not that it sounds like you're going to need it.' They trooped out into the hall where Adam heard Simon ask them all in the hallway if they were clear.

'Clear.'

'Clear.'

'Clear.'

And then they were gone.

It was like a miracle, Adam thought to himself, switching off the video and basking in the silence. *It was like a fucking miracle!* He looked at his watch – it was six-thirty, which gave him a whole half-hour to . . . Adam got up and stretched, let his muscles relax along the length of his arms and back. He would stroll upstairs, he would take his time, things had worked out perfectly. He would be clear, he would be clear, he would be *clear*!

Adam walked up and into his room. Should he turn on some music? What was the point! Lying down in his bed, Adam was almost casual about undoing his trousers. Why not try and *enjoy* it? he asked himself, his mind almost racing on ahead into the evening to the moment when Kate would grab hold of him and *whimper*. Soon, his right hand was clamped around his erection, a wad of tissue paper in his left. *No hurry,*

he told himself, *no hurry at all – he had all the time in the* . . .
Adam froze suddenly.

There it was again, the sound of the front doorbell.

There was a pause. And then it rang a third time, Kate's
voice sounding out in the street below. 'Adam? Adam? Are
you there?'

She was early. She was *early!* Gulping, Adam thought about
ignoring her voice (how long could it take – she wouldn't have
to wait more than a few moments, would she?) but when he
gazed down at the wilting flesh in his hand (so weak and limp
compared with the hard knot of excitement that had built up
right in the base of his pelvis where it would lurk until the
time came), he knew that it would be futile. Outside in the
street, Kate's voice sounded out once more.

WHITE WEDDING

Fighting games allow players to battle each other's characters . . .
Do you want to be a blonde, sandal-wearing Greek woman in a
miniskirt, or a supernatural pirate with two enormous broadswords?
A Croatian behemoth or a Hawaiian Sumo wrestler? Bruce Lee in
a gold-lamé leotard . . . ?

Steven Poole, *Trigger Happy: The Inner Life of Videogames*

1

Out behind the hotel, I'd just finished reading the printout of Clarity's email when I caught sight of Jimmy bumbling through the glass doors and out into the Vegas heat. *Is that what I look like?* I asked myself, as if it had never occurred to me before. Jimmy spotted me almost immediately, but then it wasn't as if it was hard: like him, I was eighteen stone of lard gently sweating in the sun.

Jimmy was dressed in one of his four Leeds United shirts and a pair of Bermudas and I watched his rudderless approach through the aisles of loungers. Even from a distance, I could see how hungover he was: the bulky cocktail in his right hand trailing beside him like a medicinal drip; the red mottling smeared across the pallid surface of his face; the wayward stumble.

'Morning, mate.'

'Morning, Jimmy.'

He paused to catch his breath, his damp cheeks puffing in and out, the polyester of his shirt already transparent against the doughy flesh of his arms and his back.

'You were up early.'

'Jimmy, there's some . . .'

I tried to tell him about Clarity's email, but he interrupted me with a wave of a his fat fingers.

'Enjoying your last morning of freedom, mate? I understand, say no more.'

His head twisted above his chins and he caught the eye of one of the cocktail girls who roamed the scorched concrete in white bikinis and synthetic 'grass' skirts that barely fringed the tops of their thighs. One of them clicked her way over to us and Jimmy slurped at his Mai Tai as he ordered another.

'Thanks luv.' His sunglasses tracked the swish of her green tassels and stacked calves as she sashayed off towards the bar. And then he manoeuvred his body down on to the lounger next to mine and lay back with a sigh, a seam of sweat already built up along the folds of his forehead and on the sausagemeat of his cheeks.

'Great night last night, eh?'

'Jimmy . . .'

'I felt *fooked* when I woke up this morning. Didn't recover until I'd had breakfast.'

Jimmy slapped his belly with a contented smile and I watched it wobble.

'Jimmy, there's something I've . . .'

Now some of the others appeared across the pool – Robbie and Jules, who worked at the arcade with Jimmy and me, Mandy and Damon who I knew from College – all of them with hands wrapped around colourful drinks. Jimmy stood up and waved his Mai Tai like a flag, sounding out an 'Oi oi' in greeting and soon they were all thrusting their hands towards me.

'Morning, Boomer . . .'

'Congratulations, mate . . .'

'You've made it to your big day . . .'

'Are you nervous . . . ?'

'Have we got time for a few drinks before we go to the chapel?'

Only Jimmy and I had been to Las Vegas before and the voices of the others buzzed with excitement.

'Have you seen the buffet breakfast here? All you can eat for five ninety-nine . . .'

178

'You should have seen the girl selling cigarettes down by the blackjack tables this morning. She was checking me out . . .'

'They're prostitutes, Robbie . . .'

'No they're not . . .'

'They might as well be . . .'

'I tell you: *she was checking me out* . . .'

'They've got Hitler's car up there,' said Jules. Obviously, he'd made it to the Classic Auto Show up on the sixth floor. 'A bullet-proof 1939 Mercedes 770K. And an Alfa that belonged to Mussolini *and* a Packard that belonged to Emperor Hirohito. It's like a fascist car rally up there.'

'Was Hirohito a fascist?' Mandy asked. 'I thought he was a god until 1946 when he was forced to renounce his deified status by the Allies. After that, wasn't he just an impotent symbol?'

Jimmy offered round Regals which only Robbie accepted. Then Al and Ian strolled out through the glass doors and on to the concrete, Kris and Charmain following hand-in-hand a little way behind. There were more handshakes, more congratulations, more excited voices.

'We've just been to the Luxor . . .'

'Tomorrow we're going to have a "Round Table Breakfast" at the Excalibur . . .'

'You sit there and have breakfast with these people dressed up as medieval Lords and Ladies who say "Forsooth" a lot and "By my troth, good sir" and so on while you drink foaming tankards of orange juice and eat your pancakes with skillets . . .'

'Great night last night . . .'

A three-way argument broke out between Ian, Jules and Al as to whether a *skillet* was a leather shirt, a piece of medieval cutlery or a type of frying-pan. On the other side of the group, Kris pointed out that Arthurian mythology predated medieval history by at least five hundred years ('depending on how you look at it'), a period of time your average American could only possibly hope to understand in Disney dimensions.

'No wonder they turn historical figures into cartoon animals. Foxes, lions, ducks, chickens, bears. History's about as intelligible a proposition as Mickey Mouse to this lot.'

I looked down at the printout I was holding. Between my thick fingers I could feel the paper soaking up the dirty film of grease that had been building up on my hands, imagined the paper clamped between my thumb and tensed index finger turning the same colour as the insoles of my trainers. *Should I tell them all about Clarity's email?* They'd be disappointed for me, and they'd all be very good about feeling sorry for the fat boy whose fiancée has just . . . *I should tell them about Clarity's email!* Now the others talked about the wedding anyway. The girls talked about what they were going to wear while the boys talked about what they were going to drink, pulling open a newspaper to catch up with the football scores back home. *Did Jimmy have his speech ready? Did Robbie have time to play roulette before the limousines arrived to take us to the chapel?*

'What are you wearing, Boomer?' Damon asked

'Are you nervous?' Mandy asked. 'I can't wait to see what Clarity's wearing. I bet she looks stunning.'

It was then that Jimmy proposed a toast. 'Hey everyone, don't . . .' I started, but Jimmy told me not to be shy.

'To the bride and groom.'

Everybody drained their glasses (in the general excitement, nobody noticed me ignore mine and spread myself back on my lounger. How could I tell them?) and Jimmy signalled to the waitress.

'So what are we all drinking?'

'I'll have a 57 T-Bird . . .'

'A Kamikaze . . .'

'Sunburn . . .'

'I'll have a beer . . .'

'A Caipiriñha for me please . . .'

'A Strawberry Daquiri . . .'

'A Banana Daquiri . . .'

'A Down Under Dreamsickle . . .'

'What the *fook* is that?' spluttered Jimmy.

'Irish Cream, Orange Juice and a splash of soda,' replied Mandy. Jimmy shrugged his thick shoulders.

'Whatever . . . and another Mai Tai for me. What about you, Boomer?'

I held up my Bloody Mary – I'd barely touched it.

'You not drinking today?' he asked. A round of jeers about 'last-minute nerves' circled the group. *Get 'em down you!*

'Where're we having a drink afterwards again?' Robbie asked.

'For the millionth fucking time – Caesar's.'

'I only fucking asked.'

'So, Boomer, married life *awaits*. You ready to get hitched, mate?'

I sat up, picked up my drink and stared into it. Bubbles of lime juice swirled amongst the grains of pepper and pools of sherry while little powdery islands of celery salt floated across its surface.

'I . . . er . . . erm . . . *Yes*. I mean, *I'm* ready anyhow.'

'You don't sound it, mate.' Jimmy punched me on the shoulder. 'Stop poncing about and have a *real* fucking drink.'

'No, I'm serious, listen. *I'm* ready. I just don't think that Clarity is.'

'What do you mean . . . ?'

'What's happened . . . ?'

'Has she rung you?'

'No,' I replied, vaguely aware of the ring of worried faces looking back at me. 'She sent me this email.'

I finally held up the piece of paper for all to see.

'I tried to ring her room in Caesar's Palace earlier this morning. They say she never checked in.'

'What about Anita and Lottie?'

I put the email down on the lounger in front of me.

'They haven't shown up either. So I went and checked my email and I found this waiting for me.' I stared at the folded printout as did everyone else.

'What does it say?'

'Well, I'll put it this way: we've got a spare ring.'

2

Dear Jason . . .

•

I try to ring you from my bed. A receptionist comes on the line, introduces himself as Randy and asks me how I am, asks how he can help me.

'Hi. My name's Jason Boomer. Could you put me through to Clarity McClellan?' I ask. 'I don't know what room she's checked into, but she would have arrived yesterday morning.'

Randy puts me on hold, Dean Martin singing 'That's *Amore*' cutting across the background sound of the lobby. A few seconds later there's a click and I expect to hear you come on the line, your voice husky with sleep. But it's Randy again.

'I'm sorry, Mr Boomer, Miss McClellan hasn't honoured her reservation at this time.' I ask about Lottie and Anita who were booked to share a room and I get the same response.

Where are you?

I put the phone down, tell myself that you must have tried to ring when we were all out last night and that there'll be a message waiting for me at reception, a call saying that there's been a problem with the connecting flight, with bad weather or lost luggage, a family crisis maybe, or a hostage situation on the tarmac that can't be avoided.

•

It seems criminally clichéd to tell you this isn't an easy 'letter' to write. When you get to the end of it, I hope you get your own sense of how difficult it's been for me.

•

Down in the lobby thirteen floors below, the phalanx of slot machines juddering away behind me, I ask a receptionist if there's been a message left for me, trying not to let my voice crack.

'No,' she replies, scanning through a card index. 'Nothing at this time, sir.' *At this time! At this time!* I ask if there's a terminal where I can check my email and she gives me directions to the Business Services Center.

'Walk back the way you came, toward the rear of the hotel, past the roulette and craps tables on your right, past the dollar slots on your left and down through the mini-mall until you get to elevator bank G. There, you take the elevator up to the third floor, then come out and . . .'

I find it eventually, log into my account and find a message waiting for me.

Sender: C McClellan. Subject: [none].

'Dear Jason,' you start and the first thing that strikes me is that you've called me 'Jason'. *Jason?* Haven't I always been 'Boomer' to you? From our first night together until . . .

•

By now you'll know I'm not in Vegas. The fact is I'm not coming.

I don't want us to get married.

183

There. I've said it. I hurts me to write it and it hurts me to think of you in Vegas without me. Do you remember when we were last there? I almost can't believe how quickly it all happened. The four days we spent there were like a dream. I thought I might explode from how I felt about you. Every second with you felt, and has felt, like something special. And this is the way it was right from the start, right from when we first met. Was it only 6 months ago?

•

You're right. Things happen quickly.

I remember Jimmy shaking me in our hotel room on the final day of the *Blipz Magazine* Videogames Tournament last July.

'Time to wake up, mate,' he says quietly. I don't tell him I've been lying there for hours, wondering about the Final.

'How are you feeling?' he asks. 'You nervous?'

'I . . . I . . .' I notice a little muscle tension in my fingers and wrists as I rub my eyes.

'You need some breakfast, mate,' he says, slapping me on the back. 'Room service? Or shall we go downstairs?'

I ask Jimmy to order something from downstairs while I shower and by the time I'm dressed, a waiter's brought up a tray of food: a two-litre bottle of Coke; two blueberry waffles, each one the size of a frisbee and smeared with whipped cream; a pot of coffee; a couple of Snickers. Quietly Jimmy and I munch our way through it all, Jimmy flipping through the latest copy of *Power Up* while I scan a new issue of *Batman: Legend of the Dark Night.* When we're finished, Jimmy picks up his magazine and walks out on to the balcony to smoke a cigarette while I turn on the console that we've plugged into the hotel TV.

'So who's this "Clarity McClellan" you're fighting?' he asks, pixelated by the mesh of the flyscreen.

'I dunno.' You were just a name on board to me then. 'She's unknown, English . . .'

184

I never try to know about an opponent before I play them. That way, all it boils down to is what happens out there on the screen.

'Who'd she beat in her semi-final?' Jimmy asks.

'She beat Hans Andersen yesterday in two straight fights. Andersen was fighting as Yoshimitsu.'

'*She beat Andersen?*'

'Two fights . . . so I'm told.'

'And what are *you* doing?' Jimmy's now inside the room, staring at the controller in my hand.

'I thought I'd get a little practice in before we go over to the Hilton.'

'But you *never* practise on the day of a fight!'

I shrug. But Jimmy's right. I never practise on the day of a fight. Everyone has a different way of preparing for a competition, I guess. Some players get stoned while others go swimming. Some research their opponents while others believe that the key to success is to drift out into the most anonymous arcade they can find, the roots of the game where the loners lurk with their customised special moves and left-field technique. There are some players who spend hours reciting memorised input codes for ten-string hit manoeuvres as if they were re-learning their times-tables, as if they were trying to train their mind to operate to the rhythm of *Tekken*. And there are those who practise like maniacs right up until the last minute, getting up early on the day of a tournament fight to spar all morning. Usually, like yesterday when I was waiting to play the semi-final, I just sit and flick through comics all morning to take my mind off the game ahead. But *this* morning I feel too tense to read.

I don't feel any better when Jimmy and I arrive at the Hilton just before noon. In the cab, Jimmy chuckles as he's paying the driver. He can't believe that I've made it to the Final and I tell him that I can't believe it either and by the time we reach the *Tekken* arena my head is buzzing. There's already a strong crowd milling around the spectator galleries, a few famous faces from the past (Jeff Pass who won the final two years ago; Ricky Simmons who was a *Streetfighter* World Champion three seasons in a row), a handful of groupies, gangs of pale skateboarders in ripped jeans, metal fans and petrolheads, software executives in suits whispering earnestly into each other's ears, journalists, photographers. I formally announce my arrival to the referee and he tells me that the other finalist hasn't arrived yet.

Now Shaun Warren, one of the *Blipz* editors, approaches with a tape recorder and asks me how I feel, tells me that I fought 'one helluva battle' yesterday in the semi-final. Somewhere, a flashbulb explodes, a camera, a live webcast.

'We thought it was going to be a massacre after we saw the first fight,' he says.

'So did I,' I say.

I'd fought as Jin Kazama while this season's top seed, Kim Chang-ho, had fought as Hwoarang. Last year, I'd faced him in the quarter-finals and he'd wiped me out, dispensing *overdamage* with an array of devastating kick attacks that were dispatched in unblockable sequences. A year later, all I was concentrating on was not letting the same thing happen again, an attempt that had immediately looked futile.

'He chewed you up early on in the first fight,' Shaun says, 'then spat you out with a ten-string hit combination and it looked as is if he was going to do it to you again in the second. When he suckered you into that Neck Snapper and pushed your damage up to eighty percent, the word in the stands was that you were *dead*.'

Again I nod.

186

'What was going through your mind?' he asks.

I tell Shaun it was a matter of not giving up and of *thinking* one's way to victory.

'Hwoarang players are always the most susceptible to vanity,' I say. 'Hwoarang's programmed with the ability to execute the most spectacular kinds of extended kick sequences. As a result, some Hwoarang players get distracted by the possibility of pulling off glamour kills.'

'Are you saying that the top seed from Korea was overconfident?'

'I think he got sloppy at the point where he could have won the fight.'

'Well you sure made him pay. From that point on, you were *ruthless*.'

'I hit a rhythm,' I shrug. 'Maybe I was lucky?'

What else can I say? In the third fight, I just waded in and put Hwoarang down in a matter of seconds, Jin always in a position where Hwoarang couldn't really touch him, each move arriving at my fingertips before he could duck, dodge or block. When he tried to counter-attack, I just sidestepped and punished him. When he tried to throw, I reversed him and counter-attacked myself. Sometimes it's like that.

'And now you're the favourite,' Shaun continues. 'Does it make it harder when you know that you're three rounds away from ten thousand dollars and a sponsorship deal?'

It's then that I see *you* for the first time.

Suddenly I'm stuttering.

'Err . . . I-I-I . . .'

I tell Shaun that I don't really know how I feel to be so close to the first prize, that I've never been in a final before, and I watch over his shoulder as you introduce yourself to a steward.

Then you're both walking towards me. You tap the referee

on the shoulder. 'Hi,' you say. 'I'm here for the final?' you say, as if you need to ask permission.

Shaun and the guy with the camera back away for a group shot, the referee hesitating slightly before shaking your hand, and it's then I realise I'm staring at you. You can't be more than a couple of inches over five feet, in a yellow summer dress the colour of pale butter, daisies printed on the cotton, hazel brown eyes and hair like a scrambled ball of dry straw shooting out of your head.

You extend your hand and I realise I'm *still* staring at you as I shake it, your fingers like matchsticks between the fleshy curves of my fat paw.

'Hi. Clarity McClellan.'

You smile, and I stutter.

'J-Jason Boomer,' I reply.

'Nice to meet you.'

You tell me that you were watching in the gallery yesterday.

'That was gutsy,' you say. 'But I knew you'd win. Do you remember that moment in the second fight when he pulled off that Neck Snapper? Everyone around me in the stand thought you were *out*. But I knew you'd win.'

You smile again, your thin lips (slightly dry, I notice, and almost cracking) parting to reveal tiny teeth.

'I hoped you'd win,' you say.

•

And this now brings me to the heart of things – why have I changed my mind? How could I suddenly turn my back on the person who has felt like a part of me from the moment I first knew he existed?

•

More journalists appear, each with questions. A writer from *wayofthewarrior.com* asks if I think the fact that both finalists are British heralds a new era of European dominance in beat-'em- up gaming – and there's even a woman from the *Sunday Times Magazine* asking me how I feel about 'fighting a girl'.

'It doesn't really enter my mind *who* I'm fighting,' I tell her as I look across to see you signing an autograph for a young skatepunk in the audience. 'Up there on the screen, it's one character against the other.'

Then we're asked to stand together to have our photograph taken (*am I blushing?*), a ridiculous pair staring into the flashbulbs, you with your scarecrow hair and your wispy arms and your sandals, me like a giant doughnut in a Megadeath t-shirt towering above you. The photographer asks us to move closer together so he can get a tighter shot. Does your hand brush against mine?

We're each given five minutes to prepare ourselves.

'So *that's* the mysterious Clarity McClellan,' says Jimmy. 'Well, she doesn't look like any *Tekken* player I've ever seen. She looks like one of the girls from *The Little House on the Prairie*. Anyway big man, you can take her.' He slaps me on the back. 'Good luck. Just *relax* . . .'

The referee comes over and says it's time to start and I walk over to the machine and join you at the controls as the computer flashes into the Character Selection Screen.

'Right . . . who's gonna call?' the referee asks, standing behind us.

I nod in your direction and he spins a quarter up into the air.

'Heads.'

The coin lands heads up.

'You choose first,' you say, looking me in the eye.

'OK, you heard the young lady. I'm gonna stand back now and let you guys get down to it. You know the rules . . . first to win two fights . . . good luck to both of you.'

The lights dim, two beams picking us out in the darkness,

the ranks of spectators going silent. As always, I slide my cursor across to Jin Kazama and hit the left punch button. Now I wait for you to choose your character. Who were you going to be? Julia Chang? Nina Williams (her counter-attack would be her best weapon against Jin Kazama)? Or were you going to be one of the guys? Heihachi Mishima with his ferocious Tile-Breaker Punch . . . Lei Wulong with his Tornado Kicks, his Dragon Blast and his Drunken Master special moves? Your cursor flicks negligently across the screen in front of us, and also on the giant screen suspended from the ceiling above us, until it comes to land on the face of Ling Xiaoyu and the crowd behind us gives out a sigh of anticipation. It's going to be a battle of conflicting styles, Jin's raw power pitched against Ling Xiaoyu's hustling agility and her capability for lightning-quick counter-strikes. I take a deep breath, tense and relax my hands, spread my fingers out beside the control-stick and buttons and I'm staring up at the screen, mentally preparing an opening attack sequence, when I feel you tap me on the shoulder.

'Good luck,' you say, and suddenly I'm looking into your eyes, wondering whether you're just trying to break my concentration and telling myself that *no one* wishes anyone else 'good luck' in *Tekken*, that the game's about the ruthless desire to beat the other player into a lifeless mess. But I'm looking into your eyes and I'm saying 'You too' as if it's the most natural thing in the world, as if I've met you before. And then we're both looking at the screen in front of us, Ling Xiaoyu in her schoolgirl's uniform, Jin stripped down to his waist, pulling his studded gloves tight around his fists, a giant tongue of flame leaping up his right trouser leg, streaks of black lightning branded on to his rippling bicep. This is it, I tell myself, this is it . . .

Round 1 . . . FIGHT!

Suddenly I'm closing in on you. I've got a prepared sequence in my head and I let my fingers fly at the buttons. I want to get the drop on you right from the start. I want control of the battlefield. I want to deliver maximum damage. The only way you can hurt me is if I stand back and let you.

And if I come in close . . . ? A Backhand Punch, a Spin Kick to the head that picks up the momentum of the first punch and doubles it, a crunching *Majinken* punch to your ribcage that twists you sideways. I don't hesitate and follow up with a throw, grabbing your arm, burying my elbow in your neck and catapulting you down on to the floor. As you roll back to your feet (your damage meter creeping towards the halfway mark), I'm already asking myself how long you're going to take to recover. Now you try a two-punch Bayonet – a simple move that I block easily – followed by a Backstep 'n' Roundhouse that I almost see too late, dodging only split-seconds before you make contact. Still, it leaves me open for a second and you duly connect with a series of Windmill Slaps, your slender arms scything through the air across my face and taking you down into a Phoenix Crouch. You then try for a Splits Sweep but I read this early, jump over your scissoring legs and deliver a Twin Lancer combination and an unstoppable horizontal *Donuki* punch that blasts you back across the screen on to the ground. I charge immediately. Just as I thought, you've lost your rhythm and you panic, crouching too early (expecting the obvious sliding kick) and making it all too simple for me to leap into the air instead and twirl through a sequence of Phantom Kicks . . .

K-O!

The computer growls and there's a round of applause and a few wolf-whistles from behind us as it runs through a replay. Up above, the action is repeated on the massive screen: two towering figures, six feet high, playing out the last attack. I try to stare at my hands, but there's this temptation to look across at you. Usually I'd prepare myself for the next fight, try not to get too confident, try to ignore the braying from the stands and just *focus* on the glowing screen. But I need to look across at you. Are you humiliated? I've just taken you down with a near perfect score in the first fight of a World Championship Final . . . *how does that feel?* Will you dismiss it and spit back a response in the next fight? Or are you broken, unnerved, lost? I turn my head to see you staring up at the giant screen as it replays the final torrent of kicks, your eyes tracking each foot as it connects in slow-motion, your lips slightly parted, the corners of your mouth twitching (into a smile – *into a smile?*), the tiny saw-edged tips of your teeth glistening in the same flickering light that strobes through your eyelashes. Your nose twitches (I can't take my eyes off you. Even with everyone watching, I can't take my eyes off you . . .) You move a hand to your hair, pull a strand back behind your ear, your skin, a swatch of freckles across your nose.

Jin Kazama . . . WINS!

My eyes snap back to the screen out in front of us.

Round 2 . . .

Here we go again. There's the split-second pause. I feel both of us tense beside each other, both of us breathing in slowly, waiting for . . .

FIGHT!

I decide to attack straight away again, not wanting to surrender initiative. Maybe I'm only seconds away from victory, I think, *just a few well-executed moves* . . . I close in on you with a simpler opening, a double *Majinken* punch combo and another horizontal *Donuki* punch, a 'Body Piercer' that takes your damage meter up to forty per cent. *If I could just connect another* . . . I pause for a beat before inputting the second attack (I want to time it *just right*, I tell myself) and then try

192

to Shoot The Works just as you're getting up, all four limbs striking in rotation. But you're up faster than I expected and parry all four blows before skipping backwards out of range. There are purple sparks as I lunge towards you hoping for a grapple (I plan a couple of Cyclone 'Bitch' Kicks followed up by a Can-Can Kick and a juggle attack) but you jump back leaving us standing facing each other.

Nothing happens for a second. Who's going to move first? I crouch so that I can rise up into two *Tsunami* Kicks but you anticipate and thrash me out of the air with a sweeping Cloud Kick. While I'm recovering, you move through a Phoenix Crouch into a double forearm smash and as I'm stunned backwards I'm already thinking that my moves are getting too predictable. You pause for a second – *why should I wait?* I move in: ten-hit combos with variations. *Left foot to the stomach, a right jab that hurls me into two kicks that* . . . you block my first attempt so I repeat the attack, but this time pull out of the manoeuvre early and reverse my body back into a *Kasumigeri*. Again, you block each strike. Now we both start throwing a few simpler punches amid a flurry of feints and sidesteps . . . suddenly you cut across me, two jabs to the face . . . a reverse flip that has you flying through the air and landing on my shoulders, your thighs straddling my face. You slam your fist down on to my crown and I crumple. When I finally stagger to my feet, you jab again, this time throwing in a Reverse Punt that has me floating high in the air and gives you all the time in the world to charge in and finish me off with a Sky-Scraper Kick when I finally fall back towards the ground.

K-O!

There's a haze of flashbulbs from behind us and I can feel the anticipation in the crowd rising as the third fight becomes a sudden-death decider. During the slow-motion replay, I ask myself how the hell I lost the last round but there doesn't seem to be a definite moment where I threw the fight away. One moment I was a couple of moves away from victory. The next you were anticipating my attacks as if they were your idea in the first place. And then I tell myself that it doesn't matter what happened, that we're fighting the best-of-three which means I'm still only one round away from victory. *Make or break, Boomer*, I tell myself, *make or break . . .*

Ling Xiaoyu wins . . .

There's a split-second before the deciding round starts and I tell myself to do nothing else but prepare to jump back and take up a defensive stance. What are you doing?

Round 3 . . .

A deep breath, I twist my head so that you're a faint blur at the edge of my vision . . .

FIGHT!

Okay, I think, let's *end* this. I try to launch into a *Majinken* followed by a Demon Killer (it should give me the chance to juggle you up into the air and follow up with a series of *okizeme* attacks) but you swat the first punch away. That shouldn't be a problem in itself, I think, the Demon Killer should still connect . . . *but you drop down into Phoenix Stance and roll to one side before closing in for a throw.* Because you catch me on my blindspot, you inflict extra damage. What will your follow-up attack be? As I'm rolling back up on to my feet, you're already circling me before unleashing a Phoenix Strike, both hands flying towards me, both hands crackling with energy and flinging me back across the screen. *How the hell did you create the time for that?* I glance at the damage meters – you've taken me up to fifty per cent while I've yet to land a punch.

Suddenly the spectre of being taken down with a perfect score becomes frighteningly possible. I roll back to my feet and come straight back at you with a jab that connects and a sidestepping Thunder Strike. I'm looking to *juggle 'n' float* but you back away, swat away my next punch with a left-handed Knife Chop and then go down into a Phoenix Crouch. *Okay,* I think, *I learned my lesson from the last time . . .* I immediately try a Can-Can Kick – something to scoop you off the ground and up into the air where I can pile in with some heavy punches – but you're suddenly back-flipping out of range like a gymnast. I press forward, looking to connect with a double uppercut, but you cartwheel to one side. I sidestep, knowing that you're a blink away from landing a Reverse Punt, and swing a gloved fist towards your head only to swipe at empty space as you leap up over my head and land behind me. Again, you could land a two-punch combination before blasting me up into the air but you simply land a backslap for minimal damage before backing away.

One more attack, I tell myself, and I'm finished. What should I try and do? I try a few simple moves, two- and three-punch combinations, a series of Phantom Kicks, a Gut Punch, a double uppercut rising out of a defensive crouch. You swat and block, dancing out of the way as I vainly lob myself at you. Suddenly Jin Kazama feels slow. Suddenly *I* feel slow. I attempt another assault but you block each move almost before it's even started and just as I see a chance to land a kick, you've moved through a combination and I'm lying on the floor unable to get up . . .

Ling Xiaoyu . . . WINS!

It's over.

You turn to look at me . . .

•

What can I say? I got scared. I woke up a week ago and I realised I was frightened to death. I thought about spending the rest of my life with you, about what that meant and why I was even thinking of such a thing, and

I suddenly had a feeling that somehow our getting married wasn't MY choice any more, that in some way it was a decision that was being made for me.

•

Behind us, there are cheers. I don't need to look up and watch the slow-motion replay. If I want to, I can replay the perfection of your final attack on the insides of my eyelids, the double slap and the Belly Chop forcing me backwards, the electricity gathering between your fingertips as you draw your arms up and round through the air, a ball of light, your Palm Strike driving me twenty feet back across the floor to the sound of a thousand whips cracking (I see stars, I see stars), your body holding its final position like a gymnast at the end of a tumble.

Now we're both turning away from the control panels and a crowd rushes towards you with a trophy and a blown-up cheque that almost threatens to hide you completely. I can hardly bear to look at you. You reach across and offer your hand – I take it for a moment, hold it among my fat knuckles – and then you're swept away by the referee and the guys in suits. The crowd are on their feet, their applause swelling as you're handed the trophy, the flashbulbs flaring across your face. At some point, someone takes my photo and I mumble something about the better player winning.

•

Can you believe this: I got ANGRY about the fact that you are who you are and that this person slotted into my life so perfectly. It made me feel predictable, out-of-control, frightened. I tried to talk myself out of it – but couldn't. Anita tried to talk me out of it – but couldn't (when I said to you last week that I was helping her get over her split with Michael, I was white-lying, it was the other way around. She was trying to talk me out of . . . THIS).

So I've changed my mind. Maybe I need to grow up. Maybe we both need to get a little older, I don't know . . . But one thing's for sure: if I'd gone through with things, I'd be lying to both of us because once I'd started doubting us, I couldn't stop.

•

Later, back at the Imperial Palace, Jimmy and I stare at the pool, drinking beers and watching the reflection of the sky as the temperature finally starts to drop. My 2nd prize cheque for two thousand dollars lies on the table between us, next to Jimmy's which is made out for a thousand dollars (he finished fourth in the Driving Sim Challenge). Jimmy asks me if I'm okay for the thousandth time.

'I'm fine.'

'You . . .'

'I'm sure.'

'I've never seen anyone fight the way she did in that third round. Poise, timing, variation, three-dimensional sense . . .'

I don't say anything. Jimmy tells me that he's arranged for us to meet some guys from Special Intelligence, the electronics company where his brother works, and that we're all going have a few cocktails together before going on to the end-of-tournament party at the Hilton. I tell him I'm not going.

'You're not coming?'

'I'm not coming. I think I'm just going to eat a buffet-dinner, wander around the casino and get an early night.'

Jimmy offers to have dinner with me and then go on to the Hilton later but I tell him not to change his plans.

'And you'll be okay?' he asks.

'I'll be fine. I just didn't expect to lose today,' I say, forcing a laugh, 'I'll be over it by tomorrow.'

Later, I push the food around my plate in one of the restaurants and then amble my way back along the aisles of cranking droids to the bar where I maintain a neat stack of dollar bills by my beermat and watch the towers of the candy-striped chips rise and fall at the nearby roulette table.

It's then that I notice that you're sitting at another bar across the casino floor from me, a crowd of blackjack tables between us. You're alone, a mystified look on your face as if you're puzzling over something, sipping from a green drink that matches the colour of the dress you've changed into. I wonder if I should I walk over to you, whether you'd be pleased to see me. Are you already waiting for someone? A friend? *A boyfriend?* Will you look at me and flinch like everyone else?

Before I know it, I'm rolling my way through the tangle of tables towards you.

'Hi.'

'Hi.' You stare back at me.

'You're staying here too?'

'It's the cheapest place I could find on the Strip.'

'Me too. Anyway, I just wanted to say congratulations. We didn't get a chance to talk earlier.'

'Thanks.'

'I've never seen anyone fight the way you did in the third round . . .'

'Thanks . . .'

'I mean, to be totally honest, it was . . . er . . . the best I've . . .'

'Boomer, you'd better stop before you make me blush.'

I stop.

'How do you know to call me "Boomer" and not "Jason"?'

'I heard your friend call you "Boomer" earlier.' You laugh. 'I like it, it's funny. Have people called you that your whole life?'

'Pretty much. What about "Clarity"?'

'Born with it and stuck with it. I don't really like it, it's like

being part of a bad hippie joke. And I've tried to shorten it –
but what would I shorten it to? *Cla? Clarry?* There's "Claire",
but that seems like a different name altogether.'

You don't seem to be hurrying to get away from me so I sit
down on a barstool and offer to buy you another drink. You ask
for a Midori Sour and I ask you why you're not at the party at the
Hilton. You say that you don't really go to parties, dipping your
lips to the straw, the liquid in your glass rising like mercury.

'What about you?' you ask.

'What about me?'

'Why aren't you at the Hilton?'

I don't say anything, stare down at my Mai Tai. The umbrella
hooked over the rim of the glass has hula girls printed on to its
paper panels.

'Boomer,' you say, 'are you angry with me for winning this
afternoon? Do you want to talk to me about it?'

'No, I'm fine, I really am,' I say, taking a deep breath and
twisting on my seat to look at you. 'I mean, I'm *disappointed* . . .'
I start, but then realise that I couldn't care less about the Final
when I see you looking back at me, pulling your shawl round
you a little more tightly.

'Have you looked around Vegas yet?' I ask.

You shake your head, say that you've hardly left your room
over the last three days.

'Me neither. Do you want to go for a walk along the Strip?'

You nod and we head towards the door, leaving our drinks
barely touched on the bar. Outside, the air is hot and dry
and you unwrap your shawl, draping it over an arm as we
slip into the steady stream of the other couples already out
on the street.

'Can I say something to you?' I ask.

'Sure.'

'This year was your first *Tekken* finals, right? I mean, I haven't seen you here before.'

You nod.

'I just think it's amazing that you've won in your first year. You must have beaten Tony Santos and Marek Jozwiak.'

'Tony Santos in the second round, Marek Jozwiak in the quarter-finals,' you say.

'So where the hell did you learn to play *Tekken*?'

You've always been into computer games, you tell me as we cross the street in front of Caesar's Palace. You grew up by the coast in South Devon, Torbay, a little place called Goodrington, nothing more than a cluster of holiday homes, caravan parks, chip shops and ice-cream parlours. By the time you were eight, you were telling your mother that you were reading on the beach and really sneaking into the beach-front video arcades for long hot summers of *Robotron* and *Galaxian*.

'It lasted until I was eleven,' you tell me. 'Three blissful years. And then I got caught by my mum. She freaked, told me that the arcades weren't for girls like me, that they were "drug dens", that I was never to go back. So I promised that I wouldn't. But I did, almost straight away, and got away with it for another three years until I got caught again.'

You laugh, say that it wasn't as if you were up to anything *bad*. You were still top of your class, you tell me, and always would be, though you make it sound as average an achievement as doing your laundry.

'So why all the hassle?' you ask me.

We stop inside New York, New York for coffee-cake and you tell me that it soon didn't matter. By the time you were sixteen, your parents had given up trying to stop you. And a year later, you'd been offered a place by Somerville College, Oxford to study History and your parents pretty soon stopped minding about anything. You got the A levels you needed, a degree three years later, and you've just finished a masters degree on the American Revolution.

'An academic genius *and* the *Tekken* World Champion,' I joke.

'I'm not really World Champion,' you say, 'unless I can successfully defend my title in Stockholm in November. And anyway, I don't do much else besides play computer games and read books. It's not like I'm much good at anything else.'

•

Maybe that helps explain things a little better, maybe it doesn't. I know I can't tell you to forget me. And if I feel guilty telling you that I'll be thinking of you every second of every day, it's because I know it can't help you understand my decision any more clearly. But you know I believe in the truth, and that's the way it will be . . . me thinking of you, thinking of you and knowing that I might have made a terrible, terrible mistake. If it is, then I guess we'll have to live with it. I hope you can. I hope I can.

•

Now we wander further up the strip, to the Excalibur and to the Luxor where we drink more cocktails. You ask me questions and I tell you all about being one of the security guards at the Trocadero Centre along with Jimmy.

'The Trocadero – where's that?'

'Piccadilly Circus. Surely you know where that is?'

You shake your head, say that you've never really been anywhere outside of the West Country except Oxford, and suddenly I'm telling you all about it, the six floors of arcade games, the crowds of kids each weekend, the bored staff in colour-coded shellsuits, the gangs of waiters drifting in from nearby Chinatown during the afternoons to gamble their tips on the fruit machines and play a few rounds of *Tekken*.

You ask me what happens next. Do I want promotion or a different job and I tell you about the programming course I've been doing, two years of learning Visual C++.

'If I can't make it as a professional gamer, at least I can get a new job coding games.'

Finally our glasses are empty (our fourth drinks? our fifth?) and neither of us makes a move to order more.

'Shall we walk back to the Imperial Palace?' you ask.

Outside the Luxor, we cross the Strip and walk back along the other side. I'm speechless when I feel you slip an arm through mine and you don't talk either for the whole twenty minutes that it takes to get back to the hotel. *What are you thinking?* Do you want me to kiss you – or are you merely being friendly? Do I even know *how* to kiss you (I can't remember the last time a girl put her arm through mine, let alone the last time anything more happened)?

And then we're back at the Imperial Palace, walking through the mayhem of porters and waiting cabs and into the hotel lobby. From where we're standing, we're equidistant from both the bar and a bank of elevators.

Another pause.

'I . . .'

'So . . .'

The both of us stop and laugh a little nervously.

'You first . . .'

'No. *You* first!'

You tell me that you were thinking of going upstairs to your room.

'Me too. What floor are you on?' I ask, staring at your face but unable to read what you're thinking.

'Fourteenth. You?'

I laugh. 'The fourteenth too.'

Feeling a little foolish, we walk over to the elevators and step inside where I press the button and the door closes. Again, you slip your arm through mine and I wonder whether I should kiss you. But I imagine the pitying expression you'll have on your face when you have to tell me gently that it 'wasn't what you had in mind at all' and don't make a move towards you. Then we reach the fourteenth floor and the doors slide apart.

'What room are you in?' you ask.

'Er . . . me and Jimmy are sharing 1414.'

'I'm in 1427 – I think that might be across the corridor from you. Isn't that a funny coincidence!'

I laugh nervously and we duly stroll along the corridor towards our rooms. I notice that we walk apart now and tell myself that I was right, that you were just being friendly the way some women are, that nothing could fill you with more horror than the idea of me making my clumsy pass at you.

Then we're standing outside room 1414, directly opposite 1427.

'I was right,' you say.

'You were.'

Through the thin door to my room, I can hear the sounds of laughter and drinking, the sounds of a computer game squawking away. Jimmy must have brought some people back for a few drinks.

'Well, I've had a lovely evening,' you say.

'Me too. And congratulations on winning today.'

'Thanks,' you say. Now you're trying to stretch up and kiss me on the cheek, but you can't reach, even on tip-toe, and before we know it we're in each other's arms and trying to kiss and trying to get your door key out of your purse and let ourselves into your room all at the same time.

•

203

Don't try to reply. I won't be on this address any more. I'm going travelling, Japan first to do some playtesting for a software company, then through Asia, checking out the Arcades and learning a few new games. PLEASE don't try to follow me.

•

Later, as the rising sun comes up over the desert horizon, we're lying in your bed and it's my turn to tell you about how I grew up playing computer games. Perhaps it all started when my mum left suddenly (my mum had gone . . . *where?*) and I would have to stay in our neighbour Jackie's front room after school. That was the first time I remember playing a computer game. Usually I would sit there watching cartoons until Dad got back from the site. But one day, when I was about nine, Jackie's husband Ken (short for Kenzo – he was the first Japanese guy my father could remember living in Bromley) had just returned from a business trip with a primitive computer console and a game called *Pong*. You say you remember *Pong*, two vertical lines, one on ether side of the screen, each batting a dot of light across to the other as if it were a tennis ball. *As for me?* I remember the feeling of never wanting the first time I played it to end. It felt good, swatting the dot back across the screen and beating the machine, and Dad had needed to drag me away when he finally arrived back from the building-site.

After that, I played *Pong* each day before tea until I was ten and Dad said I was old enough to come home from school on my own. After that, I would go to the chip shop round the corner from our house where I would play *Scramble*, or to the petrol station where they had an *Asteroids* machine and I soon learnt to *two-tap* and *lurk* so that my ten pee would last for an hour.

Was it healthy to take so much pride in having logged the ten all-time highest scores on the machine?

1.	BOO	501,280
2.	BOO	450,420
3.	BOO	385,320
4.	BOO	360,280
5.	BOO	360,200
6.	BOO	258,260
7.	BOO	100,120
8.	BOO	90,360
9.	BOO	88,380
10.	BOO	88,220

If I walked in after school to find that some PEA or JIZ or FUK or TIT had come in during the day and grabbed the eighth or ninth spot on the ladder, I would play until I'd knocked his initials off the screen. Sometimes it would take three hours and other kids would often hang about waiting for me to finish so that they could have a go. When they realised how long I was likely to be *with just one credit*, they'd try to put me off by taunting me about my weight. But I'd learnt to ignore such insults by then, learnt to shut them out (I'd already ballooned up to around thirteen stone and suffered enough abuse at school to have acclimatised to it) and just played on regardless.

After that? Soon they opened an arcade in Bromley High Street. It was mainly filled with fruit machines, but there were a few video-games and I'd go there as soon as my last lesson was over, grab a couple of Mars Bars, a pack of Golden Wonder and a can of Coke for lunch, and then settle down to a few hours of *Space Invaders* and *Defender*. And by the time I was thirteen, the first home computers and consoles were coming out and I just played at home.

You ask me how I ended up working at the Trocadero. I tell you that I left school at sixteen and started working with my dad. I was seventeen stone and six feet tall – humping bricks up and down ladders came pretty easily – and four years of being a builder earned me more than enough to buy a PC and more games. And then two years ago Jimmy's dad who worked with us told me that Jimmy was starting a programming course while he worked part-time as a security guard 'up in town'.

'You could do that,' he told me and he was right. There was another job going at the Trocadero. As for the course? Enrolling was only a matter of paying the fee and pretty soon I was moving my stuff into the spare room at Jimmy's new flat in Kentish Town.

•

No one else knows exactly where I'm going to be, not my parents, not Lottie, not Anita – you could waste too much time looking for me.

•

Jimmy asks me where I spent the night when I see him the next day and he can't believe it when I tell him.

'And you're going to stay in Las Vegas another three days?' he asks.

I nod.

'With *her?*'

'Why not? I won two thousand dollars yesterday. The plane ticket and expenses so far only add up to about half of that so I'm going to blow the rest on staying here with Clarity. Obviously, she's got ten thousand to play with.'

Jimmy's silent for a while. And then he laughs.

'*Yer dark fookin' horse!*'

And then it's just you and me in Las Vegas for three nights. We keep your room at the Imperial Palace but eat in Caesar's across the road. We take blackjack lessons in the Aladdin but lose two hundred dollars in the Mirage. We spend the nights making love (and with you curled up in my arms) and in the mornings I watch you swim ('fifty lengths at least three times a week', you tell me, 'but preferably every day'). I never want it to end.

On our last night in America, I want to ask you what you think will happen to us when we get back to England but I'm too afraid to say anything and you don't say anything either, not even over dinner which we eat in almost total silence. Later, we take a cab up to Fremont Street and walk past Winner's Wall and the Golden Nugget towards the outskirts of town where we find a bar with an old *Gorf* game that's still only a quarter a play before returning to our room an hour or so later. You still don't say much and I feel too awkward to bring up the subject of what happens next and pour myself a drink from the mini-bar instead to give myself something to do.

It's then that you turn on the console that's plugged into the hotel room TV.

'What are you doing?' I ask.

'I thought about playing some *Tekken*. I haven't played since the final, not for three days. It feels kind of strange not to have played for so long.'

You're right: neither of us have played *Tekken* since the final.

'Want to play?'

You nod towards the spare controller and I stare down at it but don't pick it up. The last thing I want to do is get thrashed by you with near perfect score after near perfect score.

'Play me!' you say again, the sound of the game loading up in the background, 'I loved that chickened reversal you pulled off against Kim Chang-ho in the semi. You were too busy concentrating but you should have seen him! His whole body froze the moment he realised that you suckered him.'

'He never expected it . . .'

'It scared him shitless! But that's Hwoarang players for you, all fur coat and no knickers . . . and *so arrogant!* They all believe that they're invincible . . .'

'It's not even a hard move to pull off if you see it coming – you just have to think one stage ahead . . .'

Suddenly I'm sitting next to you on the thick carpet (like my mum's slippers, I think to myself – her slippers are one of the few things I remember about her), the flashing lights streaming across our faces as I load up Jin Kazama in his leather jacket and leap across the dojo towards you, fist flying. I take the first fight, you take the second. I take the third but you take the fourth.

'You're not going easy on me now you're the World Champion and I'm a humble runner-up?' I say, connecting a White Heron with Arching Roundhouse manoeuvre.

'I told you Boomer: I don't consider myself to be World Champion until I've defended my title in Stockholm in November. Mind you, if you play like this, it shouldn't be too hard . . .'

When you call me Boomer, my body throbs with electricity (on screen, you're Firedancing towards me and I counter with an Electric Guard before lashing you with a set of Twin Lancer punches). When you execute a two-punch combination with backslaps and a Reverse Punt, you tell me that the most beautiful thing about *Tekken* is the fact that Ling Xiaoyu players call the Reverse Punt move 'Mistrust'.

'Mistrust,' you say, 'that's beautiful.'

After twenty fights, we're tied at ten each. I take the twenty-first, you take the twenty-second and twenty-third but I put you down with a buffered Headbutt in the twenty-fourth to tie us at twelve victories each. Twenty more fights (and an hour later), we're tied with twenty-two victories each, all the time talking about what we're doing, thinking out loud, swapping strategies and moves.

'Ling's left jab – timed at eight frames,' you tell me as you jab with your left, 'the equal fastest move in the game.'

'Her right kick's timed at ten frames.'

You try a Sunrise Fan attack but miss and I deliver the appropriate punishment.

'Now you're definitely going easy on me,' I tell you. 'The recovery time for that one is monstrous, eighteen frames or something achingly slow like that.'

'Maybe I don't want to put you off,' you say, rolling to your feet and cartwheeling away.

'Put me off what?' I ask, powering up and coming at you with a Corpse Splitter.

'Me.'

'You?'

'Me. What's going to happen to us, Boomer? Maybe you don't know, but I *need* to talk about it.'

On the screen, you close in for a Slam throw (with forearm chop) but I backstep before dancing in close to wrap my arms around your body and force you to the floor, straddling both legs across your breasts and driving in a series of punches. Twenty-three twenty-two to me.

'I don't think there's anything you could do to put me off you,' I say. 'And I can't imagine not being with you. I could visit you – in Oxford or in Devon. If you like.'

'I was thinking . . .' You pause to open the next fight with a one-two and Lotus Twist before backing away. 'I was hoping for something closer.'

By the time we're tied at forty fights each, we can't play any more, and we both lie back on the floor and watch the lights from the Strip outside play across the ceiling. You've told me that you want to move to London now that you've finished with Cambridge and I tell you that you can stay with me if you need a place to stay while you look for your own place and it's then you ask me why you would need your own place.

The next day we fly back to England and you sleep in my lap. I just stare down at you for the whole journey and stroke your hair. If I've been wondering for three days when all of this is going to end and asking myself what I've done to deserve you, I'm also telling myself that whatever I've done, I've done it *right* and that this is *never* going to end. It's never going to end.

At Gatwick we almost can't bear to say goodbye to each other. But after two weeks you move into the flat in Kentish Town and we both start practising for the Stockholm Tekken Challenge where we'll both go on to lose our respective semi-finals.

•

If we do ever run into each other, then I'll walk on over and say 'Hi',
I promise, and maybe we'll go for a beer and see where we are in our
lives. It's not that I'm leaving things open to chance (and I don't expect
you necessarily to greet me with a smile) – more that if fate does ever
find us in the same place again . . .

•

Which one of us first suggested the idea of getting married? I remember the night clearly. I get back from a late shift. I find you in bed playing *Wipeout*. I wash. I climb into bed next to you and while we race in split-screen mode you tell me how happy you are, that playing *Wipeout* in bed with me makes you the 'happiest person alive'. Things go blurred at that point. One minute we're racing around some secret courses. The next we're planning which hotel to stay in when we go back to Las Vegas to get married.

'Jimmy can be my best man.'

'Lottie and Anita can be my bridesmaids.'

'My dad will come.'

'My parents won't, I don't think: they can't even handle the fact that I'm a gamer so I can't see them flying to Las Vegas to see me get married. But I think they'd ultimately be happy for me.'

'Would you rather get married here?'

You shake your head. 'I would love to get married in Vegas. We could travel separately and not see each other for the first night. You could stay in the Imperial Palace and I could stay at Caesar's.'

'I didn't know you were so old-fashioned,' I say.

'It'll be more romantic. And then we could meet the next day at the chapel – and then we'd be married. It would be so beautiful, Boomer, it would be so beautiful . . .'

•

Look after yourself. And always believe in yourself, even if it seems I haven't been able to.

Clarity.

3

'So she's postponed it?'

'I don't think so,' I said, staring at the water in the pool and remembering watching Clarity diving into it six months earlier.

'What's she said?' asked Jimmy

I told them all that Clarity never arrived in Las Vegas, that she didn't want to go through with the wedding.

'It's just last-minute nerves . . .'

'We can call her, can't we . . . and get her back?'

I shook my head. And then I shot up out of my lounger and started stumbling towards the shadowy interior of the hotel.

'*Boomer!*'

Somehow I managed to get to away before anyone could

stop me. Maybe everyone was too shocked to react quickly enough. Maybe they realised that I needed to be alone for a while. Maybe I ran, a dumb bumbling blob grunting my way through the Imperial Palace and out on to the Strip. I stopped for breath on the edge of the sidewalk, drawing stares from the people passing by, and for a moment I remembered how once I'd had to run away from a couple of glue-sniffing skinheads who were throwing stones at me as they chased me across the local rec ground. I'd burst into the nearby café that time for shelter, stumbling and crying, only to be laughed at the by the road workers camped around the plastic tables with mugs of tea. And then I saw Caesar's Palace across the road and I marched across. Inside the lobby, I almost stormed up to the reception desk and demanded to see Clarity, as if she was sitting in her room suffering from an attack of last-minute nerves. But of course she wasn't there. She wasn't there.

Where could I go?

I drifted through the gaming tables and into a shopping mall styled like a Roman forum, white stucco pillars, fountains in the middle of cobbled piazzas, a fake blue sky overhead with cotton-candy clouds painted on it. Clothes shops. Souvenirs. Ice-cream parlours. A gallery with a cylindrical aquarium around which corkscrewed a rainbow of tropical fish. Eventually I found a bar and drank down a few beers and remembered meeting Clarity here the summer before and how we'd planned the whole trip three months later.

We'd announced our plan to get married a week after first talking about it. As it turned out, my dad hadn't wanted to come (he couldn't handle the flight, he'd said, but wished me the best of luck and hugged me and Clarity with his broad, tattooed forearms) and Clarity had been right about her parents – they hadn't wanted to come to America but invited us to stay with them in Devon when we returned. Would our friends be able to come? We weren't sure, but after telling a whole crowd of them, enough people committed themselves to make it worthwhile and we went ahead with buying plane tickets and putting down a deposit for hotel rooms and a slot at the Little Chapel of Flowers.

At the bar, I thought about reading Clarity's email again, but realised that I'd left it on the table by the pool in the Imperial Palace. Maybe the others were reading it. It was then that Jimmy found me.

'Boomer. Are you alright, mate?'

I asked him how he knew where to look for me and he shrugged, saying that he hadn't, that everyone had been out looking for me. He held out the printout.

'Here you are. None of us read it,' he added. I didn't take it so he put it down on the bar and pulled up a stool.

'I'm sorry, Boomer . . .'

'It's not your fault.'

'I know but . . .' Jimmy asked me if I'd tried calling England to see if I could get hold of her or her parents? Anita or Lottie? I shook my head.

'I've read it and I know Clarity well enough to know that if she says she can't be contacted then she's out of reach.'

We were silent for a moment.

'How are the others?' I asked. 'Everyone's come all this way. I can't believe I've let everybody down.'

'It's not like it's your fault,' Jimmy said.

'It feels as if it is.'

'They'll be okay. They are worried about you, though. *I'm* worried about you.'

'I . . . I . . .'

Jimmy put a hand on my shoulder. 'Tell me?'

'I feel as if it's my fault because I should have known better. This is how things *should* turn out for me. This is how things *always* turn out for me. I feel as if I've had my six months of happiness and now it's back to being fat and lonely for another twenty-five years. I knew it was all too good to be true.'

Jimmy looked at me.

'Did Clarity ever *once* make a comment about your *weight*?' he asked.

I shook my head.

'Not once?'

'Not once.'

'And are you saying that you didn't feel fat once while you and Clarity were together?'

I shook my head again. 'No,' I said, 'I felt happy.'

Jimmy sighed. 'Mate, you may have felt happy – but you were fat as well. *Happy* fat.'

He lit a Regal.

'Now you're *sad* fat.' He puffed on his cigarette. 'Look, mate, you may feel like shit, and I admit that I haven't read her letter to you. But I don't think Clarity left you because of anything like that.'

We sat in silence for a little while. Jimmy asked me if I wanted another drink and I shook my head.

'You're right, Jimmy: I feel like shit.'

'I don't think you're going to feel any different for a while,' he said. 'I'm not going to lie to you and I can't put it any other way. But let's go back to the hotel and take it from there. We'll let the others know that you're okay and call the chapel and tell them what's happened. After that we can decide whether we go back to England straight away or in a few days. We'll do whatever you want – that's one thing I can promise you.'

I looked around me at the crowds of sun-tanned people filing

214

past. For a moment, all I wanted to do was be sitting on my own with a computer game, any kind of game (it didn't matter) as long as it was an electronic world with fixed objectives and where the only issue at stake was how *good* I was and how many special moves I knew.

'Let's go,' Jimmy said again, gently, and I nodded. For a second I thought of leaving Clarity's email on the bar. I wondered if I could even bring myself to touch it. But then I thought of her and folded it into my pocket.

'Let's go,' I said, 'let's just go.'

Now we walked back out of the mall with its Roman Temples and its statues of gods and gladiators, past the bars and cafés and shops selling golfing gear and tuxedos and wedding dresses. On the other side of the gaming rooms, we found a travelator that would take us back out on to the Strip.

'You ready?'

I nodded, and as we both stepped on to the moving walkway we allowed ourselves to be carried towards the midday sun.

THE PROJECT

In an infinite universe there can exist an infinite number of
extraterrestrial human beings, and in fact an infinite number of
beings identical to myself.

Paul Davies, *Are We Alone?*

Sometimes I wonder
Why I spend the lonely nights
Dreaming of a song
The melody haunts my reverie
And I am once again with you

Nice work, Ray, you tell yourself as you haul the cab out of the dark funnel of an underpass and through the static glare of another intersection, an old song blaring at you through the radio speakers, *real nice*. Not content with losing Tess, you've made your best friend mad, you've gotten yourself thrown out of Wizard's for brawling and now you're driving drunk. The way thing's are going, surely it's only a matter of time before you get pulled over and the shit really hits the fan.

When our love was new
And each kiss an inspiration
But that was long ago
And now my consolation
Is in the stardust of a song

Could you screw things up any worse? For a moment you don't know where you are and when you look out through the windshield, you suddenly realize that in your drunken confusion you've driven back to the block where you and Tess used to live. A reflex? The only thing you could do now to make things worse is ditch the cab, walk up to your old front door and start banging on it, start screaming at the top your voice the way you did more than a few times just after Tess threw you out.

> Beside a garden wall
> When stars are bright
> You are in my arms
> The nightingale tells his fairy tale
> Of paradise where roses grew

You remember the last of these occasions. You were lonely. You were hysterical. You looked like a haggard tramp (you still hadn't found a new place to live and were sleeping in the back of the cab at the time). The door had suddenly swung inwards and your heartbeat had quickened as you thought: *at least she opened the door this time, at least she opened the door!* It was then you realized that you were staring at a stranger, an elderly man in a vest leaning heavily on his walking stick, shapes moving nervously in the hallway behind him. He told you that the last tenants had moved on (no, they hadn't left a forwarding address) and it was at that point you knew it was over.

> 'though I dream in vain
> In my heart it will remain
> My stardust melody
> The memory of love's refrain

Now you switch through the channels wanting to listen to anything but old love songs. On another station there's a discussion about the death toll from last year's monsoons and what people can do to avoid disaster this year. On the next there's pop music, the kind of stuff that kids listen to, moronic monkey chatter over a backbeat of clashing gears. On another channel the sports results are coming through . . . *the Stars beat the Meteors . . . the Comets beat the Fireballs . . . the Satellites beat the Novas . . .* suddenly you can't decide whether you're sick of the disembodied voices rattling around the inside of the cab or whether silence would be worse. You turn the radio off. You turn it back on. You turn it off again. After a few moments, you boot up the engine and pull back out into the traffic and head east for the couple of four-by-fours you call your new home.

It was all going fine, you reason, as you fly through the near-empty streets. Earlier on, you'd just dropped a couple off in the South Parallels (thirty credits with a five credit tip) when the light on the com-link on your dash flickered from green to red. It was Jeff and he was calling to see if you wanted to clock off early and drink a few beers. Sure you did, you said, and you both agreed to meet at Wizard's even though you never met anywhere else. It took ten minutes to get there. Jeff was already waiting for you with a pitcher and a couple of glasses and he came over and gave you a hug when he saw you, slapped you on the back with the gigantic wedges of his hands and the two of you shot a few frames of pool. While you were playing, you swapped stories about some of the freaks and crazies you've had in the back of your cabs the last few days, the usual hacker monologues of jumped fares, bad traffic and foul-mouthed lunatics. And after a few drinks, you were pouring out another pitcher when you looked at Jeff and considered how he's been dutifully meeting you at least two nights a week ever since Tess left, never letting on that he's worried about you and always making sure you're not on your own for too many nights in a row. And you think: *Typical Jeff,* your heart glowing, *a bear-sized guy with a bear-sized heart.* In return, you don't let on that you know he's just looking out for you and that Betsy probably doesn't need her husband spending half his free time babysitting some guy who cheated on his girlfriend the same way she doesn't really need you coming over for a home-cooked dinner every Sunday. And then, catching yourself smiling, you thought that maybe you were starting to feel better about things, that maybe you were starting to *recover*. So you told him, nothing dramatic, just one guy talking to another guy.

'Jeff,' you said, draining your glass and refilling it (spilling a bit, but not too much), 'I think I'm starting to feel better. I think I'm really starting to be myself again.'

'Yeah? That's real good, Ray,' he replied, 'I'm glad. I don't know what I'd do if Betsy ever left me, I don't know how I'd cope.'

'Well,' you said, bending down to take a shot, 'I'm starting to *cope*.'

Of course it was then that you saw Georgia Jones walk in through the steel doors, watched as she stalked up to the bar in her heels and skirt. Jeff must have noticed you tense up because you immediately felt his heavy hand come to rest on your shoulder, heard his voice in your ear.

'Easy, buddy! Best just let it go, huh?' you heard him whisper and you heard yourself tell him that you were fine as you refilled your glass and drained it and refilled it again. You remember Jeff's hand lingered on your shoulder a few seconds longer. And then he was stooping into the bright light to take his shot and you were looking over towards the bar again. There she was. You watched her wait to order a drink, your grip on your cue tightening as you saw her turn and laugh at something one of the guys sitting nearby had said. Her teeth glistened in the damp light, you noticed, as she pushed a thick stripe of black hair behind an ear and laughed again, and you wondered what dumb line the chump on the barstool had grunted at her.

And then you watched as she allowed him to buy her drink for her, watched the way she twisted her body on to the vacant stool next to him, legs crossing and the hem of her skirt riding a little higher up her thigh. *Who was he?* You thought you recognized him as one of the bruisers who worked down in Mechanics & Maintenance at the depot. And Georgia's eyes, you noticed, glanced in your direction, metallic buttons that fixed themselves on to yours for a moment before triumphantly turning away . . . suddenly you were upending the last of the beer into your mouth and walking over towards her, Jeff's voice somewhere behind you, Georgia not turning to face you until you were shouting at her across the space of a couple of meters, the chump standing and moving himself between the two of you with his hands raised. You were shouting, you remember, but what you were saying seems to have been deleted from your memory. At some point you felt Jeff's hand trying to pull you back and you remember shaking yourself free of his restraining grip. At some point the chump slammed both hands against your chest and knocked you back a couple of steps, his body lunging across the gap and his face looming into yours, the flattened trowel of his nose and the scuffed humps of his cheeks bristling against your face, his breath mingling with yours. At some point you brandished your cue at him and it was then that several pairs of hands reached out towards you and pulled you backwards. As you were dragged away, slurring and screaming, you looked back at Georgia to see her calmly meeting your gaze, her face receding into the distance as you were hurled out into the steaming night, and you couldn't help but remember those same eyes closing and the murmur of expectation that had slipped out from between her parted lips when your faces had merged outside her apartment door.

Outside Wizard's it was Jeff's turn to shout into your face: *what the hell were you thinking? Was this what you called 'coping'?* By then you were crying and almost unable to breathe. You were thinking about Tess and the way you'd both eaten that last meal in silence, the way she'd suddenly put her knife and fork down on her plate and pushed it away, her food barely disturbed. Her face had turned pale (how quickly her face had voided itself of colour, you thought, your body suddenly tingling with alarm) and you saw her throat tremble as if there was a small creature trapped inside it and you asked her what was wrong.

'What's the matter, honey . . . ?'

'Some of the girls at work have been gossiping,' she'd interrupted. 'Th-th-there's a rumor going around that . . .'

For the millionth time, you can't believe that you were so stupid. The girls in the dispatch rooms have nothing to talk about all day. Jeff and you were always laughing about it. Jeez . . . *Tess* and you were always laughing about it. Why had you ever been foolish enough to believe that you'd be able to keep the whole thing from her?

And now you think back to the parking lot outside the back of Wizard's: why did you pick up a trash can and hurl it at Jeff's cab before driving away? Is any of this *his* fault?

You focus on the road ahead, glance into the rearview expecting to see the blinding glare of a Trooper's patrol lights bearing down on you at any moment. But the air is empty behind you and soon you pull out on to the Mariposa Skyway where the traffic is heavier, climbing up into the express lanes and jinking the cab in and out of the hulking transporters speeding their way out to The Circuit and the freight yards over on East Point. Up above, you can see the squat shapes of the off-world mining rigs as they come in to land, giant lumbering shadows amongst the swarms of Guide Pods that weave around them like fireflies, the huge surging bellow of their anti-thrust audible above the cab engine as they slowly lower themselves towards the ground. Beyond them, the skyline burns blue and yellow and orange above the city, the massed clouds writhing and bristling in the sky like giant beasts, like mutant sea monsters wrestling with each other through the depths of an incendiary sea.

•

The following day you wake up to the sound of the terminal in the next room flicking on and blaring the news in through the doorway: economic fluctuation, a collapsed block over in the Ten-Forties, the latest in the election race, satellite footage of the radiation storms sweeping across the Arctic tundra, the first reports of an industrial explosion on the moon. You lie there for a few seconds, letting the sound wash over you before you sit up in bed and it's then that you realize that you're still in yesterday's clothes. For a moment you wonder if you put them on the day before. And then you drag yourself out of bed and undress and throw it all on to the pile that's already festering in the corner of the room and wonder how you ever managed to become such a slob. *Wasn't it Tess who was always the untidy one out of the two of you?* You limp through the squalid undergrowth of your apartment and slump down on to the floor of the shower stall, tell yourself that you've got to pull yourself together or . . . *or what?* All you can see lying in wait for you is another day behind the wheel of the cab, another day drifting through the maze of city blocks and yet another fitful night of regret and self-loathing spent drowning in the meaningless blue light of the terminal screen. *How can you kill this feeling? How do you kill it? How can you kill this feeling of dumb uselessness?* Without Tess, you just feel part of the city's grinding machinery. Eating to shit, only to feel hungry again. Drinking only to feel hungover and to crave more drink. Washing yourself only to get dirty again. And there was work: mindless, repetitive, anonymous. Whole days spent in the cab processing the banked tiers of traffic on the city's streets, the fares, the credits, the aliens and spooks who climbed into the backseat twenty times a day.

Now you think about Tess and you remember the first time you met her. Earlier that morning you'd headed out to pick up a fare on Battery Drive when an empty school bus ploughed into your right fender and crumpled the front corner of the hood. After an argument with the driver (you still remember him now, a guy with a face like ploughed concrete who denied all responsibility even though you'd been stationary and he'd more or less impaled your cab on the front of his bus), you'd ditched the cab at the side of the road and caught the sub back to the depot. There were forms to be filled in – insurance, disclaimers, 3rd party verification, replacement vehicle rental – and you walked up to the office only to round a corner and run straight into a woman. It was as if she appeared out of nowhere only to smack straight into you, the mound of papers she'd been carrying scattering over the floor around your feet. Quickly, you bent down to gather them back together – but so did she and your heads clashed.

'Ouch!'

'Ouch!'

'Hey, I'm real sorry,' you said.

'That's okay,' she replied, two long fingers massaging her forehead.

'Would you believe this is the second collision I've had

today,' you said with a smile. 'Some idiot just totaled the
front of my cab. You don't happen to know if you've got
any IF110s and a VR303 amongst all this?'

They were just dispatch-clerk rosters, she told you, and you
realised that you hadn't seen her before.

'You new?' you asked.

'Just started,' she replied, 'it's my first day.'

The next thing you noticed was how tan she was, the white
dress she was wearing only emphasizing the honeyed color of
her skin. You asked her if she'd been on holiday and she told
you that she'd just been on a two-week trip to one of the
resorts along Pleasure Beach. She wasn't wearing a wedding
ring and you wondered if she had a boyfriend.

'Have a good time?' you asked. She nodded but told you
that she'd been lonely now and then.

'I went on my own. I guess I expected to meet people, but
it was mainly couples and families. Still, the rest did me a lot of
good: cleaner air, lots of sleep, leisurely meals, lots of evenings
watching the sun set slowly over the sea.'

You held out your hand and told her your name was Ray.
She said that she was called Tess and you managed to stop
yourself from asking her out then and there. And then a week
later you loitered outside the depot canteen in a pressed check
shirt and red sports jacket until you saw her walk in for her
lunch-break and then you duly slipped into line behind her.
You started talking. *How was her first week? Were the others being
friendly to her?* You told her that the girls in the dispatch center
could be ruthless with newcomers but someone nice like her
shouldn't have any problems making friends.

Then the two of you got talking about sports. Did she want
to go to watch the Novas with you? They were playing the
Asteroids the following Friday night at the Novadome and a

friend of yours who worked a security shift at the stadium could get you a pair of good tickets. It turned out that Tess *did* want to go see the Novas. And it turned out that Tess wanted to go to the pictures the following Friday and eat baloney rolls with you at the Lonely Island fair afterwards. And it turned out that Tess wanted to drink Margaritas and dance to jazz and salsa at The Fuego after that and it turned out that Tess wanted to drive out to Griffiths Point after that and park the cab and watch the fiery tails of the rockets taking off from Armstrong on the horizon along with all the other couples. And then a few months later it turned out that Tess wanted you both to live together. So did you and you both gave up your apartments for a larger one in Lower Sunset.

Now you ask yourself: what was life with Tess like? *Come on, Ray, what was it like?* It was paradise. Between the two of you, you had little money to spare. But life in the apartment seemed to *throb* with contentment and the city outside seemed like a magical toy for the two of you to play with together. Looking back, you can hardly believe that you're the same person as the man you remember back then, the guy who woke up with Tess each morning, the guy who drove her to the depot at the start of each day and the guy who brought her home each evening, the guy who took her to bed each night. But you can hardly believe that you're living in the same city as you did back then. *Back then?* Was it only a couple of months ago? You remember your life together reaching some kind of peak and the two of you suddenly lying in your bed having just made love and one of you suddenly talking about starting a family. You can't remember which one out of the two of you mentioned it first but suddenly you were both excited, the two of you almost daring the other to come right out and say it: you wanted to have a child. Neither of you cared

228

if it was a boy or a girl but both of you knew that you'd have to start saving. So you both started taking on more overtime. You started driving sixteen-hour shifts and Tess started working a few nights. You saw each other less and less, your only contact for days sometimes being the brief moments you passed each other in the hallway of the apartment or in a corridor at the depot, the two of you pausing for a weary kiss before going your separate ways.

And then Georgia Jones showed up. You remember walking into the office and seeing her there. You couldn't take your eyes off her breasts, the dark hair, the immaculate lips. The two of you started talking (a matter of basic courtesy surely?) and when she said that she'd 'see you around', her teeth lined up in a smile, you couldn't help but reply: *yeah, see you around*. And you *did* see her around. While Tess was sleeping off another double shift at the apartment, you seemed to be finding more and more reasons to stop by the depot and you'd see her *everywhere*. In the canteen. In the office. In the diner across the street. At Wizard's — but also at other hacker bars, at Travis's in The Loop and at Easy Andy's over on Palantine Hill. And then one time you passed her on the steps up to the depot's entrance lobby. You both stopped to say 'hi' (you were going in, she was coming out) and when she asked you for a ride back to her apartment you nodded with a quick look over both your shoulders.

And then a fortnight later you were eating dinner with Tess when she told you that *she knew*.

Sitting there in the shower stall, you let your head bang back on to the tiles, let the water sluice through the opening of your slack mouth. Telling yourself that it's all your fault doesn't seem to make things feel any better and as the water splashes down, you imagine a universe where you could gather your will and force the water to travel in a different direction, to flow upwards from off the top of your head and back into the shower head. In such a universe you'd be able to unravel the tangle of mistakes that you've made and you'd eventually find yourself back at that day two months ago when you walked into the dispatch room to query your payslip. Only then would you let time start moving forwards again only this time you wouldn't take any notice of the new girl in the tube dress who stared at you from behind her screen with matted eyelashes. No, you'd be polite (you'd still say hello, introduce yourself and welcome her to the firm with a standard smile) but you'd think of Tess and remember to be grateful for everything you had.

Now you get up and step out of the shower stall to dry yourself (realizing, given the stink coming off the damp towel, that you're probably only making yourself dirty again) and it's then that you hear the terminal beep. You have a message waiting. *Maybe it's Tess*, you think to yourself immediately, and then groan at yourself for being so stupid. The other thought is that it might be Jeff and you wince at the memory of the trash can bouncing off the hood of his cab the night before. But when you check, you see that the message waiting for you has been sent from 'THE DEPARTMENT OF SOCIAL EVOLUTION'. The Department of Social Evolution? What the hell is that – a charity? You read the contents of the message, and then read it again, just to make sure you understand it:

We are pleased to inform you that you have been selected as a potential contributor to an exciting scientific program that is currently being initiated by the Department along with the full support of the Government at an Executive level.

To this end, the Department would like to invite you to attend a consultative meeting with one of our Directors in order that you might learn more of this exceptional opportunity. You are under no

*obligation to respond to our request. But we would like to take this
opportunity to emphasize the unique nature of our proposition.*

*We have contacted your employers and notified them of our
intentions, arranging for you to be away from your place of work
should you wish to accept our offer. Furthermore, we would credit
you with a modest sum as a sign of our commitment to you should
you attend such an introductory meeting . . .*

What could the government possibly want with you? You
check the message for evidence of a hidden agenda but there
doesn't seem to be any. Confused, you decide to call the
number at the end of the message to try to find out some
more and almost immediately there's an efficient female voice
on the other end of the line.

'Department of Social Evolution. Can I help you?'

'Hi,' you say. 'My name is Ray Straychek. I've just received
a message from your department and I was wondering if you
could tell me what it was all about?'

There's a pause while she brings your data up on her
screen.

'Yes . . . Mr. Straychek . . . apartment 33089, Westside
Towers. Can you tell me what you would like clarified
for you?'

'Well,' you say, 'the message tells me that I've been selected
to be part of a government experiment. Can you tell me more
about it in advance?'

'Everybody's asked that,' she replies, 'but I'm afraid I'm not
qualified to tell you any more than you already know. What
I *can* say is that you've been scheduled for a meeting with
Professor Zowber should you wish to take up our invitation
and that he really is the best person to explain it all to you.'

You pause for a second, and then tell the woman that you'll
be in later. *What the hell!* you think (noting the address at the

end of the message), *at least it would be time away from the cab.*
And immediately you feel your spirits lift at the thought of
doing something different.

•

You pull the cab out on to the street and up into the
traffic, the crowds on the steeped sidewalks moving like
sleepwalkers, drained faces staring wearily into the screens of
their communicators while the sky churns above them, waves
of gray and white and black waiting to unload themselves on to
the city below. *What would Tess make of all this*, you ask yourself,
what would she make of you being part of a 'government experiment'?
But then you're always wondering what Tess is thinking and
always wondering what she's doing. When it came to thinking
and doing things, you remember, she always seemed to be the
same as you. Maybe that's changed now? Who knows.

It takes you half an hour to arrive at the address you have for
the Department of Social Evolution and when you get there
you're surprised. You expected it to be situated in the wing of
some larger administrative block but find that it has a building
all to itself, a towering structure disappearing upwards towards a
vanishing point miles above. Walking across the wide plaza and
through one of ten revolving doors into a marbled lobby, you
stride up to the reception desk and introduce yourself to one
of the several brightly uniformed women sitting in a line.

'I received a message this morning asking me to attend
an introductory meeting,' you tell her and she asks you for
your name.

'Ray Straychek.'

She taps this into her terminal. 'Ray Straychek.'

You nod. 'That's me.'

She asks you to verify your identity on a palmscanner and
then consults her terminal again.

232

'Welcome to the Department of Social Evolution, Mr. Straychek,' she says, 'and thank you for responding so promptly to our invitation. You've been scheduled to meet with Professor Zowber. He's currently in the middle of another meeting but should be available for you shortly. Would you mind waiting? He really shouldn't be very long.'

You shake your head and are directed to a bank of padded chairs on the other side of the lobby where you take a seat and glance at the other people around you who are also waiting. You hope to see some distinguishing feature that you all share, a clue as to the reason why you've all been summoned, but none presents itself. None of you seem to have anything in common except that you're *there*.

Then, after maybe fifteen minutes, a uniformed woman comes over to you and tells you that the Professor is ready and you follow her across the lobby to an elevator. Inside, she punches a code into the console mounted on the wall and there's the distant sound of momentum, if not the sensation itself. Are you being lifted into the sky or lowered into the bowels of the building? You can't tell. Moments later the steelplex doors slide apart and you find yourself being led along a dark, windowless corridor with a row of doors on your right-hand side. You count them as you pass each one and eventually the woman stops by the twenty-fourth.

'Here we are,' she says and knocks. The door opens and a man appears.

'Mr. Straychek?' he asks her. She nods. 'Please,' he says, now turning to you and gesturing towards the room beyond, 'come in.'

You walk in and find yourself in a rectangular room. The far wall is entirely transparent, a floor-to-ceiling window, and as you look through it, you realize that you must be hundreds of stories up in the air. You think of the grimy porthole back at your apartment. When you looked out of it, you saw . . . you saw a thousand other dark portholes staring right back at you, pale faces appearing here and there like dim lights. *But here?* From this height, the city grid lost its symmetry and took on a more organic form, the channels and grooves of the city streets and skyways more like the tubes of some miniature organism viewed through a microscope.

'Would you like a drink?' The man's voice from behind you.

'Er . . . yes please.'

You turn and look at the guy again. He's tall and thin and though he must be at least a decade older than you he has smoother skin and pampered sandy hair and for a second you think he's some public-relations hotshot, some kind of corporate charmer the Department have sent to schmooze you before the Professor shows up (will it be bad news, whatever it is they have to say to you?).

And then you realize: he's the Professor.

'I'm Max Zowber. Pleased to meet you,' he says as if he's been waiting for you to make the connection yourself. 'Some water?'

You nod, eyeing the tall pitcher on the desk, the only piece of furniture in the polished room besides two easy chairs that sit facing each other by the window.

'Take a seat,' he says, pointing with a manicured finger as he pours out a glass. 'It's a terrible time of year, isn't it, everyone waiting for the monsoons.' He hands you the glass and sits down opposite you. 'Though I expect it must mean a busy time for cab drivers?'

'Why?' you ask, noticing that your voice has become brittle with expectation.

'I imagine that the demand for cabs increases when the weather breaks. Day after day of heavy rainfall, no one wanting to use public transport . . .'

'It's actually the worst time of year for us,' you say, taking a sip. The water in the glass tastes like water but doesn't feel like any water that you've ever come across. It feels like something heavier, like honey or milk. 'When the rain finally falls people just hole up in their homes. No one wants to go anywhere. Things go pretty dead.'

Zowber looks at you, his eyeballs freezing for a second as if he's making an internal calculation. 'I guess you're right. I've never thought of it that way.' He eases back in his chair but continues to look directly at you. 'Anyway,' he says, 'you must be pretty confused as to why you've been invited to come here.'

You nod. 'So, where do we start?' you ask.

Zowber undoes the buttons on his suit jacket, a suit that looks as if it cost a fortnight's wages, and then folds his hands together.

'I guess we start with you telling me how much you know about the history of recent space travel.'

You pause for a second. This wasn't what you expected.

'What everyone else knows, I guess.'

'Which is?'

You cough, take another sip of water as your memory gropes its way back to the history lessons you sat doodling through when you were a kid. 'Well, as far as I know, until about a hundred years ago man couldn't realistically explore space much further than the moon. The main problem, as I remember it, was that they couldn't produce rocket engines with enough power to drive a ship fast enough to make the journey worthwhile. I mean, if it takes eight months to travel to the next nearest planet, what's the point?'

You stop. Zowber doesn't say anything so you continue.

'After that, they developed ... what are they called ... *fusion engines?*'

'"Fusion engines" is the layman's term for them, yes.'

'And the way I understand it, these fusion engines meant that ships could travel at far greater speeds. After that, scientists developed a way of shielding astronauts from the intense gravitational forces produced by traveling at such speeds. And now we can make it to the edge of the solar system, but not much further. Is that right? That's all I know.'

'More or less,' Zowber replies, 'and that's more than most people know in fact.' He stops for a second before continuing. 'For the last ninety-seven years, man has managed to travel safely at increased speeds, thanks largely to the technological advances made possible by the Richard–Felix experiments at the end of the last century. Thanks to them, and also to significant advances in the field of biophysical stasis, it became possible for mankind to travel to the edge of our system in a little under two weeks. A remarkable achievement in its own way. But one has to ask oneself: what exactly have we gained from such a possibility? Perhaps very little.'

'I thought we were able to mine the nearby planets for resources,' you say, painfully aware of how naïve you must sound. 'That's what we were taught in school anyway.'

'And you're right,' Professor Zowber replies patiently. 'The kinds of advances we've been talking about have reaped certain *material* rewards. But in broader terms, we have still gained very little. The kind of distances we're talking about are still less than infinitesimal when compared with those presented by stellar geography at even just a localized galactic level. Such distances give us no hope of meaningfully traveling much further beyond the edge of our solar system, let alone the

236

possibility of the human race exploring far enough into space to reach another planet fit for colonization or give us even the remotest chance of contacting intelligent lifeforms whose existence so far remains only philosophically probable.

'Of course, if we could travel at the speed of light or faster, this would become possible but unfortunately the last two hundred years of space exploration have been limited by a problem that is, paradigmatically, extremely twentieth-century.'

Zowber sees that he's starting to lose you and explains himself.

'In order to cover the distances required to reach even the nearest star system that looks as if it could support human life, we would have to travel at the speed of light for four and half years. Given that our current technology only allows us to travel at one percent of one percent of that speed, reaching that star system is, for all intents and purposes, impossible. Until now, that is.'

You feel the hairs on the back of your neck stir.

'What? You've developed . . . *warp* engines?' you ask, now wondering more than ever before why the hell you've been summoned to this meeting. Zowber chuckles.

'No, not quite.' He leans forwards in his chair. 'Putting fiction aside for one moment, scientists are still experimenting with various possibilities for superluminal speed travel . . .'

'Superluminal?'

'Faster-than-light.'

'Oh, I see.'

'Various government departments, as well as several corporate concerns with obvious vested interests, have been testing the theoretical envelope that scientists proposed over two hundred years ago: will man ever be able to travel faster than the speed of light?

'We've tried to cover every angle,' he continues. 'We've reconsidered every one of our assumptions with regards space-time relations, reinvestigated our understanding of Absolute Time and *simultaneity*. We've explored Alternative Gravity theories, electromagnetism. We've experimented with various types of fuels and propellants, with exotic matter that produces negative energy densities in space, with . . .'

Zowber stops mid-sentence.

'I'm sorry,' he says to you, 'maybe I should put it to you a different way.'

He gets up, walks over to the desk and returns to his seat with a single sheet of paper taken from a hidden drawer. This he holds up in front of your eyes by two opposing corners.

'You see this piece of paper, right?'

You nod.

'Now imagine that this piece of paper is space and we are at *this* corner.' He inclines his head towards his left hand. 'Now imagine that the diagonally opposite corner represents our intended destination, a place we want to get to, a planet four and a half light years away, for instance. What I've been saying so far is that for the last two hundred years, we haven't had the technology to travel from one corner to the other quickly enough for the journey to take less than the length of several thousand human lifetimes. Scientists have been trying to come up with ways of traveling more quickly across the gap between the two corners, or else investigating our understanding of the gap in case it turns out that the gap wasn't what we thought it was . . .'

'And now you're going to tell me that you can jump across the gap in a second,' you interrupt. 'Or something like that.'

Zowber lowers his hands and looks at you. 'Not quite,' he says, 'it's more a case that the gap sometimes isn't as large as we thought it was.' He raises the piece of paper again and holds it in front of your eyes. 'For centuries, almost everyone believed that space was a fixed environment. However, for the last two hundred or so years scientists have understood that space is always expanding, that if this piece of paper represents a portion of space then this piece of paper is gradually getting larger and larger.

'Now here's the exciting part. In the last decade or so, scientists have realized that the fabric of space itself is subject to another effect. It moves. In a word: it *ripples*.'

'Ripples!'

'Like a wave.'

Both of you stare at the piece of paper he's holding up between your faces. Slowly, he begins to manipulate it between his fingers so that it starts to curve and undulate between his hands and you realize that you are holding your breath.

'How . . . you mean . . . why does it do that?'

'So far,' Zowber replies, 'we don't really know. Scientists have long suspected that gravity could effect the topology of space-time but not to the massive scale that our instruments have been revealing over the last few years. The forces that seem to be causing these . . . ripples . . . appear to be one level up in the hierarchy of cosmic processes so the scientific community have labeled them as *metagravitational*.

'Now look,' he snaps your attention back to the piece of paper, 'remember our two points in space, the one representing where we are now and the one representing the point where we would like to travel to but can't.'

Your eyes follow as he simulates a ripple through the piece of paper that's large enough to bring his fingers together.

'If one of these ripples was big enough,' you say, suddenly excited that you seem to be finally understanding something, 'then it would essentially mean that the distance between the two points was shorter – short enough for a rocket to cover the distance within a human lifetime.'

'*Exactly*. Of course, it's only possible if we know how to cross the gap between the two points rather than have to go the long way around, the route represented by the surface of the piece of paper.' Zowber suddenly smiles at you. 'But I'm glad to say that we do.'

You stare at his fingers and at the space between them. So far, what he's told you makes sense. Just. But what is it he wants from you?

'So you have your two points in space,' you say, 'and you have your rocket. And you even have your wormhole or tunnel through space that saves you having to go the long way around . . .'

'We prefer to call it a *window* rather than a *wormhole*.'

'A "window" then.'

'Yes.'

You pause for a moment. 'I'm not exactly astronaut material,' you say. Zowber chuckles again.

'No, you aren't. Not exactly.'

'So why am I here?'

'Ten years ago we started being able to predict these metagravitational ripples,' he says to you and you get the feeling that there's a whole lot more to know. You're not wrong. In the same kind of language as before (though now you feel that when he uses the word 'we' he seems to be referring more specifically to himself or to some team of scientists that he belongs to rather than the scientific community in general), Zowber explains to you how a research group discovered a star system containing a planet that looked as if it could sustain human life but could never be reached using conventional methods. It wasn't four and half light years away: *it was four thousand five hundred light years away.*

'Once we knew that a metagravitational ripple would essentially bring this planet into reach, we examined it intensely by way of long-range telescopes. It was then we realized that the planet could sustain human life . . .'

'Y-y-you want me to travel to this planet?' you ask.

'Not exactly.' Zowber notices your alarm and his voice softens. 'Please don't worry,' he says. 'There's nothing sinister about what I am going to tell you . . .'

'You'd better tell me then.'

Zowber puts the piece of paper down. 'To put it as simply as possible, the window to the destination planet has been open for about seven years and will be for about another seven. Initially, we sent a probe through the window. We didn't know what the result of this first experiment would be. But, sure enough, it seemed to survive the journey intact and sent back clear communications signals from its new location. The slight time delay on these signals encouragingly suggested that although the probe had initially traveled through the window, the return message traveled across what we might call conventional or linear space.'

'The surface of the piece of paper.'

'That's right, the surface of the piece of paper. Then we sent several reconnaissance probes through to verify our assumptions as to the nature of the target planet, the composition of its soil and atmosphere and so on. After that, we sent yet another probe – though this time we programmed it with flight instructions to return back through the window. That worked too. After that, the logical next step was to send through a team of astronauts.'

Zowber sighs.

'They didn't come back. Monitoring devices on board the probe suggested that they didn't even *materialize* on the other side even though the probe did. We're still investigating what this means, but it seems clear so far that organic material doesn't survive the journey for some reason that we still don't know about.'

'And what was the next step?' you ask coldly.

'We didn't know for a while. Everyone was pretty dismayed by what happened to the first team of explorers. A lot of people called for the cessation of all further research activity and everyone involved was certain that any further loss of life was unacceptable. Research was suspended for a while. And then someone came up with an idea that seemed feasible. What if there was a way to transmit the blueprint for an organic object through the window rather than the organic object itself? We looked at medical technology and principally the technology used to synthesize the organic tissue that medical science currently uses to replace damaged or dysfunctional organs. Then we developed that technology so that it could theoretically synthesize a complete body . . .'

'A cloning machine?'

'If you like.'

'Aren't those illegal?'

'Of course. Obviously we had to make certain legal guarantees – but the unique nature of how we're applying the technology seemed to satisfy almost all the moral opponents to this next stage of the plan.'

'What happened next?'

'We launched a ship carrying the cloning machines through the window. This emerged near to the destination planet and positioned itself in orbit around it. Then we transmitted data containing a sample genetic matrix out to the ship across conventional space. To begin with, we opted for limited trials and were successful. We transmitted the code for a human liver and sure enough the cloning machine generated a fully functioning human liver. After that, we tried other human organs – the spinal column, the renal system, the heart and so on – and were successful each time. The next step was to attempt to send across the complete gene map for an entire human body. We calculated this using averages derived from statistical information and duly transmitted the data except this time the machines failed to successfully generate a cloned organism. We tweaked the figures, tried again and failed again.'

You ask what went wrong and Zowber tells you that it's complicated but it seems as if an artificially constructed gene map results in a cloned organism that is physiologically too unstable to survive. *Inviable* is the word he uses.

'Which is why you're here,' he tells you. 'It appears that the machines need an already functioning and naturally generated gene map in order to replicate an organism successfully. There-fore the Department of Social Evolution is asking thousands of citizens to decide whether they would agree to volunteer their genetic information so that it can be transmitted across to the target planet. In short, we're hoping to build a race of colonists generated from the templates of citizens living right here and right now.'

You're speechless.

'That's probably quite a lot of information for you to take in all at once. Is there anything you want me to clarify?' he asks quietly.

'Let me get this straight: you want to make a copy of me and then beam that copy of me out to the other side of the galaxy. Is that right?'

'Well, approximately *half*way across *our* galaxy.'

'I don't know what to say . . .'

'Some people we've spoken to want to run out the room and forget they heard any of it.'

'Part of me does too.'

After a moment's thinking, you ask Zowber why you've been selected as one of the candidates for cloning and he tells you that the process has been more or less carried out at random. The scientists have only two broad criteria affecting their selection process: they're looking for as wide and varied a cross-section of genetic templates as possible and they obviously want to exclude as much pathological data as they can from the outset.

'Look,' Zowber says to you, walking over to the desk and refilling your glass, 'it's not surprising that the whole proposition makes you feel pretty strange. It can still feel unreal at times, even to mc, and I'm a trained scientist who's been working with these kind of ideas for twenty-five years. What I suggest is that you go away and think about all the things I've told you. You're under no obligation, though the Department certainly feels obliged to give you the chance to consider what we've been saying before you either dismiss or accept our proposal.'

You sit there.

'Why don't you spend some time thinking about it?' Zowber says. 'Come back in a few days and tell me how you feel. You could ask any questions you might have thought of and I could try and answer them.'

•

You're led back to the elevator by the same uniformed woman as before and as you pass by the twenty-four doors on your left, you wonder how many interviews are taking place at that exact moment throughout the gigantic building.

244

And then you're out on the street, eventually climbing into the battered leather seat of your cab and drifting out into the gray city. You don't even think about logging in with the dispatch center to say that you're available for any work. It hardly seems worthwhile compared with absorbing everything you've just been told. All you can think about is the idea of being transmitted across the galaxy. *What would it feel like?* you ask yourself, but then realize you have no idea. The last thing you asked Zowber before leaving his office was what the whole colonization program was called. Perhaps you weren't asking out of simple curiosity, perhaps you were just trying to get a handle on things?

'A few people were inclined towards calling it something like "The Exodus Plan" or "The Adam Experiment",' he told you, 'but thankfully it's not the sixties any more and we do things a little less dramatically. So we call it "The Project". Nothing more, nothing less.'

You then asked him why there was a need for The Project. Why try and colonize another planet in the first place? What was the ultimate point behind the whole exercise? What was the scientists' motivation? You immediately wondered if there were some impending catastrophe threatening the planet that Zowber wasn't telling you about, a gigantic asteroid on a collision course or some massive and imminent breakdown in the planet's atmosphere. But Zowber put your mind at ease. There wasn't an apocalypse waiting out there in space and the planet was going to continue toiling along just as it had for thousands of years: the thinking behind The Project was apparently 'scientific and humanitarian', an entirely benign first attempt to explore and colonize deep space.

Sitting behind the wheel of your cab, you breathe a sigh of relief. But it still doesn't help you get any sense of what it will feel like to be transmitted across the galaxy and by the time you reach your block you've failed to make any more sense of what might happen to you.

Back in your apartment, you slump into a chair. What would it feel like? *What would it feel like?* For a while, all you can think about is *The Cosmic Drifter*, a comic strip you used to read when you were a kid that featured a superhero who traveled through space by simply willing it to happen. He would concentrate for a moment, his body tensing before it collapsed into a single beam of energy that sped out into the darkness, his atoms imploding in a race to get to the other side of the galaxy.

But then you tell yourself that this isn't what will happen to you at all. This is not what Zowber explained to you. They were simply going to make a copy of you, an exact physical replica, and now you can't help but wonder how it would feel to know that there were two of you.

Automatically, you now raise yourself out of the seat and start to clear the scattered dregs of your possessions that lie around the floor of the apartment, anything to give you something to do while you consider The Project. The task takes a few hours and soon the place looks almost fit for human inhabitation. You even manage to scrub down the shower stall and spend an hour at your terminal clearing your backed-up correspondence. There's even a message from Jeff waiting to be answered and typically there's no mention of your stupidity the night before, just a note saying that he tried to call you over the radio earlier in the day to see if you were okay. You think about telling him about The Project but in the end just call him in his cab to apologize. Down the line, Jeff tells you that he was worried about you when he couldn't get hold of you out on the road and you tell him that you're sorry about hurling the trash can at his cab, that you want to pay for any damage. But he dismisses your offer, telling you that you both know that his cab 'always looks like a piece of shit' and you agree to meet up in a few nights' time.

After you've spoken to Jeff, you slump back into your chair and flick on the terminal only to turn it off again. The news. Gameshows. Pornoflicks. More footage of the radiation storms. A public-information documentary about the monsoons. None of it seems to matter to you for now. None of it helps you get a grip on the idea of existing in two places at once. The realization that your double might exist, not in some parallel universe, not in some other dimension, but simply a great distance from where you are now causes you to shudder with . . . with *fear?* Eventually you get up, your head spinning with possibilities and questions that you can't seem to answer, and you walk into your bedroom, taking off your clothes and hanging them in the closet before climbing into bed. *What if you ever met yourself?* you wonder. *And what chance would your clone have of surviving on the new world?* The last thing you think before you finally fall asleep is that you haven't thought about Tess for hours, not once since you walked into the Department of Social Evolution. And then you're not thinking of anything.

•

'I didn't expect to see you so soon,' Zowber tells you. 'Most people we've spoken to have taken at least a few days before they've given us an answer.'

'Really? I thought about what we discussed all yesterday and all last night. There didn't seem to be much point in waiting any longer to get back to you with my questions.' You're talking to him in the same room as before, sitting in the same chairs and drinking the same heavy water.

'And what are they?' Zowber asks.

'Well, obviously I've been pretty confused. I guess the idea of being cloned makes me feel . . . *afraid*.'

Zowber nods, and replies that you've reacted normally.

'The idea of being cloned obviously violates the sense you've had of yourself as an individual,' he tells you. 'A sense that you've had of yourself all your conscious life. Also, maybe the fear is a result of misunderstanding something that we've discussed.'

'I thought that too,' you reply. 'The first thing that worried me was the chance that I . . . that I might meet myself. Is that dumb?'

'Not really.'

'Every time I think about that, I feel . . .'

You hesitate. You don't know what to say.

'Perhaps we should split your question into two parts and consider two appropriate answers,' he says. 'First of all, I want to suggest to you that to describe the human being cloned from your genetic template as "yourself" is to overstate the truth of the matter.'

'What do you mean?'

'The clone, for want of a term, is only a *physical* replica of you. It will look like you but it won't necessarily think exactly like you or act exactly like you. Far from it in fact. And you will have no sense of its consciousness either. After all, it will be living in a totally different environment to any you've encountered. To put it another way, you'll be two discrete organisms in two very separate locations.

'As for the chance of you meeting this cloned replica of yourself, I would say that there is no chance of this. Sure, it's not as if in some real sense the clone will be living in a separate dimension to you — the target planet exists in the same galaxy as we do, the same plane of existence if you like.

But it is theoretically *impossible* for you to reach that part of the galaxy. Organic matter doesn't survive passage through the window. And if you were to attempt to travel to the target planet through conventional space, it would take you a minimum of one and a quarter million years traveling at the top speeds currently available to mankind.'

'One and a quarter million years?'

'A long time. A long way,' Zowber tells you. 'So unless we work out a way of traveling at superluminal speeds in your lifetime, it seems safe to assume that it is extremely unlikely that you could ever travel to meet your clone, or vice versa.'

'And you say the window's only open for another seven years?'

'Give or take a few hours.'

You're silent for a while, trying to understand the distances being described, the quantities of time. It's almost impossible.

'I don't know if this sounds stupid,' you say.

'Try me.'

'Well, it's just that I feel . . . *protective* of this other "me". I hate the idea of a copy of myself going somewhere that I don't know, somewhere that might be dangerous.'

'That's not stupid at all. Nor is it really that surprising.'

'Will I ever be able to have a chance of monitoring my clone on the other planet, check that I'm still alive?' you ask. Zowber shakes his head.

'The logistics of offering such a facility are too complex,' he says.

'Can I at least know what the other planet is like?'

Zowber smiles. 'Of course you can.'

He takes a small console from out of a jacket pocket and presses a button that causes a panel in the far wall to slide back and reveal a screen.

'There it is,' he says as an animated diagram of a star system glitters into view, 'the third most central planet out of nine, orbiting its star at an average distance of about a hundred and fifty million kilometers.'

The animation zooms in towards a blue planet and its solitary gray moon.

'It's a beautiful place really,' Zowber tells you, almost sighing. 'Like a mirror-image of our own, but untouched and unspoiled. What else can I tell you? It has a stable meteorological environment with an acceptable yearly range of average surface temperatures for sustaining human life. Eighty-five percent of its surface is covered in water, not the polluted sludge we've ended up with on this planet, but oceans of clean water rich in biodiversity and minerals. The land formations, such as they are, have reached a stage of stability in terms of their tectonic maturity and present potential colonists with vast landscapes rich in fauna and flora.'

'It sounds like paradise,' you say.

'Is that a scientific term?'

You look at Zowber and see that he's joking.

'No, you're right,' he continues, clearing his throat. 'Like you said, it really is a beautiful place.'

'How are the clones going to live? Are you just going to . . .' You wave your hands in the air. 'Are you just going to dump them on the planet's surface and see if they survive?'

'A good question. First of all I have to say that what I'm about to tell you is a little outside of my specialist field. Essentially it's anthropological in nature. But I can offer you a reasonable account of what we intend that will make sense.'

You shrug.

'Okay,' Zowber says. 'What we've planned is this. Once we have the cloned population assembled, we intend to organize them into tribal groups and place them in their own territories within the most habitable parts of each continent. We're not sure exactly what will happen but we're aiming to simulate the conditions that the human race experienced about forty thousand years ago here on our planet.'

'Why forty thousand years?'

'That was the last time our species evolved genetically. After that, we hope that the colonists will develop along similar cultural lines to how the human race developed here.'

'But how will they know what to do?' you ask, imagining yourself for a moment in a desert, naked and alone and dying of hunger. 'How will they know how to eat and hunt and cook and defend themselves from predators? How will they know how to do *anything*?'

'Our primary method will be to educate them, principally by way of rudimentary symbol systems which we hope they will interpret as the work of primitive ancestors.'

Zowber presses another button on his console as he turns to face you and the diagram on the screen is replaced by images of stick men and childish images of various animals daubed on to rocks.

'Cave paintings?'

'Cave paintings, sculpture, carved tablets, elementary scrolls. It's amazing really,' he says. 'We know that as a species we used these media successively to communicate back to ourselves our sense of ourselves – and also to communicate this information to other members of our developing society. Given this, we're going to fabricate a whole primitive cultural system on the target planet, a simulation of ancient culture as it existed on *this* planet between forty and twenty-five thousand years ago. What we hope is that the cave paintings and other primitive artefacts will serve as a kind of "instruction manual" for the colonists, that they will assume these proto-information-systems are the work of pre-existing generations and insert themselves into the evolutionary timeline accordingly. If everything goes to plan, they'll see the cave paintings depicting scenes of hunting and cooking and other social processes such as child-rearing and food-sharing and eventually start imitating them, believing the diagrams to have been painted on to the walls by their ancestors. Natural evolutionary processes should then also start to have an effect, which is to say that those colonists who learn to take our cues will stand more chance of surviving. Instinct will also undoubtedly play a role too, especially in matters of language development and so on.'

'What if the clones don't catch on?'

'We've designed a series of more interventionist strategies that we can employ during an initial incubation period of the colonization. For instance, we've established a plan whereby we'll artificially synthesize various primitive tools and then distribute them around the colonists' habitats: axe-heads and hunting weapons, flints and other fire-making tools, simple clothing and cooking implements. Again, we assume the colonists will believe that the objects have been made by forebears or innovative contemporaries. And again, we hope our artificially constructed "instruction manual" will play a massive role here, helping the colonists to work out what these objects are so that they can use and copy them. In a similar way, we'll have fabricated rudimentary shelters for them to live in rather than leaving them to fend for themselves.'

You tell Zowber that it sounds as if a lot of the clones are going to die and he agrees. But he tells you that a lot of them are going to survive as well.

'It's not as if they're going to suddenly wake up on a barren planet surface in the middle of nowhere and have to work everything out for themselves,' he says. 'They're going to find themselves in a lush savannah environment subtly moderated to help them survive, an environment artificially contrived to give them the best possible chance of thriving and developing. In many ways, they've got a better chance than our prehistoric forebears ever had because we'll be watching them every step of the way. We've even arranged for camouflaged machines to operate on the planet surface, remote-controlled machines that will deposit food and materials in nearby locations should the colonists initially need assistance, though obviously we want to be as withdrawn as possible.'

Zowber stops and then asks you if any of what he's said makes you feel more comfortable. You nod, in as much as you understand that the scientists are essentially attempting to replicate what happened *here* on this planet and that your clone is going to be a 'caveman copy' of you. The idea's almost comical.

'Will you guys ever try and contact them?' you ask Zowber.

'We debated that one for a while,' he replies. 'A lot of people couldn't see the point of committing so much time and energy unless we were going to maintain contact right from the start. But there were some of us who thought that this was a unique opportunity to see what would happen if the human race were given another chance. How would they develop? What could they come up with that we haven't been able to? In the end both sides reached a compromise.'

'How did you do that?'

'Well, we first agreed that we weren't going to make direct contact with the colonist population. Such contact would inevitably place the colonist population under our control, something no one in the Department wanted. To put it simply: it goes against the grain of the ethos out of which The Project was inspired. But it was also agreed that along with the tools and shelter and cave paintings, we'd also plant certain other types of objects in the colonists' immediate environment, artefacts that had no practical use but could be interpreted as what we might call religious symbols. The colonists' need for a moral and spiritual framework should ultimately attach itself to these points of focus and start to develop. To put it another way, we're going to give them "gods".'

'Why do you want to do that?'

'We hope that by coding certain kinds of information into the meaning of these "religious artefacts" we could eventually direct the colonists to start thinking about the existence of intelligent life elsewhere in the galaxy and to start looking for it, that if we can coax early generations of colonists into believing that there are higher cosmic entities at work in their universe, then it's only a matter of time before they start wondering if there are more tangible entities out there waiting to be discovered. Yet again, we hope that such a process runs in a similar fashion to what has happened here on this planet. And obviously such an activity lies *extremely* far off in the colonists' future, tens of thousands of years. But it's worth getting these things established right from the start.'

'Are you saying you're going to give them a religion that will make them come looking for us?'

'Well, our very distant successors anyway. They may never take the hint. But then again, they might.'

Neither of you say anything for a while.

Then you say that you'll do it.

Zowber is slightly surprised and asks you if you want to tell him your reasons and you say that you don't often get the chance to have a caveman double. More seriously, you say that it's too extraordinary an opportunity to pass up. 'It's not like there's a catch,' you tell him.

'Well, we do anticipate some lingering emotional disorientation amongst some of our volunteers, something similar to the sorts of reservations you showed earlier. So we will be offering a counseling facility to all our volunteers. But we hope that after a while it will ultimately feel like a dream to you all: slightly familiar, slightly unreal. Does that make sense?'

•

Later, down in the lobby, Zowber gives you the details of this counseling facility in case you need it and shakes your hand.

'I'm glad you chose to volunteer, Ray. Thank you very much.'

'That's okay, Professor,' you reply. 'To be honest, the whole experience has made me feel strange – but it's also made me feel kind of special.'

'That's because you've undertaken an involvement that *is* special. You're amongst the very first human beings ever to be offered an opportunity such as this.'

Then Zowber lets go of your hand and walks back towards the elevators while you turn and walk towards the revolving doors, taking a moment to glance over at the people in the lobby waiting for their interviews.

Outside the Department building, you stretch and blink. After telling Zowber you wanted to go ahead and be part of The Project, he buzzed an assistant who took you to another office where you signed several forms. After that you were taken to a preparation suite, an almost bare white room where you showered and changed into a hospital gown before being led by a nurse into another small room where you were left alone. A voice from a hidden speaker asked you to strip and lie on a metal panel. It felt strange initially. But then the panel retracted into the wall, feeding you into the dark interior of a tube that was warm with whispering circuitry, and you were surprised that you felt no panic. *Look straight ahead*, a female voice breathed, *look straight ahead* . . . a pair of visors descended onto your eyes and suddenly everything except the edge of your vision was blacked out. For a moment, you strained inside. For a moment you saw some kind of green ignition flare at the rims of your eyeballs and your muscles started to tense . . .

You felt stiff immediately afterwards, contracted, as if your entire body had minutely recoiled from something, and Zowber explained in the recovery room that you were only unconscious for a second, just enough time for the computer to take a sample of all the relevant tissue. Zowber called it a *momentary aphasia*: the process stunned your brain with a blast of light at a certain frequency that disconnected your consciousness from the relevant pain receptors. He also told you that a scan of your gene map already revealed that it was free from 'any problems' and that your data would be transmitted out to the target planet along with that of other successful applicants the following week. You said that you couldn't believe that it would be so soon and Zowber replied that there was little reason for a delay.

Now you stretch one more time, feel the bones in your spine and shoulders clicking, and then turn to start walking back towards the block where your cab is parked. It's then that you see a figure hurrying away from you, a woman who's just come out of the Department building.

Tess?

It couldn't be her, you think.

Tess?

'Tess!' you shout out. Is it your imagination or does the woman bunch her shoulders and accelerate away at the sound of your voice. Suddenly you're running after her, zig-zagging through the crowd, and finally catch up with her further down the street.

'Tess? *Tess!*'

Tess turns to face you and you can't believe that you're looking at her again. You never thought you would get the chance. But there she is. You want to grab hold of her but don't in case you scare her and you feel your hands flapping uselessly at your sides.

'What do you want?' she asks, now moving towards you.

'I . . . I . . . err . . . how are you?'

'I'm good. Now what do you want?'

She doesn't sound angry, more like she's in a hurry to get away from you.

'I wanted to . . . I don't know what I wanted. You've moved.'

'Well, you were banging on the door every night. What did you expect me to do?'

'Don't you want to stop and talk?'

'If I wanted to stop and talk, I'd have called you, wouldn't I?' Tess stares you in the eye. 'Look, I gotta . . .'

'You came out of the Department building,' you say, desperate not to let the conversation falter. If you can just keep her talking . . .

'You've been asked to volunteer for The Project, haven't you?' you say.

Tess doesn't say anything, but looks at her feet for a second.

'You *have*! Me too!'

'So what?'

'*So what!* Are you going to do it?'

'I've already done it. We're getting beamed out next . . .'

257

We?

'What's his name?' you splutter. 'Who is he?' And then you realize what she means.

'Boy or girl?' you ask. Slowly.

'Girl.' Tess now looks at you defiantly. 'And yes: it's yours.'

'Mine?'

'Who else's? It wasn't me that was screwing around.'

Your head's spinning. 'How long? How long have you been pregnant?'

'Two months. I knew the day I found out about you and that slut. I knew the day before in fact and was going to tell you. And then I found out about . . .'

She lets her voice drop.

'But now you're pregnant,' you say, your stomach quaking, your hands trembling. 'Surely we can . . .'

'I'm going now,' she interrupts.

'You can't,' you sob. 'Surely I've got . . .'

'You've got *nothing*, Ray. Nothing.'

'But . . .'

'The Department has taken our genetic reading, mine and the baby's. Once they've called me to confirm that we've been beamed out, I'm terminating . . .'

'You *can't!*' You grab hold of her shoulder but she swats your hand away, tells you that you relinquished your responsibilities *way back.* You're about to grab her shoulder again, looking to do anything to get her to stop for a second and make her talk to you when you're suddenly aware of a presence looming up behind you.

Stand back . . .

The growl of a Trooper's amplified voice.

Stand back . . .

You turn to face the Trooper, hands raised in innocence, and your eyes take in several things all at once: the visor, the studded gloves, the steelplex kneepads, the gigantic speeder parked up behind him and the massive weapon dangling from his belt. But you also keep half an eye on Tess, afraid she'll disappear into the crowds while you explain yourself.

Are you okay, ma'am . . . ?

Tess nods. 'It's fine, officer. We're just old friends who've fallen out.'

There's a pause while the Trooper checks that the situation is what he thinks it is and you think you can see his eyes move on the other side of his visor, a throb of tension moving along gunmetal points of his knuckles.

I suggest that you move along home, ma'am . . .

Suddenly she's gone. She's gone. Then the Trooper's helmet turns to face you again and you wonder if he'll haul you in just for the sake of it, haul you in and throw you in the tank just to scare the shit out of you . . .

Citizen, you . . .

Suddenly an alarm sounds off somewhere. For a moment you wonder what else you've done wrong. And then you realize that the sound you're hearing is the sound of the Monsoon Sirens starting up all around you. The Trooper's helmet appears to freeze for a second, dipping slightly towards one shoulder as he seems to be receiving a message on his radio . . .

You'd best hurry to your vehicle or nearest public transportation facility . . .

You nod, daring to glance over your shoulder for only a second at the direction that Tess ran off in with your child inside of her. Everywhere around you, people are running for cover, bright spots of color scattering in different directions. Already the sky is starting to pulse, as if the clouds are flexing

259

their muscles. And when you finally duck your head down to get into your cab, you feel the first globs of sticky rain hitting the back of your neck.

Then you're in your cab, pounding your fist against the dash, pounding away until your hands ache. You hit yourself (who else is there?) on the chest, on the head, and you slam a fist against the frame of the door again and again until you draw blood. And then you just sit there crying, the rain hammering down on to the roof of the cab, an endless roaring drum-roll, thunder thrashing through the sky above you. Should you drive home? What would you do then? And what would you do tomorrow? Or the day after? For a moment you think about calling Jeff – but what could he say to you that would make any difference?

Now you boot up the engine and tear the cab through the streets. Before long, you're out on the Eight-Eighty-Eight, nosing the hood through the flaming mist of red tail-lights and scorching headlamps, the flicker of the passing lane-beacons strobing over your face. The rain rolls off the windshield, the wipers toiling their way through the thick sludge of dirt and oil and burnt gas thrown up by the passing juggernauts plunging west and out of the city. Soon you've left civilization behind. Maybe you can make one of the cities lying out there in the gloom in twenty hours – maybe you'll just keep driving. Outside, you get faint glimpses of the toxic earth, blasted rock formations, a cursed landscape under a bruised sky, your eyes focused on the glittering backwash in front of you. All you can imagine is the three of you – Tess, yourself, and the child – strolling through a sun-drenched valley humming with life, the kind of valley you've only read about in history books and fairy tales.

Sunlight. Sweet-tasting air. Running streams.

Space.

For a moment, you see the three of you all together, holding hands as you pick your way over the lush ground. And though you know that there's no reason to believe that the three of you will live together far away on the other side of the galaxy, you can't help but think that you might.

THE TRAIL

What ravishes me is an outline of a body . . .

Roland Barthes, *Fragments of a Lover's Discourse*

This is how it happened. I still don't know if it makes sense yet, but this is how it happened.

Last Tuesday, I sold another painting, a twenty-by-eighty *interpretation* of Wile E. Coyote from the *Roadrunner* cartoons as a Broken Wino. It was my third sale in as many months.

'If it keeps on like this, it's going to be a good year for me,' I thought, as Henrietta (my agent) dropped off the cheque and drove away in her blue Saab. And that night I duly went out with the Boys to celebrate. We started off drinking Caipiriñhas in The Back Bar on Dean Street before moving on to The Chase on Wardour Street for dinner where we drank a couple of bottles of wine each and flirted furiously with the waitresses. After that, we all went back to Jake's place in Bloomsbury where we continued to get drunk and at some point I crashed out in the spare room only to find myself awake again just before six the next morning with a rabid headache and a bladder like a timebomb. Why does indulging in the merest drop of alcohol over my ten-unit limit mean that I *always* wake up preposterously early? Jake can drink for a solid eight hours and sleep like a baby till five the next day while I'm doomed to waking up spaced and drained not too long after the birds have started their infernal singing outside.

I got up, had a piss and then drank as much water as I could while writing a short note for Jake. Then I stepped out into the pearly dawn light and took my first deep breaths of the day. 'Breakfast,' I thought. 'Now there's an idea!' *If I can just fill my stomach and get home to Shepherd's Bush . . . maybe I could have a snooze* . . . I sauntered down towards Soho, down Tottenham Court Road and Charing Cross Road before taking a right along Old Compton Street and ending up at a little Italian café I know on Winnett Street where they serve up the best panini west of Genoa. A cappuccino and some Parma ham and rocket on toasted ciabatta did a lot to help me feel human again. After that, I drank another cappuccino while I read for three-quarters of an hour (I've been re-reading *Children and Television* by Robert Hodge and David Tripp) and then settled the bill before walking up to Oxford Circus. 'Thank God it hasn't got too busy,' I thought, as I entered the tube station, bought a ticket and stepped on to the escalator going down to the Central Line platforms. I always feel cheated when I'm on the underground during the rush hour. After all, isn't that one of the reasons why I do what I do: to *never* be in the underground during the rush hour?

It was then that I saw her.

She was standing on the 'up' escalator on the other side of the metal divide. And she was *beautiful*: tawny corkscrews of hair spiralling out of her head in random directions, each one like a delicately twisted filament; eyes like two swirls of dark cocoa. I couldn't take my eyes off her and I thought she would notice me staring at her as the escalators drew us level. But she didn't (she was engrossed in a book that I couldn't see the title of). And then we glided past each other and I suddenly wondered if I could sprint down the rest of the way and race back up the other side and try to talk to her. *Surely I was destined to talk to her?* I had one of those feelings I sometimes get when I see a beautiful or intriguing stranger: the feeling that if I don't somehow talk to them right then and right there, then my life has lost something for ever.

I didn't go up to her of course. How could I? I was in London. Once, when I spent an Australian summer in

Perth, I couldn't believe how friendly everyone was. Starting a conversation with *anyone*, male or female, was as easy as saying 'G'day' and 'How're you doing?' But in good ol' tight-lipped London? She'd think I was hassling her, another sleazy bloke with dark intentions.

And in any case, I'm useless at random encounters and can never make the first move. I never know what to say and everything sounds like a terrible chat-up line. If I can get into conversation with a woman by way of some other agent or by some unexpected *force majeure*, by way of introduction through a mutual friend, for instance, or by sitting next to someone at a dinner party or by having to share a taxi or if the woman herself deigns to make the first move (and of course there was that one time I got trapped in a lift with a Didi from Mornington Crescent that led to ten days of student gigs and snakebite-fuelled sex) . . . well, then I'm okay. I can more than hold my own in terms of conversation, can be intermittently witty and am occasionally even considered highly desirable.

Jill, a platonic girlfriend of mine (she said I was too much like her brother for her ever to be interested in me, but that she could see what other women liked about me) once said that she thought this was true too and put it down to the fact that I was chronically shy but that when I settle into conversation with a woman, I have the ability to make her feel as if she's the 'only woman in the world' while I'm talking to her. Jill said that this aspect of me was – what was it she said? – *powerfully seductive!* Well, maybe that's true. Maybe it isn't. Whatever, I know that when I really fall for a woman, I *really* fall for them regardless of whether I've known them ten minutes, ten days, ten weeks or (on two occasions so far) ten months. I want to know all about them. I don't want them to fit into a conceived notion of what I think a woman should be like (I haven't got one) and I'm a good listener. What can I say? I can't help being interested in what someone thinks or wants or feels.

Anyway, I digress. By the time I'd tossed the ideas back and forth in my mind, I'd reached the bottom of my escalator while the woman with the corkscrew hair had reached the top of hers and disappeared from view. She was gone and it was beyond debate: whether I was good at talking to women or not couldn't change the fact that the chances of seeing her again in a city of ten million people were only a whiff greater than none at all.

•

Then it happened again.

I laid up in bed for the whole of Wednesday, watching the Cartoon Network, *Teletubbies* DVDs and re-runs of *Sesame Street* while I recovered from my hangover. And then I spent each of the following days taking it easy, but nonetheless managing to put in a few hours on my next piece, a ninety-by-ninety painting that *re-presented* the cartoon birds from *Roobarb and Custard* as an Existential Chorus of Judgement. I didn't throw myself at it and was more than happy to splash away with my paints for a few hours as soon as I got up and let the rest of the day dissolve into a twilight of lethargic contemplation. On Sunday, I even let myself take the day off, woke up around ten and watched TV until two before strolling out to a nearby restaurant for some brunch.

It was there that I saw her.

I'd almost gone somewhere else, to either Chez Marcelle, a Lebanese place in Olympia, or to the pub for a roast (when it comes to meat and potatoes, I'm very *meat 'n' potatoes*). But as I walked past one of my favourite cafés, Antonio's on Goldhawk Road, I saw that my favourite table by the window was free.

'Great,' I thought and I walked in. Antonio makes a superb Eggs Florentine and I ordered some and a machiatto and opened up my copy of *Children and Television*, savouring the prospect of at least an hour's unadulterated satisfaction of both mind and stomach. It was then that I heard an agitated female voice at the table opposite mine break the silence.

'Eddie? It's Charlotte . . .'

'A mobile-phone user,' I thought to myself, 'how *nineties*.'

'I'm just ringing to say that I can't make it to the cinema today . . . yes, I know it's last minute, but something's come up, something that I can't put off . . . well I'm *sorry* but I can't . . .'

Her voice stopped suddenly and I guessed that Eddie had hung up on her. Quickly I peered over the edge of my book to see what Charlotte looked like and found myself staring at a woman in her late twenties in grey trousers and a cropped jumper. Once I started staring at her, it became difficult to stop. She had butter-blonde hair and pale milky cheeks, the uppermost curves of which were slightly reddened, a light dusting of inflammation across the skin that spoke of cigarettes and drink and late nights. Her eyes were the colour of frosted zaffer, her lips a naked pink, a cigarette gripped tightly between bitten nails (no wedding ring, I noticed).

She put her mobile-phone back in a leather satchel that rested against the leg of the table and then stared out of the window, smoked, her fingers twirling a silver fountain pen above an open notebook and a half-drunk espresso. Was she a writer? Or a poet? She was just staring out the window, smoking, her eyes looking down occasionally to consider what she'd already written before . . . suddenly Charlotte scribbled something in her notebook, a number and a squiggled bit of writing that I couldn't read. Then she stuffed it into her bag along with her pen and bolted her coffee before getting up and pulling on a blue duffel-coat. '*What was that,*' I wondered, '*inspiration?*' I watched as she flipped some coins on to her table, easily more than enough to cover her bill, and then purposefully strode out of the glass door on to the pavement. I twisted in my seat. Which way was she was heading? She crossed to the far side of the street and then walked up the Goldhawk Road towards the station and before I knew it, I was wiping my mouth, dropping a tenner on the table and walking out after her.

'*Now what the hell are you doing?*' I asked myself. '*You've definitely crossed a line!*' I told myself to turn back, that if I stopped straight away then I could dismiss the whole thing as a stupid moment of self-indulgence and walk away guilt-free. *But there she was!* Twenty metres in front of me and I was still trailing her. Shit! I realised that I'd left my book on the table. I could still go back and get it – *but then Charlotte would be gone . . .*

'Turn back!' I urged myself more gently, trying the Art of Gentle Persuasion. 'Go back and get your book from the restaurant and then go home and have an aspirin or something . . .' *But what if this was love?* I quickly realised that this was ridiculous and that I could only compare what I was doing with the kind of romance one saw in cheesy adverts. But hadn't *everything* about her face seemed immediately familiar to me from the moment I first saw her? Surely that meant something? *It wasn't as if I was doing anything to hurt her . . .* Charlotte now jumped on a 94 bus that pulled up at a stop a few yards ahead of her. Should I jump on? Or should I let it go?

I realised, as I leapt on to the running-board, that if I'd accused myself of 'crossing a line' earlier, then that line was now a point receding quickly into the distance and into the past along with the bus-stop. *But it was all so exciting too!* I'd immediately seen that Charlotte had climbed the stairs to the upper deck of the bus and I quickly slipped myself on to one of the bench seats on the lower deck, pretending to read a discarded newspaper. 'Good thinking,' I told myself. *What kind of ticket did I want?* Think quickly! I bought one that could take me all the way to Oxford Circus and I reasoned that I could wait until I saw Charlotte get off the bus and then just pick up the trail again. More great reasoning! And when she got off the bus, I could harmlessly engineer some randomly harmless moment in which I could engage her in harmless conversation and see what harmlessly developed from there.

Now I wondered about Charlotte's phone call in the café. 'Something had come up that she couldn't put off' – that was what she had said to Eddie before he hung up on her. What had she meant by that? I realised, my heart fluttering, that I couldn't possibly live without finding out. *Okay then*, I said, making a pact with myself, *you find out what it is she's got to do that she can't put off, that means she can't go to the cinema with Eddie (whoever he is!). And then you call it quits. After that, you go home and you never do this again.*

A few more minutes passed, the bus stopping at the bottom of Ladbroke Grove and then once more at the top of the hill. Then it pulled over on Notting Hill Gate and Charlotte came down the stairs from the upper deck and stepped off on to the pavement.

I was ready.

I waited until she'd started walking (I peered round the side of my newspaper and tracked her progress) and then I got up out of my seat and jumped out on to the pavement just as the bus started to pull away, giving myself a twenty-yard gap as she walked away towards the corner of Pembridge Road where she turned left. A few yards further on, she paused by the zebra crossing and I hung back and watched as she walked into the Italian restaurant on the other side of the mini-roundabout. Where could I go? I looked around and saw a cappuccino bar across the road.

And I laughed because a minute later we seemed to be moving in parallel. Charlotte took off her duffel-coat and hung it over the back of her chair. I took off my jacket and hung it over the back of mine. She ordered a latté. So did I. Then Charlotte took out her notebook and pen, lit a cigarette and started staring out of the window again. *What was she thinking?* 'She must be a writer,' I thought to myself as I poured sugar into my coffee and stirred it. 'Was her writing the thing that she hadn't been able to put off?' If so, I liked it. I was the same. As an artist, one sometimes has to sacrifice relationships in the real world to allow the space and time for one's inner world to flourish. Some people didn't understand that. But I did.

Now I focused on the expression of her face. Her eyes seemed strangely still, as if she was actually picturing something internally, as if she was always concentrating, and this fascinated me. It was almost as if I could track the rhythm of her thoughts by watching each twitch of her eyelids and nose, each itch she scratched, the way her breathing rose and fell.

She sat there for an hour and I never took my eyes off her.

Then she got up (she'd done little more than sit there gazing at the street before writing down a couple of lines of her poem or story into her notebook) and walked back to the main road, crossing to the other side and waiting for a bus going back to the Goldhawk Road. I duly followed her and was pleased that two 94s came at once. I got on the second and followed her as far as far as Shepherd's Bush Green where she got off and started walking up the Uxbridge Road before turning down Devonport Road. Where was she going? And what was the thing that she couldn't put off? Had it already happened? I let her get a full forty yards ahead of me and watched as she got her keys out of her bag and let herself into number 27, a typical West London two-up-two-down. *Now what did I do?* It was getting dark, I told myself, I couldn't possibly stand there all night and I'd fulfilled my earlier contract with myself. Or had I?

•

After ten minutes of standing there looking at the house, I suddenly felt foolish. Why the hell was I standing there? My fingers where starting to ache with cold and I badly wanted a coffee and to wrap up in a blanket in front of my TV. So I walked home and cooked Crab Cioppino and drank half a bottle of wine in the living-room before collapsing into bed at around nine-thirty. *Maybe I didn't want to face up to what I'd done earlier in the day ... maybe I was just spending too much time on my own in the studio ...* whatever, I woke up around three the next morning and then lay there in a daze, I seemed to alternate between praying for sleep to arrive again and dreaming that I was awake and restless. Neither satisfied. My bed felt large and cold and when the birds started singing in the street outside and the room was swimming with damp half-light, I knew (as I often do) that my chances of drifting back into a deep, nourishing slumber were getting slimmer with every second. Also, I couldn't get Charlotte out of my mind. Was the house I'd seen her walk into hers (she'd had keys and she'd let herself in with an identifiable familiarity)? It could have been Eddie's, or a place she shared with another lover. Maybe she was having an affair with Eddie? Maybe they were just friends.

Eventually I climbed out of bed, showered, dressed and then sat in my kitchen with a short and incredibly sharp ristretto. The clock on the wall told me it was six o'clock and I pictured the house I'd seen Charlotte disappear into the night before. And then I grabbed my keys and another copy of *Children and Television* from off the shelf where I kept them and walked out to the car. Again, I reasoned that I couldn't exactly stand in the freezing cold waiting indefinitely to see if Charlotte reappeared, and instead drove over to Devonport Road in my black GTi and parked a little way down the street. 'Would she even be there?' I wondered as I sat staring out through the windscreen. She might have left later on last night (it was perfectly possible, perfectly reasonable) though it was unlikely, if she'd spent the night there, that she would have left before half-past six on a Monday morning . . . a light went on in an upstairs window. Then a figure appeared. A silhouette of a woman against the thin gauzy curtain. *It was her!* Or was it? I watched the house, a sweat building on my palms as my excitement gained momentum. After twenty minutes the light in the upstairs window was turned off but another appeared moments later downstairs. *Then the curtains were suddenly pulled back and I saw Charlotte standing there for a few seconds before turning away!* My heart pumped. I sat in the car gulping down my nervousness for ten minutes, picking at the dead skin around my fingernails. Then her front door swung open and she walked through it, turning to lock it before walking out on to the pavement. Where would she go? I watched her walk up the street towards me and was suddenly afraid that she'd spot me and recognise me from the day before. But she was too engrossed in getting her car keys out from her bag and I watched as she unlocked the door to a white Volkswagen Beetle. So she was driving somewhere . . . *where?* I started my engine and let it tick over while she pulled out into the street and then I followed her out on to the Uxbridge Road.

Again it seemed thrilling to be following her and I even laughed as I pursued her round Shepherd's Bush roundabout and up Holland Park Avenue. *It was so easy!* I must have seen a million films where one character tails another, a million cops and private eyes and spies following their quarry through traffic. But now *I* was doing it and it seemed that it was only as difficult as taking the decision to do it in the first place.

The lights on Holland Park Avenue were green all the way and I let two cars cut in between my Golf and her Beetle so that she wouldn't see me. Was she going to Notting Hill Gate again? Or was she doing nothing more sinister than simply going to work? This was more likely . . . *but I had to find out.* I didn't have to wait long. On Notting Hill Gate, she turned left down Pembridge Road and then parked her car on Kensington Park Road, ten yards away from the restaurant she'd sat in the afternoon before, and I pulled over a little way ahead before twisting in my seat to see what she was doing.

She wasn't doing anything. From where I was, I couldn't see if she had her notebook open, but she was staring through the window of her car with the same fixed expression that she had yesterday. 'What a dreamer!' I told myself, but also wondered more than ever before what it was she was up to. She certainly didn't seem to be going to work, though I realised that she could be waiting to give someone a lift. A colleague? A lover? Children? I watched her for almost an hour but learned nothing more. Charlotte just sat there, as she had done the day before, until almost eight o'clock when she switched on her engine and pulled back out into the road. I did the same and soon we were back on Holland Park Avenue but this time heading back down the hill. Was she going back to Shepherd's Bush? As it turned out, she did drive back that way, but then continued on down the Goldhawk Road to Chiswick where she seemed to be heading for the motorway. Suddenly I was faced with having to make a decision. What if she turned on to the motorway? Would I follow her? I trailed her car (we seemed to be in a procession of slow-moving traffic, a white van, a red Fiat Coupé and a grey Morris Minor between me and Charlotte, a red Audi, a 391 bus and a lumbering navy-blue Peugeot estate up ahead that drove impossibly slowly and seemed to be holding us all up), all the while not sure how far I was prepared to go. When she reached the Chiswick roundabout, I was sure that she was going to sail round it and up on to the on-ramp of the M4. But she took a left instead and drove over Kew Bridge before making a right and pulling over beside Kew Green and turning off her engine.

'Okay,' I thought to myself as I waited twenty yards away. 'What happens now?' All she seemed to be doing was staring out of the window again and suddenly I was starting to feel ridiculous. What was Charlotte up to? Was I wasting my time? It was then that I saw the most intriguing thing: instead of simply chain-smoking while she stared out of her window, I saw Charlotte burrow into her bag and take something out. A Walkman? A Dictaphone? She raised the object, whatever it was, to her face and it took a few moments for me to realise that she looking through a pair of mini-binoculars.

Curiouser and curiouser.

I strained my eyes to see what she was looking at and saw that she had the binoculars trained on something on the other side of Kew Green. I squinted across the grass too and saw a row of large expensive houses on the other side, a row of cars parked in front of them. Charlotte seemed to be scanning them and I looked again. What was so extraordinary about them? A blue Range Rover, a silver Mercedes, a black BMW, a red Audi . . . *a red Audi!* The same colour and model as the one that had drifted through the traffic in front of her earlier on. I sat back in my chair with astonishment: *was she following someone?* I couldn't believe it for a moment and searched for the rational explanation. She could be checking up on a potentially adulterous husband or lover. She could have just broken up with someone, was emotionally devastated and couldn't help but follow them for a while – that would certainly explain the contemplative expression that she seemed habitually to wear. Maybe she was a private eye? They existed . . . I didn't have time to think about this any further because she suddenly turned on her engine and drove away around the green. Quickly, and with only the shortest glance at the red Audi on the other side of the grass (yes . . . it *was* pulling away!), I turned the key in the ignition and followed.

The red Audi now headed back towards Central London through Chiswick, but couldn't get too far ahead of Charlotte and me because the traffic had slowed to a crawl at the roundabout and on the High Road. I guessed that the driver of the red Audi was driving to work, whoever *he* was, and it suddenly occurred to me that it was possible that *he* was Eddie, that Charlotte might have rung him up to say that she couldn't meet him and then followed him to see what he did when she wasn't around. Perhaps Eddie was her boyfriend and she had grown suspicious that he had a lover? As we all drove along King Street and through Hammersmith, I imagined the conversation Charlotte and I would have in bed after first sleeping with each other. She'd tell me, in a moment of intimate vulnerability, that she'd discovered that her ex had been two-timing her and

I'd wrap a reassuring arm around her even though I'd been watching from the sidelines all along (and of course I would have to engineer that 'harmless' meeting with her in the first place, perhaps ten days after she broke with Eddie so that I could swoop in and start applying some Tender Loving Care just as her anger started to turn to longing).

Soon we were on High Street Kensington, driving past the cinema and the Commonwealth Centre, past the shops and cafés, before Eddie's red Audi (I was sure it was him no matter how many times I reminded myself that it was only a *possibility*) signalled left and pulled over which meant that Charlotte pulled over and I pulled over. Charlotte again brought her binoculars up to her face and tracked Eddie as he dodged through the traffic and walked into a camera shop on the other side of the street. Was this where Eddie worked? No, it didn't seem to be. As I watched through the glass, Eddie browsed for a while (he looked like an arrogant little shit if the truth be told: one of those over-fed lawyer types in a brown suede blouson jacket and not the sort of man that Charlotte deserved at all) and then he talked to an assistant when she became free. This assistant then went into a backroom for a minute before coming out with a small black case which she gave to Eddie who then ran back across the road and got back in his car. *Where are we going now?* I muttered as he slotted himself in behind a black cab. I hadn't a clue, I realised. Was that why I was on this ridiculous adventure: because every second meant I was heading further into the great unknown?

Eddie continued along Kensington Gore, past the Albert Hall and on towards Knightsbridge before parking his car by the army barracks, getting out and disappearing up a narrow alleyway with an attaché case and the box from the camera shop. Charlotte followed him. I followed her. And as we all crossed the road and proceeded into Hyde Park, I couldn't help but worry. I was out of the car now and the park was still fairly empty. If Charlotte hadn't noticed me in her rearview mirror already, then all she had to do was turn around . . . I dropped back until I was almost fifty yards behind her, Eddie the same distance in front of her. Where was he going?

There was nothing more I could do but tag along. Up above us, the sky had brightened considerably and it was strange to be in the open air after having spent so much time indoors recently or stuck in the car. People passed by, joggers and dog-walkers, nannies with children, the odd park-keeper with his wheelie-bin and spade. Up ahead Eddie walked as far as the Serpentine and then turned right and walked round the edge before coming to a standstill. Trailing behind him, with her satchel slung over her shoulder, Charlotte quickly walked into the tea-room fifty yards away, all the time watching Eddie as he put down his attaché case and opened it up. Best keep my distance, I thought and sat down on a park bench on the far side of the water. Damn! I was too far away to see what was going on properly. I saw a telescope at the water's edge a couple of yards away from me – did I have ten pence? I scrabbled around in my pocket as I walked over to it and fished out the only coin I had in my pocket: a fifty-pence piece. But then I found that I needed a twenty-pence coin anyway and couldn't believe it: *when had these things started costing twenty pence?* It was daylight robbery. I looked around me – surely there was someone who might have some change? I saw two tourists and rushed over to them.

'Hi there? Do you have change for fifty pence? I need it for the telescope.'

'Excuse me?' They were German, I thought, or maybe Dutch, and I brandished my coin at them.

'Change? *Cambio? Weschel?*' I jabbered but they already seemed to understand me, the husband unzipping his belt-bag and pulling out two twenty-pence pieces and a ten-pence piece.

'Thanks. *Bedankt. Merci. Danke.*'

I ran back to the telescope and jammed in a coin. It took a little time to get a handle on how to focus the damned thing and I used up the first of the twenty-pence pieces working it out. Then I slotted in my second coin. *Okay*, I murmured, the ticking of the meter loud in my ears, *let's see what's going on.* For a second I was worried that neither of them would still be where they were earlier, but then I managed to fix the lens on the tea-room and zoomed in on Charlotte sitting there with a cup of coffee and the binoculars and her notebook. No change there then. What was Eddie doing? I swivelled the telescope. Eddie had unpacked a camera and attached a long zoom lens and was peering across the water. What was he looking at? Was he a photographer, taking shots of the park, the wandering ducks and the reflections of the sky and trees? I panned back to Charlotte – she was still sitting there – and then back to Eddie, the telescope still ticking in my ear. Eddie had his face jammed against his camera (he'd unpacked a small tripod and was crouched down on the ground on one knee) and ... I looked more closely. He couldn't be taking pictures of the ducks, not at that angle: *the lens was aimed too high.* Slowly, I carefully tried to follow his line of vision and panned along the waterline: nothing ... nothing ... nothing. Just trees and grass and railings and litter bins and a few stupid pigeons. I carried on turning the telescope, not moving it too fast so that the image didn't blur ... *suddenly there was a flash of colour, red and blue.* I looked up and across the water: there was someone standing about two hundred yards along the bank from Eddie, a woman with short dark hair in a long red coat and jeans. I dipped my head back to the eyepiece and scanned the space between them. *Yes!* Eddie was definitely looking at her, a woman, maybe thirty, and she had her back to both him and me, was staring at something in the distance on the grass over towards Bayswater . . . with a pair of binoculars.

The ticking stopped. Everything went black. I took my face away from the eyepiece and looked over my shoulder.

ENDGAME

Are you still harking back to where you came from or where you are? Well you can't have two homes.

Lord Tebbit

It's almost six o'clock on a broiling Wednesday evening.

'Dad! Dad!' the kids shout, already over-excited about the semi-final. Rajiv has his Alan Shearer shirt on, the one Mary and I got him for his last birthday, Pravin's wearing his Arsenal pyjamas, and they both run out of the lounge as soon as they hear me coming down the stairs and heading towards the front door for work.

'Dad! Dad! What lucky t-shirt are you wearing?' they ask.

'This one.'

I open my jacket, unbutton my work shirt and show them. 'OUR HEROES' it says, with a picture of the entire Italia '90 squad underneath: Waddle, Lineker, Gazza, Terry Butcher, Shilts, Paul Parker . . . the whole lot. *The Sun* sold them mail order after the last time England got to a semi-final and me and Pete got one each to remind us what a good time we'd had in Turin that summer.

'Dad?' Pravin tugs at the sleeve of my jacket.

'What is it?'

'Please stay and watch the football.'

Now Mary comes out of the kitchen, tells the boys to calm down for the hundredth time, and then turns to me, pushing a strand of hair from my forehead.

'Deepak,' she says, 'why don't you skip work and watch the game with them?'

I touch her hand, kiss her fingers and tell her that I'll take a night off at the weekend to watch England win the final.

I almost change my mind as I shut the front door behind me and walk down the path to the car. Part of me still can't believe that I'm going to miss the game! And do we really need the money? Two shifts into the week and I've already made as much as I'd expect to get in any normal week in June or July. *But you can't turn down work when there's money to be made!* Most summers, you can expect to sit on your arse in the control room for a couple of months, twiddling your thumbs and choking on everyone else's cigarette smoke while they win and lose a fortune at cards. The phones are dead. The radio's dead. All the punters are on holiday and in terms of work it might as well be January. But this year's been different, what with all the tourists in town for the Championships and everyone drunk every night and in high spirits. Talk about making hay while the sun shines.

I climb into the car, shut the door and turn on the radio. Lesley's on the box and there's the immediate commotion of jobs being dispatched and cleared, her voice cutting through the static and hiss.

'Alpha two-nine, two-nine . . . are you still P-O-B? If not then I've got a pickup for you at 14 Shandon Road, no buzzer, going to Albert Bridge Road. If you're quick, I've got you a pickup at Petworth Street straight after for quarter-past going up to the West End. It's a phone-out so call me when you get there, over. Alpha four-five? Aren't you clear yet? Get a fuckin' move on, darl'.'

I pull out on to Trinity Road and call in. 'Evening Lesley, One-One out and about.'

'Evenin' One-One. Didn't expect you to be out tonight, thought you'd be watching the match.'

'I'm a martyr to the cause, Lesley, a martyr to the cause. Busy tonight?'

'You know it, darl', mad rush, everyone trying to get home for the football. Where are you?'

I tell her and she gives me a pickup down Chestnut Grove on the other side of the Common.

'It's going up to Chelsea,' she says, 'and I've got a lot of work on the other side of the river so be as quick as you can.'

•

Why *Boston Cars?* Why, for that matter, *Olympic Cabs*, *Herald Radio Cars* or *Pegasus?* Pegasus won't send you a flying horse and our control room on Nine Elms Lane is a million miles from New England. Lesley tells me that Donnie, our guv'nor, has got this thing about the sitcom *Cheers!* But who really knows? One thing I'll say for *Boston Cars* though: of all the firms I've been with round here (and I've been at a few, bucket-shops like *Oasis Cabs* on Stockwell Road where my Carina has been the best car on the fleet, real fly-by-nighters like *Cavalier Cars* and *Privilege* over on Kennington Butts) they're probably one of the most professional. Reasonable circuit-fee, fair controllers like Lesley and Nadi who can't be 'fed' (too stoned to be dishonest if the truth be told), good account clients and no pickups from 'Pubs 'n' Estates' which means we get less than our fair share of runners, nutters and psychopaths. It may not be much but it's a lot better than some, if you know what I mean.

The Balham job's a group of northern lads going up to the Trafalgar Arms on the Kings Road to watch the match on the big screen there, the four of them already stinking of beer as they climb in and one of them asks if he can smoke almost immediately. I catch his eye in the mirror, say that I'd rather he didn't and expect an argument. But he's surprisingly polite about it (it's amazing how many get nasty about this more than anything else, especially after a few drinks) and he slides the cigarette back into its packet before all of them start on about Stuart Pearce's penalty against the Spanish the weekend before. It takes half an hour to get across the river and into Chelsea because of the traffic, and as I push the cab through the choked streets, I can see that all the black cabs and buses are full and that almost every pub is overflowing.

After them, I do another job coming back down the other way, taking a couple in their mid-twenties from a Fulham address down to Clapham Common South Side. She's smartly dressed, well spoken and with a confident rhythm to her voice (a Chelsea girl with a City job?) while he's scruffier, wearing jeans and a crumpled shirt and carrying a bottle of wine and a four-pack in a plastic bag. 'Are you okay?' the girl asks once he's opened the door for her and slammed it before getting in the other side.

'I can't believe Serena's going ahead with her dinner. I mean *tonight* of all nights!'

'It's her birthday.'

'Yeah? England are in the sodding semi-final of the European Championship . . . against the Germans. Do you even know what that *means?*'

'I'm sure they'll have a television there,' she replies as I make a left turn out on to the Chelsea Embankment. 'And I'm sure you won't be the only person coming tonight who'll want to watch it.' The boy grunts and looks out of the window.

•

The old cabbie cliché of having 'seen it all before' must almost be entirely true and especially for those of us driving the night shift. Maybe after five years I shouldn't be amazed at some of the conversations I overhear, the arguments to which I'm a silent witness, the backseat showdowns observed through the vibrating frame of my rearview mirror. For *them* it's dead time, a necessary interval between events spent in yet another anonymous car, the space between the important stuff, between work and home, between the party and bed (alone or otherwise), between locking the house up and catching the plane. No wonder people let things slip.

I know some drivers try and get into conversation with all their fares, say it helps the time go quicker, makes things more interesting. But I guess I'm more private, a speak-if-you're-spoken-to kind of guy. Perhaps this explains why people act as if I'm not there, why I see even more than my fair share. Sometimes I feel like a ghost, a transparent spectator, the ignored onlooker who gets a front-row seat for a million 'private' moments.

•

Lesley then sends me on a couple of local jobs, a group of girls going across Battersea and a pickup on Cringle Street who wants to get to Clapham Junction. By now the streets are like I've never seen. They're full, sure, more than they usually are at this time in the evening if the truth be told. But there's an extra urgency in the way the cars move off at the lights as the amber comes on below the red, an efficient, unfamiliar briskness as drivers let other drivers join the stream of traffic and concede right of way. There's a courteousness that you never expect to see on London's streets. Suddenly everyone has a similar purpose. For once everyone's moving in the same direction, as if everyone understands that everyone else has to be somewhere, *anywhere*, as long as they're in front of a television screen within the next half an hour.

Twenty minutes later, I clear another 'local' on Prince of Wales Drive. The two guys are in such a hurry to get inside before the start of the match that they give me a fiver and tell me to keep the change. And then everything goes quiet. The roads are suddenly empty except for the lone red bus rumbling down Latchmere Road, the odd solitary figure walking a dog, beams of sunlight blinking through the trees in Battersea Park.

I pick up the radio, my mind thinking of Wembley, the players coming out of the tunnel and minutes away from kick-off.

'Lesley? One-One here – I've just cleared on Prince of Wales.'

'Thanks for the call, One-One. It's all gone dead for now – the game's about to start – but you're fourth on the plot so I'll let you know when a job comes up.'

I'm only a few blocks away from base so I decide to drive round the corner, park the Carina and walk up to the control room anyway. At least I can watch a bit of the game there while I wait. Inside, Leslie and Nadi are sitting watching the small television along with five of the other drivers.

'Alright there, Gus?' nods Preyesh. At work they've called me Gus ever since Lesley had a batch of pirate copies of Disney's *Cinderella* and someone thought I looked like one of the cartoon mice that trail around after her.

'Hi Preyesh.'

I say hello to the others, to Kojo and Clement, to Ben and to Hassan, and they all stop arguing for a moment to shake hands.

'Thought you'd be inside watching the game,' says Kojo.

I shrug my shoulders.

'No way are England going to win tonight,' says Clement, sipping from a mug of steaming red tea and dragging on a cigarette. 'Germany never lose. That Sammer in the defence – he *good*.'

The control room has been a hotbed of football debate for weeks, with Kojo and Clement usually at the heart of it. Of course, being Nigerian, they can't keep their opinions to themselves, and it was exactly the same during the World Cup two years ago, except that the drivers had the opportunity to support Cameroon, Nigeria, Saudi Arabia or Morocco back then

290

if they wanted. Now that's it's the European Championships, there's little else for them to do except argue.

'Anderton and McManaman are too weak,' adds Kojo. 'They are like little boys. You watch the Germans *crush* them.'

We're interrupted by the sight of the teams lining up. What team's Venables playing? Ince in, both Nevilles out. Three at the back with McManaman and Anderton playing as wing-backs. If Kojo's right, then it could all go horribly wrong. But if we're good enough? If we play like we did against the Dutch or that second half against Scotland? I'm almost too nervous to sit down, and part of me desperately wishes I was at home. *What happens if we lose?*

There are national anthems, the Wembley crowd predictably booing the Germans' and Barry Davies predictably remarking that it only serves to strengthen their resolve. And then the Germans get things started and suddenly our defence win the ball. Within a couple of minutes, England are surging forward, McManaman taking possession and probing down the left wing. Two German defenders jockey him towards the corner flag, forcing him to roll the ball back to Stuart Pearce who knocks in a deep looping cross only for it to get headed clear. But then the ball flies towards Paul Ince who deadens its trajectory with his chest before smashing it back towards the goal. Suddenly I'm on my feet. The ball's dipping in towards the German crossbar, travelling at high speed, and Köpke is forced to punch it over the bar for a corner.

'I don't believe it!' I shout, unable to stop myself. 'That was close.'

Clement remarks that Ince is a 'big strong black man' while Kojo suggests that it was a lucky strike, but then they're silenced as Gascoigne delivers a bending corner kick, Tony

Adams flicking it on at the near post into the path of Shearer who heads it through the flailing defenders . . .

GOAL!

I can't believe it. *We're one up within three minutes!* As Shearer peels away from the goal-line, right hand raised above his head in his trademark celebration, I think back to that balmy night in Turin. Andreas Brehme scored on the hour and the twenty minutes that England chased the game until Lineker equalised was the longest twenty minutes that I can think of, all of us in the terraces that night tearing our hair out under the watchful eye of the *carabinieri*.

But now? *Now it's the Germans' turn to chase the game!* Kojo says that the Germans will score straight away but for ten minutes he's proved wrong. England still dominate, Shearer leading the line, Gascoigne making a series of crunching tackles and managing to carry the ball through the Germans' reeling midfield on a couple of occasions.

'We're doing it,' I mutter. 'We're doing it!'

And then the Germans seem to change gear. Suddenly Reuter's carrying the ball infield, laying off a pass to his left. It's Helmer that receives it and he crosses as the rest of the German midfield swarms into the penalty box, Kuntz beating the offside trap and slotting the ball home.

'He fuckin' *walked* past Pearce,' says Preyesh.

'I told you so,' says Kojo, lighting another cigarette.

'That's typical,' I murmur. I can't believe it. For a moment, it looked as if England could consolidate their lead, as if they believed that the final was their destiny, that they refused to believe in the myth of the Germans' renowned efficiency. And then suddenly the Germans seemed to redress the balance by merely *willing* it.

Ten minutes later the Germans are still managing to dominate, their midfield finding a better shape than before and Sammer making more and more powerful runs into England territory, when the phone rings. Lesley picks up, takes down the details and then turns to Preyesh who's sharing a joint with Nadi.

'Preyesh, you're first up, mate. I've got Derek Langton on the phone and he wants to get to Borough High Street on account.'

Preyesh shakes his head. So do Kojo and Clement who're second and third on the plot, saying that they don't want to do any account work.

'Takes too long to get paid,' mutters Clement.

'What about you?' Leslie asks me. I stare at the screen as Shearer manages to get a shot in, the first England chance for maybe ten minutes, but then tell her that I'll do it.

•

Outside, the roads are still empty. I turn on the radio and hear the sound of the crowd chanting in the background.

Come on England. Come on England.

The commentators agree that England have now recovered from the equaliser and are starting to match the Germans again. Then one of the commentators' voices suddenly rises in pitch. It's an England corner, Anderton swinging the ball to Sheringham in a classic Spurs manoeuvre and Sheringham smacking the ball first time at the near post only to see it deflected by a defender's shin at the last moment. And then I'm outside Derek Langton's house on Edna Street. I ask Leslie to call him and after a minute he appears. He dips his head when he sees me and then climbs into the passenger seat.

'How are you, Deepak?'

'I'm good, thanks.'

'Anything happened in the last minute?'

Derek Langton knows I'm into football because he's a

293

Manchester United supporter, a real one (he's from up there originally), a season-ticket holder who travels up from London every Saturday when they're at Old Trafford. Once, when he'd missed his train, he called up and booked a car to take him the whole way to Manchester and I ended up taking the job for two hundred quid. United were home to West Ham that afternoon and a stag-night had meant that he'd slept through his alarm. Still, he couldn't face missing the game and we left his house at five-to-twelve, talking about football the whole way and pulling up outside Old Trafford a couple of minutes before kick-off.

'An England corner,' I tell him. 'Sheringham forced a save. Now it sounds pretty even again.'

'I couldn't believe it when we scored.'

'I couldn't believe it when they equalised.'

As we pull away, Derek tells me he didn't expect to see me working tonight. I tell him that there's too much work but that I've managed to watch most of the first half in the control room and that there's always the radio.

'What about you?' I ask.

'Would you believe that the alarms have gone off at work and I'm the fall guy who has to go and investigate?'

Now we're flying along the south bank of the river, along Nine Elms Lane and the Albert Embankment before cutting across along Lambeth Road towards Borough Road and Borough High Street. And all the time, we're listening to the radio, both teams now locked in a fierce stalemate. Finally we arrive at the car-park behind his offices just as the half-time whistle sounds.

'Can you do a wait-and-return?' Derek asks. 'I'll let you know if I'm going to be more than a couple of minutes.'

'Take as long as you like.'

He walks off and disappears for ten minutes and I sit there

listening to the half-time analysis. None of the commentators want to predict the result, though both are impressed by McManaman and Anderton. It's been frenetic they say, both teams playing at a breakneck pace. Is Gascoigne a liability, costing the team as much as he can give to it? Will the Germans continue to sit so deep? There are adverts and more discussion. And then Derek appears on the other side of the passenger window.

'Have you sorted it?' I ask him and he tells me that the engineers have arrived and reset the system.

'Let's get back to Battersea and not miss any more of this game than we have to,' he says climbing into the front seat. On the way back, we listen to more discussion. And soon we're back at Edna Street and I hand Derek the docket to sign only for him to pull out his wallet.

'Seeing as its you, Deepak, I'll do it for cash. I can claim it back out of petty cash tomorrow.'

'That's real good of you,' I say.

'No problem.' He pauses for a second. 'So, do you think we'll win tonight?'

I tell him that it's a bit too close to call right now and he tells me glumly that he agrees.

'After the last time I'm not taking anything for granted,' I say. 'You get so excited . . . and then you lose. It breaks my heart.'

'I know what you mean. Sometimes it's hard to imagine us winning,' he says, dipping a hand into his pocket for his front-door keys. 'Sometimes England are brilliant and sometimes they play as if they're the worst team on the planet. It's as if they don't know who they are, as if they don't know what kind of football they should be playing and all they're left with is passion and luck.'

'Well, let's hope passion and luck are enough and that we all go to bed happy,' I say and we shake hands before he gets out of the car and walks up to his front door.

●

I walk back into the control room to find Kojo, Clement, Hassan and Preyesh still sitting there.

'Paul Ince just had another long-range shot,' Hassan tells me.

'Yeah – I heard, on the radio.'

I sit down on the spare chair and focus on the screen. England have the ball and seem to have camped themselves on the edge of the German penalty box.

'It's been like this since half-time,' Preyesh tells me. 'Every time they get the ball either Adams or Ince wins it back. Other than that, we're outplaying them again.'

He's right. England have pinned most of the German players back behind the ball, Anderton and McManaman firing in crosses from the flanks or else making diagonal runs into the penalty box and forcing a string of tackles and clearances. On the hour, Gascoigne receives the ball on the edge of the box and teases it through the legs of three defenders before cutting it back from the byline only to see Dieter Eilts head it away from the waiting England strikers.

At that point Kojo and Clement put down their mugs and tell Lesley they're going home. Soon after, the phone rings and Nadi takes down the details.

'Alright guys, I've got a cash job going from outside the business village in Warriner Gardens out to Swanley in Kent. Preyesh?'

Preyesh looks up from the screen, taking his lips away from another joint.

'What?'

'I've quoted him thirty quid for a twenty-mile run.'

'If he doesn't want it, I'll do it,' I say.

Preyesh tells me to take it, that he can't be bothered right now and he's made enough money earlier in the day. So I get the pickup address from Nadi and walk back out to the car.

•

As I pull up in Warriner Gardens, the sky's turned a deep shade of indigo-blue. I give the horn a short tap and soon a man in his thirties comes walking out to the car.

'*Boston Cars?*' he asks. I nod and he gets in.

'Where are we going?' I ask.

'White Oak Hospital in Swanley. Do you know where that is?' he asks.

'I was going to do the A202 out to Lewisham and take it from there,' I tell him.

'That's great. My wife has just gone into labour, would you believe? Six weeks early!'

'That's amazing.'

'Probably. I just can't believe that it's happened tonight! I mean, *England* are playing.'

I tell him that sometimes one's responsibilities get in the way of football and he tells me that his responsibilities are *always* getting in the way of football. For a minute I think he's joking, but then I realise that he's being totally serious.

'Do you remember the last time we played the Germans, back in 1990?'

'I was there,' I say.

'What! In the *Stadio delle Alpi*?'

I nod. 'It was one of the most exciting nights of my life, right up until the point the Germans knocked us out on penalties anyway. At least I got to see Gazza cry.'

'I watched it in Germany.'

On the radio, the crowd is singing again.

Come on England. Come on England.

'You watched it in Germany!'

As we drive east, and then head south down Camberwell New Road, the man tells me how the company he works for sent him to visit a factory in Leverkusen on the day of the game.

'I used to work for this firm that imports German cooking equipment, not domestic stuff but the stuff that they use in kitchens in hotels and restaurants. Anyway, I was desperate for promotion so there was no way I could get out of it.'

He says that the inspection of the plant was scheduled for the afternoon of the semi-final and he thought he'd never get a chance to watch the match.

'As it turned out, me and the two guys I was sent with found out that they were screening the game in the plant canteen. So we asked the management if we could watch the game with the workers and they said that it was fine. So there we were, three of us and about a hundred Germans sitting in front of this giant television. You've never seen anything like it. By half-time the tension was unbelievable. Neither side had scored.'

I ask him what it was like, being with such a large number of opposition fans.

'It was weird. They sat in a massive group on one side of the canteen while we sat in a nervous huddle on the other. Nothing was said directly – but every time they came close to scoring, they'd all be on their feet, head in hands, some of them clapping.'

'What about when *we* came close?'

'To start off with, we were quite intimidated. I mean, there were a hundred of them. But as the game continued we couldn't stop ourselves getting more and more involved. And then Brehme scored.'

'The free-kick . . .'

298

'Paul Parker charging the kick down . . .'

'I couldn't believe it when the ball deflected off his shin and looped up over Shilton's head . . .'

'You should have seen us in the stadium, five thousand fans silenced . . .'

'You should have seen that canteen. A hundred Germans on their feet cheering.'

Again, I think back to that night in Turin, the twenty minutes of jangling nerves and heart palpitations as England pushed and probed.

'By the time Lineker equalised,' he says, 'we couldn't contain ourselves. The three of us were on our feet, screaming and cheering each replay of the goal. I swear I almost did a little jig right there on the canteen floor, in front of this massive crowd of German factory workers. And that was it. The gloves were off. For the last ten minutes of normal-time and the thirty minutes of extra-time it seemed to be as much about showing your support right then and there in the factory as it did about the football on the television screen. We would cheer every one of our near misses, and they'd cheer theirs. Every time the Germans pulled down one of our players, we'd be on our feet screaming at the referee. And every time we pulled down one of theirs, they'd do the same. You should have seen the uproar on both sides when Gazza got booked.

'And then there were the penalties,' he says, his voice dropping.

'These days I can't watch,' I say.

'Me neither,' he replies. 'But that night we watched them all. Lineker, Beardsley, Platt . . .'

'And then Pearce and Waddle.' I sigh.

'When Waddle shot his penalty over the crossbar, I remember sinking on to my knees. I couldn't understand how we'd lost, how after the games against Belgium and Cameroon – and then after that titanic hundred and twenty minutes against the Germans – we were going to come away with *nothing*.'

Both of us are silent for a second. And then I ask him how it was in the canteen, also thinking of how Pete wept openly beside me in the stands as we watched Bobby Robson walk from player to player, shaking their hands and putting a comforting arm round their shoulders. He says that he had his eyes shut for a while. Neither him, nor Doug nor Keith (the two guys he was with) said anything for minutes, and that all he could hear was the German factory workers cheering and laughing and hugging each other.

'Do you know what it makes me think of?' he asks.

I shake my head.

'It make me think of all those players sitting in the centre circle watching the last penalty. One moment, they're all sitting there together, the German team and the England team, all of them exhausted after two hours of football and ravaged with nerves. Suddenly, half of them are *devastated* while the other half are going wild with relief. Can you imagine what it's like to be Stuart Pearce at that point, surrounded by celebrating Germans wanting to shake your hand and swap shirts when all you want is for the ground to open up and swallow you? Well it was a bit like that for the three of us.'

'What did you do? What happened next?'

He pauses. 'It was amazing. The three of us looked at each other. I can't remember exactly, but I think Doug mumbled something like "Fuck this!" And then the three of us stood up and faced all the factory workers. We hadn't planned it, but we were about to give them a round of applause only to find most of them clapping us and some of them walking towards us to shake our hands.'

After that, he says that the three of them went out with twenty of the Germans and got 'blind drunk'.

By now we're driving through Peckham. The man tells me he's called Dave and I tell him to call me Deepak while the commentators on the radio observe that the Germans are about to make a substitution, Thomas Hässler for Mehmet Scholl. And then suddenly we're in the last ten minutes of the game. Dave wonders out loud if we'll manage to score before full-time but we agree that extra-time feels inevitable. Both teams seem to be cancelling each other out.

Then the whistle blows for the end of normal-time.

'I don't believe it. Not *again*,' Dave sighs, 'I'm not sure I can take it if this one goes to penalties.'

'It won't,' I say. 'We'll score.' But I know that I don't believe it. Then extra-time starts and within two minutes McManaman crosses the ball in from the right only for Anderton to smash it against the post and the ball to come rebounding back out and away from the German goal-line. Dave has his head in his hands and so would I if I didn't have to drive. A minute later, Helmer delivers a cross that flies through a crowd of bodies lurking on the English goal-line but thankfully rolls harmlessly on for a goal-kick. Dave and I are silent now, our minds only concentrating on the feverish voices of the commentators. They sound drained, tired.

'It's going to be penalties. I *know* it,' Dave says, suddenly cut short by the announcement that the Germans have counter-attacked and that Andreas Möller has forced a corner.

'Oh Christ!' he says. 'I've got a bad feeling about this one.'

On the radio, we hear that that the Germans have thrown everyone forward and I feel my stomach boil. Then the kick's taken and the commentator's voice starts up like a greyhound bolting out its trap . . .

It's a good one . . . it's swinging in . . . it's in! It's in . . . !
Kuntz has . . .

'Fuck!'

'I can't . . .'

But it's okay. The referee's disallowed the goal. There was
some pushing in the box and England have a free-kick.

'I can't take much more of this. I really can't,' says Dave.

The second period of extra-time starts. A few minutes later,
Sheringham plays a deep ball into Shearer who's drifted out wide
to the right wing. He plays it in first time and Köpke leaps to
grab it but misses. One of the commentators is screaming that
Gascoigne's sliding in at the far post. *Will he get to it?*

He's inches away from scoring but again the ball rolls on
harmlessly wide of the post for a goal-kick.

'That could have been . . . that could have been *beautiful*,'
says Dave as I relax my grip on the steering wheel.

And then the whistle finally blows for the end of extra-time
and Dave and I realise that it's penalties.

Penalties.

'Who do you think'll take them?' Dave asks.

'It'll be the same as in the Spain game last Saturday,' I say.

'Where are we?'

'Somewhere near Bexley.'

'We've got to watch this haven't we? I mean, there's got to
be a pub somewhere nearby, hasn't there?'

The two of us stare out through the glass into the darkness –
but neither of us can see any nearby buildings with a light on, let
alone a pub we can run into to watch the end of the game.

'Let's pull over,' Dave says.

'What about your wife?' I ask.

'Well, I don't think ten minutes is going to make much
difference,' Dave replies, and then smiles a nervous smile.

'And I'm not sure we should be on the road while all of this is going on.'

I nod and pull the car over. And then we're sitting there, in near darkness except for the lights on the dashboard and on the radio, neither of us saying anything. Shearer takes the first and neither of us believes that he'll miss. He doesn't, sending Köpke the wrong way, but then neither does Thomas Hässler straight afterwards. David Platt's next and he scores, but then so does Thomas Strunz.

'Pearce next,' I say. 'He'll want to get this one after missing in Turin.'

We listen as Pearce blasts his penalty-kick past the German keeper. Redemption. Then Stefan Reuter's next. Dave reckons that Seaman could save this one, his voice shaking, and he's not far wrong. On the radio, we hear that Seaman dives the right way, but also that the ball flies in even though he manages to get his fingertips to it.

'Fuck. Fuck. *Fuck!*'

'Gazza next,' I say. And sure enough, Gazza steps up to the spot and curves his just inside the right-hand post, the commentators describing him as he turns to the crowd and tries to rouse them. But Ziege gets his before Sheringham and Kuntz both convert their spot-kicks too.

And now we face sudden-death here at Wembley.

The commentators sound as breathless as Dave and me. I notice that Dave has his fists clenched.

'Who's going to take the sixth penalty?'

'I don't know. McManaman? Anderton? It's got to be one of the attacking players hasn't it?'

It's Gareth Southgate to take the sixth penalty for England . . .

'I can't believe it! Southgate . . . a *defender*.'

Now we're silent. On the radio, it sounds as if Wembley's

fallen into a deathly hush as well. One of the commentators describes Southgate placing the ball and then walking back a short distance before turning and running towards it . . .

'*Come on* . . .'

'*Come on* . . .'

Southgate hits it low and to his left. Köpke dives low and to his right and suddenly what neither of us have dared imagine comes into startling focus. England have to keep the next penalty out or that's it: months of anticipation and three weeks of manic support reduced to a moment. Dave mutters that Seaman will save it. 'What about Spain last week,' he says. 'What about the save against Scotland? What about Arsenal last year in the Cup Winners' Cup against Fiorentina? *He'll do it, he'll do it, he'll do it!*' Me? I cross my fingers, only for Andreas Möller to step up and roof his spot-kick past our flailing goalkeeper.

And then that's it. England are out.

Dave and I don't say anything for a while. We just sit there for a minute or so not saying anything. And then I start the engine and pull back on to the road and we drive away in near silence. It takes ten minutes to drive the rest of the way to the hospital and when we get there, Dave pays me and we both shake hands.

'Best of luck with your baby,' I say. 'I never asked: is it your first?'

He nods.

'I've got two,' I say.

'How is it? Being a father?'

'It's okay. It's better than okay.'

Dave smiles. 'It was nice to meet you, Deepak,' he says. 'And a pleasure to hear England lose in your cab.'

'What a night for it, eh?' I smile back. 'Let's hope we get it right in '98.'

•

On the way back, I turn off the radio and drive back towards London in silence. Foot's Cray. Sidcup. New Eltham. The road signs appear and disappear in a haze of sodium, the two hours of anticipation and excitement already in the past. Is that how I deal with it? Just put it in the past and immediately remember it as history?

Lesley's voice comes on over the handheld.

'One-One . . . One-One! You there, Gus?'

'Hi Lesley. Yeah, I've just cleared in Swanley and I'm on my way back into London.'

'S'a shame about the football. Anyway, I'm just calling to say that they've started rioting in Trafalgar Square.'

'Who has?'

'Skin'eads. Or something like that. Anyway, I'm not accepting any more fares to or from the West End at the moment and I don't suggest you lot go anywhere near there either. The place is overrun with *animals*.'

'I'll be sure to give it a miss.'

'Well, it's not like it's a problem is it, darl'? There's plenty of work south of the river so call me when you get to Lewisham and I'll tell you what I've got.'

A few minutes later, I'm in Eltham. At a junction, I bring the car to stop and stare up at the red light, half wondering what it would have felt like if Anderton's shot had gone in rather than hitting the post, or if Gascoigne had converted Shearer's cross . . . then the amber light comes on and I relax my foot on the clutch only to see a group of people still crossing . . . *damn!* I quickly apply the brake. But before I can curse myself for being so careless there's a massive bang on the bonnet. I look up to see two skinheads shouting at me through the glass, one of them in an England shirt, the other in a shellsuit slapping his hands down on the front of the car. I think about reversing, but another car's come to a rest behind me and I don't think the driver's seen what's going on. Suddenly there's the sound of the door being opened and I feel myself being hauled from my seat.

'Fuckin' Paki!'

'You almost hit my fuckin' girlfriend, you fuckin' *cunt*!' The skinhead in the England shirt spits while the other has his hands on my lapels and throws me against the railing surrounding the traffic island in the middle of the road.

'Look guys,' I start, not struggling, not starting anything. If I can just talk to them . . .

'Cunt!' he shouts. Somewhere in the background, I hear a girl's voice shrieking, another one saying, 'He's just a cab driver Vince, leave 'im.'

'L-l-look, I'm so . . .'

'*CUNT!*'

Now everything starts to blur. I get a glimpse of his yellow teeth (one missing, I notice, and one chipped and as black as an olive) and the gold stud through his earlobe and the dots tattooed across his knuckles as his knee hits me in the stomach. As I fall to the ground, I notice how much chewing gum has been squashed flat on to the tarmac. And then I can't feel anything for a moment before I find myself looking up at two snarling faces, spit dripping from their lips, every breath sending a shot of pain through my chest. A boot flies in, and another (and another).

'Want some more?'

'Fucking cunt!'

They kick me again, but somehow all I feel or see or understand now are their faces, the jaundiced whites of their eyes and their pale white faces battered with acne. Do they know that the haircut makes their ears stick out? How stupid to be thinking about their ears. Somewhere, I hear another shriek, one of the girls screaming for them 'not to do it'.

'Don't do it,' she screams. 'Don't do it!'

But they do.

Acknowledgements

I would especially like to thank the following at this time. Jeff Hargreaves for his continual support and generosity; Damian Peel and the Peel family for theirs; Joanna Johnston for her inspirational contributions to 'Higher Society' and 'Ink'; Charles Lambert for his key contribution to 'The Project'. I would also like to take this opportunity to thank Angus Graham-Campbell, Mark Moore, Ian Crocombe (Mr Knox.com), Stephanie Cabot, Dan Franklin and everyone at Random House.

Finally, I would like to acknowledge the tremendous support of Hannah Griffiths and Paddy Grey.

RISK,
INTERVENTION
and CHANGE

HIV prevention and drug use

Health Education Authority
in association with
the National AIDS Trust

Tim Rhodes

Tim Rhodes is Research Fellow at the Centre for Research on Drugs
and Health Behaviour, Charing Cross and Westminster Medical School,
University of London.

© Health Education Authority, 1994

Health Education Authority
Hamilton House
Mabledon Place
London WC1H 9TX

ISBN 0 7521 0121 8

Typeset by Type Generation Ltd, London
Printed by The KPC Group, London & Ashford Kent

Contents

Preface

This publication is the result of work commissioned by the Health Education Authority, in conjunction with the National AIDS Trust. Its purpose is to provide an overview of developments in the research and delivery of HIV and drug work. Additionally, it aims to place this work within the current framework of service provision and addresses how HIV prevention strategies among drug injectors may be most successfully progressed. As such, we hope that *Risk, Intervention and Change* will be of use to both purchasers of health services, and also the providers of such services – both statutory and voluntary.

The reality is that drug users remain at risk of infection from HIV through the sharing of needles, syringes and other injecting equipment, and through unsafe sex. Nearly 10 per cent of people who have tested HIV positive in England and Wales are injecting drug users. The figure is higher in Scotland (50 per cent) where there was rapid epidemic growth among drug injectors in the 1980s, similar to that experienced in New York and Italy.

However, the latest assessment in the Day report (1993) indicates that the UK has moved down the league table of rates of infection in Europe, to second from bottom. Central to this is a marked reduction in projected new infections among injecting drug users when compared to estimates in the 1980s. There is now considerable evidence that prevention strategies such as targeted HIV/drugs education campaigns and needle and syringe exchange schemes have had some success, and represent perhaps the most effective components of the Government's anti-HIV measures to date.

There is, however, much to learn, as the task of changing health behaviour is an immensely complicated and difficult thing to do. For example, research continues to show that drug users, like the majority of the population, have difficulty changing their sexual behaviour and so may be putting themselves and their sexual partners at risk through unsafe sex. Further, the prevalence of problem drug taking continues to increase, bringing a generation of young people who are newly exposed to the risks of HIV infection and drug related harm.

So where next in HIV and drugs prevention? This is a question for national strategic planning and also for purchasers and providers of HIV and drugs services.

This and other questions concerning the future direction and priorities of HIV and drugs prevention work are posed by this timely and important publication, which aims to inform the debate about on national strategy and local planning and purchasing in this field.

Dr Les Rudd
Director of the National AIDS Trust

Acknowledgements

For help and comments on the consultancy report, I would like to thank Sue Barnes, Ruth Lowbury, Lindsay Neil and Jane Stevens of the HEA; Les Rudd, Director of the NAT; Gerry Stimson, Director of the Centre for Research on Drugs and Health Behaviour (CRDHB); and Martin Donoghoe, also of the CRDHB. For assistance in editing and revising the consultancy report into this current format, I would like to thank Alan Quirk of the CRDHB. I would also like to thank Steve Monk for administrative assistance.

1   Policy, prevention and the process of change

The HIV epidemic has encouraged a process of change in the policy and practice of many UK drug services. This change has occurred at a number of distinct levels and has included shifts in the formation of drug policy and in the organisation of drug treatment and prevention services. The immediacy of the health-related harms associated with HIV have demanded a re-orientatation and a re-conceptualisation of the drug problem and of the drug user. These changes have encompassed an increased recognition of the importance of community-based responses to HIV prevention and a realisation that a reliance on interventions encouraging abstinence from drug use is impractical.

It is a decade since the emergence and identification of HIV and at least five years since UK drug policy and practice began a process of change in response to HIV and AIDS. Such changes in policy and practice are emergent and ongoing. They are a gradual process similar to the ways individuals adopt changes in their own lifestyles and behaviour. As noted by John Strang:

> "Change must be recognised as a process of adaptation rather than as a simple one-off event: it follows that there will be factors which increase or decrease the likelihood of movement through the process, and factors which influence the speed of this movement"
>
> (Strang, 1990a: 213)

It is timely to review the movement and speed with which individuals, communities and organisations have responded to the challenges posed by HIV infection and AIDS. It is important to identify the key factors which facilitate the scope and parameters of change at individual, community and institutional levels. This calls for a review of responses to HIV prevention and drug use with regard to the behaviour of individuals and communities, the aims and achievements of interventions and the planning and implementation of health promotion strategy. This task can be seen to consist of three distinct stages: risk, intervention and change. Without an understanding of the nature and extent of risk with regard to drug use and health behaviour it is difficult to plan or carry out appropriate intervention responses. Without an understanding of the ways in which interventions can influence the health and illness of individuals and communities, it is difficult to envisage or encourage a process of adaptation or change.

In reviewing state of the art understandings of risk, intervention and change, this book hopes to map out possibilities for future research and intervention developments in HIV prevention with drug users. It aims to achieve this by briefly outlining the policy context in which change has been encouraged and achieved (this chapter), by summarising recent research on the prevalence of HIV infection and HIV risk behaviour among drug using populations (Chapters 2 and 3) and by reviewing recent HIV prevention and community-based harm reduction interventions targeting drug users (Chapter 4). The implications of the review for the design and development of future HIV prevention research and intervention initiatives among drug users are discussed in Chapters 5 and 6 and summarised in Chapter 7. The review is by no means exhaustive but aims to review recently published literature highlighting key findings and their implications. Key published reports and papers on HIV prevention and drug use are listed in the Appendix.

POLICY AND THE SHIFTING PARAMETERS OF PRACTICE

The Advisory Council on the Misuse of Drugs (ACMD) has remained the single most influential body with regard to developments in British drug policy (Farrell and Strang, 1992). Established as an independent body of experts to the Home Office under the Misuse of Drugs Act in 1971, the ACMD aims to inform future policy and practice with regard to the management, treatment and prevention of drug use. This has been achieved through governmental endorsement of recommendations contained in its four reports focusing on drug treatment, rehabilitation, prevention, and AIDS and drug misuse (ACMD, 1982, 1984, 1988, 1989).

  The process of revision and change encouraged by the advent of HIV infection has been characterised by an emergence of pragmatism in British drug policy (Stimson, 1990). The need for pragmatism in public health responses to drug use arose because of the increasing risks of HIV transmission associated with injecting drug use. This is reflected in the recommendations contained in the ACMD report *AIDS and Drug Misuse: Part 1*:

> *"The advent of HIV requires an expansion of our definitions of problem drug use to include any form of drug misuse which includes, or may lead to, the sharing of injecting equipment"*
> (ACMD, 1988)

The ACMD of 1988 thus recommended that the management of drug problems be characterised by practical responses designed primarily for the protection of public health:

> *"We have no hesitation in concluding that the spread of HIV is a greater danger to individual and public health than drug misuse"*
> (ACMD, 1988)

The ACMD shift towards a policy of pragmatism has had an important influence on the ways in which the public health problem of HIV and injecting drug use has been viewed (Stimson and Lart, 1991). It has been part of a process of change in the re-conceptualisation of how drug services respond to the drug user. Most importantly, this has encouraged a re-orientation of service delivery towards the prevention of HIV:

> *"... services which aim to minimise HIV risk behaviour by all available means should take precedence in development plans"*   (ACMD, 1988)

This precedence has emphasised the need for services to reach out, understand and respond to the drug user outside of the immediate constraints necessitated by drug treatment regimes:

> *"We must recognise that, for the time being, many drug misusers will not be sufficiently motivated to consider abstinence and that many drug injectors will not be sufficiently motivated to change their route of administration. We must therefore be prepared to work with those who continue to misuse drugs to help them reduce the risks involved in doing so, above all the risk of acquiring or spreading HIV"*   (ACMD, 1988)

Practical responses such as these have strengthened the move towards understanding the drug user as a rational individual able to make choices about his or her health behaviour. This has meant that drug services have re-oriented themselves towards targeting drug users as *rational* decision-makers in the production (and reduction) of HIV risk behaviour. The concept of *choice* has become central to public health interventions in the AIDS era. The aim of HIV prevention initiatives targeting drug users is to create the environments in which drug using individuals and communities can be enabled or empowered to make 'healthy choices' about their behaviour and lifestyles.

Approaches to the prevention of HIV infection among drug users have thus made explicit the need to "work with those who continue to use drugs" (ACMD, 1988). This has led to the re-emergence of 'harm-reduction' as the cornerstone of HIV prevention policy targeting drug injectors and drug users. Building on previous ACMD reports which noted the importance of harm reduction in the prevention of drug use (ACMD, 1984), the ACMD reports *AIDS and Drug Misuse* (1988, 1989) emphasise the need for *community-based prevention* and *harm reduction* responses.

Harm reduction is variously defined, but it is best viewed as the programmes and policies which attempt to reduce the harms associated with drug use (Strang, 1993). With regard to reducing the health harms associated with injecting, the approach encourages a hierarchical approach from stopping or reducing the sharing of used injecting equipment through to stopping or reducing injecting drug use itself (see Chapter 3). In keeping with this approach, HIV prevention interventions aim to ensure that drug users have the knowledge and means necessary to make 'healthy choices' within this hierarchy of goals.

An increased commitment to community-based service provision is of pivotal importance in reaching and responding to hidden populations of drug users who may have little or no contact with existing treatment or prevention services. This commitment was made considerably easier in practice by the Central Funding Initiative (CFI). In response to ACMD evidence of a lack of co-ordination in community-based drug services (ACMD, 1982), central government funding (the CFI) was allocated to regional health authorities (RHAs) in 1984 for developments in drug services. Managed with a considerable degree of central flexibility and local autonomy, the CFI effectively introduced a new tier of 'lower-threshold' and 'user-friendly' community-based drug services (MacGregor *et al.*, 1991). These CFI-funded services provided the foundations for developing community-based HIV prevention interventions in response to ACMD recommendations on AIDS and drug misuse:

> *"One clear benefit of the CFI promotion of the new services was that it allowed a base from which AIDS work could be developed and allowed a smoother and more rapid response to this major public health issue than might otherwise have been the case."*
>
> (MacGregor *et al.*, 1991)

As noted by Farrell and Strang (1992), the majority of developments in drug services were funded after the CFI. At the time of conducting the evaluation of the CFI, MacGregor and colleagues note that there were about 300 drug services in England, of which approximately half were located in the non-statutory sector (MacGregor *et al.*, 1991). A little under half (43 per cent) of these were counselling and advice services, a quarter (24 per cent) were community drug teams, 13 per cent were rehabilitation services and 10 per cent were drug dependence units (DDUs). The major service developments in HIV prevention since this time have been syringe exchange (Stimson *et al.*, 1988) and outreach work (Rhodes, Hartnoll and Johnson, 1991).

The momentum of change in HIV-related drug service developments has begun to slow. It is now almost a decade since the CFI initiative and the onset of the HIV epidemic. Drug services are now at a time of consolidation and re-assessment. Five years on from the first and second ACMD reports on *AIDS and Drug Misuse*, it is timely to review the effectiveness of current UK harm reduction and community-based HIV prevention strategies.

In October 1993, the ACMD report *AIDS and Drug Misuse: Update* was published. The report returns to territory outlined in the first and second reports reviewing progress and introducing new recommendations for change. The report endorses the need for consolidation, recommending a shift in the current direction of policy towards re-emphasising the prevention of drug use alongside current HIV prevention activity:

> *"Greater efforts are now needed to reduce the extent of drug use itself, and particularly of drug injecting, together with a wider recognition that all interventions to discourage drug misuse will contribute to HIV prevention."* (ACMD, 1993)

Recently termed the "Back to Basics Report" by an editorial in *Druglink* (Druglink, 1994), *AIDS and Drug Misuse: Update* suggests that "efforts to prevent or reduce drug misuse *per se* [have] been overshadowed by responses to the urgent needs of injectors". As shown in Figure 1.1, drugs service policy recommendations have shifted from prioritising the prevention of HIV above that of drug use to re-emphasising the prevention of drug use – particularly injecting drug use – as a dual objective of harm reduction and prevention activity. These policy shifts which help define the parameters of drug service provision are embedded in wider historical shifts in HIV and AIDS policy. Policies have moved through three distinct phases from a position of 'panic' (1982–1985), 'emergency', 'political priority' and 'crisis management' (1986–1987) through to 'consolidation' and 'normalisation' (Strong and Berridge, 1990; Weeks, 1989). The ACMD report of 1993 encourages a consolidation of HIV prevention practice as part of the routine of drug service provision and as part of the fundamental objectives of preventing problem drug use.

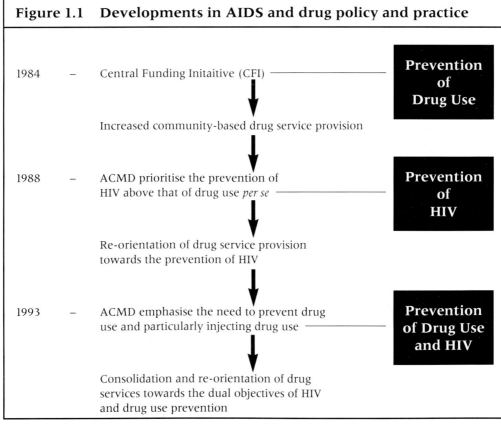

Figure 1.1   Developments in AIDS and drug policy and practice

1984 – Central Funding Initaitive (CFI) ——————— **Prevention of Drug Use**

Increased community-based drug service provision

1988 – ACMD prioritise the prevention of HIV above that of drug use *per se* ——————— **Prevention of HIV**

Re-orientation of drug service provision towards the prevention of HIV

1993 – ACMD emphasise the need to prevent drug use and particularly injecting drug use ——————— **Prevention of Drug Use and HIV**

Consolidation and re-orientation of drug services towards the dual objectives of HIV and drug use prevention

CONSUMER CARE AND *THE HEALTH OF THE NATION*

The objectives of harm reduction to reduce the harms associated with drug use at the level of the individual, community and society have emerged alongside policy developments advocating greater commitment to consumer choice and consumer care. These shifts have been encouraged by recent NHS and community care reforms (NHS and Community Care Act, 1990), adoption of a Patients' Charter (Department of Health, 1992a) and the setting of national health targets for HIV, AIDS and sexual health in *The Health of the Nation* (Department of Health, 1992b). These developments are in essence designed to establish an internal market of health services in response to demonstrated consumer needs so as to encourage and enable consumer choice about health and service use.

The NHS and Community Care Act is the basis for these reforms. By separating the purchasers of drug and HIV prevention services from the providers of services, it is hoped that services will be commissioned (and thus provided) on the basis of ongoing needs assessment in response to local public health need. Services are thus contracted between purchasers and providers and regulated and evaluated in terms of health targets and outcomes. The setting and implementation of health targets are central to defining the future direction of HIV prevention service developments and to demonstrating the effectiveness of health promotion practice.

Viewing HIV infection as "perhaps the greatest new public health challenge this century" (Department of Health, 1992b), the Government document and strategy *The Health of the Nation* provides an initial framework for the setting of targets for health gain in the area of HIV, AIDS and sexual health. The one target which relates specifically to drug use aims to measure reductions in the rates of sharing among injecting drug users (see Chapter 5). The shift towards establishing an internal market of services based on the demonstrated successes of service provision and of consumer need raises the question of which targets are most appropriate for HIV prevention services among drug users and how such targets should be set and met.

The aims and objectives of *The Health of the Nation* strategy provide the context in which future HIV prevention interventions among drug users are to be planned and implemented. They provide broad guidelines on HIV, AIDS and sexual health which aim to inform purchasers' purchasing decisions and providers' intervention strategies. It is important to review the parameters and achievements of current HIV prevention interventions so as to assist the formation of target setting and assessment. The recent shifts in drug service policy recommended by the ACMD (1993) also provide a framework for how the targets and parameters of HIV prevention work among drug users should be defined, regulated and evaluated. In reviewing the current situation with regard to risk and intervention it becomes possible to appreciate the possibility and feasibility of change. A review of what is known gives an indication of how current policy shifts may influence future HIV prevention practice for better or for worse. This is the first step towards maximising health and minimising harm for individuals and communities affected by drug use.

2 HIV prevalence among injecting drug users

This chapter briefly reviews research on the prevalence of HIV infection among injecting drug users in the United Kingdom. There are few published studies which have investigated the prevalence of HIV among non-injecting drug users. In view of North American studies which associate HIV risk and HIV prevalence with the use of non-injecting drug use, and in particular cocaine and crack use (see Chapter 3), this can be considered a priority for future epidemiological and prevalence research focusing on drug use and HIV infection.

HIV TRANSMISSION AMONG INJECTING DRUG USERS

Injecting drug use has become increasingly important in the world-wide transmission dynamics of HIV (Wodak and Moss, 1990: Des Jarlais *et al.*, 1992; Stimson, 1993). The growth of the epidemic among drug injectors in Western developed countries has been rapid (Des Jarlais, 1992) and in many areas continues to increase (Stimson, 1991). As of 1990, there were reports of HIV infection or AIDS among injecting drug users in 30 countries in Europe, the Americas, Africa, Asia and Australia (Des Jarlais, 1992). In Europe and the United States, drug injectors are currently the second largest group of reported cases of AIDS. In 1993, the World Health Organization European Centre for the Epidemiological Monitoring of AIDS estimated that 37 per cent of newly diagnosed cases were among injecting drug users. As shown in Figure 2.1, the proportion of cumulative AIDS cases thought to be injecting drug users in the UK are considerably lower than in most other Western European countries.

The rate or growth of HIV transmission among injecting drug users has been shown to be particularly rapid in countries and areas lacking in methods of prevention and prevalence control. In some countries and cities, drug injectors are the largest single group of people with HIV infection or AIDS. These include cities such as New Jersey, Connecticut in the United States, Edinburgh, Italy and Spain in Europe and Bangkok in Thailand (Freidman and Des Jarlais, 1991). Edinburgh provides a UK case example prior to media and public health recognition of HIV infection and AIDS, where HIV prevalence rose to estimates of approximately 50 per cent among drug injectors between 1983 and 1985 (Robertson, 1990). Bangkok provides a more recent example of rapid epidemic growth. While there were no reported cases of HIV infection among injectors in 1986, prevalence rates had risen to 16 per cent by early 1988 and were as high as 43 per cent by September of the same year (Stimson, 1993a; Anderson, 1990).

Figure 2.1 Proportion of cumulative AIDS cases in Western Europe thought to be injecting drug users (March, 1993. WHO) (includes AIDS cases diagnosed among gay/bisexual injecting drug users)

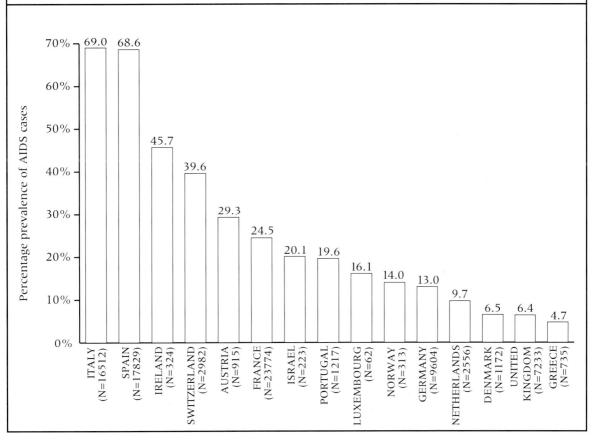

UK large-scale HIV surveillance

The absence of denominator populations of drug injectors clearly limits the methodological validity and reliability of HIV prevalence estimates. In the UK, such estimates are derived from voluntary reporting from diagnosing physicians, voluntary reporting from testing laboratories, large scale unlinked anonymous surveys of sentinel populations, and from linked and unlinked anonymous studies based on non-randomised primarily treatment-based convenience samples. More recently, these estimates have been supplemented by multi-site serial period prevalence studies of drug injectors recruited simultaneously from treatment and non-treatment settings (see below).

The surveillance of the spread of HIV infection in the UK thus relies heavily on the voluntary reporting of diagnosed cases of HIV and AIDS to the Communicable Disease Surveillance Centres in England (CDSC) and the Communicable Disease (Scotland) Unit (CD(S)U). These data have been collected routinely since 1982 for AIDS cases and since 1984 for HIV cases. It is important to note that the AIDS data reflects the pattern of *past* HIV infection, given the variable length of incubation. While new reports of HIV infection are more likely to reflect current transmission patterns, they rely on reports of voluntary testing in genito-urinary medicine (GUM) clinics, other hospital departments and in general practice.

Since surveillance reporting began, and as of March 1993, a total of 7341 AIDS cases (6827 male (93 per cent); 514 female (7 per cent)) were reported to CDSC in England and CD(S)U in Scotland. Of these, 4572 (63 per cent) were known to have died (PHLS, 1993a). The majority of reported AIDS cases were attributed to sexual intercourse between men (75 per cent), while 6 per cent were attributed to injecting drug use. Of the 514 cases of AIDS in women, 20 per cent were attributed to injecting drug use (PHLS, 1993a). There was therefore a greater proportion of cases of AIDS attributed to injecting drug use among women than men.

As of March 1993, there were 19,524 reports of HIV-1 infection in the UK. Of these, 60 per cent were attributed to sexual intercourse between men and 13 per cent to injecting drug use (including 1 per cent attributed to injecting drug use *or* sexual intercourse between men) (PHLS, 1993a). Among cases of HIV in women (13 per cent of total cases), 30 per cent were attributed to injecting drug use (PHLS, 1993a).

There are marked geographical variations in the proportion of reported cases attributed to injecting drug use. Of the 1921 HIV cases reported in Scotland, for example, 50 per cent are attributed to injecting drug use, while of 12,376 cases reported in the four Thames Regions (accounting for 63 per cent of total HIV reports), 9 per cent are attributed to injecting drug use (PHLS, 1993a).

UK studies of HIV prevalence among drug injectors

In recognition of the methodological limitations in current UK HIV surveillance, Waight *et al.* (1992) collected data on all HIV tests, irrespective of result, to provide denominator estimates of prevalence and incidence. Of 10,048 HIV tests categorised under injecting drug use, 259 tested HIV antibody positive, giving a prevalence rate of 2.6 per cent. Geographical differences were found, with a prevalence rate of 5.4 per cent (101/1885) in London and 1.9 per cent (158/8163) outside London (Waight *et al.*, 1992).

In addition to routine surveillance and the above denominator study, a major on-going voluntary, unlinked anonymous testing programme is being undertaken among sentinel populations in England and Wales. This includes a large scale survey of HIV prevalence in multi-site samples of drug injectors (PHLS, 1993b). The study found an overall prevalence of 1.2 per cent (18/1531) among injecting drug users in 1990, 1.8 per cent in 1991 (25/1402) and 1.8 per cent (44/2461) in 1992 (Figure 2.2).

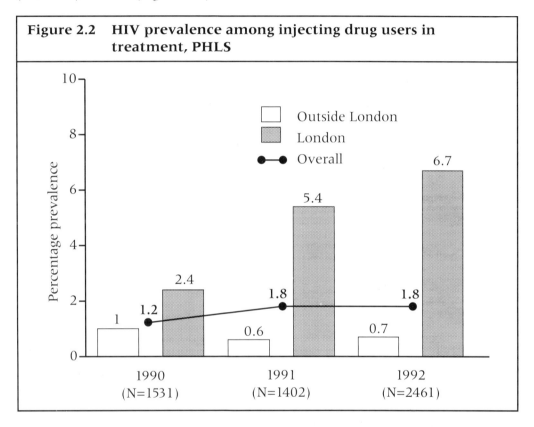

Figure 2.2   HIV prevalence among injecting drug users in treatment, PHLS

Women had a higher prevalence than men in 1990 (1.9 per cent; 0.9 per cent) and 1992 (2.1 per cent; 1.7 per cent) but not in 1991 (0.6 per cent; 2.1 per cent). As shown in Figure 2.2, HIV prevalence was higher in London than outside London in 1990 (2.4 per cent; 1.0 per cent), 1991 (5.4 per cent; 0.6 per cent) and 1992 (6.7 per cent; 0.7 per cent) (PHLS, 1993b). These data support the findings of Waight *et al.* (1992) which suggest higher rates of HIV prevalence among female than male injecting drug users and higher rates in London than elsewhere. They are restricted in that they rely primarily on samples drawn from treatment and service settings. They are also limited in that they include clients attending services who have *ever* injected drugs. This means that they can only be used as crude indicators of the prevalence of HIV among current drug injecting populations as a whole.

The majority of UK reports of HIV prevalence among injecting drug users are based on highly selective samples recruited primarily from drug treatment clinics

(Hart *et al.*, 1989a), rehabilitation agencies (Webb *et al.* 1986) and general practice (Robertson *et al.*, 1986; Skidmore *et al.*, 1990). Estimates based on treatment recruited samples in London have ranged from 0.7 per cent (Webb *et al.*, 1986) to 6.7 per cent in 1992 (PHLS, 1993b). Outside London, these estimates have ranged from 0.6 per cent to 1.0 per cent (PHLS, 1993b). HIV prevalence estimates based on treatment recruited samples in Edinburgh in the mid-1980s have ranged from 38.0 per cent (Peutherer *et al.*, 1985) to 51.0 per cent (Robertson *et al.*, 1986). One other estimate found 64.0 per cent of injecting drug users attending a general practice to be HIV positive (Skidmore *et al.*, 1990). More recently, HIV prevalence estimates of 31.0 per cent (Ronald and Robertson, 1992) and 25.0 per cent (Bird *et al.*, 1992) have been reported. HIV prevalence rates among drug injectors in treatment in Glasgow were estimated in 1986 to be 0.7 per cent (Robertson *et al.*, 1986).

There are serious potential methodological limitations in estimating prevalence on the basis of samples recruited primarily from treatment settings. The minimisation of potential bias is possible using samples of injecting drug users recruited through multi-site community-based sampling strategies. These studies aim to

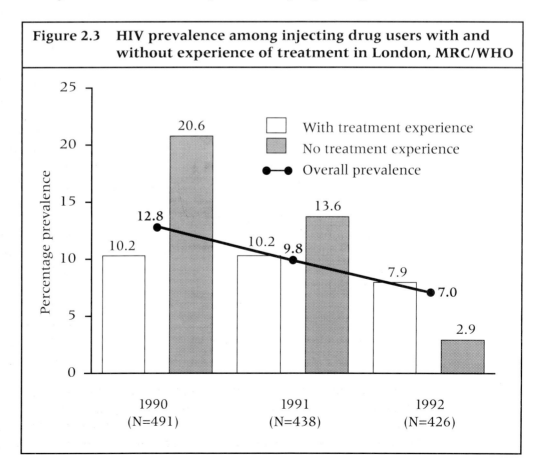

Figure 2.3   HIV prevalence among injecting drug users with and without experience of treatment in London, MRC/WHO

recruit in multi- rather than single sites and from treatment and non-treatment/helping settings so as to include drug injectors with current, previous and no treatment experience.

UK studies using multi-site sampling strategies have found higher than previously reported HIV prevalence among drug injectors. In London, estimates have ranged from 12.8 per cent in 1990 (Donoghoe *et al.*, 1993; Rhodes *et al.*, 1993a) to 9.8 per cent (Donoghoe *et al.*, 1993) and 12.0 per cent (Strang *et al.*, 1992) in 1991, to 7.0 per cent in 1992 (Donoghoe and Hunter, personal communication). In contrast, a HIV prevalence rate of 3.0 per cent was found among non-injecting drug users in London (Strang *et al.*, 1992). A meta-analysis of HIV prevalence findings among injectors in London undertaken by the Public Health Laboratory Service estimated a prevalence of 8.0 per cent (Stimson, 1993). Figure 2.3 summarises these findings.

Evidence suggests that HIV prevalence is higher among drug injectors with no experience of drug treatment than among those who have current or previous experience of treatment (Figure 2.3). In 1990, a HIV prevalence of 20.6 per cent was found among those with no treatment experience compared with 10.2 per cent prevalence among those with previous or current treatment experience (Donoghoe *et al.*, 1993; Haw *et al.*, 1992). In 1991 these same differences were 13.6 per cent prevalence against 10.2 per cent prevalence (Donoghoe *et al.*, 1993; Rhodes *et al.*, 1993a). However, in 1992 the same study found a higher rate of HIV prevalence among drug injectors currently (8.0 per cent) and previously (7.5 per cent) in treatment than among those with no treatment experience (2.9 per cent) (Donoghoe and Hunter, personal communication). At the time of writing, the study has yet to complete data analysis and has yet to provide explanations for a reversal in higher HIV prevalence trends among injectors with no treatment experience. It is also interesting to note that the study associates higher HIV prevalence among younger injectors (under 20 years) and among those with shorter injecting careers (less than 5 years) (Donoghoe *et al.*, 1993).

Comparable multi-site recruitment studies have also been undertaken in Glasgow and Edinburgh. These show overall HIV prevalence rates among injectors in Glasgow of 1.8 per cent in 1990, 1.2 per cent in 1991 and 1.0 per cent in 1992 (Taylor *et al.*, 1994; Frischer *et al.*, 1992) and among Edinburgh injectors of 20.4 per cent (Bath *et al.*, 1994). The Edinburgh study found HIV infection to be significantly more likely among injectors aged between 27 and 36 years and among those who started to inject between the years 1978 and 1981 (Bath *et al.*, 1994). HIV prevalence also increased with the number of times drug injectors had been imprisoned and the study concluded that continued sharing in prison was of particular concern.

These studies indicate the continued importance of multi-site sampling in increasing the reliability of prevalence estimates among injecting populations with and without experience of drug treatment. These estimates themselves would be improved with more 'random' recruiting. This necessitates investigating the possibilities for methodological developments, either through undertaking denominator population studies using 'capture-recapture' methods (Frischer, 1992; Hartnoll *et al.*, 1985) or through random nomination and structured randomisation techniques. In addition, there are few UK cohort studies among injecting drug users, and thus few studies monitoring the incidence of new HIV infections.

Given the potential for increases in HIV prevalence among certain populations of drug users and the potential for second generation transmission among drug users and their sexual partners, the co-ordination and collation of multi-indicator prevalence data at a local and national level is of critical importance. The Regional Drug Misuse Databases provide an opportunity to integrate data within a region (and nationally) on a variety of key measures associated with extent and nature of use and treatment experience (Donmall, 1990). Such data, collated on a systematic and regular basis, is essential for the planning of local (and national) resources, for identifying key changes in local patterns of use and for informing appropriate prevention and intervention responses. The ACMD in 1993 emphasised that anonymised surveys for HIV prevalence provide purchasers and planners with vital epidemiological data to assist in estimating the health needs of local populations. The report recommended that:

> *"anonymised surveys of HIV prevalence should be undertaken more widely, including surveys of drug injectors both in and out of contact with treatment services"* (ACMD, 1993)

HIV TESTING AND AWARENESS OF HIV STATUS

Findings from recent research in London show that many drug injectors are unaware of their HIV status. Research among 104 injectors confirmed HIV positive by anonymous saliva found that approximately 70 per cent were unaware of their positive status and that 16 per cent thought themselves to be HIV negative (Rhodes *et al.*, 1993b). Half (52 per cent) had never received a named test for HIV antibodies. These are important findings, particularly in the context of research which suggests that those who are aware of their HIV positive status may be more likely to make drug and sexual risk reduction changes (see Chapter 3).

Multi-site recruitment studies in London show that approximately half of drug injectors report having been tested for HIV (Donoghoe *et al.*, 1993; Rhodes *et al.*, 1993b). Rates of HIV testing are considerably lower among drug injectors who have never been in treatment, and drug injectors who are currently in treatment are roughly twice as likely to have been tested for HIV (Donoghoe *et al.*, 1993). These studies also show that HIV positive injectors with no experience of drug treatment are less likely to be aware of their positive status than injectors who were or had been in treatment.

Findings that the majority of HIV positive drug injectors are unaware of their positive status emphasise the important role that community-based drug and outreach projects have in raising awareness of counselling and testing facilities and in encouraging referral into existing treatment and health services (see also Chapter 4). As concluded by the ACMD in 1993:

> *"...the public health advantages of wider availability of HIV testing, both anonymised and named, are as important as ever. The advantages to the individual of being tested are, in our view, clearer than they were when we considered the issue in 1988. We recommend the expansion of opportunities for voluntary HIV testing... a more proactive approach to testing in areas of known or suspected high prevalence... [and] more widespread use of anonymised HIV prevalence surveys"*

Increasing the accessibility of HIV testing facilities is required in conjunction with increased access to education and prevention interventions (see Chapter 4). As concluded in the study of HIV positive drug injectors in London mentioned above:

> *"The association between experience of contact with a treatment or helping agency, history of HIV testing and HIV positivity suggests that an expansion of existing HIV testing and associated counselling facilities alone may not be adequate, but that greater emphasis should be placed on the expansion and increased accessibility of prevention, education and treatment services in the community"* (Rhodes *et al.*, 1993b)

Prevalence of hepatitis B and C viruses

Concerns about the prevalence of hepatitis B (HBV) among injecting drug users have largely been eclipsed by concerns with regard to HIV. Studies undertaken by the Public Health Laboratory Service among drug injectors attending treatment centres in England and Wales found a HBV prevalence rate of 33 per cent in 1990 and of 31 per cent in 1991 (Noone *et al.*, 1994). Virtually all of the 33 participating centres in the study reported drug injectors who were antibody positive to HBV antigen and the prevalence of HBV ranged from 9 per cent to 52 per cent in 1990 and from 14 per cent to 54 per cent in 1991. The study also found that among injectors in London, HIV infection was less likely among those with HBV infection than among those without, whereas outside London no association was found between the prevalence of HIV and HBV infection. This may indicate that injectors with past HBV infection have minimised risk behaviour or that the sample is biased through loss from death or migration of injectors positive to both

HBV and HIV viruses (Noone *et al.*, 1994). Further research needs to investigate the feasibility of using HBV infection as a risk marker for HIV.

Unpublished data from the ongoing World Health Organization multi-site prevalence study among drug injectors in London shows a higher prevalence of HBV. Among injectors recruited to the study in 1992, a prevalence of 51 per cent (178/347) was found (Donoghoe, personal communication). These data highlight concerns, shared by the ACMD in 1993, that a high prevalence of hepatitis B virus may be likely among many populations of injectors even if the prevalence of HIV is stabilising or in decline. This emphasises the importance of screening as part of drug treatment services and a commitment to improving the general health of drug users. As noted by the ACMD:

> *"The prevalence of hepatitis B among drug injectors is high in some areas and we therefore recommend that drug injectors and their sexual partners should be encouraged to seek hepatitis B immunisation"*   (ACMD, 1993)

In addition to hepatitis A and B, the hepatitis C virus (HCV) has been identified (Choo *et al.*, 1989). This has been shown to be responsible for the vast majority of previously categorised non-A and non-B (NANB) hepatitis among drug injectors. HCV, which can be transmitted in blood as well as through unprotected sexual intercourse, is known to be a major cause of liver disease (cirrhosis), including hepatocellular carcinoma. About 10–20 per cent of people with chronic active HCV are likely to develop cirrhosis within 5 to 30 years (Benhamou, 1993) and about 15 per cent will develop hepatocellular carcinoma.

There are few studies of HCV prevalence among injecting drug users. Evidence in Australia points to a HCV prevalence among drug injectors of 68 per cent in Victoria (Crofts *et al.*, 1993) and of 100 per cent among people injecting for more than eight years in New South Wales (Bell *et al.*, 1990). Studies in Europe show a HCV prevalence among injectors in Rome of 68 per cent (Girardi *et al.*, 1990), in Amsterdam of 74 per cent (Van den Hoek *et al.*, 1990) and in Athens of 82 per cent (Malliori *et al.*, 1993).

To date, there has been only one published study on HCV prevalence in the UK. Of 120 drug injectors tested in West Suffolk, 58 per cent were HCV positive (Staff, 1993). Given the high rates of prevalence found elsewhere but nonetheless suspected in the UK, estimating the prevalence of HCV among drug injectors in the UK should be seen as a priority for future epidemiological research.

3   HIV risk and health behaviour

This chapter provides an overview of recent research on the HIV risk behaviour of drug users, focusing on the risks associated with injecting drug use and sexual behaviour. By way of an introduction, the chapter gives a brief overview of common theoretical explanations of health behaviour and behaviour change. This gives a framework within which to understand the perceptions and behaviours of drug users with regard to HIV and AIDS. This understanding provides the foundations upon which to build appropriate intervention and prevention responses (see Chapter 4).

MODELS OF HEALTH BEHAVIOUR AND BEHAVIOUR CHANGE

There are a number of competing theories of health behaviour and behaviour change. These generally fall within two broad areas: those offering *individualistic* explanations and those offering *social* explanations.

Individualistic explanations

Most psycho-social models of health behaviour are individualistic in focus in that they seek to explain and predict the health behaviour of individuals by reference to their personal characteristics (Morgan, Calnan and Manning, 1988). The best established of these is the Health Belief Model (Becker, 1984; Becker and Joseph, 1988). This model highlights the role of risk perception, perceived illness susceptibility, perceived illness severity and the perceived costs and benefits associated with preventive action. Health belief models presume that once individuals perceive the risks associated with an illness and have the means to avoid them, they will realise the benefits of preventive action and accordingly act to avoid risk. This is often referred to as the 'knowledge and means' approach to understanding behaviour and behaviour change.

Similar models, such as the Theory of Reasoned Action (Fishbein and Azjen, 1975) and the Theory of Planned Behaviour (Azjen, 1988), extend the analysis of health beliefs to include the influence of significant others and peer opinion on individual decision-making and behavioural intentions. While these attempt to recognise the importance of factors other than personal characteristics in decision-making about health behaviour, they are still based largely on the assumption of individual rationality. This means that psycho-social models of risk and health behaviour tend to view 'risk taking' as the result of a *rational* decision-making process based on an assessment of the perceived costs and benefits of risk-action.

Most explanations of HIV risk behaviour among drug users are based on individualistic models of health behaviour and behaviour change. The central ethos of the harm reduction approach to date has thus been to enable the drug taker to make *rational choices* about his or her drug taking behaviour. The drug taker is encouraged through a decision-making process in which a hierarchy of choices are offered. These choices range from starting to clean shared equipment through to stopping drug use altogether (see Figure 3.1).

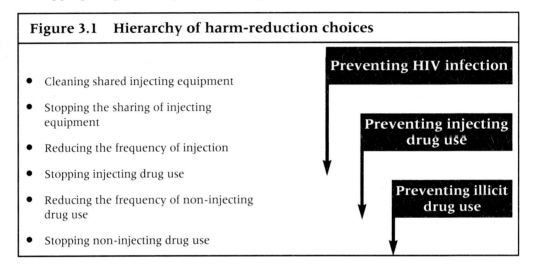

Figure 3.1   Hierarchy of harm-reduction choices

- Cleaning shared injecting equipment
- Stopping the sharing of injecting equipment
- Reducing the frequency of injection
- Stopping injecting drug use
- Reducing the frequency of non-injecting drug use
- Stopping non-injecting drug use

Preventing HIV infection

Preventing injecting drug use

Preventing illicit drug use

As decisions are made at each of these levels the drug taker begins the hierarchy of transitions which have to be made away from drug-related harm towards a healthier (and ultimately drug and HIV-free) lifestyle. The 'healthy choices' offered by harm reduction are viewed as being one and the same as the 'rational choices' (unhealthy choices are deemed 'irrational'). Individualistic models of health behaviour therefore target individuals as rational decision-makers with the aim of encouraging rational (i.e. healthy) choices about health behaviour.

Social explanations

What these individualistic models fail to capture is that the concept of rationality is neither neutral nor static. Instead, individuals' perceptions of what is 'rational' and of what is 'risky' are determined by a variety of wider everyday social, cultural and material factors. Expectations and legitimations of what is socially acceptable and normal (e.g. about what is 'risky') are not the same for *all* individuals but vary within and across different social groups and networks of drug users and by different situational and social settings. First, there are variations between individuals. What is normal or acceptable about risk for the heroin injector may be different for the heroin chaser; what is seen as risky by the heroin dealer may be different to what is seen as risky by the woman prostitute. Second, there are variations between peer groups or social networks of drug users. What is normal about risk for one group of crack and cocaine users may be different to what is seen as risky for other groups; what is normal for one network of heroin users is different for another.

   This means that perceptions of what is normal, risky or rational behaviour are often different in interpersonal relationships (e.g. sexual relationships) from those in peer group or friendship networks (e.g. drug dealing networks) and occupational or material relationships (e.g. prostitution). Social models of health behaviour are therefore more inclusive than individualistic models in that they attempt to understand the interaction between the individual, their health beliefs, and the social, cultural and material context of behaviour (see Figure 3.2).

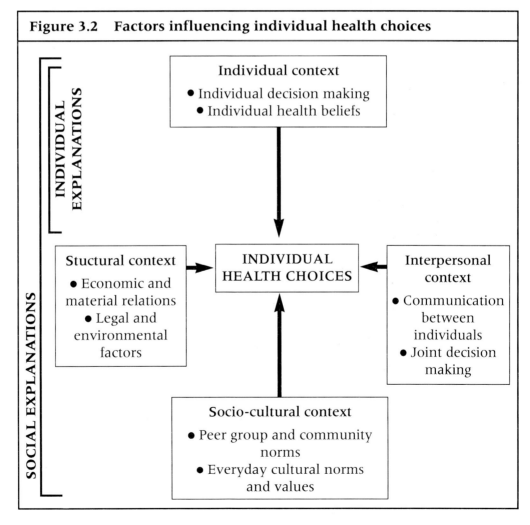

Figure 3.2   Factors influencing individual health choices

INDIVIDUAL EXPLANATIONS

SOCIAL EXPLANATIONS

Individual context
- Individual decision making
- Individual health beliefs

Stuctural context
- Economic and material relations
- Legal and environmental factors

INDIVIDUAL HEALTH CHOICES

Interpersonal context
- Communication between individuals
- Joint decision making

Socio-cultural context
- Peer group and community norms
- Everyday cultural norms and values

Individualistic models of risk behaviour can be seen to be inadequate to address the complex problems of behaviour change. They recognise a cognitive decision-making process in risk perception (based on self-efficacy, motivations etc.) but they fail to capture either the social dimensions of risk-related encounters or the complexity of interpersonal and social interactions (Rhodes and Stimson, 1994a). Risk behaviour usually involves at least two participants. At the very least, models of HIV risk behaviour need to account for how individuals *interact* with other individuals in the negotiation and production of risk. It is becoming increasingly evident that such negotiations (if they are 'negotiated' at all) are based on more than a simple cost and benefit analysis of personal harm (Bloor *et al.*, 1992; Rosenstock *et al.*, 1988; Becker and Joseph, 1988). Individual HIV risk behaviour does not occur in a vacuum but is influenced by the norms, opinions and persuasions of other individuals and groups in different situational and social settings.

Research implications

This has important implications for research on HIV risk behaviour among drug users. To date, most research has been initiated and designed to survey the prevalence of HIV risk behaviour. While such an epidemiological focus is clearly necessary in public health terms, it is becoming increasingly clear that it provides only part of the picture. Survey-based prevalence research is unable to describe fully the social contexts in which risk occurs, how risk is negotiated or how and why risks are perceived, managed or simply ignored (see Chapter 5). In short, such research is singularly unable to sufficiently explain or influence the *process of change* (Rhodes and Stimson, 1994a).

HIV RISK ASSOCIATED WITH INJECTING DRUG USE

There is now a well established link between the sharing of unsterile injecting equipment and HIV transmission. HIV positivity has been statistically associated with syringe sharing and the frequency of injecting with used equipment (Stimson, 1991). HIV infection has also been shown to be associated with the indiscriminate sharing of equipment (e.g. with 'strangers') and the number of people with whom injectors report sharing (Stimson, 1991; Des Jarlais and Friedman, 1987). Equipment sharing continues to be an important factor in determining the dynamics of HIV spread among drug injecting populations. By 1991, it was estimated that 10 per cent of cumulative worldwide HIV infections were due to the sharing of injecting equipment (Bureau of Hygiene and Tropical Diseases, 1991).

In some regions of South and South East Asia, such as Madras, Thailand and Manipur State, drug injection has only become prevalent in the 1980s (Stimson,

1993a). In these regions, the shift from smoking to injecting heroin has been associated with the introduction and rapid spread of HIV among injecting drug users. In Manipur State, for example, there was a dramatic increase in injecting drug use in the 1980s. HIV infection was first identified among drug injectors in the State in 1989 but by mid-1990 the HIV prevalence rate among injectors had risen to over 50 per cent (Stimson, 1993a). This demonstrates the continuing importance of mapping the introduction and diffusion of injecting drug use and of HIV transmission associated with the sharing of injecting equipment.

In Edinburgh, a city where estimates of HIV prevalence among injecting drug users were as high as 51 per cent among treatment populations, sharing was known to have taken place among large gatherings of drug injectors, in part because of a lack of availability of sterile equipment (Robertson, 1990). While equipment availability is an important determinant of sharing, high levels of HIV prevalence have nonetheless been found among injectors in some cities with good availability (Tempesta and Di Giannantonio, 1990). This makes clear the fact that needle sharing is not simply a function of awareness and needle and syringe availability. Understanding why drug injectors share injecting equipment requires more than a 'knowledge and means' approach to explaining HIV risk.

Levels of sharing

There is mounting evidence that drug injectors are changing their drug use and injecting behaviour in response to HIV infection and AIDS. The proportions of drug injectors sharing injecting equipment continues to decline overtime (Donoghoe *et al.*, 1991) and sharing has become less the norm and less indiscriminate (Burt and Stimson, 1993). Studies of London drug injectors between 1984 and 1986 show that as many as 59 per cent (Sheehan, Oppenheimer and Taylor, 1988) and 67 per cent (Mulleady and Green, 1985) of injectors reported sharing injecting equipment in the previous four weeks. Studies among attenders and non-attenders of syringe exchange schemes indicate that between 59 per cent and 62 per cent of injectors were sharing in a four-week period in 1988 compared with between 21 per cent and 25 per cent in 1990 (Donoghoe, Stimson and Dolan, 1992).

More recent research shows a continued decline in the proportion of drug injectors who report sharing. Data from an ongoing survey in London found levels of sharing over a six-month period to be 13 per cent lower in 1991 than in 1990 (34 per cent compared with 47 per cent) (Hunter *et al.*, 1992). In the same period, the study also found reductions in the average number of people with whom injectors had shared.

There are important regional differences in reported rates of sharing. In 1988, levels of sharing in Scotland, for example, were notably higher than those reported in England (76 per cent compared with between 59 per cent and 62 per cent). A recent study of injecting drug use in London and Glasgow suggests such differences remain: 25 per cent of London injectors shared used equipment at least once a month compared with 49 per cent of Glasgow injectors (Rhodes *et al.*, 1993a). The sharing of used needles and syringes comprises two distinct activities: borrowing and lending. In both London and Glasgow, a greater proportion of drug injectors report lending used equipment to others than borrowing others' used equipment (38 per cent compared with 35 per cent in London; 57 per cent compared with 43 per cent in Glasgow) (Rhodes *et al.*, 1993a). While this might suggest attempts to reduce personal HIV risk, surveys in London in 1990 and 1991 show that injectors made greater reductions in lending than in borrowing (Hunter *et al.*, 1992).

Evidence for a continued decline in levels of sharing is supported by qualitative and ethnographic work with drug injectors. One such study, indicated that sharing is becoming less the norm among injectors, occurring in unusual or exceptional circumstances (Burt and Stimson, 1993). Drug injectors were found to employ a variety of strategies to protect themselves from HIV risk. These 'strategies of protection' included personally marking syringes, sharing with selected people, assessing the HIV status of prospective sharing partners, hiding syringes for emergency use and not sharing when blood was visible in the syringe (Burt and Stimson, 1993). The study proposes that community-wide changes in the 'social etiquette' of injecting and sharing behaviour have occurred.

Social context of sharing

It is important to note that all studies have found that a minority of drug injectors continue to share. This raises questions about why sharing continues and whether it is possible to encourage further reductions in levels of sharing. In addressing these questions, studies need to understand the specific situations and circumstances in which sharing continues to occur. This helps to elucidate what situations influence whether or not sharing takes place and what it is that needs to be changed if further reductions in sharing are to be made.

A number of situational factors have been shown to influence whether sharing takes place. Of these, the most important is access to sterile equipment. This appears to be particularly important for those whose drug dependence is severe and who may be in more urgent need for drugs at times of withdrawal (Gossop *et al.*, 1993). In general, where and when availability is poor, sharing rates will be higher (Stimson, 1989). Where syringe availability is relatively good, sharing tends to take place under certain social circumstances and conditions.

The most frequently cited exception to changes in the 'social etiquette' of sharing is that many injectors continue to share in particular social relationships, such as with sexual partners and close friends. In these relationships the passing on or receiving of injecting equipment may not be seen as 'sharing'. Qualitative work in Glasgow, which notes differences in the social dynamics of sharing among men and women, shows that women in particular see sharing with sexual partners as nothing unusual and not worthy of comment (Barnard, 1993). This may in part be because such sharing is viewed as part of a wider pattern of reciprocity and 'sharing' within relationships (Zule, 1992). As noted by Barnard, sharing is a "socially embedded behaviour which is responsive to the many rights and obligations" within social relationships. Norms and expectations about sharing injecting equipment and about the 'risks' associated with these actions are influenced by social relationships and social circumstances.

Studies in New York also show that the nature of social relationships between drug injectors are important determinants of sharing. Friedman and colleagues show that younger less experienced injectors were more likely to share among themselves, than were older, more experienced injectors (Friedman, Des Jarlais and Sterk, 1990). These social relationships are important for mapping the epidemiology of HIV transmission. Despite higher levels of HIV risk behaviour, younger less experienced injectors were less likely to be HIV positive. But as the younger injectors become more experienced they were more likely to inject (and share) with older, more experienced injectors. As Friedman *et al.* suggest, the nature of drug injectors' social relationships influence both levels of HIV risk behaviour and the likelihood of HIV transmission.

The social context of drug use is thus an important determinant of HIV risk behaviour associated with injecting. This is forcefully demonstrated by the ethnographic work undertaken by Ouellet (Ouellet *et al.*, 1991) and Jimenez (1989). They describe how different Chicago shooting galleries have their own unique set of social and organisational norms and 'rules' for renting out injecting equipment and other paraphernalia. These different social structures impinge directly on participants' likelihood of HIV risk and HIV transmission. This indicates that the social context of drug use is just as important as a target for intervention and change as the individuals who use drugs themselves.

Research also shows the importance of the social context of drug use in influencing the sharing of other injecting paraphernalia and in influencing drug use practices. Qualitative studies in London have shown that many injectors who attempt to stop sharing needles and syringes, continue to share other equipment such as filters and spoons (Power *et al.*, 1993). Drug injectors may share equipment other than needle and syringes without realising that this may increase the risk of HIV.

Frontloading

Grund *et al.* (1991) identified a practice known as 'streepjes delen' or 'frontloading' among Dutch heroin injectors. This is where a single preparation of drugs is shared equally by loading one syringe barrel directly from the front of another. 'Backloading' is this process in reverse, where the solution from one syringe is injected into the back of another (plunger removed). Frontloading, which has been associated with HIV transmission (Jose *et al.*, 1992), may go unnoticed in studies which assess the prevalence of 'sharing' between injectors. As yet there are no published studies of the prevalence of frontloading among injectors in the United Kingdom. Unpublished data show that, in a six-month period, 37 per cent of London injectors reported sharing the drug solution between syringes (i.e. frontloading or backloading) (Hunter and Donaghoe, 1994). Of drug injectors who did not borrow injecting equipment in the six-month study period, 27 per cent reported frontloading or backloading. Preliminary data also suggest that frontloading occurs among injectors in Glasgow, where the practice is known as 'halfing' (Green *et al.*, 1993). The importance of frontloading as a risk factor in HIV transmission has yet to have been recognised in UK studies of injecting drug use.

Cleaning equipment

The decline in reported levels of sharing among drug injectors in the last five years has been accompanied by a more recent increase in attempts to clean borrowed injecting equipment. Findings from a London study, show that between 1990 and 1991, the proportion of London injectors who reported cleaning used injecting equipment rose from 87 per cent to 91 per cent (Hunter *et al.*, 1992). While this is encouraging, the study also notes that only a third of injectors in 1990 and a fifth in 1991 used recommended decontaminants such as bleach (see Chapter 4). This suggests the need for careful communication of guidelines for cleaning equipment both to staff of drugs services and to drug injectors and their sharing partners.

Drug transitions

Because of the health harms associated with the injection of drugs, it is becoming increasingly important to consider the possibilities and processes involved in moving away from injecting drug use to non-injecting drug use. It is equally important to examine the factors which encourage or prevent transitions from non-injecting drug use to injecting drug use. Studies are underway in the UK and the USA to study transitions in drug use from one route to another (Strang *et al.*, 1992). Preliminary findings from the Drug Transitions Study in London show that transitions are more common from chasing or smoking heroin to injecting than in reverse (45 per cent compared with 25 per cent) (Griffiths *et al.*, 1992).

This highlights the importance of research in determining when and how transitions to injecting are made and how HIV prevention interventions may encourage not-yet-injectors to remain as such (Strang *et al.*, 1992). There are few reported HIV-related harms associated with non-injecting drug use. Some North American studies show that the frequent smoking of crack and cocaine produces dry, cracked and bleeding lips which may increase the risk of HIV transmission (Holden, 1989). Despite this, most HIV risks associated with non-injecting drug use are thought to be less directly associated with the route of administration than they are with the effects of drug use (particularly stimulant use) on sexual behaviour and sexual safety.

HIV RISK ASSOCIATED WITH SEXUAL BEHAVIOUR

The primary focus of research, intervention and prevention among drug users has been injecting drug use and the sharing of injecting equipment. It is only comparatively recently that research and intervention projects have recognised the increasing public health importance of the HIV risks posed to drug users and their sexual partners through the sexual transmission of HIV. As has been noted:

> *"The sexual mediation of HIV infection is a problem that seems relatively neglected by drug workers and their clients alike"* (Klee *et al.*, 1990a)

The sexual transmission of HIV is likely to be of increasing significance in the future dynamics of epidemic spread, particularly among injecting drug users and their sexual partners (Des Jarlais, 1992). In the United States, it is estimated that injecting drug users are the source of HIV in at least three-quarters of hetero-sexually transmitted cases of AIDS (Des Jarlais and Friedman, 1987; Moss, 1987). In the United Kingdom, a drug injecting partner is reported for over 60 per cent of first generation cases of heterosexual transmission (Evans *et al.*, 1992). Sexual transmission is going to be particularly important in the second decade of AIDS among injecting drug users:

> *"In most areas where HIV has spread among injecting drug users, the drug users have become the source for both heterosexual and perinatal transmission of HIV"* (Des Jarlais, 1992)

The recent ACMD report *AIDS and Drug Misuse: Update* gives closer attention to the importance of the sexual transmission of HIV among drug users. It notes that:

> *"drug users are an especially important target group for promoting sexual change... As a group, drug users... have an increased risk of acquiring and transmitting HIV infection through sexual intercourse"* (ACMD, 1993)

Drug effects and sexual risk

Prior to HIV infection, sexual behaviour research among drug users concentrated on the pharmacological relationship between drug use and sexual activity. In general, these studies suggested that frequent opiate use was associated with a reduction in sexual activity and sexual interest (Mirin *et al.*, 1980) while stimulant use was associated with an enhancement of sexual interest and sexual activity (Gawin and Ellinwood, 1988).

A number of more recent studies investigating HIV and sexual risk, support an association between stimulant drug use and increased levels of sexual desire and activity (e.g. Fullilove *et al.*, 1990; Chaisson *et al.*, 1989). However, some have found increased sexual desire associated with amphetamine use but no increases in sexual activity (Klee, 1992). Others have found either no effects or decreases in sexual desire and activity associated with stimulant drug use (e.g. MacDonald *et al.*, 1988; McCoy *et al.*, 1990).

There are an increasing number of studies which associate the use of drugs with sexual risk behaviour. It has been commonplace, for example, for studies to note the 'disinhibitive effects' of alcohol on condom use. McEwan *et al.* (1992) associate alcohol use with a likelihood of having unprotected sexual intercourse and with having a greater number of sexual partners. Stall *et al.* (1986) found that gay men who engaged in 'high risk' sexual encounters were twice as likely to have used alcohol or other drugs. However, studies also show that the relationship between alcohol use and safer sex compliance is far more complex (Myer *et al.*, 1992; see Reinarman and Leigh, 1988). Some studies, for example, show no empirical associations between alcohol use and unsafe sex while others show *positive* associations between alcohol use and safer sex (e.g. Weatherburn *et al.*, 1992; Leigh, 1990). It has been noted that alcohol has the potential to *encourage* the initiation of safer sex if individuals perceive themselves to have inhibitions in suggesting and negotiating safer sexual encounters (Rhodes and Stimson, 1994b).

Assertions about the effects of stimulant drugs on safer sex compliance are also commonplace. But like alcohol, the research findings suggest a complex relationship which is at best only partially understood. A number of North American studies have found positive associations between cocaine or crack use, HIV infection and sexual risk behaviour. Chitwood and Comerford (1990), for example, found that injectors of cocaine were twice as likely to test HIV positive than were injectors of opiates. Wolfe *et al.* (1990) found that injectors recruited in drug treatment who used crack were more likely to have exchanged sex for money than injectors not using crack, while Watters and Cuthbert (1992) report similar associations between crack smoking and sexual risk behaviour among a sample of female injectors recruited outside of treatment.

Other studies, however, show no simple associations between cocaine or crack use, HIV infection and sexual risk behaviour (e.g. Marx *et al.*, 1991; Hartgers *et al.*, 1991; Wolfe *et al.*, 1992). Of crucial importance is that there are few studies of sexual transmission which show there to be causal links between cocaine or crack use in people without a history of injecting drug use. Such studies are necessary if the relationship between stimulant drug use, sexual risk behaviour and HIV infection is to be better understood. As Marx *et al.* (1991) conclude in a recent review of the US literature on drug use and sexually transmitted diseases:

"It is not known whether drug use is a marker for high risk sexual behaviour, drug use leads to high-risk sex, high-risk sex leads to drug use, or some combination"

In the light of these findings, it is important to note that most explanations of the relationship between drug use and sexual behaviour fail to distinguish between pharmacological and popular perceptions of the 'effects' of drugs on sexual behaviour (Rhodes and Stimson, 1994b). The determinants of the relationship between drug taking and sexual risk remain unclear and their understanding "rests as much upon commonsense understanding as on empirical evidence" (Rhodes and Stimson, 1994b). It is the task of future research to investigate the nature of the relationship between drug use and sexual risk with the aim of delineating the interaction between pharmacological effects and individual and commonsense understandings.

Levels of sexual activity

The majority of drug injectors are sexually active. One recent study found 80 per cent of drug injectors to have had vaginal or anal sexual intercourse in the six months prior to interview (Rhodes *et al.*, 1994a). Approximately two-thirds of drug injectors reported having had vaginal intercourse at least once a week. Other UK studies also show the majority of drug injectors to be sexually active: 77 per cent (Donoghoe *et al.*, 1989); 82 per cent (Klee *et al.*, 1990a); 86 per cent (Coleman and Curtis, 1988).

These findings suggest that there may be some exaggeration in the popular perception that opiate injectors are sexually inactive. Indeed, the proportion of drug injectors who are sexually active has been found to be comparable with the proportion who are sexually active in the British adult population as a whole (Rhodes *et al.*, 1994a). The average number of non-commercial sexual partners reported by London drug injectors in a six-month period (2.1 partners) is slightly greater than those reported in the British adult population over a similar time period (Rhodes *et al.*, 1994a). Strang *et al.* (1994) also found overall levels of sexual activity (including heterosexual anal intercourse) among heroin and cocaine users to be higher than those in the adult population, while the mean number of sexual partners reported by Glasgow injectors was also found to be slightly greater (Goldberg, Frischer and Green, 1993).

Levels of condom use

Levels of condom use among drug injectors and their sexual partners are similar to those reported in the heterosexual population as a whole. Studies also show that injectors are more likely to use condoms with casual partners than with primary partners. Recent findings in London, for example, show that in a six-month period, two-thirds (68 per cent) of drug injectors never used condoms with primary partners and over a third (34 per cent) never used condoms with casual partners (Rhodes *et al.*, 1994a). Other reports indicate that 79 per cent of injectors in Glasgow (Rhodes *et al.*, 1993a) and 75 per cent of injectors in the West Midlands (Klee *et al.*, 1990a) never use condoms.

Most United Kingdom studies conclude that condom use remains at insufficient levels to prevent the potential for sexual transmission of HIV between drug injectors and their sexual partners. This is particularly the case given the average rates of partner change reported by drug injectors and the significant minority of injectors who continue to share used equipment with people other than their sexual partners.

Involvement in prostitution

An involvement in injecting drug use may often overlap with an involvement in prostitution. Studies in London have found that 14 per cent of women prostitutes contacted at a sexually transmitted disease service were injecting drugs (Day *et al.*, 1988) as were 33 per cent of women prostitutes contacted through street-based outreach (Rhodes *et al.*, 1991a). Estimates among women working as prostitutes elsewhere range from 25 per cent (Kinnell, 1989) to 59 per cent (McKeganey and Barnard, 1992).

Conversely, estimates have been made of the proportion of female drug injectors who are involved in prostitution. One recent study shows 14 per cent of female injectors in London and 22 per cent in Glasgow to be involved in exchanging sex for money or drugs in a six-month period (Rhodes *et al.*, 1993a). There is less evidence of injecting drug use among male prostitutes (Bloor, McKeganey and Barnard, 1990).

It is known that women prostitutes are considerably more likely to use condoms with paying partners in commercial transactions than they are with non-paying partners (Day *et al.*, 1988). Recent estimates among female drug injectors working as prostitutes in Glasgow show almost 100 per cent condom use with clients compared with 9 per cent 'always' condom use with steady partners and 22 per cent 'always' with casual partners (Taylor *et al.*, 1993). A similar study of female drug injectors working as prostitutes in London found that 70 per cent reported always using condoms with clients (Rhodes *et al.*, 1994b).

HIV infection among women working as prostitutes has been shown to be closely associated with injecting drug use (Padian, 1988; McKeganey *et al.*, 1992). There are as yet few UK studies which have systematically investigated the epidemiology of HIV prevalence among drug injecting and non-injecting prostitutes or among drug injectors involved in prostitution.

Sexual partners of drug users

There is a high degree of sexual mixing between drug injecting and non-injecting sexual partners: approximately half of the sexual partners of injectors are estimated to be non-injectors (Rhodes *et al.*, 1994a). The vast majority of these partners are women. This is in part an artifact of injecting drug use being a predominantly male activity and in part because some male injectors show specific preferences for *non-injecting* female partners (McKeganey and Barnard, 1992). Such preferences may also be more likely with primary (i.e. more important, longer term) partners than with casual partners (Rhodes *et al.*, 1994a).

There may be increased sexual health risks for the non-injecting sexual partners of injectors (in particular for female primary partners) because contact with an injecting drug user may be their only significant risk factor. It is within primary relationships that condom use is lowest and a significant minority of injectors (between 16 per cent and 19 per cent, Rhodes *et al.*, 1993a) report sex with both primary *and* casual partners in a six month period.

Sexual behaviour change

In marked contrast to the changes in drug use reported earlier, there are only scant indications of change in the sexual behaviour of drug injectors in response to HIV and AIDS. Some follow-up studies point to reductions in the number of sexual partners and sexual encounters or increased levels of reported condom use (Skidmore *et al.*, 1989). In general these have been limited changes and studies also report either no change or increased levels of sexual risk behaviour over time (Des Jarlais *et al.*, 1992).

There are a combination of reasons for the lack of sexual behaviour changes made by drug users. First, drug users' perceptions of risk may give more weight to more immediate or important risks associated with injecting drug use and everyday lifestyle (Connors, 1992). Second, it may be more difficult to encourage changes in sexual norms than in norms about drug use within networks defined primarily in terms of drug use (Rhodes, 1994b). Third, there may be greater difficulties associated with attempts to translate knowledge about sexual risk into action than there is with risks associated with injecting (Stimson *et al.*, 1988). Fourth, the primary focus of intervention and education on modifications in injecting behaviour has encouraged a shared responsibility between injectors about the risks associated with sharing. Such interventions have yet to give equal emphasis to the promotion of sexual safety and sexual responsibility.

HIV status and sexual behaviour change

Drug users who are aware that they are HIV positive show higher levels of condom use, particularly with primary partners, than drug injectors who know themselves to be negative or who are unaware of their HIV status. In Amsterdam, for example, injectors who knew they were HIV positive reported fewer commercial sex partners and more frequent condom use with private partners (Van den Hoek, Van Haastrecht and Coutinho, 1990). No such differences were found in reported levels of syringe sharing (Van den Hoek, 1989).

That awareness of HIV status can facilitate sexual behaviour changes is an important finding, particularly given that the majority of HIV positive drug injectors may in fact be unaware of their HIV positive status (see Chapter 1). While in the UK there are few studies examining the health behaviour of HIV positive drug users, a study of 104 drug injectors who were confirmed HIV positive by anonymous saliva testing showed that 73 per cent never used condoms with their primary partners and that 20 per cent never used them with their casual partners (Rhodes *et al.*, 1993b). Those who were aware of their status were more likely to use condoms than those unaware of their status (58 per cent compared with 18 per cent with primary partners and 88 per cent compared with 75 per cent with casual partners).

Social context of sexual encounters

The social context of sexual encounters is an important determinant of sexual risk and safer sex compliance. Research has shown social factors to influence sexual risk behaviour among drug users at a variety of levels.

At one level, peer group endorsements have been shown to be a particularly important determinant of whether sexual behaviour changes are attempted, achieved or sustained by drug users. Safer sex compliance was found to be more likely among drug users who were in situations where the use of condoms was endorsed by partners, close friends and peers (Abdul-Quader *et al.*, 1990; Friedman *et al.*, 1991). Whether the female sexual partners of drug injectors attempted or achieved sexual behaviour changes was also found to be associated with environments in which peer group and social norms were supportive of safer sex and condom use (Abdul-Quader *et al.*, 1992; Tross *et al.*, 1992). Mounting evidence suggests that social norms about sexual behaviour may be more important determinants of risk reduction changes than norms about drug use or injecting. Within networks of drug users, norms about sexual behaviour and sexuality may be more difficult to change than norms about drug use and drug related practices (Rhodes, 1994b).

Drug users' perceptions and management of sexual risk have also been shown to be determined by the social context of everyday drug using lifestyle. Preliminary findings from an ongoing qualitative study in London indicates that sexual risks are prioritised and acted upon in the context of a *range* of risks and harms associated with buying and dealing drugs, using and injecting drugs and violence within and outside of relationships (Rhodes and Quirk, 1994). Drug injectors (like some drug workers) may not concern themselves with the risks associated with sexual behaviour (McKeganey, Barnard and Watson, 1989).

Of central importance in bringing about sexual behaviour change is the negotiation of sexual safety. This is perhaps the most important aspect of the process of sexual behaviour change. Qualitative studies have shown how social norms in gender relations have influenced women and men's capacity to control sexual negotiations and risk within sexual encounters. Research by Kane (1991) and Wermuth *et al.* (1992), for example, indicates how the female partners of male drug injectors often take responsibility for initiating and sustaining risk reduction strategies both for themselves and for their sexual partners. Qualitative work among cocaine and crack users also illustrates how gender roles within drug using relationships are framed by wider heterosexual relations (Moringstar and Chitwood, 1987; Carlson and Siegal, 1991). These norms and expectations often impinge directly on whether women have equal choice and equal control over negotiating sexual safety within relationships.

A review of research shows the relationship between drug use and sexual risk to be the function of a complex interaction of individual and social factors (Rhodes and Stimson, 1994b). There remains a lack of research into sexual risk and sexual behaviour change. In keeping with current ACMD recommendations, such research is necessary to help interventions develop effective health promotion about safer sex for drug users and their sexual partners.

PRISON, INJECTING DRUG USE AND HIV RISK

A substantial proportion of drug users experience incarceration at some point in their drug use careers and at any one time a substantial proportion of the prison population is made up from current or former drug users. Surveys of injecting drug users in London show that between 61 per cent and 76 per cent reported having recently been incarcerated (Stimson *et al.*, 1988; Dolan *et al.*, 1991). One study showed that 7.5 per cent of the prison population in England and Wales (approximately 3,400 people) had injected drugs within the six months prior to entering prison (Maden, Swinton and Gunn, 1991). A study among inmates recruited from eight Scottish prisons showed that 27.5 per cent had a history of injecting drug use prior to imprisonment, 8 per cent had injected at least once while in prison, and 15 per cent expected to inject drugs after release (Power *et al.*, 1992). One other study of a prison population in Scotland suggests that as many as 35 per cent of inmates had injected drugs prior to imprisonment (Dye and Isaacs, 1991). The high degree of overlap between an involvement in drug use (and particularly injecting drug use) and incarceration has highlighted concerns about the prevalence of HIV risk behaviour in prisons (Turnbull, Dolan and Stimson, 1991).

In a review of HIV prevalence among inmates in European prisons, Harding noted that the proportion of people who were seropositive in prison tended to be in excess of 10 per cent which far outweighed rates of seropositivity outside prison (Harding, 1987). A survey of 452 recently released prisoners in England and Wales also found higher rates of HIV prevalence among prison populations, and in particular among people with a history of injecting drug use (Turnbull, Dolan and Stimson, 1991). This study found 15.5 per cent of female injectors and

8 per cent of male injectors to be HIV positive. Extrapolated data from the study gave an estimated HIV prevalence among injecting drug users in prison of 10 per cent (Turnbull, Stimson and Dolan, 1992). Anonymous HIV surveillance by saliva among inmates in Saughton Prison, Edinburgh found an HIV prevalence rate of 4.5 per cent (Bird *et al.*, 1992). All HIV infections were among inmates who had injected drugs.

Similar patterns are found elsewhere. One study in a Maryland prison found drug injectors to be eight times more likely to be HIV infected than non-injectors (Vlahov *et al.*, 1989). Studies of the New York State prison system show that approximately 95 per cent of inmates with AIDS report a history of injecting drug use (Bureau of Communicable Disease Control, 1989). In South Australia, 85 per cent of inmates with HIV infection were reported to be injecting drug users (Gaughwin *et al.*, 1991).

It is now established that many drug injectors continue injecting while in prison. Surveys indicate that between 25 per cent and 30 per cent of people who inject drugs prior to imprisonment continue to do so when incarcerated (Turnbull and Stimson, 1994). However, of most importance is that the prison environment may act as an impediment to drug injectors' attempts to reduce HIV risks associated with injecting. Prisons may act as 'risk environments' because of the scarcity of injecting equipment and effective cleaning materials (Turnbull and Stimson, 1994). While prison may decrease overall levels injecting among injectors (because of the institutional constraints of pursuing illegal activities) it may increase the likelihood of sharing for those who continue to inject. As has been noted, in comparison to risk behaviour outside prison, imprisonment decreases the prevalence but increases the risk (Turnbull, Dolan and Stimson, 1992).

This is confirmed by numerous studies. Recent research shows that 73 per cent of injectors report injecting with borrowed injecting equipment while in custody and 78 per cent report lending used equipment to others (Covell *et al.*, 1993). Most UK studies show high levels of needle sharing among people who inject drugs in custodial environments: 79 per cent (Carvell and Hart, 1990a); 76 per cent (Dye and Isaacs, 1991); 76 per cent (Power *et al.*, 1992). Studies in Australia have shown that on average 42 per cent of injecting drug users continue to inject in prison, that 80 per cent of these share equipment at sometime during their stay, of whom less than a third attempt to clean shared equipment with bleach or boiling water (Gaughwin, Douglas and Wodak, 1991). Concerns that prisons increase the likelihood of HIV risk behaviour and HIV infection among drug users are shared by the ACMD. While prison environments may help to reduce drug use or encourage transitions from injecting to non-injecting drug use, it is also the case that:

> *"the prison environment may promote unhealthy changes such as the first episode of inject-ing or the first sharing of needles and syringes"* (ACMD, 1993)

HELP-SEEKING BEHAVIOUR

The notion of 'clinical iceberg' refers to the fact that it is only a small proportion of those with a potential need for health services who access them. The processes by which individuals come to recognise 'illness' and the responses or actions taken by individuals as a result is known as 'illness behaviour' (Mechanic, 1968). One aspect of illness behaviour is help-seeking.

The majority of drug users remain out of contact with drug treatment and helping services (Frischer, 1992). It is therefore important to consider the extent to which those who do not seek help for their drug problems are in need of help, and conversely the extent to which those who do seek help are able to improve their health by reducing the harms associated with drug use. It is important to investigate the determinants of help-seeking behaviours themselves. This is necessary to help design appropriate health education and prevention strategies for reaching drug users in need of health services. Such work is an urgent priority in the context of HIV prevention.

Determinants of help-seeking

As noted earlier, models of health behaviour attempt to explain the factors which determine the health and illness of individuals and societies. Different models make different assumptions about the factors which determine whether or not an individual seeks help about an illness. Individualistic models (see above) emphasise a cognitive process of decision-making about the costs and benefits of help-seeking. More recent models tend emphasise more social factors such as the importance of individuals' interactions with significant others (peers, family, friends) and the influence of lay support and referral systems in determining patterns of help-seeking (see Dingwall, 1976; Fabrega, 1974).

Decisions about whether or not to seek help do not simply depend on an individuals' awareness of service availability or on their own 'health-beliefs'. While awareness of services has been shown to a factor influencing the help-seeking of drug users (Sheehan, Oppenheimer and Taylor, 1988), there are many other situational and social factors of influence such as the perceived accessibility and appropriateness of services (Jackson and Rotkiewicz, 1987), perceptions of service and treatment effectiveness (Shehan *et al.*, 1988), and perceptions of health and welfare (Hartnoll and Power, 1989). Help-seeking is determined by a combination of social as well as individual factors. These include the influence of peer opinions, social norms and 'lay referral systems' (Friedson, 1970), cultural norms about health, illness and service need (Zborowski, 1952), and social inequalities with regard to service access and care (Tudor Hart, 1971).

Reviews of the literature on patterns of help-seeking among drug users are provided elsewhere (Hartnoll, 1987, 1992). One of the most crucial factors in the help-seeking of drug users is that most drug users have an inequality of access to health services. It is often difficult for drug users to access health services as easily as it is for non-drug users. Furthermore, some drug users have easier access to drug specialist services than others. What determines whether some drug users have a greater ease of access to services than others? What determines whether some drug users seek help while others remain 'hidden' or 'hard-to-reach'?

One factor often reported as being an important determinant is the severity of problem drug use. Many studies suggest that help-seekers are more likely to have severe problems associated with drug use and are more likely to be worried about their health. Other studies show there to be no differences between help-seekers and the non-help seeking peers of help-seekers with regard to severity of drug dependence (e.g. Hartnoll and Power, 1989; Rounsaville and Kleber, 1985). Hartnoll and Power (1989) report that the only key differences between help-seekers and non-seekers were that those who did not seek help were more likely to employ coping strategies to control their drug use, to spend less money on drug use, to be more enterprising at supporting themselves financially, to be better at avoiding arrest and to experience less criticism from their friends. They conclude that help-seekers were more likely to have experienced significant drug-related negative events in their lives within approximately three months prior to seeking help. Prior to this time, there were no demographic or behavioural differences between help-seekers and non-seekers.

Help-seeking and HIV risk

Most studies of help-seeking behaviour among drug users were undertaken either prior to HIV infection and AIDS or relatively early in the development of the epidemic. Studies undertaken since then have concentrated less on the help-seeking behaviour of drug users themselves and more on the ability of 'lower threshold' and 'user friendly' services to seek-out hard-to-reach and hidden populations of drug users (Hartnoll, 1992).

A growing number of studies report that drug users with no experience of seeking or receiving help are more likely than those with experience of help to be HIV positive (see Chapter 1). One recent study in London found a HIV prevalence of 20 per cent among drug injectors with no experience of treatment or help for their drug use compared with 8 per cent HIV prevalence among drug injectors with previous or current experience of treatment or help (Haw *et al.*, 1992). Differences have also been found between help-seekers and non-seekers in levels of reported HIV risk behaviour (e.g. Power *et al.*, 1988), though these differences are by no means consistent across studies and study designs (Samuels *et al.*, 1992; Alcabes *et al.*, 1992).

Implications for intervention

It is clear that there are limitations in dominant models of primary prevention which operate on the assumption that given an individual's recognition of the severity of an illness they will necessarily and appropriately seek help. The emergence of HIV infection and AIDS has encouraged the evolution of lower threshold services oriented towards harm reduction which aim to seek-out hard-to-reach drug users through the use of pro-active and innovative contacting strategies (see Chapter 4). This has shifted the parameters and meaning of concepts like 'help' and 'seeking' common to treatment oriented models of disease prevention and illness behaviour. As Hartnoll (1992) contends, it is timely to review conventional notions of 'help-seeking' in line with the public health oriented approaches now common to most HIV prevention strategies. While it is vital to understand the determinants of help-seeking behaviour among drug users to help provide more appropriate intervention responses, in the interests and immediacy of public health there is a greater urgency to reach-out to drug users who do not and will not seek help. In the words of the ACMD:

> *"We must move beyond the concept of drawing drug users into services to develop a broader response which, above all, incorporates a range of early interventions"* (ACMD, 1993)

4 HIV prevention and health intervention

This chapter describes the range of HIV prevention interventions targeting drug users. These include primary health care, counselling, testing and prescribing services and community-based prevention initiatives such as syringe exchange and outreach work. The chapter gives greater attention to reviewing the feasibility and effectiveness of community-based and drug service interventions than initiatives based within generic and non-specialist services.

MODELS OF PREVENTION AND HEALTH INTERVENTION

Prevention is usually defined as operating at three distinct levels: primary, secondary and tertiary. At each level, health education performs three complementary functions. At the level of primary prevention, health education aims to persuade people to avoid behaviours which carry an increased risk of HIV. This involves encouraging individuals to adopt healthy lifestyles and to maintain health behaviour. At the secondary level, health education aims to provide advice to people perceived to have put themselves or others at increased risk. This involves encouraging individuals to adopt safer practices, to comply with health recommendations and to seek appropriate help in the event of health related harm or illness. At the tertiary level, health education aims to encourage the healthiest possible lifestyles for those who have HIV infection and AIDS.

   The concept of harm reduction straddles each of these levels of prevention. In practice, harm reduction interventions have placed most weight on the primary and secondary prevention of HIV, while tertiary prevention has become subsumed under the provision of HIV-related treatment and care. These priorities are reflected in current drugs policy recommendations which emphasise that the "opportunity and need for prevention remain" (ACMD, 1993), which is in keeping with earlier recommendations that "all services in contact with drug misusers should inform them of the risks of HIV and how they can avoid and reduce these risks both sexual and injecting" (ACMD, 1988).

Health promotion

There have been a number of attempts to categorise health education (Tones, Tilford and Robinson, 1990). These have led to an accepted typology of four models of health education: information-giving, individual empowerment, community action and radical-political (Beattie, 1991; Tones, Tilford and Robinson, 1990; French and Adams, 1986). These models each make different assumptions about health behaviour and behaviour change and each emphasise different intervention strategies in the process of achieving and sustaining change. As shown in Figure 4.1, they range from primarily individualistic models which emphasise the importance of information-giving, awareness-raising and individual empowerment to primarily social models which emphasise strategies of community action and community change (Beattie, 1986, 1991).

Figure 4.1   Individual and social models of health intervention and change

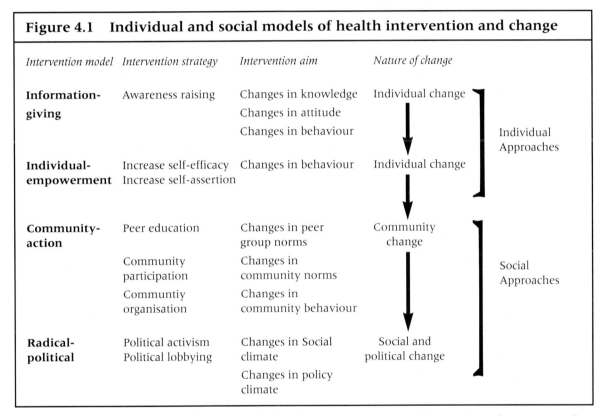

Information-giving and *individual empowerment* models are based on an understanding of health behaviour which parallels that of health-belief models (see Chapter 3). Their aim is to enable or empower individuals to have the knowledge and means to make healthy choices about their behaviour and lifestyles. In contrast, *community action* models of intervention recognise the need for social explanations of health behaviour which recognise the influence of social norms and values in determining health and in achieving change (see Chapter 3). They also recognise the need for community involvement and community organisation in defining and controlling the parameters of change and in sustaining change over time. Whereas individual empowerment interventions target individuals for individual change, community action interventions target whole communities and populations for community change (Rhodes, 1994a). Interventions may also aim to achieve changes in social, fiscal and legislative policy (e.g. soliciting laws in prostitution) or in the wider social and political environment which influences the ways individuals and communities behave. These strategies fall within the category of *radical-political* models of health education, which move from a position of community action to political action in an attempt to facilitate more fundamental social changes in society.

Individualistic and social models of health intervention are often seen to work in opposition to one another. However, it is important to recognise that effective health intervention demands an *integrated strategy* which is multi-faceted and multi-disciplinary in approach. This has led to the emergence of the concept and theory of 'health promotion', of which individual, social and political health interventions are all parts (Bunton and MacDonald, 1992). Health promotion calls for intervention strategies which are oriented to the task in hand, employing information-giving interventions with individual or community empowerment interventions as required. A consummate health promotion practice co-ordinates a range of health education components with the overall aim of facilitating individual, community and public health.

The tenets of health promotion were first outlined by the World Health Organization in the *Ottawa Charter for Health Promotion* (WHO, 1986). As shown in Figure 4.2 these principles can be summarised as healthy individuals; healthy services; healthy communities; healthy environments; and healthy policy. These form the principles of health promotion today and provide a strategic framework for HIV prevention. It is these principles which help towards understanding the effectiveness of current HIV prevention interventions among drug users. They may also provide a strategic basis for developing and planning future HIV prevention targets and for measuring HIV prevention outcomes (see Chapter 5).

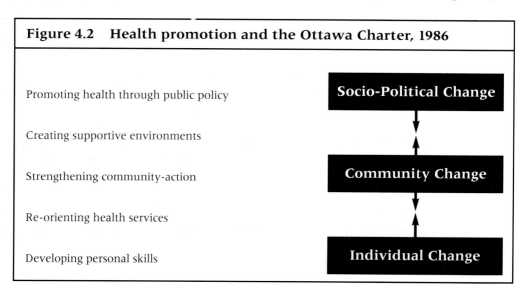

Figure 4.2   Health promotion and the Ottawa Charter, 1986

Promoting health through public policy — **Socio-Political Change**

Creating supportive environments

Strengthening community-action — **Community Change**

Re-orienting health services

Developing personal skills — **Individual Change**

METHADONE PRESCRIBING AND THE PREVENTION OF HIV

The prescription of methadone as a substitute opiate drug is a harm reduction strategy. This is because the prescription of oral methadone (as a linctus) helps the drug user to avoid the harms associated with injecting and the prescription of injectable methadone (physeptone) helps avoid the harms associated with injecting 'street' drugs. The potential that methadone prescribing provides as a harm reduction strategy was as relevant at the time of its introduction in the mid-1960s as it is today in the context of HIV infection and AIDS ((Dole and Nyswander, 1965; Berridge, 1989).

Prescribing and harm reduction

The commitment to philosophies of harm reduction in the time of HIV and AIDS has encouraged a change in methadone treatment and prescribing practice. The aims and objectives of methadone treatment interventions have shifted from abstinence-oriented outcomes towards the outcome of maintaining harm-free, non-illicit drug use (Ward *et al.*, 1992). This focus on reducing the risks and harms associated with drug use (rather than on reducing and stopping drug use) has also encouraged change in the ways methadone treatment is offered and delivered. A commitment to 'lower threshold' prescribing and 'user friendly' services has made methadone treatment more accessible and more available to opiate users. These changes have been characterised by 'flexibility' in prescribing and have included low threshold (in some cases 'no threshold') entry into treatment programmes, less extensive screening, more relaxed treatment regimes and in some cases, the provision of sterile injecting equipment and cleaning kits (Ward *et al.*, 1992).

The contemporary 'paradigm of prescribing', which is informed by the twin objectives of harm reduction and HIV prevention, emphasises the multi-faceted roles that prescribing can play (Strang, 1990b). As well as relieving withdrawal in the process towards reducing drug use, it can function as a 'bait' to capture and retain drug users in treatment and as a promoter of change in their drug use, HIV risk and health behaviour. In the light of evidence which suggests lower levels of HIV risk behaviour and HIV prevalence among drug injectors who are in contact with drug treatment interventions (see Chapter 3), these objectives can be considered an integral part of low threshold prescribing programmes. The potential role that prescribing has in HIV prevention was noted in the ACMD report of 1988:

> "We conclude that prescribing can be a useful tool in helping to change the behaviour of some drug misusers either towards abstinence or towards intermediate goals such as a reduction in injecting or sharing"

The majority of methadone prescribed in the UK is oral methadone. In seeing part of the purpose of prescribing as "attracting more drug misusers to services and keeping them in contact", the ACMD also noted that (in exceptional cases) the "prescribing of *injectable* drugs may be necessary to keep the individual in treatment and/or ease the change from injecting the drug of dependence to taking a substitute orally" (ACMD, 1988). This position was reaffirmed in the latest ACMD report:

> *"We are of the firm view that the major health gain to be provided by methadone mainte-nance programmes is in the form of non-injectable drugs and that injectable prescribing should remain a minority clinical activity for exceptional circumstances"* (ACMD, 1993)

The role of methadone prescribing in HIV prevention is therefore to reduce the harms associated with injecting illicit drugs and to see these targets as interme-diate outcomes in the process towards reducing and stopping opiate use. It is timely to review the effectiveness of methadone prescribing in doing this and to re-assess the role of prescribing in future HIV prevention interventions.

Methadone and HIV prevalence

There has been little UK based research on the effectiveness of methadone as a method of HIV prevention. A number of North American studies have associated lower rates of HIV prevalence among drug users in methadone maintenance pro-grammes. In cities where HIV prevalence is relatively high among drug injectors, retrospective studies have associated length of time in treatment with lower rates of HIV positivity (Des Jarlais *et al.*, 1989; Schoenbaum *et al.*, 1989). One study in New York City, for example, found that drug users who entered into treatment before 1982 were less likely to be HIV positive than those who entered treatment in later years (Abdul-Quader *et al.*, 1989). Another study in New York showed that no clients of a methadone programme were HIV positive, despite the fact that almost all had hepatitis B infection (Novick *et al.*, 1990). This may suggest that while nearly all had shared injecting equipment at some time, sharing has probably not occurred since the introduction of HIV and their entry into methadone treatment.

Other studies have found that clients in methadone treatment were less likely to be HIV positive than those in detoxification programmes (Marmor *et al.*, 1987) or those yet to be receiving methadone (Chaisson *et al.*, 1989). Although research suggests that HIV prevalence differences only hold true for those on long term maintenance (Ball *et al.*, 1988), studies have also found no such differences between longer and shorter term methadone clients (Hartgers *et al.*, 1990).

Methadone and HIV risk

Research has also suggested that methadone prescribing can reduce HIV risk behaviour. The largest study to look at differences in injecting and sharing among drug injectors in methadone treatment compared to injectors not in treatment was conducted by Ball *et al.*, (Ball *et al.*,1988; Ball and Ross, 1991). Findings indicated that reported rates of injecting and equipment sharing were markedly reduced among those in treatment. Findings from an Australian study showed that 20 per cent of injectors in treatment reported sharing equipment in the last month compared with 68 per cent of injectors not in treatment (Darke, Hall and Carless, 1990).

Studies also show that drug users successfully maintained on methadone reduce their levels of HIV risk behaviour over time. Of the 633 methadone clients studied over a three year period by Ball *et al.* (1988), 36 per cent had not injected again after one month of treatment and 22 per cent had not done so after one year. Other studies support reductions in injecting and sharing to be associated with methadone treatment (Selwyn *et al.*, 1987; Abdul-Quader *et al.*, 1987). In one of the few English studies, Klee *et al.* (1991) report that methadone maintenance was associated with a reduction in sharing, but only for older, longer-term patients.

Despite mounting evidence of the effectiveness of methadone prescribing in reducing injecting and sharing, it is important to note that a proportion of clients continue to engage in HIV risk behaviour (Klee *et al.*, 1991). Studies also show no reductions in clients' reported sexual risk behaviour (Darke, Hall and Carless, 1990) and there is little evidence to associate methadone treatment with either reductions in the numbers of sexual partners or with safer sex compliance.

Methadone treatment in HIV prevention

It is important to determine not only whether methadone treatment is an effective method of HIV prevention, but also what it is that makes some methadone programmes more effective than others. In this respect, the most incisive studies are those of Ball and colleagues (Ball *et al.*, 1988; Ball and Ross, 1991). In comparative studies evaluating the effectiveness of six methadone treatment programmes in different US cities, Ball *et al.* found specific characteristics of the different programmes to account for variations in reductions in HIV risk behaviour. The most important components were methadone dosage levels, the range and quality of counselling and support services, and the quality of relationships between workers and clients. The other most important factor is the length of time in treatment and an emphasis on maintenance rather than a reduction in prescribing.

As recently pointed out by Ward *et al.* (1992), all of these characteristics were highlighted as being of crucial importance when methadone was first introduced. The studies by Ball *et al.* show that clients on higher dosage levels were more likely to have reduced their levels of injecting and HIV risk behaviour. They show that adequate dosage levels fall between 60–100mg per day. These findings are supported elsewhere. Brown *et al.* (1989), for example, found that low dosage levels were associated with an increased likelihood of HIV positivity and Joe, Simpson and Hubbard (1991) found that clients on lower doses were more likely to drop out of treatment. Newman (1991) notes that "lower doses are associated with a significant likelihood of persistent illicit narcotic use".

Despite the evidence on dosage levels, there is a "reliance on dosages known to be sub-optimal" and "many clinicians in methadone maintenance programmes routinely prescribe methadone in doses known to be inadequate for optimal therapeutic effectiveness" (Newman, 1991). The research evidence indicates that dosage is an important determinant not only of treatment effectiveness but also of HIV risk behaviour and HIV transmission.

With regard to duration of treatment, studies have found that clients who leave programmes prematurely are likely to relapse to pre-existing levels of injecting (Ball *et al.*, 1988). For effective HIV prevention, it is crucially important to encourage as many drug users as possible into treatment and to retain as many as possible once they seek help (Strang, 1990b). Apart from dosage, the most important determinants of capture and retention are the nature and length of treatment offered and the environment within which such treatment is delivered and organised. Key factors are good and frequent contacts between workers and clients and a commitment to establishing clear and realistic treatment targets for clients, including maintenance rather than reduction.

In response to mounting evidence that methadone treatment can work as a method of HIV prevention if certain criteria are followed, the ACMD has stated:

"The benefit to be gained from oral methadone maintenance programmes, both in terms of individual and public health and cost-effectiveness, has now been clearly demonstrated, and we conclude that the development of structured programmes in the UK would represent a major improvement in this area of service delivery" (ACMD, 1993).

Methadone prescribing is one of the few areas in which the ACMD has identified the need for re-assessment and development since the earlier reports in 1988 and 1989. The ways in which methadone is prescribed and treatment is delivered requires co-ordination and change. At present, methadone treatment in the UK is provided in a disparate and fragmented fashion. What is needed are structured methadone programmes which systematically incorporate the programme characteristics known to be effective. This requires a move away from many of the current practices, such as inadequate dosage, which are common to many treatment programmes in the UK.

PRISONS: CHANGING THE RISK ENVIRONMENT

The research evidence reviewed in Chapter 3 illustrated that while the prevalence of HIV risk behaviour among injecting drug users may be reduced while in prison, for those who continue to inject the chances of sharing unsterile injecting equipment are greatly increased. Custodial settings can be seen as 'risk environments' (Turnbull and Stimson, 1994) in that they impede individuals' attempts to reduce risk. Not only do they necessarily constrain individual freedom, they constrain individual health. Upon release many prisoners return to pre-custodial levels of injecting drug use, sexual activity and HIV risk behaviour. Not only do prisons constrain individual health, they may also constrain public health. As reported by the ACMD, the research evidence:

"points towards a significant level of HIV risk behaviour within prison which suggests that HIV may be spreading within the custodial setting, and could further spread back into the community when seropositive prisoners are released"   (ACMD, 1993)

HIV prevention in prison

In 1993, the ACMD saw prisons as representing "an important missed opportunity in the national strategy to combat the spread of HIV". The issue of HIV prevention in prison environments is a complex one. The pragmatics of recommending the distribution of condoms, injecting equipment and cleaning materials cannot be considered as public health pragmatics alone. Just as prison environments influence individual risk behaviours, such interventions would also be subject to the norms, regulations and constraints of the prison environment. The ongoing problem of facilitating HIV prevention interventions within prison environments is the conflict between correction and health; between public law and safety and public health (Brewer, 1991). While the research evidence points to the need for public health interventions to help change the prison environment, this requires more than public health pragmatism and good HIV prevention strategy. In the longer term it may also require changes in the law. Effective HIV prevention strategy needs to target prison environments as well as prison policy: it needs contextual as well as policy change.

For this reason few prisons have endorsed public health recommendations advocating the distribution of injecting equipment, decontamination materials or condoms (Brewer and Derrickson, 1992). It is therefore impossible to determine the effectiveness of such interventions within prison environments. To date no prison anywhere in the world has sanctioned either the distribution or exchange of injecting equipment (Gaughwin and Vlahov, 1993). British drug policy recommends against the distribution of injecting equipment.

The ACMD has emphasised that "the Prison Service should address the issue of the provision of decontaminants in prisons with urgency" (ACMD, 1993). To date there are no documented examples of such interventions in Britain. One or two prisons in Australia provide bleach but there are as yet no research or evaluation findings (Gaughwin and Vlahov, 1993). Condoms are available in prisons in 16 European countries but not in Britain. Preliminary evidence from prisons elsewhere (United States and Canada) suggest that their distribution has not had adverse consequences (Gaughwin and Vlahov, 1993). The ACMD has urged the Prison Service, as they did in 1988, to "make provision for inmates to have confidential but easy access to condoms" (ACMD, 1993).

Assessing the feasibility and potential effectiveness of HIV prevention interventions in prisons is fraught with ethical, medical and legal difficulties, and with little or no research evidence, this task is made no easier. The current position of the ACMD is that increased availability of injecting equipment will result in increased injecting while restricted availability may encourage people to move from injecting to non-injecting drug use while in prison. Evaluations of equipment distribution interventions outside of prison have established that increasing availability does not result in increased prevalence of injecting (see under 'Syringe exchange'), but the situation in prison is clearly more volatile.

Each intervention strategy appears to have its advantages and disadvantages. Restricting equipment availability in prison might bring about transitions towards non-injecting drug use but these transitions may not be maintained after release. These may be small rewards when it is known that restricted availability increases the likelihood of needle sharing for the sizeable proportion of injectors who continue to inject in prison. While making decontaminants available in prison makes injecting safer, such a strategy may deter some injectors from making a transition towards non-injecting drug use. But this is the primary rationale for recommending the distribution of decontaminants above that of injecting equipment. The possibility that availability of cleaning materials may prevent reductions in the prevalence of injecting in prisons for similar reasons as increased availability of equipment (i.e. access to clean equipment) goes unmentioned in the latest ACMD report.

It is also important to note the limitations of decontaminants in the effective cleaning of injecting equipment. Most guidelines recommend bleach as being the most effective agent in inactivating HIV. Recent research, however, has shown that bleach is only effective when used in certain concentrations and under certain conditions (see below under 'Syringe exchange'). For decontaminants to be effective, cleaning equipment requires both time and care, and it is uncertain whether prison environments and the conditions under which people inject drugs in prison are conducive to this. Many prisoners, for example, may inject outside of their cells to reduce the likelihood of being searched or seen. They may be injecting in areas without easy access to water for the flushing out of equipment.

Planning HIV prevention strategy within the prison environment is not simply a balance between law enforcement and public health but is also a delicate balance between the risks and harms of intervention and non-intervention. The selection and development of appropriate intervention options clearly depends on the prison environment. For some public health advocates, the decontamination option is an intermediate one, permitting some reduction in harm but retaining some of the risks. Those who advocate the distribution of condoms and injecting equipment in prisons may see important omissions in this debate as it is documented by the ACMD. It is worth commenting that elsewhere in the report (when debating outreach), the ACMD note:

> *"We reiterate the view expressed in our Part One report that any advice should make it clear that cleaning cannot offer full protection against infection and is no substitute for using unused sterile injecting equipment"*

There is currently little HIV prevention activity within British prisons beyond advice, education and information-giving. Even these responses are subject to the institutional and social constraints of the prison environment and of prison culture. The move towards the decontamination of injecting equipment is clearly the next step to minimising the risks and reducing the harms associated with injecting drug use in prisons. While decontamination strategies may be an incomplete solution to preventing HIV in prisons, they are the most immediate, realistic and effective options available.

Methadone treatment in prison

One intervention which can be effective as a method of HIV prevention is methadone maintenance treatment (see above). Recent policy developments in the Prison Service recommend the availability of short-term methadone detoxification for opiate users on entry into prison. The ACMD has endorsed these recommendations suggesting "that this practice should be adopted more widely" and encouraging the Prison Service to consider:

> *"making longer term methadone treatment available for those remanded or with short sentences who were in receipt of such treatment before custody"*   (ACMD, 1993)

The objectives of methadone treatment in prison have recently been outlined by Hall, Ward and Mattick (1993). First, methadone can provide a continuation of treatment received prior to incarceration. They emphasise that treatment regimes in prison should share the same entry criteria and treatment goals as treatment available outside. Second, methadone treatment can stabilise prisoners on methadone while in prison with the aim of preventing relapse upon release. Third, methadone can reduce the prevalence of injecting drug use with the aim of reducing the risk of HIV transmission in prison.

There is little published research or evaluation material about the effectiveness of methadone treatment in prisons. One exception is the ongoing evaluation of the New South Wales Prison Methadone Programme in Australia (see Hall, Ward and Mattick, 1993) which has found that prisoners who receive methadone report that their levels of drug use have decreased. Few of the prisoners on the programme have been found to use drugs other than their prescribed methadone. The effectiveness of the programme in reducing HIV risk behaviour has yet to be systematically evaluated. To date, findings show that approximately half of the prisoners receiving methadone report sharing equipment while in prison. In the absence of control or comparison groups it is difficult to assess whether reductions in levels of drug use and sharing are specifically associated with being in the methadone programme. Despite this, the authors note that sharing rates might usually be as high as 90 per cent (see also Chapter 3).

PRIMARY PREVENTION, COUNSELLING AND HIV TESTING

The ACMD has noted the importance of 'broadening the constituency' of drug users reached by harm reduction and HIV prevention interventions (ACMD, 1993). This requires a multi-faceted approach which encourages early identification and early intervention in the primary prevention of drug-related problems.

Key strategies which assist in this approach are advice, education and counselling interventions. These are based largely within specialist drug services although opportunities also exist for early intervention within generic services, particularly in general practice. The Central Funding Initiative (CFI) of 1984 encouraged a rapid expansion in community-based drug services (see Chapter 1). Key developments included the expansion of community-drug teams and advice and counselling agencies. Evaluation of the CFI initiative in 1990 estimated there to be approximately 135 advice and counselling teams, 75 community drug teams, 200 syringe exchange schemes (see below), 50 residential rehabilitation units and 33 drug dependency units (MacGregor *et al.*, 1991).

General practice

General practitioners (GPs) are ideally placed to provide advice, education and counselling to recreational and problem drug users. The GP's role as a health educator is well established and substantial opportunities exist to develop this role in relation to HIV, AIDS and drug use. The Royal College of General Practitioners (RCGP) has estimated that 97 per cent of the general population are registered with a GP, and of these, approximately two-thirds consult a practitioner at least once a year (RCGP, 1986). Practitioners are the main providers of family planning in the UK (DHSS, 1984) and have a substantial contact with opiate users, including those who inject (Glanz and Taylor, 1986; Neville, McKellican and Foster, 1988).

Unpublished data from a survey of London drug injectors in 1992, indicated that 78 per cent of drug injectors were registered with a GP and that 62 per cent had visited a practitioner in the last three months (Donoghoe, personal communication). In the last three months, 43 per cent had been prescribed drugs by a GP. Of these, approximately half had been prescribed methadone and half tranquillisers. The potential role of the GP in primary prevention of HIV and of drug use is emphasised by the ACMD:

> *"All general practitioners have drug users among their patients, whether they have identified them as such or not. GPs are the key to early and easy access to care for drug users, as they are for any other patient, and they remain central to the overall strategy of achieving behavioural change"* (ACMD, 1993)

Despite the considerable opportunities in general practice for early identification of drug use and the provision of HIV related advice, counselling and prevention interventions, research indicates that there remain a number of obstacles to effective prevention work (Rhodes *et al.*, 1989; Glanz and Taylor, 1986; Gallagher *et al.*, 1988). Studies show that GPs often lack the necessary knowledge and skills to undertake preventive and clinical work associated with HIV infection and AIDS (Anderson and Mayon-White, 1988; Milne and Keen, 1988). For example, a national survey found practitioners to have considerable difficulties in discussing issues associated with sexuality and safer sex, particularly with gay men and lesbians (Rhodes *et al.*, 1989). While studies indicate variability in practitioners' knowledge and skills to do HIV-related work, many practitioners do not express an interest in health education and prevention being part of training programmes about HIV and AIDS (Milne and Keen, 1988).

One of the most frequently cited obstacles to effective HIV prevention work with drug users in general practice is a reluctance to work with drug users. Despite RCGP and ACMD recommendations, one national survey showed a decline in the number of practitioners offering care to drug users and found that the majority of practitioners had difficulties in conducting such work (Glanz and Taylor, 1986). Another national survey found that approximately half of practitioners said that they would not accept patients they knew to be injecting drugs onto their practice lists (Rhodes *et al.*, 1989). This study also showed that 60 per cent of practitioners were willing to distribute condoms and under half of practitioners were willing to distribute sterile injecting equipment from their practice. As noted by the ACMD, practitioners often view drug users "as a single, unmanageable group of chaotic opiate injectors who are manipulative, time-consuming, disruptive and aggressive towards staff and other patients" (ACMD, 1993).

The potential role of the GP in providing HIV prevention and counselling advice to drug users is under utilised. GPs are in an excellent position to offer brief opportunistic HIV-preventive interventions as part of general consultations and to identify and educate younger drug users and potential recruits into drug use. Many experimental and recreational drug users are not adequately covered by existing health education programmes or by specialist drug services. For many injecting drug users GPs are their primary and sometimes their only access to health and medical services (Glanz and Taylor, 1986). Practitioners are reminded by the ACMD that they "have a contractual responsibility to provide general medical services to all patients on their list, including drug users" and are "encouraged to respond to the specific needs of this particular client group" (ACMD, 1993).

Advice, counselling and HIV testing

Advice-giving and counselling are a core component of service provision in drug services and can be seen to have two complementary functions in the context of HIV and AIDS (Green, 1990). The first is to prevent the spread of HIV by encouraging and sustaining behaviour changes among drug users. The second is to maximise drug users' psychological and social well-being.

One key area neglected within drug services is work about sexuality, sexual behaviour and safer sex. Aware of the difficulties interventions have had in bringing about changes in the sexual behaviour of drug users (see Chapter 3), the ACMD has reiterated the importance of focusing on sexual health in HIV prevention work, stating that:

> *"purchasers should incorporate a requirement that safer sex counselling be made available in all drugs services, and at the same time require suitable monitoring procedures to ensure that this counselling is delivered"* (ACMD, 1993)

There is little evidence on the extent to which safer sex advice and counselling is undertaken within drug services. Similarly, there is little evidence on what passes for 'counselling' or on which counselling methods are most effective with drug users. Preliminary research in this area shows that drug workers may be reluctant to initiate discussion about safer sex with drug users and that drug users often do not expect to receive such education when contacting drug agencies (Rhodes and Green, 1994). Many drug workers may see safer sex education and sexual counselling as a 'specialist skill' to be undertaken by external 'experts' and 'counsellors' (Cranfield and Dixon, 1990). This means that many drug users do not receive safer sex education by virtue of never having contacted an agency for this purpose, while those who do seek help relating to their drug use are more likely to receive such education on a re-active rather than pro-active basis. While most drug workers systematically undertake individual assessments of clients' drug and alcohol use, few consider investigating client sexual histories (Cranfield and Dixon, 1990). The ACMD has recommended that "at the very least, safer sexual practices should be discussed with a drug user when contact is first made... perhaps in the context of assessing the client's overall risk behaviour..." (ACMD, 1993).

The evidence suggests the need for increased drug service training with regard to educating and counselling about safer sex and sexual behaviour. It also suggests the need for further research to investigate the effectiveness of different communication and counselling formats in HIV prevention work with drug users (Silverman *et al.*, 1992).

In particular, there remains confusion between the relative effectiveness of HIV test counselling and HIV testing with regard to behaviour change (Piot, 1990). Evidence suggests that HIV testing is beneficial, although behaviour changes may often be small and sometimes short-lived. Much of this evidence is based on samples of gay men, and there are a number of North American and Dutch studies which show a reduction in unsafe sexual practices among gay men who learn they are HIV positive (e.g. Schechter *et al.*, 1988; McCusker *et al.*, 1988; Van Griensven *et al.*, 1989). Reported changes are most marked among those who test HIV positive, less in those who do not learn of their results and least discernable in those who test and learn they are HIV negative.

Knowledge of antibody test results have been shown to be associated with reductions in HIV risk behaviour among drug users. Among injecting drug users learning they are HIV positive, for example, reductions in the frequency with which injecting equipment is shared has occurred (Van den Hoek, 1990). It is not clear, however, whether knowledge of an HIV positive status would merely add to an already chaotic lifestyle for many drug users who are out of contact with treatment and helping services (Mulleady *et al.*, 1989).

Relatively high levels of unawareness of HIV positivity among drug injectors has highlighted the need for lower threshold community-based HIV counselling and testing facilities. This is particularly important for drug users who remain out of contact with drug agencies who may be less likely to have access to testing facilities and who are less likely to be HIV tested (Donoghoe *et al.*, 1993). The ACMD has recommended increasing the availability of testing facilities in a wider variety of settings to make voluntary HIV testing "more accessible and appropriate to the needs of drug users" (ACMD, 1993).

Existing outreach projects may provide the appropriate foundations for increasing the accessibility and availability of counselling and testing services (Rhodes *et al.*, 1993b; see below under 'Outreach'). Alternative testing facilities would perhaps be most effective if placed in selected outreach projects in areas of high prevalence of injecting and/or HIV. Such facilities would require integration into primary and general health care services as well as education and prevention services within drug services. The 'lowest' threshold HIV testing services in the UK remain those operating as 'special' or satellite clinics based in community drug teams and outreach projects. While a selection of the more established outreach projects in the United States offer HIV testing by outreach workers trained specifically for this purpose, it is as yet too early to encourage such interventions in the UK (Rhodes *et al.*, 1993b).

SYRINGE EXCHANGE: CHANGING EVERYDAY DRUG USE

The syringe exchange has often been represented as one the icons of UK harm reduction strategy. The development of syringe exchange schemes in England and Wales can be seen as one of the first practical steps towards preventing HIV among injecting drug users. It was a community-based response which aimed to reach drug injectors who did not come into contact with existing drug services. It aimed to provide them with the knowledge about the risks associated with injecting and the means to avoid these risks by having easy access to clean injecting equipment. It was an attempt to encourage fundamental changes in the everyday drug using practices of most drug injectors.

The Department of Health endorsed the development and evaluation of 15 pilot syringe exchange schemes in England and Wales in early 1987. Despite rising levels of HIV infection among drug injectors in certain UK cities (primarily Edinburgh) such a pragmatic policy response was bold. The pilot exchange programme sparked controversy because it formed the basis of a shift away from previous policy which saw increased syringe availability being directly related to increases in the prevalence of injecting drug use. The Government could be seen to be indirectly involved in supplying the tools which were required to undertake an illegal activity. The policy which framed the response was designed first and foremost to protect public health (Stimson, 1990). Drugs policy in the late 1980s saw the prevention of HIV to be more important than the prevention of injecting drug use (see Chapter 1).

The Department of Health-funded evaluation of the pilot exchange schemes was completed in 1988 (Stimson *et al.*, 1988). The study reported that the exchanges had encouraged reductions in the frequency of injecting and HIV risk behaviour. Tentatively, the pilot evaluation suggested that the exchanges "could be of cumulative importance in reducing the spread of HIV". These findings proved enough to convince most remaining sceptics of the wisdom of increasing the availability of injecting equipment to drug injectors (Ghodse, Tregenza and Li, 1987; Hart, 1990).

Further impetus to the development of the approach was given by the first ACMD report on *AIDS and Drug Misuse* (ACMD, 1988). This stated that:

> *"the benefits of reduced sharing which will occur if needles and syringes are made easily available alongside health education will outweigh the risks involved in any increase in the injecting population"*

Satisfied that increasing the availability of equipment was a justified response in epidemic times, the ACMD recommended that "further exchange schemes be set up drawing on the experience of the more successful pilot projects" (ACMD, 1988). In response the Department of Health issued guidelines and recommendations for establishing schemes in regional and district health authorities. By 1990, it was estimated that there were approximately 120 schemes in England and Wales (Lart and Stimson, 1990). More recent estimates put this figure at approximately 200 (MacGregor *et al.*, 1991; Donoghoe, Stimson and Dolan, 1992).

The historical and policy climate which surrounded the development of syringe exchange was one of comparative tranquillity and pragmatism (Stimson, 1990). The relative lack of central co-ordination and direction over the 'syringe exchange experiment' (Stimson *et al.*, 1990) meant that exchange programmes were tailored in response to local needs and circumstances. Models of service delivery and organisation were diverse. These initiatives were innovative and localised and yet fragmented in that they lacked co-ordination in terms of national strategic response. They remain of historical note in that they provided the foundation for the public health pragmatism which has continued to characterise UK HIV prevention and harm reduction strategies for injecting drug users.

Syringe exchange and client contact

The Department of Health-funded evaluations of syringe exchange schemes are described in full elsewhere (Stimson *et al.*, 1988; Donoghoe, Stimson and Dolan, 1992). These evaluations indicate that the schemes were relatively effective in contacting clients. Findings showed that between 1987 and 1988, 40 per cent of syringe exchange attenders had never before contacted a drug service for help or treatment (Stimson *et al.*, 1988). As would be expected this proportion dropped over time, and between 1989 and 1990, 26 per cent of attenders had never before sought help for their drug use (Donoghoe, Stimson and Dolan, 1992).

Evaluation of one of the busiest syringe exchanges in England (based in central London) has pointed to the importance of adopting a comprehensive approach to service provision for capturing and retaining clients (Hart *et al.*, 1989b). The study shows that a flexible approach to the provision of injecting equipment, condoms and advice is required along with user-friendly communication strategies and options of referral into other services. While the proportion of first-time attenders at exchanges who have no previous experience of help continues to decline over time, exchanges have provided excellent opportunities for onward referral into other statutory and non-statutory health services (Carvell and Hart, 1990b). This emphasises that the syringe exchange is one component in a wider package of HIV prevention and harm reduction strategies.

Although the exchanges reached many drug-injecting populations (including anabolic steroid users) (Korkia-Kenwood and Stimson, 1993), it is important to note that the schemes have had difficulties in attracting younger injectors, female injectors, injectors of non-opiate drugs (particularly amphetamines and cocaine) and injectors from ethnic minority groups (Donoghoe, Stimson and Dolan, 1992). Most important is that the schemes have had most difficulty in reaching and maintaining contact with drug injectors most vulnerable to HIV and those who continue to engage in risk behaviour. These injectors can perhaps be viewed as the people most in need of syringe exchange services. The evaluations show that syringe exchanges are unable to reach and provide injecting equipment to all those in need (Stimson *et al.*, 1991). This indicates the need to improve on current strategies of exchange and distribution and to develop additional methods of reaching and providing services to drug injectors who are 'hard-to-reach' (see below under 'Outreach').

Syringe exchange and HIV risk

Increasing the availability of injecting equipment through syringe exchange schemes has not been associated with an increase in the prevalence of injecting. Equally importantly, syringe exchanges have not been associated with a fall in the numbers of drug injectors entering drug treatment. These statements are made on the basis of evaluation findings across Europe and elsewhere (Van Haastrecht *et al.*, 1989; Stimson, 1989). Findings from Amsterdam, where exchanges were established in 1984 to prevent Hepatitis B infection, show that since the implementation of exchange schemes the prevalence of heroin users in the city has remained stable (at about 3000) although the number of drug users entering treatment has doubled (Buning, 1990).

The ultimate measure in effectiveness of HIV prevention interventions is a fall in HIV incidence and HIV prevalence. There is only suggestive evidence that syringe exchanges are associated with a decline in HIV transmission (Haastrecht *et al.*, 1989; Stimson, 1989; Wolk *et al.*, 1988). Measures for the effectiveness of syringe exchange have for the most part been intermediate, made on the basis of reported levels of injecting, sharing and associated HIV risk behaviours.

The Amsterdam syringe exchanges have had an encouraging impact on reductions in HIV risk behaviour (Hartgers *et al.*, 1989, 1991; Van Haastrecht *et al.*, 1991). In a follow-up study of drug injectors attending exchange schemes, Hartgers *et al.* (1991) found that over the course of one year, reported levels of injecting did not increase but reported levels of sharing were reduced. Attenders were less likely to borrow unsterile equipment than non-attenders and 74 per cent of attenders compared with 26 per cent of non-attenders always used sterile equipment.

Evaluation of syringe exchange in England shows that drug injectors who attend exchanges report lower levels of sharing, fewer sharing partners and a longer period of elapsed time from the last sharing occasion (Donoghoe, Stimson and Dolan, 1992). But it is also important to recognise that attenders of the schemes had lower levels of HIV risk behaviour than non-attenders *prior* to attendance. The schemes thus attracted injectors who were already making risk reduction changes. Furthermore, reductions in levels of risk behaviour have occurred not just among attenders of exchanges but also among non-attenders (Figure 4.3). As shown in Figure 4.3, levels of reported syringe sharing in the previous four weeks among attenders dropped from 28 per cent in 1987–1988 to 21 per cent in 1989–1990, while levels of sharing within the same time periods among non-attenders dropped from 62 per cent to 38 per cent (Donoghoe, Stimson and Dolan, 1992). These findings support ethnographic work which suggests that syringe sharing is becoming less the everyday norm for drug injectors and that the 'social etiquette' of injecting behaviour is changing (Burt and Stimson, 1993; see Chapter 3).

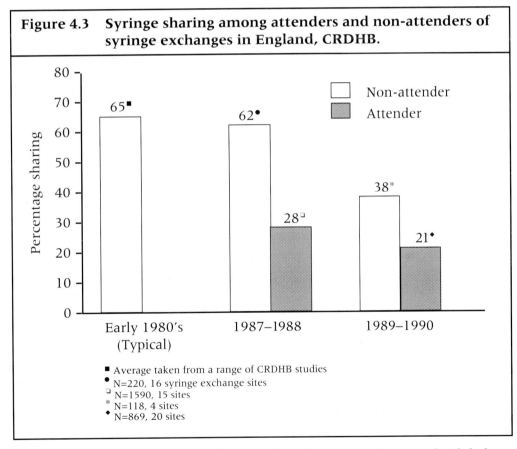

Figure 4.3 Syringe sharing among attenders and non-attenders of syringe exchanges in England, CRDHB.

■ Average taken from a range of CRDHB studies
● N=220, 16 syringe exchange sites
◻ N=1590, 15 sites
* N=118, 4 sites
◆ N=869, 20 sites

Evidence shows the schemes to have had less impact on the sexual risk behaviour of drug injectors. Here there are also fewer discernable differences in the sexual behaviour of attenders and non-attenders, although one London evaluation shows that attenders reported fewer sexual partners than non-attenders and that attenders with multiple sexual partners reported increased condom use over time (Hart *et al.*, 1989). Studies show that exchange workers, like many other drug workers, often find initiation of discussion about sex and safer sex difficult (Stimson *et al.*, 1988). Exploratory qualitative research indicates that while opportunities for safer sex education may exist, both clients and workers may be reluctant to enter into discussion about safer sex and sexual health (Rhodes and Green, 1994).

Syringe exchange in HIV prevention

Five years on from the evaluation of the pilot exchange schemes, the ACMD has emphasised that "needle and syringe exchange schemes should continue to be developed in response to identified need" (ACMD, 1993). Research and evaluation in the UK indicate that there are a number of limitations in current distribution and exchange strategies. Responding to these limitations has implications for the future organisation and delivery of syringe exchange interventions (Stimson *et al.*, 1991).

First, the current supply of sterile injecting equipment cannot meet current demand. Second, it is difficult, particularly in rural areas, for all drug injectors in need of equipment to have easy access to exchanges. Third, exchanges have had most difficulty in reaching drug injectors who continue to engage in HIV risk behaviour. They have also had difficulties in reaching and retaining contact with female injectors, younger injectors, black and ethnic minority injectors and injectors of amphetamines and other stimulant drugs. Fourth, exchanges have had less success in providing sexual health and safer sex education services or in responding to the needs of the sexual partners of injectors. Lastly, a significant minority of injectors continue to share and sharing continues within certain social relationships and in certain social situations (see Chapter 3).

These limitations have three main implications for future syringe exchange interventions. First, they point to the need for expanding the number of distribution points for the exchange and disposal of injecting equipment. It has been estimated that syringe exchange schemes in England and Wales supplied approximately two million syringes between 1989-1990 (Stimson *et al.*, 1991). A survey of retail pharmacists estimates that a further two million syringes were supplied throughout England and Wales in the same year (Glanz, Byrne and Jackson 1989). Based on conservative estimates of the number of drug injectors in the UK, Stimson *et al.* (1991) have estimated the need for an annual distribution of 18 million syringes.

Syringe exchanges can be seen as part of a larger distribution network which includes pharmacy schemes and outreach interventions (see below). This also highlights the possibility of exchange attenders themselves acting as agents of change among non-attending drug injectors. Clients of exchange schemes may assist in distributing needles and syringes to non-attending drug injectors, as volunteers or 'peer educators' within their own drug using and social networks (see below under 'Outreach').

Second, current limitations point to the need for changes in the ways in which exchange interventions attempt to bring about changes in injecting behaviour. Most importantly, this includes the need to target changes in the social situations which encourage continued sharing among injectors. Targeting changes in the social context of sharing (see Chapter 3) requires a shift from targeting individuals with a 'knowledge and means' approach towards community action approaches which may encourage further changes in the everyday norms – or 'social etiquette' – of injecting drug use (see 'Outreach').

The future role of syringe exchange in the prevention of HIV is as one component in a wider package of community-based prevention strategies designed to change the social norms and social context of risk behaviour. Increasing the availability of needles and syringes is part of the picture. To complete the picture it is necessary to create the situations in which individuals not only have the 'knowledge and means' to use clean equipment but in which it is also socially acceptable, desirable and possible not to share equipment. In addition to increasing availability, this requires changes in the social norms which are supportive of sharing. To achieve this it is necessary to move beyond targeting individual drug users to targeting the specific drug-using networks, peer groups, friendships and other social relationships (e.g. between sexual partners) where such norms prevail.

Pharmacy distribution and exchange

Given that demand for injecting equipment far outweighs current supply, it is increasingly important to consider the role of the pharmacist in the distribution, exchange and disposal of equipment (Glanz, Byrne and Jackson, 1989). Recent research among London injectors indicates the importance of pharmacy distribution (Hunter *et al.*, 1992). This study showed that 47 per cent of injectors in 1990 and 42 per cent in 1991 used pharmacies as their main source for sterile equipment compared with 30 per cent of injectors in 1990 and 37 per cent in 1991 who used syringe exchanges.

Most pharmacists supply syringes but few participate in syringe exchange. It is important to encourage further participation in pharmacy exchange because of the need to dispose of used equipment effectively. Surveys show that the level of participation in exchange schemes by pharmacists depends largely upon the individual pharmacist (Glanz, Byrne and Jackson, 1989). One of the most frequently cited reasons given by pharmacists for not participating in exchange schemes is their concern for financing and arranging the disposal of returned equipment. While the ACMD recommends that "pharmacists increase their level of involvement in needle and syringe exchange schemes", the report also points to the need for "health and local authorities to ensure that adequate facilities are available for the disposal of used injecting equipment" (ACMD, 1993).

Bleach interventions

Many interventions recommend to drug injectors that they decontaminate shared injecting equipment. The most commonly recommended decontaminant is bleach. Bleach interventions are most common in the United States. This is because syringe availability has been restricted in many states through laws against possession of 'narcotics paraphernalia' which have prohibited the establishment of syringe distribution and exchange.

Research evidence from San Francisco, where bleach distribution became an established part of HIV-prevention interventions in the mid-1980s, shows that bleach has been successfully incorporated into existing everyday patterns of injecting drug use. Ongoing evaluation studies of bleach distribution by outreach teams, found that 3 per cent of drug injectors used bleach in 1986 compared with 68 per cent in 1987 (Watters, 1988). Similar results in Worcester City, Washington, show that bleach use increased from 29 per cent of injectors in November 1987 to 70 per cent in November 1988 (Connors and Lewis, 1989). As noted in Chapter 3, while the vast majority of drug injectors in London attempt cleaning borrowed equipment, only a third in 1990 and a fifth in 1991 did so with bleach (Hunter *et al.*, 1992). Moss (1990) suggests that long-term use of bleach in San Francisco may have had a protective effect on HIV positivity, although there is little conclusive evidence about the association between bleach use and HIV incidence or HIV prevalence.

There are a number of problems associated with bleach interventions (Rhodes, Hartnoll and Johnson, 1991). Initially, the communication of a hierarchy of instructions with regards to a choice of decontaminant was noted to have encouraged confusion. The recommendation to use ethanol to clean equipment, for example, was sometimes interpreted as drinking alcohol. Recommendations to boil syringes in water in the event of bleach or ethanol being unavailable were also found to be imperfect because the boiling of many syringes caused them to buckle.

Flushing the syringe with bleach has been the internationally accepted method of inactivating HIV in injecting equipment (Newmeyer, 1988). However, the efficacy of this method has recently been questioned (Donoghoe and Power, 1993). Evidence from one study shows no differences in the rate of HIV incidence among injecting drug users using decontaminants all the time compared with those never using decontaminants (Vlahov *et al.*, 1991). One other study found that a 10 per cent solution of bleach was not effective in removing blood from syringes using a six-second cleaning with bleach followed by two six-second rinses with water (Contoreggi *et al.*, 1992). In response, the US National Institute on Drug Abuse (NIDA) has issued new recommendations on syringe hygiene which stress that "cleaning with disinfectants, such as bleach, does not guarantee that HIV is inactivated" (NIDA, 1993). To maximise the effectiveness of bleach, NIDA recommend that syringes are soaked with full-strength household bleach for at least 30 seconds.

While bleach, if used consistently and carefully, may reduce the possibilities of HIV transmission, it is thought that bleach is largely ineffective in inactivating hepatitis viruses. Preliminary evidence suggests that the prevalence of hepatitis B and C among drug injectors in the UK may be over 50 per cent (see Chapter 1). The potential ineffectiveness of disinfecting equipment with bleach could be of crucial importance in the further spread of hepatitis infections.

OUTREACH: CHANGE IN THE COMMUNITY

The majority of drug users remain out of contact with existing treatment and helping services. Agency-based initiatives, such as syringe exchange, are reliant on drug users seeking help. As mounting evidence indicates higher levels of HIV prevalence and, in some cases, higher levels of HIV risk behaviour among drug users who do not seek help from drug services (see Chapters 1 and 3), it is increasingly important to develop innovative strategies for 'reaching the hard-to-reach' (Rhodes and Hartnoll, 1991).

HIV outreach work can be broadly defined as:

> *"A community-based activity with the overall aim of facilitating improvement in health and reduction in the risk of HIV transmission for individuals and groups who are not effectively reached by existing services or through traditional health education channels"*
> (Rhodes, Hartnoll and Johnson, 1991)

Outreach thus aims to target individuals and groups without an equality of access to service provision. These include the traditionally more difficult to access groups of drug users and women and men working as prostitutes, as well as those defined less in terms of specific HIV risk behaviours but who are nonetheless out of contact with helping services, such as homeless young people, black and ethnic minority groups, prisoners and women. Evidence suggests that younger, recreational and female drug users are under-contacted by current outreach interventions, as are users of non-opiate drugs, particularly amphetamines.

Outreach is an important strategy in the aim to 'broaden the constituency' of drug users contacted by primary prevention interventions (ACMD, 1993). In 1988, the ACMD saw the role of outreach to be one of reaching-out to drug users with the aim of bringing them back into contact with existing services. The report stated:

> *"The most effective way of educating drug misusers about HIV, and changing their behaviour so as to minimise the risks, involves first bringing them into contact with a helping agency. At present, only a small minority of drug misusers are in touch with services"*
>
> *(ACMD, 1988)*

The ACMD working group recommended that drug services "experiment with a variety of [outreach] approaches and monitor their effectiveness in reaching drug users not in touch with services" (ACMD, 1988). By mid-1988, Department of Health funded research estimated there to be 122 projects in Britain undertaking outreach work to contact individuals affected by HIV and AIDS (Hartnoll *et al.*, 1990). A third of these had developed specifically in response to HIV and AIDS. Two-thirds of the projects targeted injecting drug users and 62 per cent saw harm minimisation as one of the primary objectives of their work. Over half of the outreach projects were located in the voluntary sector, and just under a quarter in the NHS.

Outreach services have expanded rapidly over the last five years. It is now viewed as an essential component of HIV-prevention strategy both inside and outside the NHS. As a complement to most health education interventions outreach has much to offer. Like syringe exchange, it is an extension of a pragmatic response in the public health prevention of HIV. Because it is an extra-agency response (unlike most syringe exchanges) it has the potential to offer education within the social contexts in which risk behaviour occurs. It aims to reach drug users out of contact with, and in need of, health services. This gives it the potential to respond quickly to client need. It is a client-centred approach, which provides the opportunity for idiosyncratic advice-giving and education. Most outreach interventions work on the principle of reaching out to people with the aim of providing them with the means to make healthy choices. This is likely to be more effective than merely providing individuals with health information alone or assuming that they will seek help when experiencing sufficiently serious health problems. Outreach is therefore important in the primary prevention of HIV and drug use in that it aims to "influence greater numbers of drug users at an earlier stage in their drug using career" (ACMD, 1993).

Outreach service provision

Almost all outreach projects aim to provide harm reduction and safer sex education and most projects distribute condoms and injecting equipment. Few distribute bleach although many provide advice on how to clean injecting equipment. These services are commonly provided through three distinct outreach approaches. These are summarised in Figure 4.4 as detached, domiciliary and peripatetic (see Rhodes and Stimson, 1994c).

In addition to extra-agency strategies many outreach projects also have drop-in facilities. Others have regular community-based satellite clinics and mobile

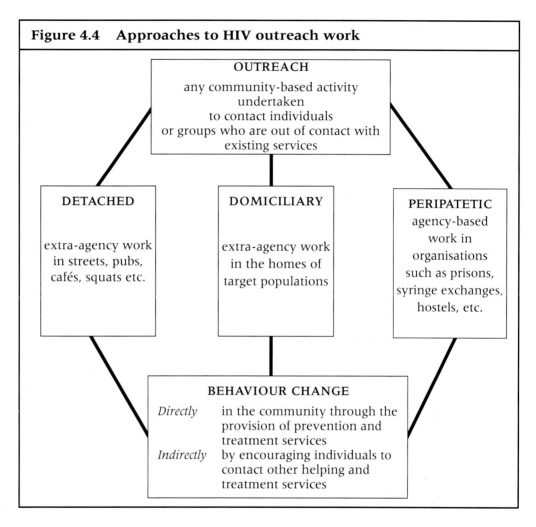

Figure 4.4   Approaches to HIV outreach work

OUTREACH

any community-based activity undertaken
to contact individuals
or groups who are out of contact with
existing services

DETACHED

extra-agency work
in streets, pubs,
cafés, squats etc.

DOMICILIARY

extra-agency work
in the homes of
target populations

PERIPATETIC
agency-based
work in
organisations
such as prisons,
syringe exchanges,
hostels, etc.

BEHAVIOUR CHANGE

Directly   in the community through the
provision of prevention and
treatment services

Indirectly   by encouraging individuals to
contact other helping and
treatment services

units. These strategies have been found to be useful in providing opportunities for extended 'off the street' contact with clients and for the provision of primary health care, STD and HIV testing and counselling services (Buning, Van Brussel and Van Santen, 1990).

Despite the urgency with which UK outreach services have been developed, there is little evaluation of the effectiveness of outreach targeting drug users. Evidence suggests that outreach services are feasible and valuable for identifying and reaching hidden populations where HIV risk behaviours are prevalent (Rhodes, Hartnoll and Johnson, 1991). An evaluation of an outreach team in central London found that approximately half of clients contacted through detached work were not in contact with other health or helping services (Rhodes, Holland and Hartnoll, 1991).

UK evaluation also shows that outreach can be effective in providing prevention services through detached work. Outreach may also provide client referrals into existing statutory and non-statutory based services. It is therefore considered a particularly effective method of bridging gaps in service provision between statutory and non-statutory sectors and between social and medical services. Many clients contacted through outreach work have more immediate needs than HIV services such as needs for housing, and legal or financial assistance. These more pressing needs have been found to limit the appropriateness and effectiveness of some HIV-related outreach interventions (Rhodes and Holland, 1992). This has raised the question of how HIV outreach might work as part of a wider package of service delivery which targets changes in the social factors which impede the effective promotion and adoption of HIV prevention interventions.

Evidence indicates that referral of clients contacted through outreach work into existing centre-based services should not be seen as the justification or primary aim of outreach work (Rhodes and Holland, 1992). Instead, it should be viewed as one objective of many. This is because clients have a variety of needs of which referral into existing HIV-related, STD and drug services is one. In addition, for some clients existing services will remain inappropriate to their needs, while for others they will be perceived to be inaccessible irrespective of need. This highlights the limitations of viewing outreach as merely a mechanism to encourage individuals into existing services. In response, the ACMD no longer views referral into existing services as being the prime objective of outreach work. As stated in the latest report (ACMD, 1993):

> *"...it is time to look at new ways of working towards the overall aim of outreach, that of improving health and reducing HIV risk among drug users out of touch with services"*

A review of research on interventions in Europe and the United States has shown that outreach has the capability to provide prevention and other health services directly in the community, and that these objectives are complementary with the referral of clients into existing services (Rhodes, Hartnoll and Johnson, 1991). Findings, particularly from the Netherlands, demonstrate the usefulness of integrating primary health and drug treatment as part of community-based responses to HIV prevention, such as outreach (Buning, Van Brussel and Van Santen, 1990). These services can include general health check-ups, STD treatment and advice, HIV testing and HIV counselling as well as methadone prescription and drug treatment. By providing them directly in the community, they become more accessible to clients of outreach services. Only a small proportion of clients who are contacted through outreach are referred to other services and only a small proportion of these clients access services when referred (Rhodes and Holland, 1992). This suggests the continued importance of broadening the constituency of drug users who are in contact with general health care services as well as HIV prevention services. There is both the need and potential for outreach to offer services beyond that of referral and street-based health education. It is important to recognise the limitations of agency-based responses and the importance of integrating general health services as part of community-based interventions.

Limitations in current outreach

HIV outreach is currently in a state of change. The rapid development of outreach targeting drug users in the UK has been accompanied by a growing recognition of its limitations (Rhodes, 1993, 1994b; McDermott, 1993). The third ACMD report on *AIDS and Drug Misuse* places greater emphasis on the potential role of outreach than previous reports. The report's recommendations on outreach are arguably the most challenging and important for purchasers and providers of community-based HIV prevention services for drug users. In the introduction, it is noted that despite "innovative and imaginative developments... outreach work has not yet reached its full potential" (ACMD, 1993). It states the "need for consolidation and a reassessment of the objectives, organisation and delivery of outreach interventions".

Current outreach work among drug users remains limited for two reasons (Rhodes, 1994a). First, outreach is limited by the numbers of drug users it reaches. Not all drug users remain within reach. Because it is a client-centred intervention the numbers of potential contacts are limited to the drug users individual outreach workers are able to contact. It is inefficient and impractical to expect outreach workers to contact *all* drug users within a specified target population. Equally important is that evaluation indicates that it is the 'easier-to-reach' of 'hard-to-reach' drug users which are most likely to be contacted and that those most in need of services often remain untouched by outreach interventions (Rhodes, Holland and Hartnoll, 1991). Future interventions need to consider how to reach drug users who are most in need of services and who remain out of reach from existing outreach projects.

Second, outreach is limited by the methods and strategies it commonly uses to facilitate change. Because most interventions focus on individuals and target changes in individual knowledge, opinion and behaviour, they have a limited capacity for changing peer group and social norms about drug use and risk behaviour. Research has shown that whether individuals attempt or achieve behaviour changes often depends on whether these changes are endorsed or encouraged by their peer group (see Chapter 3). This is because community-wide social norms and beliefs tend to influence the beliefs and behaviours of individuals and the effectiveness of interventions targeting individual behaviour change (Rhodes, 1993; Friedman *et al.*, 1992a). It is therefore extremely important for future interventions to facilitate changes in peer norms which impede risk reduction and to encourage endorsement in peer norms which are supportive of safer sex and safer drug use.

Peer education and community change

To overcome these limitations, future outreach services need to reach a larger constituency of hidden drug users and influence peer group and social norms about risk behaviour. This demands shifting the focus of outreach away from the individual drug user and towards social networks or communities of drug users. If intervention needs to facilitate changes in what is considered normal within a specific social network of drug users it needs to target whole social networks and not just disparate groups of individuals. By targeting 'communities' of drug users, outreach aims to influence commonly held beliefs about HIV and drug use such that behaviours which minimise HIV risk come to be seen as the 'community norm'. This challenge represents a major shift in the aims and focus of outreach work. This is clearly stated in the ACMD report (ACMD, 1993):

> *"Our new vision of outreach is that it should be more than a vehicle for bringing people into contact with services, and more than an agent for delivery of services at the point where HIV risk behaviour takes place. The aim of outreach should be to achieve change at the community level, influencing behaviour away from high-risk activities, as much as to secure individual behaviour change"*

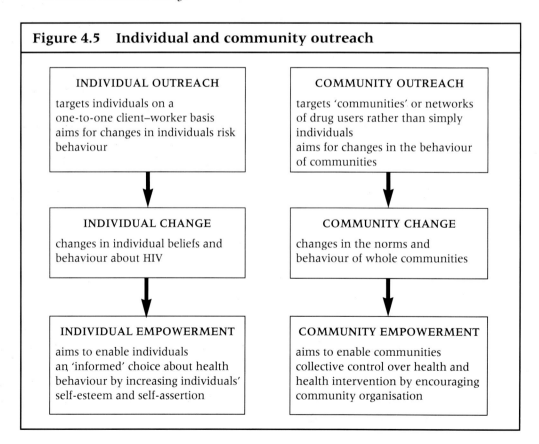

Figure 4.5   Individual and community outreach

Whereas most existing outreach interventions can be categorised as Individual Outreach aiming for individual behaviour change, this new vision of outreach can be described as Community Outreach aiming for 'community change' (see Figure 4.5). Community change has thus been defined as "change in the norms of communities as a whole... rather than changes which are restricted to individuals within that community" (Rhodes and Stimson, 1994c).

Peer education is one of the most commonly advocated methods of facilitating community change. It is also perhaps the most cost effective way of reaching a wider constituency of drug users. As noted in the ACMD report, the new role of outreach workers is to "identify those among their target population who could act as peer educators" with the aim of helping "clients *themselves* to bring about changes in other injectors with whom they are in contact" (ACMD, 1993). As recently noted, the task of outreach can be seen to be similar to "pyramid selling", allowing for *geometric* progression through communities (Stimson, 1993b).

There are few established examples of peer education projects among drug users. The most well documented projects are the 'Indigenous Leader' demonstration projects funded by the US National Institute of Drug Abuse (NIDA). These employ current or former drug users as peer educators ('AIDS Prevention Advocates'). They are selected because of their key status as 'opinion leaders' within specific drug-using social networks and are charged with the responsibility of encouraging socially responsible beliefs and behaviours among their peers. Because these interventions aim to target key status individuals within a peer group or social network with the aim of changing group norms and opinions as a whole, they can be said to be oriented towards 'communities' rather than individuals (Rhodes, 1994b). In targeting multiple access points to a network and in utilising multiple channels of communication, the approach aims to generate a gradual cascade of changes throughout a network with the aim of achieving collective changes in the everyday norms and values associated with HIV-risk and sexual health behaviour.

There is limited evaluation of the effectiveness of peer education as a method of facilitating community change among drug users. Evaluation of one of the most established NIDA projects based in Chicago provides the most compelling evidence for community change. Not only has this project been associated with a reduction in HIV risk behaviour within social networks of drug users over time, but it has also been associated with a stabilisation and reduction in the rate of new HIV infections among target populations (Wiebel *et al.*, 1993). Other evaluations show that peer-based syringe exchange projects can be more effective in reaching new clients and in distributing and exchanging equipment than non-peer-based programmes (Herkt, 1993; Grund *et al.*, 1992). Preliminary evidence from a peer organising initiative in Brooklyn indicates that collective participation has been associated with greater levels of risk reduction among drug users than street-based outreach with no collective organising component (Friedman *et al.*, 1992a, 1992b).

Research suggests the use of 'indigenous' outreach workers (current or former drug users) facilitates the contacting of, and communication with, hard-to-reach clients (Wieble *et al.*, 1988; Friedman *et al.*, 1990). Despite this, only 10 per cent of outreach projects in Britain currently employ indigenous workers (Hartnoll *et al.*, 1990). In the UK, peer education programmes might begin on a volunteer basis with peer educators targeting individuals new to their social networks and new to drug use, particularly injecting drug use. Help-seeking research indicates that important determinants of help-seeking are peer support and advice and awareness of the availability of services. The passing on of advice to individuals early in their drug use careers and to individuals new to injecting may be of considerable importance in encouraging early demands for treatment or help and in encouraging transitions away from injecting drug use. More experienced drug users already have an established informal role in educating and advising less experienced drug users (e.g. initiation into injecting) and this provides outreach with an appropriate target for encouraging initial peer led and self-help education.

UK outreach has much to learn from interventions which are reportedly effective in using peer education methods and in achieving community change (Rhodes, 1993). These include projects using self-help, community development and organising strategies designed to increase drug users' involvement and control over the development and implementation of interventions (Rhodes, 1994b). Peer education interventions among drug users can learn from the successes of self-help initiatives within gay communities such as STOP AIDS (Frutchey, 1990), MESMAC (Prout and Deverell, 1994), New York's Gay Men's Health Crisis (Kayal, 1993) and Gay Hero peer education projects (Kelly *et al.*, 1992). These projects have designed intervention strategies based on community development and social diffusion methods in health promotion (Rogers and Shoemaker, 1971). They are grass-roots responses which have actively encouraged strong collective identity and ownership over the nature and extent of change. While this currently remains a distant objective of many outreach interventions among drug users, peer education offers the most realistic and effective methods for reaching a wider constituency of drug users with the aim of achieving community change.

5   Developments in research: understanding change

Understanding the process by which change becomes possible is an important first step towards planning interventions to facilitate change. As noted in Chapters 3 and 4, the factors or situations which influence the possibility or likelihood of change in individual or community health behaviour are many and varied. They range from the provision of information and the acquisition of knowledge about the need to change risk behaviour through to changes in the environment (such as changes in soliciting laws) which help create the situations in which individual behaviour changes become possible. Intervention strategy relies on an understanding of *which* factors are important – and of *how* these factors interact – to create the possibility for change.

This chapter examines developments in research with regard to understanding risk, intervention and change. The chapter focuses on the ways in which research can gain an understanding of how changes in risk and health behaviour become possible. This is a pre-requisite to understanding how interventions can initiate, achieve and sustain changes towards healthy behaviour among drug users (see Chapter 6).

SETTING AND MEASURING TARGETS FOR CHANGE

It was noted in Chapter 1 that change is not a single or one-off event but is best viewed as an adaptive and multi-directional process (Strang, 1990a). This means that a number of intermediate or temporary transitions are often made in the process towards achieving ultimate change. Ultimate outcomes or targets in behaviour change may be the same for many drug users (e.g. to stop sharing injecting equipment) but the path of intermediate outcomes may vary widely across different individuals and communities in different social and material contexts. In view of the importance of assessing the success with which interventions are influencing drug users' attempts to make behaviour changes, it is fundamentally important that the targets and outcomes of interventions match those made by drug users themselves. Intervention targets should be set at key transition points on the path of change, but need to remain adapative to the different routes taken by different drug users in different contexts when moving towards behaviour change.

The NHS and Community Care Act (1990) deems purchasers of services responsible for assessing the health and service needs of populations resident in a given district or locality. Services are to be provided in repsonse to the needs of populations and not – as was the case – in response to the demand for district treatment and prevention *per se*. Having assessed the needs of a population, purchasers are responsible for commissioning to providers the required services. This is achieved by negotiating a contract. A contract for HIV prevention services involves the setting of health targets by which services are regulated by purchasers. Evaluation of effectiveness and the demonstration of the achievement of targets and outcomes is thus critical to shaping future service developments and the parameters of HIV prevention service delivery.

Target setting is central to *The Health of the Nation* strategy. The formation and assessment of intervention targets are seen as being the main route to securing the health of the nation. The setting and measuring of health targets are without doubt crucial to the monitoring and evaluation of effectiveness of interventions, and thus also, to the future purchasing of services. The strategic targets for HIV, AIDS and sexual health outlined in *The Health of the Nation* are two fold. First, their objectives are to reduce the incidence of HIV infection, STDs and unwanted pregnancy, and second, their objectives are to increase the effectiveness and efficiency of STD monitoring and service delivery associated with family planning, GUM and STD services (Department of Health, 1992b). The only target pertaining to drug use is as follows:

> *"To reduce the percentage of injecting drug users who report injecting equipment in the previous four weeks by at least 50 per cent by 1997 and by at least a further 50 per cent by the year 2000 (from 20 per cent in 1990 to no more than 10 per cent by 1997 and no more than 5 per cent by the year 2000)"* (Department of Health, 1992b)

This immediately raises the question of the specificity and appropriateness of targets relating to HIV prevention and drug use. *The Health of the Nation* targets provide no more than an indirect indicator of the health of drug using populations. Measuring the proportions of injectors who *report* sharing is obviously an indequate measure of success alone, particularly if interventions aim to understand and influence the range of intermediate transitions relevant to risk reduction changes in drug injecting lifestyles (see Chapters 3 and 4). Measuring rates of sharing alone gives no indication of change in other health behaviours relevant for minimising HIV and STD risk or among drug users who do not use or share injecting equipment. It is therefore crucially important that a range of appropriate targets for HIV prevention work among injecting as well as non-injecting drug users are set at local as well as national level. Such targets require a level of specificity which is of practical use in assessing and planning local and national intervention repsonses. Mounting research indicates the importance of intervening early in an individual's drug use career and it is equally important for interventions to focus on the modification of transitions in injecting to non-injecting use behaviours as it is for interventions to focus on modifications in existing injecting behaviour. Targets need to be tailored to the specifics of HIV prevention work with drug users but also require a general applicability to measuring the extent to which interventions can prevent the use or injection of drugs *per se* (Strang, 1991).

The Health of the Nation also provides an impetus to examining the interplay between drug use behaviours and sexual health. Both transitions in drug use behaviour and the interplay between drug use and sexual risk can be considered

---

Figure 5.1   Targets for HIV prevention intervention with drug users

Outcome targets

- reductions in prevalence of HIV, Hepatitis A/B/C, STDs and unwanted pregnancy
- reductions in prevalence of injecting drug use
- reductions in prevalence of illicit drug use

Intermediate targets

- reductions in time elapsed between addiction and first treatment demand
- reductions in proportion of drug users leaving treatment prematurely
- increases in proportion of drug users who clean shared equipment
- reductions in proportion of drug users who share used injecting equipment
- reductions in the reported frequency of injection
- increases in transitions from injecting to non-injecting drug use
- reductions in the frequency of non-injecting drug use
- increases in the proportion of drug users who report using condoms

---

Service targets

- increases in proportion of contacts with women and younger drug users
- increases in proportion of contacts with non-opiate and non-injecting drug users
- increases in proportion of contacts with gay drug users and with the sexual partners of drug users
- increases in proportion of clients educated and counselled about safer sex
- increases in proportion of appropriate contacts in which condoms and injecting equipment distributed
- increases in proportion of clients educated and counselled about availability of HIV, STD and Hepatitis B testing
- increases in proportion of drug injectors tested for HIV
- increases in proportion of contacts educated and counselled about safer drug use and transitions in drug use

key areas of focus given the current (and future) significance of the sexual transmission of HIV and STDs. It is important that these and related concerns (such
as hepatitis transmission) are not eclipsed by health targets which focus exclu-
sively or primarily on injecting drug use and the sharing of injecting equipment.

In keeping with the customer ethic of NHS reforms, it is essential that appropriate targets for intervention are identified on the basis of consumer research
and consumer involvement. Intervention targets in the shape of intermediate
and global outcome measures can only be of practical use when they reflect the
actual transitions made by drug users when making risk reduction changes. If
targets are not specific enough or if they do not reflect the many adaptations
made by drug users when minimising risk as part of their everyday lifestyles, such
measures will lack their ability to properly measure or assess drug users' service
needs and requirements. This is in keeping with *The Health of the Nation*:

> "The ideal form of targets... is that they should be related to actions known to be effective,
> be achievable but challenging and be monitorable through indicators... Improving under-
> standing of the ways in which changes in health are measured is central to the development
> of epidemiologically based evaluation of health policy"
>
> (Green Paper, Department of Health, 1992c)

Appropriate targets are thus 'action-based', formulated on the basis of careful
research, monitoring and evaluation (see below). In considering the importance
of setting targets relating to the prevention of HIV as well as of drug use per se
(ACMD, 1993; Strang, 1991), the targets as shown in Figure 5.1 can be seen to
be centrally relevant to most HIV prevention targeting drug users (see also Farrell
and Strang, 1992; Lucas, 1992; Department of Health, 1993). Beyond these,
tailor-made targets would need to be decided in the light of consultations with
service users, non service users, key experts, purchasers and providers and on
the basis of appropriate needs assessment and research.

RESEARCHING RISK, INTERVENTION AND CHANGE

The aim of effective HIV prevention research strategy is to inform the ongoing
development, implementation and evaluation of health promotion planning and
intervention. In the context of considering health promotion strategy targeting
drug users, the practice of 'HIV prevention research' can be viewed at three
distinct levels.

As shown in Figure 5.2, the first level is research which informs public health
planning by advancing *epidemiological* understanding of the determinants and distribution of HIV disease. The second level is *social and behavioural* research which
informs health promotion and intervention strategies by advancing understandings of the *social context* and interpersonal dynamics of risk and behaviour change.

The third level is research which informs future health promotion and intervention strategies and targets by undertaking *evaluation* of the process and outcomes of specific interventions. Each of these are discussed below. Each approach can be viewed as a necessary component of the other and all can be considered essential components of an integrated HIV prevention research strategy designed to inform the undertaking of *needs assessment* at national and local level.

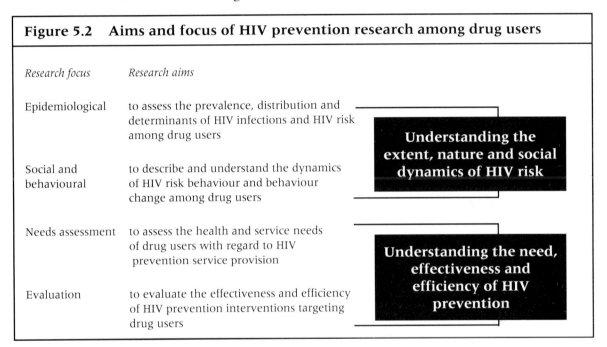

Figure 5.2   Aims and focus of HIV prevention research among drug users

Research focus	Research aims	
Epidemiological	to assess the prevalence, distribution and determinants of HIV infections and HIV risk among drug users	**Understanding the extent, nature and social dynamics of HIV risk**
Social and behavioural	to describe and understand the dynamics of HIV risk behaviour and behaviour change among drug users	
Needs assessment	to assess the health and service needs of drug users with regard to HIV prevention service provision	**Understanding the need, effectiveness and efficiency of HIV prevention**
Evaluation	to evaluate the effectiveness and efficiency of HIV prevention interventions targeting drug users	

Prevalence and epidemiological research

Epidemiological research is concerned with the study of the prevalence, distribution and determinants of HIV infection among drug users. Such research has provided baseline quantitative indicators on levels of HIV risk behaviour among drug users and their sharing and sexual partners. For example, it is now well established that the sharing of injecting equipment is an important *determinant* of HIV infection among injecting drug users; that the *prevalence* of sharing is on decline; and that the *distribution* of sharing behaviour is uneven throughout different localities in the UK. These indicators have been essential in modelling epidemic trends and in planning public health resources and intervention responses efficiently and effectively.

Epidemiological research continues to play an important role in the planning of public health resources. Key areas for continued study include the monitoring and surveillance of HIV, hepatitis and STD prevalence among injecting drug users with and without experience of treatment. It can be considered a future methodological imperative that studies of prevalence and risk behaviour among injecting drug users are based on community-wide samples recruited via a number of different social networks (Rhodes and Stimson, 1994a). This is essential if bias is to be minimised in future HIV prevalence estimates. Future studies investigating the possibilities for methodological improvements (e.g. randomised nomination techniques) should be considered, as should targeted studies of HIV, hepatitis and STD prevalence monitoring among non-injecting drug users with and without experience of treatment or help. One other – as yet neglected – area which can be seen as being crucial to providing improved epidemiological research is estimating levels of HIV and STD prevalence and risk behaviour among gay and bisexual injecting (and non-injecting) drug users.

Monitoring the prevalence of drug use should remain a key priority at local level. Considerable methodological improvements have been made in using indicators to assess local drug problems. The currently most efficient methods are based on a form of 'capture-recapture' involving three or more separate (but not necessarily independent) data sources (Frischer, 1992; Hartnoll *et al.*, 1985). Regions – and also districts – would benefit from assessing the extent of local drug problems, particularly if HIV prevalence data were collated concurrently. This would allow, for example, estimating both the local prevalence of injecting drug use and HIV among injecting drug users on the basis of data collated from sources such as the Home Office Addicts Index, Regional Drug Misuse Databases, general practice surveys, police arrests and HIV testing centres.

Targeting resources on the basis of local population drug and HIV-related prevalence data is considerably more efficient than currently adopted methods of planning resources on the basis of population per capita. This is particularly the case given the need to consider purchasing and providing services in response to

---

Figure 5.3   Key areas for future epidemiological research

Key study areas

- HIV incidence among injecting drug users
- STDs and hepatitis infections among drug users
- recreational, episodic and 'non-problematic' drug use
- risk associated with recreational and non-injecting drug use
- transitions in patterns and modes of drug use
- initiation into illicit and injecting drug use

Key study populations

- gay injecting and non-injecting drug use
- drug use patterns of black and ethnic minority groups
- drug use patterns of women
- health behaviour of the sexual partners of drug users

---

the needs of local populations. The systematic collation of prevalence data is thus central to building the foundations for regular ongoing needs assessment and requires the establishing of infrastructures for statistics monitoring at district and regional level.

Epidemiological research is required to assess the prevalence of continued HIV risk behaviour among drug using populations. Needs assessment of local HIV prevention requires ongoing targeted surveys of HIV risk and drug taking behaviour among current and potential target populations. Figure 5.3 summarises the key areas for continued and future epidemiological monitoring.

Considerable improvements can also be made to current epidemiological research on HIV risk among drug users (see Rhodes and Stimson, 1994a). There is a need for greater standardisation and comparability between studies in measures of 'risk'. These vary considerably even on fundamental measures such as 'safer sex'. There is also the need for improvements in sampling and study designs (Samuels *et al.*, 1992). Most studies of drug users rely on samples drawn from drug treatment centres which may introduce the possibility of bias in measures of risk (see above). Most study designs are cross-sectional using retrospective measures of risk and there are few longitudinal or cohort studies of behaviour change among drug users. If future epidemiological research is to study the process of behaviour change over time it is fundamentally important that they simultaneously include longitudinal as well as cross-sectional designs.

Perhaps the most serious criticism of current epidemiological research is that current indicators of risk are based primarily on measures of individual risk behaviour. Reliable indicators of HIV spread require a measure not just of the frequency and type of risk behaviour in individuals but also of the interaction and epidemiological efficiency of mixing patterns *between* individuals (Vlahov *et al.*, 1990). Because HIV infection is transmitted behaviourally, HIV spread is not random or uniform but subject to the ways in which different groups of individuals interact. Rather than taking the individual as the unit of analysis, improved estimates of risk and prevalence can be achieved by examining specific 'social networks' or social groups of individuals. It is the *interaction* between individuals in certain settings and social contexts which is of key importance in assessing HIV spread and in informing the design of appropriate intervention targeting and communication strategies.

Social and behavioural research

Most epidemiological explanation and prediction is based almost entirely on measures of individual risk behaviour. As noted in Chapters 3 and 4, such explanations are limited because they remain blind to a variety of other social and cultural factors which influence the ways in which individuals behave, and thus also, the ways in which epidemics spread. If research is to have an effective practical role in intervention, it must *explain* as well as assess. While epidemiological research is effective in identifying the prevalence of risk behaviour among drug users, it is often unable to explain the processes or dynamics which create, reinforce and shape risk behaviour in the first place. Psycho-social models of research – which like psycho-social models of health behaviour and intervention (see Chapters 3 and 4) – are based upon individualistic lifestyle notions of risk which are rarely adequate to address the complex social realities of risk perception, assessment and behaviour change.

There is a need for research to view and study drug users' perceptions of 'risk' as relative, both to wider peer-group, social and community norms and to situational and structural context. For research to provide an adequate understanding of risk and behaviour change it must have the capacity to describe the social contexts in which individuals engage in risk behaviour and in which behaviour changes are attempted and achieved (for a full discussion see Rhodes and Stimson, 1994a). For example, as noted in Chapter 3, an understanding of why some drug users continue to share used injecting equipment is made possible by an understanding of the social and situational contexts in which injecting and sharing takes place and not simply by an understanding of individual knowledge and intention. For intervention to be effective in encouraging behaviour change, it is important to first understand how such change is possible. This requires an understanding of the social context of risk behaviour and of the social factors which facilitate or complicate the process of change.

This is achieved by targeted social and action-oriented research interventions among specific drug using populations. Such research is often qualitative or ethnographic in orientation and may also be incorporated as part of ongoing intervention design. It aims to describe and understand the range of factors which influence individual and collective behaviour in the community. This involves describing the processes and dynamics of risk and health behaviour in the light of interpersonal interactions (e.g. 'negotiations' between individuals) and wider community or social norms (e.g. peer group norms and endorsements). This helps inform how interventions might *target* populations – for example, by identifying key opinions leaders within a social network – and how they might *communicate* with populations – for example, by making communication strategies socially and culturally specific.

Some of the key areas for future qualitative and social research are summarised in Figure 5.4. Qualitative research can be considered an under-utilised research methodology in the planning, implementation and assessment of HIV prevention interventions among drug users. It is of most practical use in understanding the processes which influence the possibility and likelihood of behaviour change.

Needs assessment, evaluation and intervention-based research

The role of evaluation, needs assessment and intervention-based research is of critical importance in the planning and distribution of public health resources

---

Figure 5.4   Key areas for future social and behavioural research

- interpersonal interaction and 'negotiation' of safer drug use and safer sex encounters
- dynamics of the relationships between drug use, sexual activity and sexual risk
- problems and dynamics of attempting and sustaining sexual behaviour change
- gender issues in negotiation and dynamics of drug-using and sexual relationships
- help-seeking and coping strategies adopted by drug users
- social norms, values and dynamics of drug-using peer groups and social networks
- influence of social setting and context on individual perceptions and behaviours
- effects of social policy changes on service delivery and effectiveness

---

and in the balancing of different HIV prevention intervention strategies. The overview presented in Chapter 4 indicates that future developments in HIV prevention among drug users necessitate improving existing drug service and community-based service delivery while considering new possibilities and new methods of intervention in the community. There are key areas in which future service-based research might be prioritorised. These are summarised in Figure 5.5.

Of key importance in the design and planning of needs assessment and evaluative research is the identification of appropriate targets and outcomes of measurement. Very much related to this are the questions of *how* 'needs' are assessed and more fundamentally, of *what* 'needs' are. Because these questions are fundamental to how an assessment or evaluation is undertaken and to the criteria of efficiency and effectiveness adopted, they require debating early in the planning and development of interventions. It is absolutely essential that all participants in the assessment process are involved in determining and agreeing intervention aims, objectives, targets and outcomes. Crucially, this includes the

---

Figure 5.5   Key areas in evaluation and intervention-based research

- peer education and peer support interventions
- outreach interventions encouraging community-action and targeting community change
- bleach and condom distribution interventions within prison
- structured methadone maintenance programmes
- integration of primary, general and community health interventions
- communication methods in counselling about HIV and drug use

---

consumers and potential consumers of a service as well as purchasers, commissioners, providers and evaluators. Since what is determined a 'need', 'target' or 'outcome' is the criteria by which a service is assessed and evaluated, it is of pivotal importance that clients, workers and managers share an understanding of intervention objectives and effectiveness. Assessment and evaluation can be seen to be a tool, not by which people are judged, but by which an intervention can aim to improve over time on an ongoing basis.

While it is as important for clients as it is for service workers and managers to identify appropriate targets and outcomes for assessment, it is equally important to include measures of process. As with social and behavioural research paradigms, evaluation ideally needs to explain as well as assess. There is little practical utility in interventions gaining a sense of *what* strategy worked (outcomes evaluation) without having an accompanying understanding of *how* strategy worked (process evaluation). Similarly, it is fundamental to the usefulness of process evaluations that they include – at the outset – surveys or studies of the opinions of service users and ideally also, of non-users of the service. It is important that HIV prevention interventions are primarily responsive to the needs and requirements of drug users and secondarily to the needs and requirements of purchasers, commissioners and providers. This demands the systematic and ongoing use of process and outcome measures which are of a high enough methodological standard to satisfy all key participants concerned.

The emphasis on developing services within the NHS in response to demonstrated consumer needs raises a number of specific problems for needs assessment in HIV prevention work with drug users (see Figure 5.6). These relate to wider concerns about the role of needs assessment and evaluative research in the contracting process. This highlights the importance of critically reviewing the methodological and practical feasibility and effectiveness of evaluation and needs assessment methodology in community-based HIV prevention interventions targeting drug users.

Most HIV prevention services are provided under contracts, with local and health authorities purchasing services on the basis of local needs assessments. There are number of potential problems associated with this process. First, the allocation of resources by residency rather than by treatment or service received

---

Figure 5.6   Key issues in needs assessment and evaluation research

- effectiveness of needs assessments in assisting purchasing and providing decisions
- feasibility of process, outcome and action-oriented evaluation methods in demonstrating effectiveness
- feasibility and effectiveness fo intervention target setting and assessment
- feasibility and effectiveness of evaluating and demonstrating effectiveness of community-based interventions

introduces untold problems for most drug services as they are often unaware of the residency of their clients. Most drug and HIV prevention services aim to cater for drug users from outside districts and regions and promise either confidentiality or anonymity. Maintaining confidentiality and anonymity is important to increasing the accessibility and user-friendly aspects of services and can be seen to preserve consumer choice by encouraging clients to make contact with services. Because assessing the demand for services against local population needs becomes fraught with difficulties, as does the contracting process with regard to clients who receive their treatment or care elsewhere, there are concerns as to whether resource allocation will reflect client need. In the long term, services will aim to be funded, provided and *located* on the basis of local population needs assessment. It is for this reason, that needs assessment of local drug using populations would benefit from improved infrastructures for systematic and ongoing monitoring of prevalence and behavioural data.

Second, there are difficulties in determining the extent to which local needs assessments undertaken by local or health authorities are representative of local needs. This is largely because of the methodological problems inherent in researching the 'hidden' nature of drug using populations. Clearly, it is difficult to plan resources on the basis of the unmet or 'as-yet-to-be' identified needs of a population of an unknown size. Once again, this emphasises the importance of generating prevalence estimates, but also of systematically integrating indicators from a variety of sources at a local level (Farrell and Strang, 1992).

Healthy contracts depend on healthy needs assessments. The crux of the difficulties in the contracting process are centred on the relationship between purchasers and providers and the relationship between local health needs, their assessment and service provision. The methodological and practical difficulties in undertaking 'healthy' needs assessments have often meant that purchasers either rely on providers' opinions rather than systematic needs assessments to inform purchasing decisions, or on providers to undertake appropriate needs assessments of their target populations. This detracts from the main aims of the reforms which were designed to encourage the purchasing of services on the basis of careful assessment of local needs and unmet needs, outside of the *a priori* needs identified by providers. One danger therefore is that the contracting process may hinder the development of new and innovative styles of services targeting the previously unmet needs of under-targeted populations. Such innovation is critical to preserving the progressive nature of drug service delivery.

Third, there may be difficulties achieving an efficient balance between the methodological constraints in evaluating HIV prevention interventions and demonstrating effectiveness to purchasers. There are fears – particularly with regard to sub-contracts to the voluntary sector – that certain interventions are methodologically and practically more difficult to demonstrate as effective (and as cost effective) than others, despite their perceived need within a community. These services also tend to be the more innovative community-based interventions, often based in the voluntary sector. They also appear to be the most progressive projects in terms of the future requirements and developments in HIV prevention, and include interventions such as outreach, peer education and consumer groups. It is crucially important that voluntary sector, self-help and community-based projects have – and continue to have – a key role in identifying service need and in providing services accordingly and efficiently in response to consumer need and demand. In order to preserve consumer choice and to meet as yet unmet needs, HIV prevention services for drug users must maintain (and increase) their degree of flexibility and accessibility of service provision. While centrally important, needs and outcomes assessment can not prioritise methodological desirability above that of the fundamental aims and objectives of interventions. It is vital that HIV prevention services for drug users remain innovative and experimental and that interventions are not nudged towards providing services which are methodologically easier to demonstrate as cost-effective and considerably less risky to purchase or provide.

6 Developments in intervention: achieving change

Healthy HIV prevention strategy aims to create the situations in which individuals and communities can exercise choice about health behaviour. Change becomes possible when individuals and communities are able to act in response to choices made about health behaviour and lifestyle. Because the ways in which individuals behave are influenced by a range of individual, social and environmental factors, achieving change demands a strategic approach to intervention which encourages change at the level of the individual, the community and the environment.

DEVELOPING HEALTHY HIV PREVENTION STRATEGY

Over the last five years, drug service policy has been characterised by a public health pragmatism to prevent HIV infection above that of drug use *per se*. This has encouraged increased flexibility in service provision and increased accessibility and availability of services. HIV prevention strategies have encouraged a new vision of health services and a re-orientation of thinking about health and health behaviour in responding to problem drug use. In essence, services have continued to move away from established medico-legal conceptions of drug use and have increasingly advocated departure from conventional individualistic notions of prevention characterised by one-dimensional notions of health, help-seeking and health behaviour. The move has been towards a more holistic view of health necessitating a multi-faceted multi-disciplinary approach to facilitating changes in the individual, the community and the health environment. While this has encouraged many changes in services targeting drug users, such changes remain in their comparative infancy, and it is timely to review the effectiveness of these developments. These developments provide the stepping stones to building healthy HIV prevention strategy.

Healthy HIV prevention strategy demands more than an *advocation* of 'health promotion' (see Chapter 4). It also requires an *application* of health promotion in practice. It is important to emphasise that the 'new' public health, of which a comprehensive and integrated health promotion is a part, advocates the need to balance individual and community action as a means of facilitating and enabling changes in individual and collective health status (Bunton and MacDonald, 1992; Nutbeam and Blakey, 1990). The new public health movement of the 1980s promised to move beyond a bio-medical understanding of health and illness towards a new understanding of social action which encompasses the social and environmental influences on health, choices and behaviour. This is a fundamental necessity if HIV-related health promotion is to be effective in recognising the complexities of how individual and community behaviour interacts with social, cultural and material contexts. While the five tenets of health promotion outlined in the WHO Ottawa Charter (see Chapter 4) are often advocated by health institutions they are rarely applied. With regard to HIV prevention with drug users, these five guiding principles encourage:

- building healthy HIV prevention policy;
- facilitating environments supportive of safer drug, HIV and sexual health behaviour;
- strengthening community action and participation;
- re-orienting drug, HIV and sexual health services;
- facilitating drug users' empowerment with regard to health and health choices.

In essence, these key principles of healthy prevention strategy can be summarised as healthy policy; healthy environments; healthy communities; healthy services; and healthy individuals. While these make good strategic sense, it is equally clear that an advocation of an integrated strategy for individual, community, environmental and political action is very different from achieving action in practice. It is abundantly clear from the research reviewed in Chapter 4 that there is little strategic emphasis in current HIV prevention work on community action or environmental change. Instead, most prevention strategies remain focused towards the re-orientation and improvement of service provision and the facilitation of changes in individual behaviour and lifestyles. With regard to the new public health and the development of harm reduction strategies for drugs services, Stimson and Lart (1991) have described the promises of health promotion as "new words" and the practices as "old tunes". Despite a wealth of research evidence which suggests the need to work *with* and not just *in* the community, existing HIV prevention interventions have done little to develop worthwhile links with the communities with which they work.

Consumer involvement and community action

While the bulk of the ACMD recommendations for change are focused on the re-orientation of service delivery (e.g. improving methadone treatment) and the facilitation of individual behaviour change away from drug use (ACMD, 1993), to their credit, they note the importance of drug using communities themselves in initiating, achieving and sustaining behaviour change. The *AIDS and Drug Misuse* report, for the first time in its five year history, introduces the idea of 'community-change' (see Chapter 4). This can be seen as endorsing moves towards what is usually described in health promotion as community development for health, the aim of which is to facilitate community action and community participation among members of affected communities themselves (Beattie, 1991; see also Rhodes and Stimson, 1994c).

The ACMD recommendations for actively involving drug users as 'peer educators' or as 'AIDS activists' are based on the need to 'broaden the constituency' of drug users reached by prevention interventions (see Chapter 4). For the ACMD, this is ostensibly about reaching hidden populations of drug users potentially in need of drug and prevention services:

> *"Clients become 'AIDS activists' with responsibility for passing on information about HIV transmission, thus facilitating changes in the behaviour of their peers. In this way HIV prevention messages, and the skills needed to adopt safer behaviours, can be passed on to the widest possible population, including recent recruits to injecting who are harder to reach..."*
>
> (ACMD, 1993)

These recommendations create opportunities not only for facilitating contacts with greater *numbers* of drug users by employing drug users as peer educators, but also lay the foundations for intervention responses which encourage consumer advocacy, involvement and organisation. The long-term aim of peer-based interventions is not simply to *involve* the consumer but to encourage a *mobilisation* of consumer involvement towards collectively organising and controlling community-based interventions (Rhodes, 1994b). The ACMD recommendations can therefore be seen as an encouraging step towards endorsing the idea of peer-led initiatives. But it is also important to recognise that they provide no more than a springboard for action. In time, peer-led initiatives may become truly 'activist' when they enable the communities they serve to have collective control over health change and intervention responses.

The advocation of community action and the supporting of healthy communities is vital to building effective health promotion strategy. While NHS strategy emphasises the importance of equity of access, consumer involvement and consumer choice this is a somewhat less vibrant version of the vision of consumer involvement in health promotion. Like recommendations from the ACMD, the underlying 'consumer ethic' of *The Health of the Nation* and of NHS contracting, create windows of opportunity for real innovation in practice. These opportunities should be seized with determination and creativity by purchasers and providers with the aim of shifting the rhetoric of consumer involvement towards reality. The fundamental health promotion principles of community action demand a re-conceptualisation of drug and HIV prevention service provision, and in particular, of the consumer and provider of prevention services. If purchasers are to meet the challenges posed by the shifting goals and targets of HIV prevention, it is necessary to invest resources in innovative interventions encouraging community development. This adds new practical dimensions to the principles of consumer .care and requires an element of risk-taking for some purchasers and providers. Such risks should be seen as small costs against the potential for much larger gains.

The move towards greater consumer involvement raises as many questions as answers. While it is clearly strategically and practically important that community advocacy becomes community action, such a strategy is difficult to put into operation. There is little experience of undertaking peer education work with drug users in the UK and on a practical level there is little clarity in how drug users are to be selected, recruited and managed as peer educators. It is also largely unclear which methods of peer education strategy will prove most effective in UK drugs work and whether such an approach necessarily avoids many of the problems which have hindered current models of outreach work (see Chapter 4). While peer education and community action interventions have been shown to be effective among drug users elsewhere (Rhodes, 1994a; Rhodes and Stimson, 1994a), systematic assessment and demonstration research is required to determine the feasibility and effectiveness of employing such strategies in the UK context. It is to this end that future prevention research, intervention and debate must be directed (Rhodes, 1993).

Healthy alliances and the integration of service response

The ACMD in 1993 prioritised the importance of improving the co-ordination of drug services. At local and district level, there is the need for greater collaboration between agencies across different sectors in the purchasing and provision of services. The notion of a 'healthy alliance' is central to *The Health of the Nation* terminology. It is also centrally important to developing effective HIV prevention strategy. In the light of increased commitments to consumer involvement in services, the notion of an alliance takes on a further – stronger – meaning than that commonly used by most NHS purchasers and providers. Not only is it fundamentally important to include drug users as active participants in needs assessment, evaluation and collaborative work but it highlights the potential for drug users' involvement in organising, and eventually 'owning', intervention responses within their own communities.

The concept of a healthy alliance is a collaboration which fosters improved co-ordination, integration and delivery of services. This is why the most important ingredient of 'healthy' alliances are drug users themselves. If services are to be needs-led, it is extremely important that drug users, service users and those working closest with target populations contribute to purchasing and providing decisions. This has implications for the design and development of appropriate inter-sectoral purchasing and providing alliances as well as for the role of commissioners and other mediating bodies in the contracting process.

Most drugs work is currently funnelled through specific voluntary and statutory agencies with little central or regional co-ordination. The lack of co-ordination betweeen agencies may provide a rocky foundation for future service developments, particularly if such fragmentation is exacerbated rather than alleviated under NHS contracting arrangements. There is a need for collaboration in the provision of HIV prevention services to drug users to ensure that services are purchased and provided in the most effective and efficient ways and to ensure that drug users have adequate access to a comprehensive network of voluntary and statutory health services. Healthy alliances are therefore important at the level of service provision, purchasing and planning.

Clients of HIV prevention and drug services demand services that are flexible, anonymous or confidential, and above all, accessible. The voluntary and non-statutory sectors have a long standing expertise in responding to these needs, and it is fundamentally important that purchasing decisions are made on the basis of equal and reciprocal statutory–voluntary sector collaboration and on the basis of consultation with key statutory and voluntary sector providers. This demands regulation, not simply of providers by purchasers, but also of purchasers by inter-sectoral alliances of key 'experts' in the field. If purchasers are to gain an insight as to what the 'market' demands, it is fundamental that alliances represent the views of key purchasers, providers and consumers from voluntary as well as statutory sectors.

It is important to recognise that the contracting of services may encourage an 'unhealthy' competition between statutory and voluntary sectors. Given that resources are clearly finite, the contractual tenets of 'cost' and 'quality', and the regulatory nature of the purchaser-provider relationship, may limit the degree to which 'innovative' non-statutory services are funded. It is therefore essential that alliances are based on equal partnerships between participants. This is necessary so as to prevent 'unhealthy' alliances. One often 'unhealthy' voluntary–statutory alliance in HIV prevention was described and evaluated by Rhodes, Holland and Hartnoll (1991). The evaluation showed that alliances based on unequal partnerships with confused terms of reference can have direct (and negative) consequences for the delivery of services to consumers.

The primary role of provider alliances are to ensure that the views of service users and non-users are acted upon. They aim to encourage an integration of service delivery so as to prevent unnecessary duplication in services and to accommodate drug users' health needs as they are identified in the community. If the needs of consumers require service change, then the purchasers and providers of service must be committed to making such changes in practice. Many statutory services have much to learn from voluntary organisations which have greater experience and expertise in managing and delivering accessible and innovative community-based interventions in response to client need. HIV prevention services are likely to benefit drug users the more accessible and available they become. This demands increased consumer accessibility to a comprehensive range of statutory and voluntary drug, HIV and general health services. The co-ordination and development of such a network of services requires collaboration in service provision, purchasing and planning.

There is a need, for example, for increasing the accessibility of sexual and generic health services for drug users. Many drug service interventions have neglected the importance of preventing the sexual transmission of HIV and other STDs. There is a continued need for interventions to maximise risk reduction changes in drug taking behaviour, but interventions simultaneously need to emphasise safer sex compliance and sexual behaviour change. These concerns are shared by the ACMD:

> "Changing the unsafe sexual practices of drug users is a crucial aspect of curbing the spread of HIV. Success here has been elusive, and more needs to be done by all services, specialist and generic, which deal with drug users. The promotion of safer sex needs to be more clearly defined, more closely monitored and regularly reviewed" (ACMD, 1993)

Similarly, many treatment and helping services would benefit considerably from increased general and primary health care service provision (see Chapter 4). This requires greater collaboration between general practitioners, other generic health workers and specialist drug services with regard to the quality of services provided to drug users in generic settings and to the quality of general health care provided in drug services (ACMD, 1993). Future interventions need to focus not just on the HIV and sexual health of drug users but on the general health of drug users. This necessitates increased service alliances between prescribing, primary and general health care, sexual health, counselling, testing and outreach services with the aim of providing drug users with immediate access to key health and prevention services.

Policy and prevention

There is a continued need for HIV prevention efforts among drug users. Research indicates the increasing importance of injecting drug use and sexual transmission in HIV spread. Research also emphasises the importance of access to health services and of treatment and help in reducing the prevalence and likelihood of HIV risk behaviour.

While there remains a need for continued HIV prevention, the ACMD recommends re-orienting prevention strategy towards the prevention of drug use *per se* alongside that of HIV. As noted in Chapter 1, the ACMD recognises that *"all* interventions [that aim] to discourage drug misuse will contribute to HIV prevention" (ACMD, 1993). Balancing the need for HIV prevention with the prevention of drug use itself is in keeping with *The Health of the Nation* guidelines on the prevention of HIV and the promotion of sexual health among drug users (Department of Health, 1993). These outline the main aims as:

- preventing people from starting to inject drugs;
- encouraging cessation of drug use, especially injecting;
- minimising the harms associated with injecting drug use;
- minimising the harms associated with unprotected sex.

Recent policy shifts have returned the prevention of drug use centre-stage alongside the prevention of HIV and STDs. This does not detract from working towards a hierarchy of changes in drug use of which the final outcome is cessation of use. However, it is necessary to emphasise the limitations of intervention strategies which rely on abstinence-oriented approaches. While interventions can operate within the hierarchy of 'healthy choices' offered by harm reduction (see Chapter 3) it is essential to recognise that the success of HIV prevention strategy to date has depended largely on community-based intervention developments emphasising secondary prevention. As this review demonstrates, the continued success of HIV prevention depends on increasing the commitment to developments *in* and *with* targeted communities themselves. It is fundamental that HIV prevention initiatives do not obstruct initiatives targeting the prevention of drug use itself. They are part and parcel of the same harm reduction continuum. Equally important, however, is that primary drug prevention initiatives to not obstruct initiatives aiming to reduce the harms associated with continued drug use. It is still the case that HIV infection is of greater potential individual, community and public health harm than drug use *per se*. In the words of *The Health of the Nation*, the HIV epidemic remains the "greatest new public health challenge this century" (Department of Health, 1992b). It is for this reason that the most practical and effective way forward is to work with communities of drug users towards facilitating community action away from the harms associated with drug use. If harm reduction is to be conceived of as a hierarchy of transitions from reducing HIV-related harm through to reducing drug use itself then the priorities and targets of interventions and drug service policy must continue to reflect this.

HIV prevention policy is designed to protect the 'public health' from harm. If it is 'public health' that is to protected then it is mobilising the 'public' which is the best antedote to harm. This demands a continuation of the pragmatism which has characterised policy developments towards re-orienting the way in which the 'drug problem' and the 'drug user' is viewed. The targeting of drug using communities and the promotion and supporting of 'community health' among drug users can be seen as one and the same as protecting and promoting the 'public health'. Health promotion at the community level necessitates a partnership between health providers and health consumers based on equality and reciprocity. Learning from the relative success of HIV prevention and drug policy to date it becomes possible to isolate the key factors which may help to protect HIV prevention strategy from harm. Healthy HIV prevention policy depends on:

- pragmatism in responding to drug users and HIV-related problems;
- recognition of the importance of public and community health over and above medico-legal interventions;
- felxibility in providing low-threshold services in response to consumer need;
- recognition of the multi-faceted nature of HIV-related problems and of the non-medical nature of drug use;

- recognition of the need for a holistic and multi-disciplinary approach to HIV prevention and of the key role of the voluntary sector and of drug using communities themselves;
- recognition of the importance of early intervention in preventing transitions in drug use and in particular to injecting drug use.

Healthy policy thus encourages *pragmatic, flexibile* and *holistic* approaches to intervention and prevention strategy. The maintaining of such a policy very much depends on the how recommendations for service delivery are co-ordinated at national and local level. While the ACMD is perhaps the single most influential policy body on drugs, it functions in an advisory capacity to the Home Office with little central integration or co-ordination. There remains a lack of central co-ordination of HIV prevention services for drug users, but a need to preserve local autonomy in service developments while fostering inter-regional integration, consolidation and support. The need for central co-ordination of HIV prevention strategy targeting drug users can be seen to be particularly acute in the light of setting and meeting health targets encouraged by *The Health of the Nation*.

The historical development of prevention policy on HIV and AIDS has emerged alongside, but quite independent from, policy developments on drugs. This fragmentation at policy level has been reflected in the way services have been funded and provided. This in effect means that there is no explicit or specific national HIV prevention strategy for drug users. There remains a need for greater integration in the co-ordination and provision of drugs and sexual health interventions towards a national strategy on HIV prevention among drug users. Such a strategy needs to focus not just on the prevention of HIV or on the prevention of drug use itself but on improving the general health and welfare of drug users and drug using communities.

7   Summary and conclusions

ACMD AND DRUGS SERVICE POLICY

The Advisory Council on the Misuse of Drugs has played a key role in defining and facilitating developments in drug and HIV prevention policy. These developments have prioritised HIV prevention above the prevention of drug use *per se* and have encouraged a pragmatism in approaches to public health and health promotion intervention.

Current HIV prevention policy among drug users remains one of pragmatism, aiming to build on what has proven to be effective over the last decade, while pushing still much needed developments in health promotion methods and service delivery. **The key developments required include moves towards community development and self-help initiatives encouraging community action and community change**. The ACMD in 1993 recommended the need to "achieve change at the community level, influencing behaviour away from high-risk activities, as much as to secure individual behaviour change".

Drugs service policy is also at a time of consolidation and re-assessment. **The ACMD noted the need for increased targeting of HIV intervention towards non-injecting drug users, recent injectors and recreational users.** It was stated that "greater efforts are now needed to reduce the extent of drug use itself... together with a recognition that all interventions to discourage drug misuse will contribute to HIV prevention". It is important that such recommendations do not detract from the importance of continued funding and development for primary and secondary HIV prevention interventions among drug users.

While on the one hand, the ACMD has encouraged innovative developments in community action, it cautions against over flexibility in prescribing practices. **There is the need for revising current methadone treatment practice towards structured methadone programmes which incorporate the programme characteristics known to be most effective.** One such factor is increased flexibility from methadone providers in the dosage of methadone prescribed.

THE HEALTH OF THE NATION **AND NHS CONTRACTING**

NHS contracting of health services requires careful examination and careful national and local co-ordination with regard to needs assessment and the setting and measuring of targets and intervention outcomes. **Evaluation and assessment is required of the effectiveness and efficiency of the contracting process in delivering HIV prevention services in response to the needs of drug users, service-users and non-service-users.**

The NHS and Community Care Act emphasises consumer care and consumer choice in service provision. This provides an opportunity for encouraging increased consumer involvement and organisation. **It is fundamental that drug users are actively involved in the development and assessment of intervention targets and strategies.**

The Government document and strategy *The Health of the Nation* emphasises the importance of setting health targets in shaping purchasing decisions in HIV, AIDS and sexual health services. **Careful consideration and co-ordination needs to be given to the setting of appropriate targets in HIV prevention work with drug users.** *The Health of the Nation* provides an opportunity to develop a range of intervention targets relating to the maximisation of the general health of a range of drug using populations.

HIV RISK BEHAVIOUR

While encouraging changes have occurred in the drug taking and injecting behaviour of injecting drug users, targeted research and intervention programmes are required to encourage further changes in sharing behaviour. These interventions require prior ethnographic fieldwork and situation assessment in order to target changes in the 'social etiquette' and social norms associated with drug use as well as targeting changes in individual health beliefs and behaviours.

Higher levels of HIV prevalence and HIV risk behaviour are found among drug injectors with no experience of treatment or help for their drug use. **This emphasises the need for community-based intervention to encourage changes in the behaviour of drug users who never or rarely seek help. This also highlights the important role that peer education and consumer-led interventions have in reaching and educating those who even outreach workers do not reach.**

Research also associates HIV risk behaviour with non-injecting and non-opiate use. Further research and intervention is required to target non-injecting and recreational users, and particularly those using stimulant drugs. **Of key importance are the factors which are associated with initiation and transitions**

into injecting drug use and the HIV and sexual health behaviour of gay drug users and their sexual partners.

There are only scant indications of sexual behaviour change among drug users and their sexual partners, despite the increasing significance of sexual transmission of HIV. There is also a dearth of safer sex health promotion and intervention targeting drug users and their sexual partners and a lack of expertise and experience in this field. **Future research and intervention is required which focuses on the interpersonal dynamics of safer sex negotiation between drug users and their sexual partners and on the relationship between drug use, sexual risk and sexual health**.

Research indicates increased HIV risk behaviour in prison environments. Prisons are environments which often constrain individual attempts at behaviour change. They can be seen as 'risk environments'. **It is timely to consider the applicability and feasibility of systematically researching the context of risk taking in prisons with view to developing and evaluating the effectiveness of intervention strategies to contain HIV risk behaviour**.

Research has shown that the majority of drug injectors who are confirmed positive to HIV are unaware of their HIV status, and that those with no experience of treatment are also less likely to have been tested for HIV. **This suggests the need for greater accessibility of HIV counselling and HIV testing services directly in the community. It also points to the importance of providing immediate low-threshold access to community-based drug treatment and helping services**.

The majority of drug users remain out of contact with treatment and helping services. The help-seeking patterns of drug users often highlight the inadequacies and limitations of medically oriented models of primary prevention. These operate on the assumption that given an individual's recognition of the severity of an illness they will necessarily and appropriately seek help. It is important to review conventional notions of 'help-seeking' in line with the public health and 'client-seeking' approaches now common to most HIV prevention strategies. This demands recognition of the limitations of many existing health and prevention services and the importance of community-based, voluntary and consumer-led services. It also points to the necessity of systematically assessing the needs of drug using populations for existing statutory and voluntary services.

HIV PREVENTION

HIV prevention interventions are part of a wider strategy of *health promotion* targeting drug users. It is timely for HIV-related health promotion practice to reflect the fundamental tenets of health promotion contained within the Ottawa Charter. **This involves greater *applied* commitment to community action,**

community participation and community organisation within drug-using communities and to the creation of healthy environments and the supporting of healthy policy. While often advocated in HIV prevention work, such a strategy is rarely adopted in practice.

Outreach requires careful ongoing evaluation with regard to the excellent opportunities it provides for identifying and responding to consumer needs in the community and for facilitating peer education, community participation and community change interventions among drug users. These may be advanced through carefully commissioned demonstration or intervention-based research projects, modelled on similar established projects within gay communities.

Health service contact with a drug treatment agency is an important determinant of HIV risk behaviour. This demands continued commitments to increasing the accessibility of treatment services for drug users, of which a commitment to flexibility in prescribing is part. **Research suggests methadone maintenance is most effective when offered as part of a structured treatment programme which includes adequate dosage, adequate length of treatment and close contact between clients and workers**. Many existing treatment programmes work to criteria (such as inadequate dosage) which undermine their effectiveness.

General practitioners are in an excellent position to offer opportunistic health education and early intervention to drug users, and in particular, to new initiates into drug use. **Stronger links between non-specialist and specialist services are required and this might be encouraged through increased and improved referral, supervision and joint management in training and integration of service provision**.

There are problems associated with providing sexual health services to drug users. **Careful evaluation and needs assessment is required of current HIV and sexual health counselling practices in specialist and non-specialist settings. Exploratory research is needed to describe the specific problems that drug workers may have in undertaking safer sex education with drug users**.

There are particular needs with regard to service training associated with sexuality and safer sex education. Training of non-specialist practitioners who work with drug users also remains a priority. General practitioners are in an excellent position to educate and advise but many remain reluctant to work with drug users or have difficulties in discussing drug use and sexual behaviour.

There is an urgent and neglected need to provide HIV prevention interventions in prisons. **Prison interventions should be carefully evaluated, perhaps as model demonstration projects and should include the provision of condoms and disinfectants for cleaning injecting equipment**.

The need for integrating drug treatment, primary care, counselling, HIV testing, safer sex interventions and social welfare advice as part of a wider community-based response to HIV prevention remains an urgent priority. It is clear that the HIV related health needs of drug users and their sexual partners are relative to wider social, housing and welfare needs. This demands a co-ordinated community-based response, of which voluntary and consumer advice services are central.

RESEARCH STRATEGY

Understanding the process and dynamics of change is an important first step to designing appropriate intervention responses to facilitate change. **Research strategies need to incorporate multi-disciplinary approaches so as to investigate the epidemiological, individual and social context of HIV risk and behaviour change** (see Figure 7.1). Qualitative approaches help to provide an understanding of the processes and factors which influence individuals' capabilities to achieve behaviour change and are under-utilised by current research in the field of HIV and drug use.

Careful consideration needs to be given to the effectiveness of needs assessments in drug and HIV prevention work. **It is essential that local and health authorities build appropriate infrastructures for the ongoing and systematic undertaking and analysis of prevalence monitoring of HIV and drug use**. These should also include measures to assess the extent and nature of unmet need in a given local population.

Careful consideration needs to be given to the setting of appropriate measures of process and outcome in the ongoing monitoring and evaluation of interventions. There are methodological difficulties in demonstrating the effectiveness of health promotion interventions, particularly those encouraging community-based changes. This demands careful consideration with regard to the purchasing and regulation of service delivery. **It is important that the methodological difficulties associated with conducting needs assessment and in demonstrating effectiveness do not eclipse the funding and provision necessary for developing innovative community-based services**.

Commissioned and co-ordinated evaluative and developmental research is required in the following areas: HIV prevalence monitoring, drug use among men who have sex with men, transitions and initiation into drug use, interpersonal dynamics and negotiation of safer drug use and sexual encounters, sexual behaviour and sexual behaviour change, peer education programmes, outreach and community change interventions and structured methadone maintenance programmes.

HIV PREVENTION STRATEGY

There is currently little central co-ordination of drug service delivery. While this has encouraged a degree of local autonomy in the purchasing and providing of services, current service provision also remains fragmented and in need of greater integration. **Co-ordination of HIV prevention strategy targeting drug users is required at national level. This demands clarifying and delineating the responsibilities of key agents in drug policy and service development and strengthening the collaborative links between them.** These key agents might include the Department of Health, the Department for Education, the Home Office, the Advisory Council on the Misuse of Drugs, the Health Education Authority, the Standing Conference on Drug Abuse and the National AIDS Trust. **There is a need for facilitating and supporting the integration of HIV prevention services for drug users into wider national and regional HIV prevention strategy.** This is particularly important given the increasing fragmentation of HIV prevention services and the need for inter-sectoral collaboration in the light of *The Health of the Nation* target setting.

Because the ways in which individuals behave are influenced by a range of individual, community and environmental factors, achieving change demands a strategic approach to health promotion which encourages individual, community and environmental change (see Figure 7.1). The

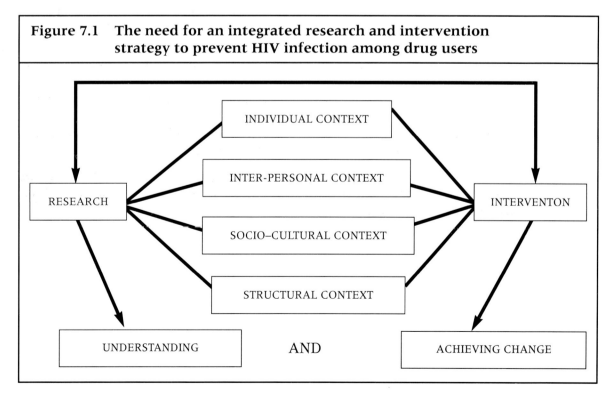

Figure 7.1   The need for an integrated research and intervention strategy to prevent HIV infection among drug users

key elements of the health promotion process are to facilitate and support healthy policy, healthy environments, healthy communities, healthy services and healthy drug users. The key elements in planning intervention strategy are needs assessment, purchasing, commissioning, providing, contracts, target setting and monitoring/evaluation. **The effectiveness and efficiency with which intervention strategy operates may be considerably improved by developing a national framework for co-ordinating, supporting and advocating healthy HIV health promotion strategy targeting drug users**.

As drug services stand today they are relatively fragmented with little central, inter-departmental or inter-sectoral co-ordination. *The Health of the Nation* encourages a need to develop a *national* strategy for HIV prevention work among drug users. Healthy HIV prevention policy among drug users can be achieved by supporting and encouraging:

- the purchasing and providing of healthy services at national and regional level by providing expert and state-of-the art review and evaluation evidence on what works in HIV prevention intervention strategy;
- the purchasing and providing of healthy services by reviewing and disseminating expertise on needs assessment and evaluation methods in the field of drug use;
- regional and district infrastructures for the collation of key prevalence data and estimates on the epidemiology of HIV and drug use;
- national and regional consensus meetings of key purchasers, commissioners and providers to review the effectiveness and organisation of the contracting process;
- healthy alliances in the purchasing, commissioning and providing of HIV prevention services;
- the setting of appropriate health targets at national and regional level in the light of *The Health of the Nation* objectives;
- regional community-development strategies which aim to facilitate community action and community participation among drug users.

The above activities would aim to support the establishment of minimum standard guidelines in the contracting and providing of HIV prevention services for drug users.

References

Abdul-Quader, A. S., Friedman, S. R., Des Jarlais, D. *et al.* (1987) Methadone maintenance and behavior by intravenous drug users that can transmit HIV, *Contemporary Drug Problems*, 14, 425–434.

Abdul-Quader, A. S., Tross, S., Des Jarlais, D. C. *et al.* (1989) Predictors of attempted sexual behaviour change in a street sample of active male IV drug users in New York City, *Fifth International Conference on AIDS*, Montreal.

Abdul-Quader, A. S., Tross, S., Friedman, S. R. *et al.* (1990) Street-recruited intravenous drug users and sexual risk reduction in New York City, *AIDS*, 4, 1075–1079.

Abdul-Quader, A. S., Tross, S., Silvert, H., Simons, P., Friedman, S. R. & Des Jarlais, D. C. (1992) Peer influence and condom use by female sexual partners of injecting drug users in New York City, *Eighth International Conference on AIDS*, Amsterdam.

ACMD (1982) *Treatment and Rehabilitation Report*, London, Department of Health and Social Security.

ACMD (1984) *Prevention*, London, Home Office.

ACMD (1988) *AIDS and Drugs Misuse Part One*, London, Department of Health and Social Security.

ACMD (1989) *AIDS and Drugs Misuse Part Two*, London, Department of Health.

ACMD (1993) *AIDS and Drug Misuse: Update*, London, Department of Health,

Alcabes, P., Vlahov, D. J Anthony, J. C. *et al.* (1992) Correlates of human immunodeficiency virus infection in intravenous drug users: are treatment-program samples misleading?, *British Journal of Addiction*, 87, 47–54.

Anderson. P. & Mayon-White, R. (1988) General Practitioners and management of infection with HIV, *British Medical Journal*, 296. 535–537.

Anderson, J. (1990) AIDS in Thailand, *British Medical Journal*, 300, 415–6.

Azjen, I. (1988) *Attitudes, Personality and Behaviour*, Milton Keynes, Open Univeristy Press.

Ball, J. C., Lange, W. R., Meyers, C. P. & Friedman, S. R. (1988) Reducing the risk of AIDS through methadone maintenance treatment, *Journal of Health and Social Behaviour*, 29, 214–226.

Ball, J. C. & Ross, A. (1991) *The Effectiveness of Methadone Treatment: Patients, Programs, Services and Outcome*, New York, Springer-Verlag.

Barnard, M. (1993) Needle sharing in context: patterns of sharing among men and women injectors and HIV risks, *Addiction*, 88, 805–812.

Bath, G. E., Dominy, N., Burns, S. M. *et al.* (1994) Fewer drug users share needles, *British Medical Journal*, 306, 1414.

Beattie, A. (1986) Community development for health: from practice to theory, *Radical Health Promotion*, 4, 12–18.

Beattie, A. (1991) Knowledge and control in health promotion: a test case for social policy and social theory. In Cabe, J., Calnan, M. & Bury, M. (Eds) *The Sociology of the Health Service*, London, Routledge.

Becker, M. H. (1984) (Ed) *The Health Belief Model and Personal Health Behaviour*, New Jersey, Charles B. Slack.

Becker, M. H. & Joseph, J. G. (1988) AIDS and behavioral change: a review, *American Journal of Public Health*, 78, 394–410.

Bell, J., Batey, R. G., Farrell, G. C. *et al.* (1990) Hepatitis C virus in intravenous drug users, *Medical Journal of Australia*, 153, 274–276.

Benhamou, J. P. (1993) Viral hepatitis: chairman's introduction, *GUT*, 34 (Supp. 2), iv.

Berridge, V. (1989) Historical issues. In MacGregor, S. (Ed) *Drugs and British Society: Responses to a Social Problem in the 1980s,* London, Routledge.

Bird, A. G., Gore, S. M., Jolliffe, D. W. & Burns, S. M. (1992) Anonymous HIV surveillance in Saughton Prison, Edinburgh, *AIDS,* 6, 725–733.

Bloor, M. J., McKeganey, N. P. & Barnard, M. A. (1990) An ethnographic study of HIV-related risk practices among Glasgow rent boys and their clients: report of a pilot study, *AIDS Care,* 2, 17–24.

Bloor, M. J., Barnard, M. A., Finlay, A. *et al.* (1992) The inappropriateness of health belief models in explaining the behaviour of rent boys in Glasgow, *AIDS Care,* 4, 1–5.

Brewer, T. F. (1991) AIDS in prison: the pragmatic approach, *AIDS,* 5, 897.

Brewer, T. F. and Derrickson, J. (1992) AIDS in prison: a review of epidemiology and preventive policy, *AIDS,* 6, 623–628.

Brown, L. S., Chu, A., Nemoto, T. *et al.* (1989) Human immunodeficiency virus infection in a cohort of intravenous drug users in New York City: demographic, behavioural and clinical features, *New York State Journal of Medicine,* 89, 506–510.

Buning, E. (1990) The role of harm reduction programmes in curbing the spread of HIV by drug injectors. In Strang, J. & Stimson, G. V. (Eds) *AIDS and Drug Misuse: The Challenge for Policy and Practice in the 1990s,* London, Routledge.

Buning, E., Van Brussel, G. & Van Santen, G. (1990) The 'methadone by bus' project in Amsterdam, *British Journal of Addiction,* 85, 1247–1250.

Bunton, R. & MacDonald, G. (1992) Health promotion: discipline or disciplines?. In Bunton, R. & MacDonald,G. (Eds) *Health Promotion: Disciplines and Diversity,* London, Routledge.

Bureau of Communicable Disease Control (1989) *AIDS Surveillance Monthly Update, New York State Department of Health,* New York.

Bureau of Hygiene and Tropical Diseases (1991)

Burt, J. & Stimson, G. V. (1993) *Drug Injectors and HIV Risk Reduction: Strategies for Protection,* London, Health Education Authority.

Carlson, R. G. & Siegal, H. A. (1991) The crack life: an ethnographic overview of crack use and sexual behaviour among African–Americans in a Midwest metropolitan city, *Journal of Psychoactive Drugs,* 23, 11–20.

Carvell, A. & Hart, G. (1990a) Risk behaviours for HIV infection among drug users in prison, *British Medical Journal,* 300, 1383–1384.

Carvell, A. & Hart, G. (1990b) Help–seeking and referrals in a needle exchange: a comprehensive service to injecting drug users, *British Journal of Addiction,* 85, 235–240.

Chaisson, R. E., Bacchetti, P., Osmond, D. *et al.* (1989) Cocaine use and HIV infection in intravenous drug users in San Francisco, *Journal of the American Medical Association,* 263, 851–855.

Chaisson, M. A., Stoneburner, R L., Hilderbrandt, W. E. *et al.* (1991) Heterosexual transmission of HIV–1 associated with the use of smokable freebase cocaine (crack), *AIDS,* 5, 1121–1126.

Chitwood, D. & Comerford, M. (1990) Drugs, sex and AIDS risk, *American Behavioural Scientist,* 33, 465–477.

Choo, Q. L., Kuo, G., Weiner, A. J. *et al.* (1989) Isolation of a C–DNA clone derived from blood–borne non–A non–B viral hepatitis genome, *Science,* 359–362.

Coleman, R. & Curtis, D. (1988) Distribution of risk behaviour for HIV infection among intravenous drug users, *British Journal of Addiction,* 83, 1331–1334.

Connors, M. and Lewis, B. (1989) Anthropological and epidemiological observations of changes in needle use and needle sharing practices following twelve months of bleach distribution, *Fifth International Conference on AIDS,* Montreal.

Connors, M. (1992) Risk perception, risk taking and risk management among intravenous drug users: implications for AIDS prevention, *Social Science and Medicine,* 34(6), 591–601.

Contoreggi, C., Jones, S. W., Simpson, P. M. *et al.* (1992) A model of syringe disinfection as measured by polymerase chain reaction for human leucocyte antigen and HIV genome, *Eighth International Conference on AIDS*, Amsterdam.

Covell, R., Frischer, M., Taylor, A. *et al.* (1993) Prison experience of injecting drug users in Glasgow, *Drug and Alcohol Dependence*, 32, 9–14.

Cranfiled, S. & Dixon, A. (1990) *Drug Training, HIV & AIDS*, London, Health Education Authority.

Crofts, N., Hooper, J. L. *et al.* (1993) Heaptitis C virus infection among a cohort of Victorian drug users, *Medical Journal of Australia*, 159, 237–241.

Darke, S., Hall, W. & Carless, J. (1990) Drug use, injecting practices and sexual behaviour of opiod users in Sydney, *Australia, British Journal of Addiction*, 85, 1603–1609.

Day, S., Ward, H. & Harris, J. (1988) Prostitute women and public health, *British Medical Journal*, 297, 1585.

Department of Health (1992a) *The Patients' Charter*, London, HMSO.

Department of Health, (1992b) *The Health of the Nation: A Strategy for Health in England*, London, HMSO.

Department of Health (1992c) *Green paper on Health of the Nation*, London, Department of Health.

Department of Health (1993) *Health of the Nation Key Area Handbook: HIV/AIDS and Sexual Health*, London, HMSO.

Des Jarlais, D. C. & Friedman, S. R. (1987) HIV infection and intravenous drug users: epidemiology and risk reduction, *AIDS*, 1, 67–76.

Des Jarlais, D. C., Tross, S., Abdul Quader, A., Kouzi, A. & Friedman, S. R. (1989) Intravenous drug users and maintenance of behaviour change, *Fifth International Conference on AIDS*, Montreal, June 1989.

Des Jarlais, D. C. (1992) The first and second decade of AIDS among injecting drug users, British *Journal of Addiction*, 87; 347–353.

Des Jarlais, D. C., Friedman, S. R., Choopanya, K., Vanichseni, S. & Ward, T. P. (1992) International epidemiology of HIV and AIDS among injecting drug users, *AIDS*, 6, 1053–1068.

Department of Health and Social Security (1984) *The Health Service in England and Wales: Annual Report*, London, DHSS.

Dingwall, R. (1976) *Aspects of Illness*, London, Martin Robertson.

Dolan, K. A., Donoghoe, M. C., Jones, S. & Stimson, G. V. (1991) *A Cohort Study of Syringe Exchange Clients and other Drug Injectors in England, 1989 to 1990*, London, The Centre for Research on Drugs and Health Behaviour.

Dole, V. P. & Nyswander, M. (1965) A medical treatment for diacetylmorphine (heroin) addiction, *Journal of the American Medical Association*, 193, 80–84.

Dole, V. P. (1989) Methadone treatment and the acquired immunodeficiency syndrome, *Journal of the American Medical Association*, 262, 1681.

Donmall, M. (1990) Towards a national drug database, *Druglink*, March/April, 10–12.

Donoghoe, M. C., Stimson, G. V. & Dolan, K. A. (1989) Sexual behaviour of injecting drug users and associated risks of HIV infection for non–injecting sexual partners, *AIDS Care*, 1, 51–58.

Donoghoe, M. C., Dolan. K. A. & Stimson, G. V. (1991) Changes in injectors' HIV risk behaviour and syringe supply in UK, 1987–1990, *Seventh International Conference on AIDS*, Florence, Italy.

Donoghoe, M. C., Stimson, G. V. & Dolan, K. A. (1992) *Syringe Exchange in England: An Overview*, London, Tufnell Press.

Donoghoe, M. C. (1993) Personal communication

Donoghoe, M. C. & Hunter, G. M. (1993) Personal communication.

Donoghoe, M. C. & Power, R. (1993) Household bleach as disinfectant for injecting drug users, *Lancet*, i, 165.

Donoghoe, M. C., Rhodes, T. J., Hunter, G. M. & Stimson, G. V. (1993) HIV testing and unreported positivity among injecting drug users in London, *AIDS*, 7, 1105–1111.

Dorn, N. & Murji, K. (1992) *Drug Prevention: A Review of the English Language Literature*, Institute for the Study of Drug Dependence, Research Monograph Monograph 5.

Druglink (1994) Back to basics report says cut drug use to curb HIV, *Druglink*, 9(1), 4–5.

Dye, S. & Isaacs, C. (1991) Intravenous drug misuse among prison inmates: implications for spread of HIV, *British Medical Journal*, 302, 1506.

European Centre for the Epidemiological Monitoring of AIDS (1993) *AIDS Surveillance in Europe*, Quarterly Report No.36.

Evans, B. G., Noone, A., Mortimer, J. Y. *et al.* (1992) Heterosexually acquired HIV–1 infection: Cases reported in England, Wales and Northern Ireland, 1985–1991. In *Communicable Disease Report*, Public Health Laboratory Service, 2(5), April.

Fabrega, H. (1974) *Disease and Social Behaviour*, Boston, MIT Press.

Farrell, M. & Strang, J. (1992) Healthy drug users and HIV prevention. In Evans, B., Sanberg, S. & Watson, S. (Eds) *Working Where the Risks Are: Issues in HIV Prevention*, London, Health Education Authority.

Fishbein, M. & Ajzen, I. (1975) *Belief, Attitude, Intention and Behaviour: An Introduction to Theory and Research*, Reading, MA, Addison-Wesley.

French, J. & Adams, L. (1986) Health education: from analysis to synthesis, *Health Education Journal*, 45, 71–74.

Friedman, S. R., Des Jarlais, D. C. & Sterk, C. (1990) AIDS and the social relations of intravenous drug users, *Milbank Quaterly*, 86 (Supp. 1), 85–110.

Friedman, S. R., Sterk, C., Sufian, M., Des Jarlais, D. C. & Stephenson, B. (1990) Reaching out to injecting drug users. In Strang, J. & Stimson, G. V. (Eds) *AIDS and Drug Misuse: The Challenge for Policy and Practice in the 1990s*, London, Routledge.

Friedman, S. R. & Des Jarlais, D. C. (1991) HIV among drug injectors: the epidemic and the response, *AIDS Care*, 3, 237–248.

Friedman, S. R., Jose, B., Neaigus, A. *et al.* (1991) Peer mobilization and widespread condom use by drug injectors, *Seventh International Conference on AIDS*, Florence.

Friedman, S. R., Neaigus, A., Des Jarlais, D. C., Sotheran, J. L., Woods, J., & Sufian, M. (1992a) Social intervention against AIDS among injecting drug users, *British Journal of Addiction*, 87, 393–404.

Friedman, S. R., Des Jarlais, D. C., Neaigus, A. *et al.* (1992b) Organizing drug injectors against AIDS: preliminary data on behavioural outcomes, *Psychological Addictive Behaviours*, 6, 100–106.

Friedson, E. (1970) *The Profession of Medicine*, New York, Dodd Mead & Co.

Frischer, M. (1992) Estimated prevalence of injecting drug use in Glasgow, *British Journal of Addiction*, 87, 235–243.

Frischer, M., Green, S. T., Goldberg, D. J. *et al.* (1992) Estimates of HIV infection among injecting drug users in Glasgow, 1985–1990, *AIDS*, 6, 1371–1375.

Frutchey, C. (1990) The role of community–based organizations in AIDS and STD prevention. In Paalman, M. (Ed) *Promoting Safer Sex: Prevention of HIV and Other STD*, Amsterdam, Swets and Zeitlinger.

Fullilove, R., Fullilove, M., Golden, E. *et al.* (1990) Drug use and sexual behaviours in a probability sample of single adults in 'high risk' neighbourhoods of San Francisco, *Sixth International Conference on AIDS*, San Francisco.

Gallagher, M., Foy, C., Rhodes, T. *et al.* (1988) *A National Study of HIV Infection, AIDS and General Practice*, University of Newcastle Upon Tyne, Centre for Health Services Research Report 37.

Gaughwin, M., Douglas, R., Liew, C. *et al.* (1991) Human Immunodeficiency virus (HIV) prevalence and risk behaviours for its tranmsission in South Australian prisons, *AIDS*, 5, 845–851.

Gaughwin, M. & Vlahov, D. (1993) Assessing the risk of HIV–1 transmission in correctional centres. In Heather, N., Wodak, A., Nadelmann, E. & O'Hare, P. (Eds) *Psychoactive Drugs and Harm Reduction: From Faith to Science*, London, Wurr Publishers.

Gawin, F. H. & Ellinwood, E. H. (1988) Cocaine and other stimulants: actions, abuse and treatments, *New England Journal of Medicine*, 318, 1173–1182.

Ghodse, A. H., Tregenza, G. & Li, M. (1987) Effects of fear of AIDS on sharing of injecting equipment among drug abusers, *British Medical Journal*, 292, 698–699.

Girardi, E., Zaccaretti, M., Tossini, G. *et al.* (1990) Hepatitis C virus infection in intravenous drug users: prevalence and risk factors, *Scandinavian Journal of Infectious Diseases*, 22, 751–752.

Glanz, A. & Taylor, C. (1986) Findings of a national survey of the role of general practitioners in the treatment of opiate misuse: extent of contact with opiate misusers, *British Medical Journal*, 293, 427–430.

Glanz, A., Byrne, C. & Jackson, P. (1989) Role of community pharmacists in the prevention of AIDS among injecting drug users: findings of a survey in England and Wales, *British Medical Journal*, 299, 1076–1079.

Goldberg, D., Frischer, M. & Green, S. (1993) Sex surveys and drug users, *Nature*, 361, 504–505.

Gossop, M., Griffiths, P., Powis, B. & Strang, J. (1993) Severity of heroin dependence and HIV risk: sharing injecting equipment, *AIDS Care*, 5, 159–168.

Green, J. (1990) Counselling the drug taker about HIV infection and AIDS. In Strang, J. & Stimson, G. V. (Eds) *AIDS and Drug Misuse: The Challenge for Policy and Practice in the 1990s*, London, Routledge.

Griffiths, P., Gossop, M., Powis, B. & Strang, J. (1992) Extent and nature of transitions of route among heroin addicts in treatment: preliminary data from the drug transitions study, *British Jounral of Addiction*, 87, 585–492.

Grund, J. P., Kaplan, C. D., Adriaans, N. F. P. *et al.* (1991) Drug sharing and HIV transmission risks: the practice of "frontloading" in the Dutch injecting drug user population, *Journal of Psychoactive Drugs*, 23, 1–10.

Grund, J. P., Stern, L. S., Kaplan, C. D., Adriaans, N. F. P. & Drucker, E. (1992) Drug use contexts and HIV consequences: the effect of drug policy on patterns of everyday drug use in Rotterdam and the Bronx, *British Journal of Addiction*, 87, 381–392.

Hall, W., Ward, J. & Mattick, R. (1993) Methadone maintenance treatment in prisons: the New South Wales experience, *Drug and Alcohol Review*, 12, 193–203.

Harding, T. (1987) AIDS in prison, *Lancet*, 2, 1260–1263.

Hart, G., Carvell, A. L. M., Woodward, N. *et al.* (1989a) Evaluation of needle exchange in Central London: behaviour change and anti–HIV status over one year, *AIDS*, 3, 261–265.

Hart, G. Woodward, N. Carvell, A. *et al.* (1989b) Needle exchange in London: operating philosophy and communication strategies, *AIDS Care*, 1, 125–134.

Hart, G. (1990) Needle exchange in historical context: responses to the 'drugs problem'. In Aggleton, P., Davies, P. & Hart, G. (Eds) *AIDS: Individual, Cultural and Policy Dimensions*, Lewes, Falmer Press.

Hartgers, C., Buning, E. C., Van Santen, G. *et al.* (1989) The impact of the needle and syringe exchange programme in Amsterdam on injecting behaviour, *AIDS*, 3, 571–576.

Hartgers, C, Van den Hoek, J. A. R., Krijnen, P. & Coutinho, R. A. (1990) Risk factors and heroin and cocaine use trends among injecting drug users in low threshold methadone programs, Amsterdam 1985–1989, *Sixth International Conference on AIDS*, San Francisco.

Hartgers, C., Van den Hoek, A., Krijnen, P. *et al.* (1991) Changes over time in heroin and cocaine use among injecting drug users in Amsterdam, The Netherlands, 1985–1989, *British Journal of Addiction*, 86, 1091–1097.

Hartnoll, R. L., Lewis, R. Daviaud, E. & Mitcheson, M. (1985) *Drug Problems: Assessing Local Needs*, London, Birkbeck College.

Hartnoll, R. L. (1987) *Help–Seeking by Problem Drug Takers: A Review of the Literature*, London, Insitute for the Study of Drug Dependence.

Hartnoll, R. L. & Power, R. (1989) *Study of Help–Seeking and Service Utilisation by Problem Drug Takers*, London, Institute for the Study of Drug Dependence.

Hartnoll, R. L., Rhodes, T. J., Jones, A. *et al.* (1990) *A Survey of HIV Outreach Intervention in the United Kingdom*, London, Birkbeck College.

Hartnoll, R. L. (1992) Research and the help-seeking process, *British Journal of Addiction*, 87, 429–437.

Haw, S., Frischer, M., Donoghoe, M. *et al.* (1992) The importance of multi-site sampling in determining the prevalence of HIV among drug injectors in Glasgow and London, *AIDS*, 6, 517–518.

Herkt, D. (1993) Peer-based user groups: the Australian experience. In Heather, N., Wodak, A., Nadelmann, E. & O'Hare, P. (Eds) *Psychoactive Drugs and Harm Reduction: From Faith to Science*, London, Wurr Publishers.

Holden, C. (1989) Streetwise crack research, *Science*, 246, 1376–1381.

Hunter, G. M & Donoghoe, M. C. (1994) "Frontloading": an HIV risk behaviour among injecting drug users in London, *Addiction*, in press.

Hunter, G. M., Donoghoe, M. C., Crosier, A. & Stimson, G. V. (1992) Drug injectors in London reduce syringe sharing between 1990 and 1991, *Eighth International Conference on AIDS*, Amsterdam.

Jackson, J. & Rotkiewicz, L. (1987) A coupon programme: AIDS education and drug treatment, *Third International Conference on AIDS*, Washington.

Jimenez, A. (1989) Shooting galleries in three Chicago community areas. In *Epidemiological Trends in Drug Abuse: Proceedings of the Community Epidemiology Work Group*, National Institute on Drug Abuse, III, 86–93.

Joe, G. W., Simpson, D. D. & Hubbard, R. L. (1991) Treatment predictors of tenure in methadone maintenance, *Journal of Substance Abuse*, 3, 73–84.

Jose, B., Friedman, S. R., Neaigus, A. *et al.* 'Frontloading' is associated with HIV infection among drug injectors in New York City, *Eighth International Conference on AIDS*, Amsterdam.

Kane, S. (1991) HIV, Heroin and heterosexual relations, *Social Science and Medicine*, 32(9), 1037–1050.

Kayal, P. M. (1993) *Bearing Witness: Gay Men's Health Crisis and the Politics of AIDS*, San Francisco, Westview Press.

Kelly, J. A., St Lawrence, J. S., Stevenson, L. Y., Hauth, A. C., Kalichman, S. C., Diaz, Y. E. *et al.* (1992) Community AIDS/HIV risk reduction: the effects of endorsements by popular people in three cities, *American Journal of Public Health*, 80, 1483–1489.

Korkia–Kenwood, P. & Stimson, G. V. (1992) *Anabolic Steroid Use in Great Britain: An Exploratory Investigation*, London, The Centre for Research on drugs and Health Behaviour.

Kinnell, H. (1989) *Prostitutes, their clients and risks of HIV infection in Birmingham*, Occasional Paper, Birmingham, Department of Public Health Medicine.

Klee, H., Faugier, J., Hayes, C. *et al.* (1990a) Sexual partners of injecting drug users: the risk of HIV infection, *British Journal of Addiction*, 85, 413–418.

Klee, H., Faugier, J., Hayes, C. *et al.* (1990b) AIDS-related risk behaviour, polydrug use and temazepam, *British Journal of Addiction*, 85, 1125–1132.

Klee, H., Faugier, J., Hayes, C. & Morris, J. (1991) Risk reduction among injecting drug users: changes in the sharing of injecting equipment and condom use, *AIDS Care*, 3, 63–73.

Klee, H. (1992) Sexual risk among amphetamine misusers: prospects for change, in Aggleton, P., Davies, P. & Hart, G. (Eds) *AIDS: Rights, Risk and Reason*, Lewes, Falmer Press.

Kleinegris, C. (1991) Innovative AIDS prevention among drug using women prostitutes, *Second International Conference on the Reduction of Drug Related Harm*, Barcelona.

Lart, R. & Stimson, G. V. (1990) National survey of syringe exchange schemes in England, *British Journal of Addiction*, 85, 1433–1444.

Leigh, B. (1990) The relationship of sex-related alcohol expectancies to alcohol consumption and sexual behaviour, *British Journal of Addiction*, 85, 919–928.

Rhodes, T., Hartnoll, R. L. & Johnson, A. M. (1991) *Out of the Agency and on to the Streets: A Review of HIV Outreach Health Education in Europe and the United States,* London, Institute for the Study of Drug Dependence, Research Monograph 2.

Rhodes, T. & Holland, J. (1992) Outreach as a strategy for HIV prevention: aims and practice, *Health Education Research,* 7(4), 533–546.

Rhodes, T. (1993) Time for community change: what has outreach to offer?, *Addiction,* 1317–1320.

Rhodes, T. J., Bloor, M. J., Donoghoe, M. C. *et al.* (1993a) HIV prevalence and HIV risk behaviour among injecting drug users in London and Glasgow, *AIDS Care,* 5, 413–425.

Rhodes, T. J., Donoghoe, M. C., Hunter, G. M. & Stimson, G. V. (1993b) Continued risk behaviour among HIV positive drug injectors in London: implications for intervention, *Addiction,* 88, 1553–1560.

Rhodes, T. J., Donoghoe, M. C., Hunter, G .M. & Stimson, G. V. (1994a) Sexual behaviour of drug injectors in London: implications for HIV transmission and HIV prevention, *Addiction,* in press.

Rhodes, T. J., Donoghoe, M. C., Hunter, G. M. & Stimson, G.V. (1993b) HIV prevalence no higher among female drug injectors also involved in prostitution, *AIDS Care,* in press.

Rhodes, T. (1994a) HIV outreach, peer education and community change: developments and dilemmas, *Health Education Journal,* in press.

Rhodes, T. (1994b) Outreach, community change and community empowerment: contradictions for public health and health promotion. In Aggleton, P., Hart, G. & Davies, P. (Eds) *AIDS: Foundations for the Future,* Lewes, Falmer Press.

Rhodes, T. & Green, A. (1994) *Safer Sex Education With Drug Users: An Exploratory Study,* London, The Centre for Research on Drugs and Health Behaviour.

Rhodes, T. & Quirk, A. (1994) All risks are relative: illicit drug use, sexual risk and social context, *British Sociological Association Annual Conference on Sexualities in Social Context,* Preston.

Rhodes, T. & Stimson, G. V. (1994a) Sex, drugs, intervention and research: from the individual to the social (forthcoming).

Rhodes, T. & Stimson, G. V. (1994b) What is the relationship between drug–taking and sexual risk? Social relations and social research, *Sociology of Health and Illness,* 16, 189–208.

Robertson, J. R., Bucknall, A. B., Welsby, P. *et al.* (1986) Epidemic of AIDS related virus (HTLV–III/LAV) infection among intravenous drug abusers, *British Medical Journal,* 292, 527–529.

Robertson R. (1990) The Edinburgh epidemic: a case study. In Strang J. & Stimson G. V. (Eds) *AIDS and Drugs Misuse: The Challenge for Policy and Practice in the 1990s,* London, Routledge.

Robertson, D. (1994) *HIV Prevention in Custodial Settings,* London, Health Education Authority (forthcoming).

Rogers, E. M. & Shoemaker, F. (1971) *Communication of Innovations,* New York, Free Press.

Ronald, P. J. M. & Robertson, J. R. (1992) Prevalence of HIV infection among drug users in Edinburgh, *British Medical Journal,* 304, 1506.

Rosenstock, I. M., Strecher, V. J. & Becker, M. H. (1988) Social learning theory and the health belief model, *Health Education Quarterly,* 15, 175–183.

Rounsaville, B. J. & Kleber, H. A. (1985) Untreated opiate addicts: how do they differ from those seeking treatment?, *Archives of General Psychiatry,* 42, 1072–1077.

Samuels, J. F., Vlahov, D, Anthony, J. C. & Chaisson, R. E. (1992) Measurement of HIV risk behaviours among intravenous drug users, *British Journal of Addiction,* 87, 404–417.

Schechter, M., Craib, K., Willoughby, B. *et al.* (1988) Patterns of sexual behaviour and condom use in a cohort of homosexual men, *American Journal of Public Health,* 36, 509–515.

Schoenbaum, E. E., Hartel, D., Selwyn, P. A, Klein, R. S., Davenny, K., Rogers, M., Feiner, C. & Friedland, G. (1989) Risk factors for human immunodeficiency virus infection in intravenous drug users, *New England Journal of Medicine,* 321, 874–879.

Selwyn, P. A., Feiner, C., Cox, C. P. *et al.* (1987) Knowledge about AIDS and high–risk behavior among intravenous drug users in New York City, *AIDS*, 1, 247–254.

Sheehan, M., Oppenheimer, E. & Taylor, C. (1988) Who comes for treatment: drug misusers at three London agencies, *British Journal of Addiction*, 83, 311–320.

Silverman, D., Bor, R., Miller, R. & Goldman, E. (1992) 'Obviously the advice is then to keep to safer sex': advice giving and advice perception in AIDS counselling. In Aggleton, P., Davies, P. & Hart, G. (Eds) *AIDS: Rights, Risk and Reason*, Lewes, Falmer Press.

Skidmore, C. A., Robertson, J. R. & Roberts, J. K. (1989) Changes in HIV risk taking behaviour in intravenous drug users: a second follow-up, *British Journal of Addiction*, 84, 695–696.

Skidmore, C., Robertson, J., Robertson, A. & Elton, R. (1990) After the epidemic: follow up study of HIV sero-prevalence and changing patterns of drug use, *British Medical Journal*, 300, 219–223.

Staff, A. (1993) Pragmatic Euphoria, *ANSA Journal*, 13, 2224.

Stall, R., McKusick, L., Wiley, J. *et al.* (1986) Alcohol and drug use during sexual activity and compliance with safe sex guidelines: the AIDS behavioural research project, *Health Education Quarterly*, 13, 359–371.

Stimson, G. V., Alldritt, L., Dolan, K. & Donoghoe, M. C. (1988) *Injecting Equipment Exchange Schemes: Final Report*, London, Goldsmiths College.

Stimson, G.V., Donoghoe, M.C., Lart, R. & Dolan, K. (1990) Distributing sterile needles and syringes to people who inject drugs; the syringe exchange experiment. In Strang, J. & Stimson, G.V. (Eds) *AIDS and Drug Misuse: The Challenge for Policy in the 1990s*, London, Routledge.

Stimson, G. V. (1989) Syringe exchange programmes for injecting drug users, *AIDS*, 5, 253–260.

Stimson, G. V. (1990) AIDS and HIV: the challenge for British drug services, *British Journal of Addiction*, 85, 329–339.

Stimson, G. V. (1991) Risk reduction by drug users with regard to HIV infection, *International Journal of Psychiatry*, 3, 401–415.

Stimson, G. V. & Lart, R. (1991) HIV, drugs and public health in England: new words, old tunes, *International Journal of the Addictions*, 26, 1263–1277.

Stimson, G., Lart, R., Dolan, K. & Donoghoe, M. (1991) The future of syringe exchange in the public health prevention of HIV infection. In Aggleton, P., Davies, P. & Hart, G. (Eds.) *AIDS: Responses, Interventions and Care*, Lewes, Falmer Press.

Stimson, G. V. (1993a) The global diffusion of injecting drug use: implications for human immuno-deficiency virus infection, *Bulletin on Narcotics*, 1, 3–17.

Stimson, G. V. (1993b) AIDS and drug use: five years on, *Third Dorothy Black Lecture*, Charing Cross and Westminster Medical School, London.

Strang, J. (1990a) Intermediate goals and the process of change. In Strang, J. & Stimson, G. V. (Eds) *AIDS & Drugs Misuse: The Challenge for Policy and Practice in the 1990s*, London, Routledge.

Strang, J. (1990b) The roles of prescribing. In Strang, J. & Stimson, G. V. (Eds) *AIDS & Drugs Misuse: The Challenge for Policy and Practice in the 1990s*, London, Routledge.

Strang, J. (1991) Injecting drug misuse: response to Health of the Nation, *British Medical Journal*, 303, 1043–1046.

Strang, J., Des Jarlais, D. C., Griffiths, P. & Gossop, M. (1992) The study of transitions in the route of drug use: the route from one route to another, *British Journal of Addiction*, 87, 3, 473–483

Strang, J. (1993) Drug use and harm reduction: responding to the challenge. In Heather, N., Wodak, A., Nadelmann, E. & O'Hare, P. (Eds) *Psychoactive Drugs and Harm Reduction: From Faith to Science*, London, Wurr Publishers.

Strang, J., Powis, B., Griffiths, P. & Gossop, M. (1994) Heterosexual vaginal and anal intercourse amongst London heroin and cocaine users, *International Journal of STD and AIDS*, in press.

Strong, P. & Berridge, V. (1990) No one knew anything: some issues in British AIDS policy. In Aggleton, P., Davies, P. & Hart, G. (Eds) *AIDS: Individual, Cultural and Policy Dimensions*, Lewes, Falmer Press.

Taylor, A., Frischer, M., McKeganey, N. *et al.* (1993) HIV risk behaviours among female prostitutes in Glasgow, *Addiction*, 88, 1561–1564.

Taylor, A., Frischer, M., Green, S. *et al.* (1994) Low and stable prevalence of HIV among drug injectors in Glasgow, *International Journal of STDs and AIDS*, in press.

Tempesta, E & Di Giannantonio, M. (1990) The Italian epidemic: a case study. In Strang, J. & Stimson, G. V. (Eds) *AIDS & Drugs Misuse: The Challenge for Policy and Practice in the 1990s*, London, Routledge.

Tones, K., Tilford, S. & Robinson, Y. K. (1990) *Health Education: Effectiveness and Efficiency*, London: Chapman and Hall.

Tross, S., Abdul–Quader, A. S., Silvert, H., Simons, P., Des Jarlais, D.C . & Friedman, S. R. (1992) Determinants of condom use in female sexual partners of IV drug users in New York City, *Eighth International Conference on AIDS*, Amsterdam.

Tudor Hart, J. (1971) The inverse care law, *Lancet*, 1, 405–412.

Turnbull, P. J., Dolan, K. A. & Stimson, G. V. (1991) *Prisons, HIV and AIDS: Risks and Experiences in Custodial Care*, Horsham, AVERT.

Turnbull, P. J., Dolan, K. A. & Stimson, G. V. (1992) Prison decreases the prevalence but increases the risks, *Eighth International Conference on AIDS*, Amsterdam.

Turnbull, P. J., Stimson, G. V. & Dolan, K. A. (1992) Prevalence of HIV infection among ex-prisoners in England, *British Medical Journal*, 304, 90.

Turnbull, P. J. & Stimson, G. V. (1994) Prisons: heterosexuals in a risk environment. In Sherr, L. (Ed) *AIDS in the heterosexual population*, Berkshire, Harwood Academic Publishers.

Van den Hoek, J. A. R., Van Haastrecht, H. J. A & Coutinho, R. A. (1990) Heterosexual behaviour of intravenous drug users in Amsterdam: implications for the AIDS epidemic, *AIDS*, 4, 449–453.

Van Griensven, G., De Vroome, E., Tielman, R. *et al.* (1989) Effects of HIV antibody knowledge on high risk sexual behaviour with steady and nonsteady sexual partners among homosexual men, *American Journal of Epidemiology*, 129, 596–603.

Van Haastrecht, H., Van den Hoek, J. & Coutinho, R. (1989) No trend in yearly HIV seroprevalence rates among IVDUs in Amsterdam: 1986–1988, *Fifth International Conference on AIDS*, Montreal.

Van Haastrecht, H. J. A., Van den Hoek, J. A. R., Mientjes, G. H. & Coutinho. R. A. (1991) The early course of the HIV–1 infection epidemic among drug users in Amsterdam, The Netherlands, *Seventh International Conference on AIDS*, Florence.

Vlahov, D., Brewer, F., Munoz, A. *et al.* (1989) Temporal trends of human immunodeficiency virus type 1 (HIV–1) infection among inmates entering a statewide prison system, 1985–1987, *Journal of Acquired Immune Deficiency Syndrome*, 2, 283–290.

Vlahov, D., Munoz, A., Anthony, J. C. *et al.* (1990) Association of drug injection patterns with antibody to human immunodeficiency vuris type 1 among intravenous drug users in Baltimore, Maryland, *American Journal of Epidemiology*, 132, 847–856.

Vlahov, D., Munoz, A., Celentano, D. *et al.* (1991) HIV seroconversion and disinfection of injecting equipment amongst injecting drug users, Baltimore, Maryland, *Epidemiology*, 2, 444–446.

Waight, P. A., Rush, A. M., Miller, E. (1992) Surveillance of HIV infection by voluntary testing in England, *Communicable Diseases Report*, 2, R85–R90.

Ward, J., Darke, S., Hall, W. & Mattick, R. (1992) Methadone maintenance and the human immunodeficiency virus: current issues in treatment and research, *British Journal of Addiction*, 87, 447–453.

Watters, J. (1988) A street-based outreach model of AIDS prevention for intravenous drug users: preliminary evaluation, *Contemporary Drug Problems*, Fall, 411–423.

Watters, J. & Cuthbert, M. (1992) Crack cocaine and associated risks for HIV–1 infection in female injectiong drug users in San Francisco, California, *Eighth International Conference on AIDS*, Amsterdam.

Weatherburn, P., Davies, P. M., Hickson, F. C. I. *et al.* (1992) No connection between alcohol use and unsafe sex among gay and bisexual men, *AIDS*, 7, 115–119.

Webb, G., Wells, B. *et al.* (1986) Epidemic of AIDS–related virus infection among intravenous drug abusers, *British Medical Journal*, 292, 1202.

Weeks, J. (1989) AIDS: the intellectual agenda. In Aggleton, P., Hart, G. & Davies, P. (Ed) AIDS: *Social Representations, Social Practices*, Lewes, Falmer Press.

Wermuth, L., Ham, J. & Robbins, R. L. (1992) Women don't wear condoms: AIDS risk among sexual partners of IV drug users. In Huber, J. & Schneider, B. E. (Eds) *The Social Context of AIDS*, California, Sage.

World Health Organisation (1986) *Ottawa Charter for Health Promotion*, WHO/Canadian public Health Association.

Wiebel, W. (1988) Combining ethnographic and epidemiologic methods in targeted AIDS interventions: the Chicago model. In Battjes, R. & Pcikens, R. (Eds) *Needle Sharing Among Intravenous Drug Abusers*, Washington, NIDA Research Monograph 80.

Wiebel, W., Jimenenz, A., Johnson, W. *et al.* (1993) Positive effect on HIV seroconversion of street outreach interventions with IDU in Chicago, 1988–1992, *Eighth International Conference on AIDS*, Berlin.

Wodak, A. & Moss, A. (1990) HIV infection and injecting drug users: from epidemiology to public health, *AIDS*, 4(S1), 105–109.

Wolfe, H., Vranizan, K. M., Gorter, R. G., Cohen, J. B. & Moss, A. R. (1990) Crack use and related risk factors in IVDUs in San Francisco, *Fifth International Conference on AIDS*, San Francisco.

Wolfe, H., Vranizan, K. M., Gorter, R. G. *et al.* (1992) Crack use and human immunodeficiency virus infection among San Francisco intravenous drug users, *Sexually Transmitted Diseases*, March–April, 111–114.

Wolk, J., Wodak, A., Morlet, A. *et al.* (1988) Syringe HIV seroprevalence and behavioural and demographic characteristics of intravenous drug users in Sydney, Australia, 1987, *AIDS*, 2, 373.

Zborowski, M. (1952) Cultural components in rersponse to pain, *Journal of Social Issues*, 8, 1–6.

Zule, W. A. (1992) Risk and reciprocity: HIV and the injection drug user, *Journal of Psychoactive Drugs*, 24, 243–249.

Appendix

KEY PUBLICATIONS ON HIV PREVENTION AND DRUG USE

This appendix lists key publications on HIV prevention and drug use. Publications are selected on the basis of their immediate relevance to the issues discussed in this review.

Overviews on HIV prevention and drug use

ACMD (1988) *AIDS and Drugs Misuse Part One*, London, Department of Health and Social Security.
ACMD (1989) *AIDS and Drugs Misuse Part Two*, London, Department of Health.
ACMD (1993) *AIDS and Drug Misuse: Update*, London, Department of Health.
Heather, N., Wodak, A. Nadelmann, E. & O'Hare, P. (Eds) *Psychoactive Drugs and Harm Reduction: From Faith to Science*, London, Whurr Publishers.
MacGregor, S. (Ed) *Drugs and British Society: Responses to a Social Problem in the 1980s*, London, Routledge.
O'Hare, P., Newcombe, T., Matthews, A. *et al.* (Eds) (1992) *The Reduction of Drug Related Harm*, London, Routledge.
Rhodes, T. & Hartnoll, R. (Eds) (1994) *HIV Prevention in the Community: Perspectives on Individual, Community and Political Action*, London, Routledge, in press.
Strang, J. & Stimson, G. (Eds) (1990) *AIDS and Drugs Misuse: The Challenge for Policy and Practice in the 1990s*, London, Routledge.
Strang, J., Stimson, G. & Des Jarlais, D. C. (Eds) (1992) Special issue on AIDS, Drug Misuse and the Research Agenda, *British Journal of Addiction*, 87 (3).

Epidemiology of HIV infection among injecting drug users

Brenner, H., Hernando–Briongos, P. & Goos, C. (1991) AIDS among drug users in Europe, *Drug and Alcohol Dependence*, 29, 171–181.
Des Jarlais, D. C. & Friedman, S. R. (1987) HIV infection and intravenous drug users: epidemiology and risk reduction, *AIDS*, 1, 67–76.
Des Jarlais, D. C. (1992) The first and second decade of AIDS among injecting drug users, *British Journal of Addiction*, 87, 347–353.
Des Jarlais, D. C., Friedman, S. R., Choopanya, K., Vanichseni, S. & Ward, T. P. (1992) International epidemiology of HIV and AIDS among injecting drug users, *AIDS*, 6, 1053–1068.
Friedman, S. R. & Des Jarlais, D. C. (1991) HIV among drug injectors: the epidemic and the response, *AIDS Care*, 3, 237–248.
Frischer, M., Green, S. T., Goldberg, D. J. *et al.* (1992) Estimates of HIV infection among injecting drug users in Glasgow, 1985–1990, AIDS, 6, 1371–1375.
Haw, S., Frischer, M., Donoghoe, M. *et al.* (1992) The importance of multi–site sampling in determining the prevalence of HIV among drug injectors in Glasgow and London, AIDS, 6, 517–518.

Noone, A., Durante, A. J., Brady, A. R. *et al.* (1994) HIV infection in IDUs attending centres in England and Wales; 1990–1991, *AIDS*, in press.

Ronald, P. J. M. & Robertson, J. R. (1992) Prevalence of HIV infection among drug users in Edinburgh, *British Medical Journal*, 304, 1506.

HIV risks and help-seeking associated with drug use

Alcabes, P., Vlahov, D. J Anthony, J. C. (1992) Correlates of human immunodeficiency virus infection in intravenous drug users: are treatment-program samples misleading?, *British Journal of Addiction*, 87, 47–54.

Barnard, M. (1993) Needle sharing in context: patterns of sharing among men and women injectors and HIV risks, *Addiction*, 88, 805–812.

Burt, J. & Stimson, G. V. (1993) *Drug Injectors and HIV Risk Reduction: Strategies for Protection*, London, Health Education Authority.

Connors, M. (1992) Risk perception, risk taking and risk management among intravenous drug users: implications for AIDS Prevention, *Social Science and Medicine*, 34(6), 591–601.

Donoghoe, M. C., Dolan, K. A. & Stimson, G. V. (1992) Lifestyle factors and social circumstances of syringe sharing in injecting drug users, *British Journal of Addiction*, 87, 37–48.

Friedman, S. R., Des Jarlais, D. C. & Sterk, C. (1990) AIDS and the social relations of intravenous drug users, *Milbank Quarterly*, 86 (Supp. 1), 85–110.

Grund, J. P., Kaplan, C. D., Adriaans, N. F. P. *et al.* (1991) Drug sharing and HIV transmission risks: the practice of "frontloading" in the Dutch injecting drug user population, *Journal of Psychoactive Drugs*, 23, 1–10.

Hartnoll, R. L. & Power, R. (1989) *Study of Help-Seeking and Service Utilisation by Problem Drug Takers*, London, Institute for the Study of Drug Dependence.

Hartnoll, R. L. (1992) Research and the help-seeking process, *British Journal of Addiction*, 87, 429–437.

Jose, B., Friedman, S. R., Neaigus, A. *et al.* 'Frontloading' is associated with HIV infection among drug injectors in New York City, *Eighth International Conference on AIDS*, Amsterdam.

McKeganey, N. & Barnard, M. (1992) *AIDS, Drugs and Sexual Risk: Lives in the Balance*, Buckingham, Open University Press.

Power, R., Jones, S. Kearnes, G. *et al.* (1993) *Lifestyles (Part Two): Coping Strategies of Drug Users*, London, The Centre for Research on Drugs and Health Behaviour.

Rhodes, T. J., Bloor, M. J., Donoghoe, M. C. *et al.* (1993) HIV prevalence and HIV risk behaviour among injecting drug users in London and Glasgow, *AIDS Care*, 5, 413–425.

Stimson, G. V. (1991) Risk reduction by drug users with regard to HIV infection, *International Journal of Psychiatry*, 3, 401–415.

Vlahov, D., Munoz, A., Anthony, J. C. *et al.* (1990) Association of drug injection patterns with antibody to human immunodeficiency virus type 1 among intravenous drug users in Baltimore, Maryland, *American Journal of Epidemiology*, 132, 847–856.

HIV risks associated with sexual behaviour

Donoghoe, M. C. (1992) Sex, HIV and the injecting drug use, *British Journal of Addiction*, 87, 405–416.

Kane, S. (1991) HIV, heroin and heterosexual relations, *Social Science and Medicine*, 32(9), 1037–1050.

Klee, H., Faugier, J., Hayes, C. *et al.* (1990) Sexual partners of injecting drug users: the risk of HIV infection, *British Journal of Addiction*, 85, 413–418.

Marx, R., Aral, S. O., Rolfs, R. T., Sterk, C. E. & Khan, J. G., (1991) Crack, sex and STD, *Sexually Transmitted Diseases*, 18, 92–101.

Moss, A. (1987) AIDS and intravenous drug use: the real heterosexual epidemic, *British Medical Journal*, 294, 389–390.

Plant, M. A. (Ed) *AIDS, Drugs and Prostitution*, London, Routledge.

Rhodes, T. & Stimson, G. V. (1994) What is the relationship between drug-taking and sexual risk? Social relations and social research, *Sociology of Health and Illness*, 16, 189–208.

Wermuth, L., Ham, J. & Robbins, R. L. (1992) Women don't wear condoms: AIDS risk among sexual partners of IV drug users, in Huber, J. & Schneider, B. E. (Eds) *The Social Context of AIDS*, California, Sage.

HIV risk, drug use and prisons

Brewer, T. F. and Derrickson, J. (1992) AIDS in prison: a review of epidemiology and preventive policy, *AIDS*, 6, 623–628.

Carvell, A. & Hart, G. (1990) Risk behaviours for HIV infection among drug users in prison, *British Medical Journal*, 300, 1383–1384.

Covell, R., Frischer, M., Taylor, A. *et al.* (1993) Prison experience of injecting drug users in Glasgow, *Drug and Alcohol Dependence*, 32, 9–14.

Hall, W., Ward, J. & Mattick, R. (1993) Methadone maintenance treatment in prisons: the New South Wales experience, *Drug and Alcohol Review*, 12, 193–203.

Power, K. G., Markova, A., Rowlands, K. J. *et al.* (1992) Intravenous drug use and HIV transmission amongst inmates in Scottish prisons, *British Journal of Addiction*, 87, 35–45.

Turnbull, P. J., Dolan, K. A. & Stimson, G. V. (1991) *Prisons, HIV and AIDS: Risks and Experiences in Custodial Care*, Horsham, AVERT.

Methadone treatment and HIV prevention

Ball, J. C., Lange, W. R., Meyers, C. P. & Friedman, S. R. (1988) Reducing the risk of AIDS through methadone maintenance treatment, *Journal of Health and Social Behaviour*, 29, 214–226.

Ball, J. C. & Ross, A. (1991) *The Effectiveness of Methadone Treatment: Patients, Programs, Services and Outcome*, New York, Springer-Verlag.

Dole, V. P. (1989) Methadone treatment and the acquired immunodeficiency syndrome, *Journal of the American Medical Association*, 262, 1681.

Hall, W., Ward, J. & Mattick, R. (1993) Methadone maintenance treatment in prisons: the New South Wales Experience, *Drug and Alcohol Review*, 12, 193–203.

Strang, J. (1990b) The roles of prescribing. In Strang, J. & Stimson, G. V. (Eds) *AIDS & Drugs Misuse: The Challenge for Policy and Practice in the 1990s*, London, Routledge.

Ward, J., Darke, S. Hall, W & Mattick, R. (1992) Methadone maintenance and the human immunodeficiency virus: current issues in treatment and research, *British Journal of Addiction*, 87, 447–453.

Syringe exchange and distribution

Carvell, A. & Hart, G. (1990b) Help–seeking and referrals in a needle exchange: a comprehensive service to injecting drug users, *British Journal of Addiction*, 85, 235–240.

Donoghoe, M. C., Stimson, G. V. & Dolan, K. A. (1992) *Syringe Exchange in England: An Overview*, London, Tufnell Press.

Glanz, A., Byrne, C. & Jackson, P. (1989) Role of community pharmacies in the prevention of AIDS among injecting drug misusers: findings from a survey in England and Wales, *British Medical Journal*, 299, 1076–1079.

Hart, G., Carvell, A. L. M., Woodward, N. *et al.* (1989) Evaluation of needle exchange in Central London: behaviour change and anti-HIV status over one year, *AIDS*, 3, 261–265.

Lart, R. & Stimson, G. V. (1990) National survey of syringe exchange schemes in England, *British Journal of Addiction*, 85, 1433–1444.

Stimson, G. V., Alldritt, L., Dolan, K. & Donoghoe, M. C. (1988) *Injecting Equipment Exchange Schemes: Final Report*, London, Goldsmiths College.

Stimson, G. V. (1989) Syringe exchange programmes for injecting drug users, *AIDS*, 5, 253–260.

Stimson, G., Lart, R., Dolan, K. & Donoghoe, M. (1991) The future of syringe exchange in the public health prevention of HIV infection. In Aggleton, P., Davies, P. & Hart, G. (Eds.) *AIDS: Responses, Interventions and Care*, Lewes, Falmer Press.

Outreach and community-based prevention

Broadhead, R. S. & Fox, K. J. (1990) Takin' it to the streets: AIDS outreach as ethnogrpahy, *Journal of Contemporary Ethnography*, 19, 332–348.

Friedman, S. R., Sterk, C., Sufian, M., Des Jarlais, D. C. & Stephenson, B. (1990) Reaching out to injecting drug users. In Strang, J. & Stimson, G. V. (Eds) *AIDS and Drug Misuse: The Challenge for Policy and Practice in the 1990s*, London, Routledge.

Friedman, S. R., Neaigus, A., Des Jarlais, D. C., Sotheran, J. L., Woods, J., Sufian, M. (1992) Social intervention against AIDS among injecting drug users, *British Journal of Addiction*, 87, 393–404.

Friedman, S. R., Des Jarlais, D. C., Neaigus, A. *et al.* (1992) Organizing drug injectors against AIDS: preliminary data on behavioural outcomes, *Psychological Addictive Behaviours*, 6, 100–106.

Hartnoll, R. L., Rhodes, T. J., Jones, A. *et al.* (1990) *A Survey of HIV Outreach Intervention in the United Kingdom*, London, Birkbeck College.

Rhodes, T. & Hartnoll, R. L. (1991) Reaching the hard to reach: models of HIV outreach health education. In Aggleton, P., Davies, P. & Hart, G. (Eds.) *AIDS: Responses, Interventions and Care*, Lewes, Falmer Press.

Rhodes, T., Hartnoll, R. L. & Johnson, A. M. (1991) *Out of the Agency and on to the Streets: A Review of HIV Outreach Health Education in Europe and the United States*, London, Institute for the Study of Drug Dependence, Research Monograph 2.

Rhodes, T. & Holland, J. (1992) Outreach as a strategy for HIV prevention: aims and practice, *Health Education Research*, 7(4), 533–546.

Rhodes, T. (1993) Time for community change: what has outreach to offer?, *Addiction*, 1317–1320.

Wiebel, W. (1988) Combining ethnographic and epidemiologic methods in targeted AIDS interventions: the Chicago model. In Battjes, R. & Pcikens, R. (Eds) *Needle Sharing Among Intravenous Drug Abusers*, Washington, NIDA Research Monograph 80.

Wiebel, W., Jimenenz, A., Johnson, W. *et al.* (1994) Positive effect on HIV seroconversion of street outreach interventions with IDU in Chicago, 1988–1992, *American Journal of Public Health*, in press.

Other titles of interest

Drug injectors and HIV risk reduction
Strategies for protection
Jill Burt and Gerry V Stimson
A report of particular interest to all those involved in HIV education and pre-vention amongst injecting drug users.

Through the findings of two studies carried out in London and Brighton and through interviews with injecting drug users, it examines recent changes of behaviour implemented by drug users to protect themselves and others from HIV. It points towards practical future health education strategies based on a gradual reduction of risk.

1 85448 901 1   £7.99

Getting to the point
Tom Aldridge and Steve Cranfield, HEA/LBTC Training for Care Unit
A set of eight manuals and a video providing a course for trainers who offer training on HIV and AIDS for staff working directly with drug users.

Titles in the set: Introduction to the course; Health care and safer injecting; Sexuality and safer sex; The HIV antibody test; Living with asymptomatic HIV; Living with sympotmatic HIV or AIDS; Family work, drug use, HIV and AIDS; Death, dying and bereavement.

Only available as a pack.

1 85448 464 8   £95.00

For orders and further information please contact: Health Education Authority, Customer Services Department, PO Box 87, Oxford, OX2 0DT. Tel: 0865 204 745. Fax: 0865 791 927.